The Early Adventures of El Borak

ROBERT E. HOWARD

Introduction by David A. Hardy
Edited by Rob Roehm and Paul Herman

THE

Robert E. Howard

FOUNDATION PRESS

For Glenn Lord (1931-2011), preserver of Howard's typescripts and manuscripts, godfather of Howard studies, and the greatest fan that ever lived.

ISBN: 978-1-955446-21-1 (Paperback)
ISBN: 978-1-955446-11-2 (Hardcover)
ISBN: 978-1-955446-32-7 (eBook)

Published by the REH Foundation Press, LLC by arrangement with Robert E. Howard Properties Inc.

https://rehfoundation.org
https://rehfpress.com

Cover illustration copyright © 2024, Mark Wheatley.

https://markwheatleygallery.com

Book prepared for publication by Ståle Gismervik, Savage Studios.

Version 2.0 - Ultimate Edition.

In loving memory of our friend and colleague
Steven Tompkins
1960 - 2009

Contents

Miscellanea

Maps, Sketches and Lists

Acknowledgments

All of the Howard stories, poems, letters and portions thereof contained in *The Early Adventures of El Borak* come from Howard's original typescripts, manuscripts, and carbons. Virtually all of the original REH papers were scanned from the Glenn Lord collection, now at the University of Texas, Austin; the Robert E. Howard collection at Texas A&M University; and the typescript collection at Cross Plains Library.

CHANGES FROM THE FIRST EDITION: In this Ultimate Edition, "Drag" has been added. Transcriptions of Howard's typescripts or previously edited versions of "The Further Adventures of Lal Singh," "Red Curls and Bobbed Hair," Untitled ("Madge Meraldson"), Untitled ("The Hades Saloon"), and "The West Tower" have been restored to typescript. In the first edition, a handwritten first draft was used for "The Tale of the Rajah's Ring"; this edition uses an incomplete typed second draft, finished with the text from the handwritten first draft. Accordingly, all texts are now from REH typescripts except "Under the Great Tiger," which is from first publication.

"The first character I ever created was Francis Xavier Gordon, El Borak, the hero of "The Daughter of Erlik Khan" (*Top-Notch*), etc. I don't remember his genesis. He came to life in my mind when I was about ten years old."

- Robert E. Howard

The Making of El Borak

introduction by David A. Hardy

There is a myth that Athena was born from Zeus's head, arriving in a shower of blood, armed and ready for battle. Francis X. Gordon, known as El Borak, is also a born warrior. One might be forgiven for thinking that he sprang straight from Robert E. Howard's head like Athena, to fight his way through "The Daughter of Erlik Khan" in the pages of the December 1934 issue of *Top Notch*. But neither stories nor writers come into being without work, practice, false starts, and experiments.

El Borak's gestation in Howard's imagination was a long one indeed. Howard described the origin of Gordon and other characters to Alvin Earl Perry: "The first character I ever created was Francis Xavier Gordon, El Borak, the hero of 'The Daughter of Erlik Khan' (Top Notch), etc. I don't remember his genesis. He came to life in my mind when I was about ten years old" ("A Biographical Sketch of Robert E. Howard," 1935). Writing of Bran Mak Morn, Howard added, "Physically he [Bran Mak Morn] bore a striking resemblance to El Borak." That is a telling comment, for in some sense it means that the Scotch-Irish Gordon is recapitulating the globe-wandering of the Picts and Celts that so filled Howard's fantasies.

But it was not until 1922 that Howard began to write of Gordon. The stories of that era show just how many variations Howard tried on Gordon. Several are about quests for lost treasure in unexplored Africa. H. Rider Haggard's "Lost Race" romances have a strong influence here. In "Khoda Khan's Tale" Gordon reveals his destination is a ruin called "Valooze." This is of course related to Valusia, the pre-historic empire ruled by Howard's Sword & Sorcery character Kull, created in 1928.

In "The Iron Terror," Gordon is plotting a revolt in Arabia in order to build a personal empire. It may be a bit of homage to George Allan England's airship-adventure *The Flying Legion*, where a group of renegade aviators plot a gold-heist from Mecca.

The theme of the usurper who wins a throne by dint of his indomitable will to power is also a uniquely Howardian one. Both Kull and Conan come to power that way; indeed, it is central to their identities. Gordon meets with an arms-dealer to purchase weapons for his rebellion. There is a brief exchange that might serve to describe many Howard heroes.

"I am no soldier," says Gordon.

The arms dealer replies, "No, you are a conqueror."

Howard's conquerors are not men who direct others from behind a desk, nor are they uniformed servants of the state. They are utterly free, wild, and ferocious in their drive to dominate their world or be destroyed in the attempt. When Howard was writing "The Iron Terror" he was struggling to find his own road. Becoming a full-time writer in the face of his parents' reservations required much determination on Howard's part. Howard was no one else's soldier; he followed a lonely road to conquer the life he wanted.

Although clearly fascinated by self-willed men who imposed their rule on the world, Howard regularly raised existential questions about conquest and imperial glory. The arms dealer says, "Like all conquerors. They came, they saw, they conquered! Where are they now? Here is the dagger that was carried by Genghis Khan. But where is Genghis Khan? So all conquerors go!"

Yet for all the ambition of *this* Gordon, in later stories Gordon would be an opponent of the sorts of adventurers who sought to build themselves a throne atop the corpses of others.

Howard gave the theme of empire building a twist in a piece titled "Intrigue in Kurdistan." The setting is a Turkish castle with an elaborate network of secret passages, a motif that would recur in several El Borak stories. Gordon instigates a Kurdish revolt, ostensibly to forge an empire with himself as ruler. Gordon's true motive is revenge for Turkish atrocities, rather than self-aggrandizement.

The shift may seem a subtle one, but it is no doubt significant for the later development of the El Borak stories. The motif of building an empire on the slaughter of entire races would return in the last, and most ferocious of the El Borak Stories, "The Son of the White Wolf" (*Thrilling Adventures*, December 1936).

"The Coming of El Borak" concerns an English woman kidnapped by Afghan tribesmen. The fragment's protagonists are Khoda Khan, the cheerful narrator, and the brooding Yar Ali Khan. Gordon appears only at the end of the fragment.

The story has one of the strongest Western-genre themes at its core: the rescue of a white woman from hostile tribesmen. Gordon is described as a gunfighter, a motif related to the waning of the frontier. But the captive-rescue motif harks back to a much earlier type of Western, exemplified by James Fenimore Cooper's frontier-hero Natty Bumppo, known as Hawkeye, and the epic captive-rescue novel *The Last of the Mohicans*. Gordon has much in common with Bumppo. Hawkeye has close affinities with Indian culture, yet retains his loyalty to the settlers. Like Bumppo, Gordon has one foot in the "civilized" world of Western culture and one foot in the tribal world of the Afghans, though in the later Gordon stories his loyalty to colonialist goals is sometimes tested. Like Bumppo, Gordon even has a special nickname bestowed on him by the natives. He is El Borak, the swift, indicating his fast-draw speed just as Hawkeye pays tribute to Bumppo's skill with the long-rifle.

While the captive-rescue motif is a time-honored one, Howard may have found his inspiration elsewhere. In 1923, about the time Howard was writing the early El Borak stories, Afghan tribesmen kidnapped a British girl named Mollie Ellis. The story was reported in *The Dallas Morning News* and Howard may well have read of it at the time. Admittedly, Miss Ellis was not rescued by a grim-faced American gunslinger. Instead, the British employed a medical missionary, Mrs. Lillian Starr, and a local civil servant, Kuli Khan.

The supporting characters from "The Coming of El Borak" are integral to the El Borak tales. Both Khoda Khan and Yar Ali Khan appear in several other unfinished stories, as does Lal Singh, a Sikh warrior. All three would re-appear in later El Borak tales. Howard also wrote a few pieces with Lal Singh as the leading protagonist. Lal Singh is a merry Sikh thief who relishes trickery as much as swordplay. Perhaps there is a bit of homage to Douglas Fairbanks's role in the 1924 film *Thief of Bagdad*.

Howard had a real affection for these characters. In addition to bringing them back in the later El Borak stories, Khoda Khan shows up in "Names in the Black Book," a story Howard wrote in 1934 during his brief fling with the detective genre. But Howard's underworld has no gangsters as such, instead it is full of swaggering swordsmen from the Jebal Druse and the Hindu Kush. "Names in the Black Book" culminates in a rousing sword-battle more typical of an El Borak story than a detective tale.

The idea of a Western gunslinger blazing trails in Asia so captivated Howard that he had to create another Texan to accompany El Borak. Steve Allison, the Sonora Kid, is a leading character in his own right. Just as there is more than one Gordon, there is more than one Steve Allison. There is the Sonora Kid, cowboy, outlaw, and gunslinger; then there is the decidedly more domesticated version of Steve Allison, jewel-thief, *bon vivant*, and doting elder brother.

The domesticated Steve Allison is part of a large family, consisting mostly of sisters. They emerge in a cycle of vignettes and fragments: "Brotherly Advice," "Desert Rendezvous," and "Red Curls and Bobbed Hair." These stories revolve around the indiscretions of the Allison girls, such as getting a bobbed hairdo or falling in love with an insincere "sheik." Steve alternates between the soft-touch big brother and the stern disciplinarian. Underneath the domesticity there is a subtext of titillation.

One should not read too much into these stories. The pulps had a boundless appetite for the risqué and taboo. The settings, whether New York or a large family of girls, were equally exotic to Howard's own life.

The wild side of Steve Allison is more properly called the Sonora Kid. This is the cowboy Steve, developed in "The Sonora Kid-Cowhand" as a man ready to fight ranch-hand bullies and wild broncs. Along with his partner, Bill "Drag" Buckner, the Sonora Kid is a gambler ("The Sonora Kid's Winning Hand"), explorer of Southwestern mysteries ("A Blazing sun in a Blazing Sky"), and evidently a wanted man ("The Hades Saloon").

Cowboy Steve and domesticated Steve begin to merge in "The West Tower," where our heroes are transmuted into highsociety jewel thieves, sort of cowboy versions of Sir Charles Lytton and Alexander Mundy. The business at hand is a party in a haunted castle hosted by a decadent, rape-obsessed German junker. Steve's sisters are nowhere in evidence; a bad hair-do is one kind of family crisis, being wanted by the police on two continents is another.

Finally there are hints of Eastern adventures, the aforementioned sheik being one example. Gazing on the Rio Grande, Steve thinks of a Malay *kris* and Arab war-cries. In his New York penthouse Steven studies ancient Assyrian art under trophies of Arab scimitars. The fragment "The Mountains of Thibet" puts the Sonora Kid and an un-named narrator (probably Bill Buckner) right on the Roof of Asia.

In the fragment "North of Khyber" jewel-thief Steve and Bill Buckner travel to Afghanistan (one step ahead of the law) to help El Borak deal with an incipient *jihad*. Howard later used a very similar concept in "Country of the Knife" (*Complete Stories*, August 1936), with gentleman-gambler Stuart Brent taking Allison's place. In both tales Howard holds El Borak back until the last possible moment.

Steve and El Borak share a few Lost Race treasure hunts. Fantastic elements such as living dinosaurs and a cursed ruin appear in a couple of the fragments. In one fragment titled "A Power Among the Islands" Gordon appears as a sailor nicknamed "Wolf Gordon," echoing Jack London's "Wolf Larsen" from *The Sea Wolf*.

A fragment simply titled "El Borak" details how Allison and Gordon met. It is one of the starker Sonora Kid tales; there are no sisters or rustic sidekicks. Steve is a broken man on the beach in Oman, degraded enough to accept a job as a killer-forhire. This sets up the Texans for a classic fast-draw shoot-out, with Oman substituting for El Paso.

Interestingly Gordon acquires a new nickname: Diego Valdez. This appears to be a reference to the Kipling poem "The Song of Diego Valdez." Valdez tells how he found his ease in adventure on the high seas. But when he becomes High Admiral of Spain the demands of authority deprive him of the wild and free life of an adventurer. The tension between duty to others, and the desire to seek adventure for its own sake, is a motif in some of Howard's best Conan stories, such as "Black Colossus" and Hour of the Dragon. Was this how Howard conceived of Gordon? When El Borak re-appeared in the '30s, he was no longer a treasure hunter or a man seeking a crown, but a very different character.

The El Borak that emerges in the stories of the mid-1930s is a man strongly devoted to others. His resemblance to Bran Mak Morn is more than physical; El Borak becomes a tribal warrior motivated by loyalty and a powerful determination to fight long odds when committed to a cause. These early fragments were Howard's proving ground for El Borak. Look at them closely for the ultimate product was a good one. El Borak may not have leapt from Howard's head like Athena, but like other mythic characters he has stood the test of time.

The Coming of El Borak

The Iron Terror

Outside the wind roared, snatching up the snow, whirling the flakes high in the air. The streets were deserted except for a few belated pedestrians hurrying home, heads bowed against the gale. Further up, in the business-proper part of town, even the crowds were scattered and few. Traffic had almost stopped. In a section where the streets were entirely bare, a house reared, bleak and dark among its lesser neighbors.

"At last!" A laboratory filled with weird contrivances. A withered old man seated at a table.

"At last!" What cared he for the wind and the cold outside? He scarcely knew of it, one of the worst blizzards that had ever swept New York.

"At last!" He rubbed his hands and chuckled.

A taxi drew up in front of the tall house that loomed so dark and forbidding.

A man alighted and made his way through the whirling snow to the door. The taxi whirled away.

The clang of an old-fashioned knocker rose above the shriek of the storm.

The man at the door shook the snow from his coat, stamped his feet and cursed beneath his breath. He raised his hand to knock again when the door swung open. An impassive Chinaman stood in the doorway.

The man handed him a card. The Oriental glanced at it and stepped aside, bowing.

"You are expected," he said, in almost perfect English.

The man stepped inside a dimly lighted hallway. The Oriental took his hat and coat. He carried no cane. The lights showed him to be a man of medium height and of a lithe, wiry build. His face was bronzed with the sun and his black eyes were clear, farseeing, with a certain compelling something about them. His whole form and features suggested an unusual mind and intellectual power combined with a tigerish physical power. His motions were quick but not hasty nor excited. Altogether, an unusual man.

The Chinaman led him up a flight of stairs, down a corridor and into a room.

"Wait here," he said and disappeared.

The stranger paced about the room restlessly. He seemed to be conscious of unseen eyes upon him and it gave him the feeling of a trapped wolf. His eyes took in the room rapidly but with every detail.

The room was not a large one. Several doors led from it. A few chairs, a costly Persian rug, a divan and a large mahogany table constituted the furniture. The walls were hung with weapons and the table was covered with them. Such a collection as is seldom seen outside a museum.

The stranger sat down at the table and began to examine the weapons upon it with an interest that was not feigned.

Then he looked up as a man came through one of the doors. An old, wrinkled man, small and withered, stooped with age, wearing a dressing gown, bedroom slippers and a red Turkish fez placed at a rakish angle on his nearly bald head.

The stranger rose.

"So you have come?" the old man said, a sneering note in his voice. "I have expected you."

He came forward to the table.

"You are interested in my collection?" he said. "What do you think of it, eh?"

"One of the most perfect I ever saw," the stranger replied, speaking for the first time.

"Ah, you think so? You are right." He waved his hands about the room, "This is but a part of my collection yet here you will find the weapons of all lands and all ages. Do you know them?"

"Yes."

"Aye, a good workman should know the tools of his trade. But," here the sneering note crept into his voice again, "do not flatter yourself."

He picked up a short dagger with a wide, wickedly curved blade. "What is this?"

"A cheray from Afghanistan, manufactured in Ghuzni," answered the stranger, scarcely glancing at the weapon.

"And this?"

"A Dyak parang-parang from Borneo."

"And this?"

"An Italian misericorde dagger."

"And this?"

"A bronze Kalmuck-Tartar peaked helmet of about the fifteenth century."

"And this?"

"A French anlace of the Middle Ages."

"And this?"

"A Zulu shield from Africa."

"And this?"

"A samurai sword of old Japan."

"And this?"

"A claymore from Scotland. But enough of this child's play!" he exclaimed impatiently. "There is no weapon here with which I am not acquainted. Few that I have not used. I know their use and their history as well as you.

"That tulwar was made by Yussef Abdullah of Kabul who prides himself on his work. That bowie knife was made in Missouri by James Black. That rapier is the work of Andrea di Ferrara. Antonio Picinino of Venice made that Italian schiavone. That Maharati gauntlet-sword was made in the workshops of Delhi.

"But I did not come here to speak of weapons."

"No." The old man seated himself across the table from the stranger, motioning him to sit down.

The old man cupped his chin in his hands, rested his elbows on the table and stared at his visitor.

"Aye," he said, scornfully, "you know the tools of your trade. The simple tools, steel and lead, edge, point and muzzle. But what does a soldier know of the higher arts of war? The triumphs of science?"

"I am no soldier," returned the stranger.

"No, you are a conqueror. An empire builder, is that not it, my friend?"

The stranger said nothing but his eyes flashed suddenly.

"Do you think I am a fool?" sneered the old man. "I know!"

"War, conquest, power! Oh, it has been done before, I admit. Alexander, Caesar, Tamerlane! All those fools. Now you. Listen!" He leaned forward, "I know more than you think for, my friend. I know that you plan to unite the tribes of Arabia and make an empire!"

The stranger leaned forward, half-casually, but his hand played with the lapel of his coat.

"And how do you know all this?" he asked.

"I ask you again, am I a fool? Why have shiploads of rifles and ammunition continually landed at out-of-the-way ports of Arabia? Why do you come to me in the night in the midst of a storm? I have ways of knowing and learning things no other man may know. Oh, yes. Empire is your goal, Mr. Gordon. Sultan Gordon sahib! How does that sound to you?"

"If you know my plans, very well," Gordon answered coolly. "But," he leaned forward and his eyes glittered tigerishly, "it is not good for any man to know too much of my plans, my friend."

The old man laughed harshly. "I will not betray you. What care I for the country that disowned me? For the nations that laughed at me? And who am I to interfere with destiny? Aye, go your way. Be what you wish to be. Another Caesar, nay, rather another Genghis Khan! But trace the roads of the conquerors and try to be free from vanity."

"My road is my own," Gordon replied.

"Aye, and you will travel it. Like all conquerors. They came, they saw, they conquered! Where are they now?

"Here is a dagger that was carried by Genghis Khan. But where is Genghis Khan? So all conquerors go!"

"All men must go," Gordon replied. "It makes no difference whether he be slave or Emperor. But the Emperor is remembered."

"Yes, men go; but the works of man, stand. Genghis Khan has been dust for a thousand years, yet here I sit and hold his dagger! And a thousand years from now men will say, 'Here is the saber Gordon swung in the fore ranks of battle? Where is Gordon now?'" and the old man laughed, a cynical, mocking laugh. Gordon smiled.

"But science prevails!" the old man exclaimed. "Science, the work of man! What are soldiers, statesmen, workers of art? They pass. Science remains. Conquerors come and go like whirlwinds. The generations of man melt like snow on a mountainside. But the triumphs of science stand through the ages, outliving the pyramids!

"You, you conqueror, you empire builder, you man with great ambitions, you come to me for aid! Aye, well you may for I have perfected an invention that makes all others seem as grains of sand to a mountain! You are skilled in the use of all weapons, you say. But what do you know of the heights of attainment the mind of a scientist may reach? A man of war may wield implements of slaughter but first the man of science must make them!"

"Now we come to the real reason of my visit," said Gordon.

"You wish to buy my invention? One thing I tell you; that it will make you master of the world—if you gain control of it."

"What is it? I found out that you had perfected some machine of war. I must see it. If I do not buy it, be assured your secret will be safe."

"I should think so," sneered the old scientist. He leaned forward, his eyes blazing with scientific zeal.

"Man, I have worked out an engine of war that dwarfs all other such inventions. Come, you shall see it, at once, at once."

He sprang to his feet with a vitality amazing in one of his age. "Come."

Gordon followed him through a door and down a short, narrow corridor. Outside a heavy door, the scientist paused.

"You are now about to see what no man but myself has ever looked upon," he announced. "If you have treachery in mind, you had better not enter."

"Lead on," Gordon answered briefly.

The scientist turned the lock and swung the door wide. Gordon stepped into a large, brilliantly lighted room. The old man followed, pulling the door to. It locked with a click.

"Look well at the door, Mr. Gordon," the old man said.

Gordon did so. It was sheathed with heavy steel and was entirely bare of knob or lock of any kind.

"The walls are sheathed with steel," the scientist said. "This is the only door. The two windows are heavily barred. I, and only I, know the secret of the door. If I were murdered here my murderer could never escape."

Gordon's eyes wandered over the great room, taking in every detail. It was filled, but not crowded, with tables, cases and stands covered with scientific apparatus. Books of scientific subjects littered the room and here and there were more weapons. Some of them of weird type.

In one corner of the room, something, some object, bulked huge and forbidding. It was covered entirely by a heavy, dark, velvet cloth but even so there seemed to be something sinister about it. Gordon's eyes rested long upon it.

The scientist strode forward and stood before the veiled object.

"Beneath this cloth," he said, "stands an invention compared to which tanks, shrapnel, gas and submarines become the toys of infants!"

Gordon approached and leaned on a table. Mechanically he noticed that on the table were three or four broadswords of the Middle Ages. Long, massive, double-edged, two-handed swords.

"Show me," he answered.

The scientist gripped the cloth and dramatically snatched it away.

There stood revealed what appeared to be a metal statue, some eight feet high.

It was in the form of a man, and as a work of art alone it was a masterpiece. The face was terrifically powerful, there were no lines or curves of fineness or weakness. A face of crude, primeval, terrible power. A malignantly powerful face.

It appeared to be of steel and was jointed; shoulder, neck, elbow, hips, knee, ankle and fingers, protected by a steel mesh, somewhat like the joint-protections of Medieval armor.

"Well," the old scientist said impatiently, "what do you think of it?"

"Why, I hardly know," Gordon replied. "I see only a statue, a remarkable statue, I admit, but still a statue, such as I see everyday, barring the face."

The old man sneered. "A statue! You fool! Look here, this 'statue' is of metal. What kind?"

Gordon tapped it. His expression showed interest.

"I thought at first it was made of Harvard steel but I am not sure."

"Harvard steel! Bosh! Steel of my own invention. Twice as powerful as Harvard steel, twice as powerful as Krupp steel. No shell can shatter it. No bullet can pierce it. Listen while I tell you the secret of the Iron Terror."

Gordon drew nearer. The old man began, turning from the figure to his visitor as he talked.

"Inside this covering of iron, this manlike form, there is an incredibly powerful engine. No such engine as you have known. Not steam or gasoline or electric. What then? Can you guess?"

"Radium," Gordon suggested, his eyes aglitter.

"Yes, radium! But radium concentrated and strengthened a thousandfold. No man on earth but I know the secret of the concentrating of radium. The engine, which I shall not describe, has antennae similar to that of a wireless, but much smaller. Here," he turned to a machine which he had uncovered. It was a complicated affair of knobs and wheels and levers. "This controls my machine. But still you do not understand. But you shall. By manipulating this machine I can send my iron figure forward at any speed I wish!

I can regulate the speed, turn it any way or bring it back. No wires connect the machine. I guide the automaton by wireless!

"Ah, you see at last! This automaton, this Iron Terror, goes straight on in the direction that I guide it. Bombs, shells, shrapnel, cannot stop it. It may be knocked from its feet but it automatically rises. It tears down fortifications, climbs walls and mountains, wades rivers. Nothing can stop it, nothing but the pressure of a finger on a certain lever of the guiding-machine. Don't you see the terrible advantage of such a machine? A river can stop a tank but my machine strides straight through it. How many armies could stand before a thousand such monsters? See, I put a sword in its hand." He took up a great broadsword and placing the hilt in the palm of the metal hand, pushed down the metal fingers one at a time. Each finger clicked metallically as it closed around the hilt.

The old scientist stepped to the guiding-machine and worked a lever.

Gordon sprang back as the great arm rose and swept down, the long sword whistling with the force of the blow. The metal arm rose and fell, rose and fell, without stay or pause. Then the old man touched a lever and the arm stopped instantly, poising the sword in midair.

The scientist laughed eerily. "A swordsman, eh? You are a swordsman yourself; what could you do against such a swordsman as that?"

Gordon shook his head.

"Are you a strong man?" the scientist asked suddenly.

"Do I look like one?" Gordon asked, somewhat impatiently; he hated personal conversation.

"No, not especially. But your slim build is deceiving. You are built for speed, not strength. Oh, you are quick. I know what the tribes name you, 'El Borak, The Swift.' But you are strong. You have slain armed men with your bare hands. Your strength is a wonder. Yet, in the grip of my automaton, you would be as helpless as would be a young girl in your arms. Look."

He touched another lever and the other arm of the automaton went through the motions of throwing something. The fingers opened, reached to the figure's side, closed, and the arm swung back and forward.

"Bombs in a sack at the side," the old scientist said, bringing the figure to a stop. "Think of a thousand automatons charging into an army, hurling great bombs incessantly. Or sending forth clouds of gas. Or even hewing with great swords."

"A marvel," said Gordon. "Unless—"

"Unless what?" asked the old scientist sharply.

"Are you sure you can keep such a thing in absolute control? It would be a horror to have it free, charging at random, casting bombs or hewing right and left with such a sword as it now holds."

"Bosh!" cried the old scientist angrily. "Do you think I am a fool?"

Gordon shrugged his shoulders and did not reply.

"So you think I am a fool, eh?" the old man exclaimed in a fury.

"No, I know you are no fool," Gordon answered. "If I have offended you I sincerely apologize. But still I cannot believe that any invention can be perfected as you say this is. You say you have absolute control of the machine. Is it not possible for it to get from under your control?"

"It is not, sir," the old scientist retorted. "It is perfectly under my control, as much as any other inanimate object."

"A man might raise a storm," Gordon said, "but he could hardly control it after he had raised it. Understand me, sir; I realize that this is the greatest invention of the age. I consider you one of the greatest scientists that has ever lived. Still, there may be a flaw."

This but increased the old man's fury. "You fool!" he fairly shrieked. "You think there is a flaw in my machine? I'll show you!"

He whirled toward the controlling machine and jerked a lever. The great automaton moved out into the room with long, regular strides!

Only its metal legs worked, the arms were motionless, one hanging at its side, the other poised in the air, gripping the great sword.

It approached the scientist.

The old man turned to Gordon. "See?" he sneered, reaching for the control lever.

As he reached, his arm struck another lever. The great arm swung down! The old scientist was too near to the figure to receive the blade but the great arm itself struck him a glancing blow on the head and descending, crashed down upon the controlling machine.

Instantly, the thing charged out into the room, the great sword swishing the air as it rose and fell!

With incredible speed Gordon leaped back and jerked out a big automatic. The crashing reports filled the room with echoes, the bullets ringing on the metal figure as they glanced and smashed against the walls.

Gordon might have been throwing pieces of paper as far as the automaton was concerned. It strode straight on. One arm wielded the sword, the other by some freakish cause, swung out in a circular motion, swung back and clanged against the metal breast of the automaton. The smashing of the control machine had turned the metal horror loose and it was running amuck!

The old scientist lay where he had fallen, half across the battered controlling machine.

Gordon leaped across the room to the door. Then as he tried it the scientist's words flashed into his mind: "—only I know the secret of the door. If I were murdered here my murderer could never escape."

Gordon realized that he was trapped! Trapped in an inescapable room with an iron monster!

Then began one of the strangest battles that ever occurred on earth. Gordon had fought battles and fights by the hundreds. Again and again he had faced and overcome tremendous odds. But never in his life had he fought such a battle as when, in a room in New York, he fought for his life against a thing such as the world had never seen, a thing more terrible than a thousand armed men.

The thing came straight across the room and Gordon avoided it with ease. It struck a table and turned aside in its course. With no hands upon its control, its course was to an extent, dependent upon obstacles and other influences. It kept no straight course, but moved in an erratic manner. But nothing was irregular about the movements of its great arms. They kept up their motions with a terrible regularity.

Gordon avoided it and ran across the room to the old scientist. He raised him and found that he was alive. Gordon glanced around. He saw a large shelf high up upon the wall. With unbelievable strength and agility he managed to place the unconscious man upon it. There, at least he was out of the reach of the Iron Terror unless the thing developed a climbing ability.

As Gordon completed his task he saw the automaton had turned once more and was coming back.

He leaped to the guiding machine and sought to work the lever. They were bent and broken and the machine itself was nearly a wreck. Gordon was astonished. He would have thought that to smash the guiding machine would render the automaton useless.

The thing advanced across the room. Its sword clanged against the wall and Gordon hoped it would shatter. But the thing merely veered about and started on another course. Desperately Gordon jerked on a bent lever—the speed of the automaton increased! More than that it charged straight across the room towards him. He let go of the controlling machine and sprang across the room just in time to avoid the sweep of the automaton's sword. Then the Terror turned and came toward him again.

A rage came over Gordon. He was not used to running from his foes. He caught up one of the great swords that lay upon a table and charged in. He swung the great sword high into the air with both hands and struck a terrific blow. There was a clash and a clang like a mighty hammer-and-anvil and the great blade shattered from point to hilt. The automaton did not even rock and Gordon felt the wind of its sword as the thing swung about and struck.

He leaped back and hurled the useless hilt from him with a curse. The Terror was advancing toward him. He backed away and felt a heavy table at his back. Just in time he cleared it with a bound, as the Terror's sword came down and severed the table in half. The automaton strode over its ruins. A great metal cauldron stood in one corner of the room. It was for chemical experiments and must have weighed at least two hundred pounds. Gordon lifted it, swung it into the air and dashed it against the automaton! Even the Iron Terror could not stand before such a missile. It was knocked off its feet and crashed to the floor. But instantly it rose to its feet again, not once ceasing the motion of its arms!

Gordon watched, fascinated. It moved swiftly across the room and came into contact with a tall case. Instantly there was a rending and smashing of wood as the moving arm encircled the case and splintered it against the metal figure. Gordon shuddered in spite of himself. It was clear that if that arm ever closed on him, it would crush him.

"What a monster!" he said, aloud, wonderingly. "The old scientist was right. And I," he laughed sardonically, "I, who intended to hurl it against my foes, and he, who made it, are its first victims. The man who fought the cannon in the ship had an easy task, I think."

He looked about for a weapon. With one eye on the figure he opened several drawers. In one he found a bomb. He poised it in his hand, musing.

He remembered the scientist's words, "No shell can shatter it."

"A waste of time," he decided. "And dangerous."

He laid the bomb down and sidestepped as the automaton crashed into the opposite wall, swung around and charged in his direction. He watched and his eyes narrowed. At least he could break its sword. A great battle-axe of the Middle Ages lay near. He snatched it up and advanced.

He leaped in from the side, swinging the battle-axe as he sprang. It clashed against the sword and the sword-blade broke at the hilt and flew ringing across the room. Wolflike, Gordon recovered himself and leaped back almost simultaneously.

But though the sword was broken the great hand still rose and fell, gripping the heavy hilt. The other arm still swung out and back.

The room was a wreck. The automaton had knocked down, smashed, hewed or splintered nearly every piece of furniture.

As it lumbered across the room once more, Gordon did what he had tried to do before. He darted past the figure, raced across the room, and began to smash the controlling machine with the battle-axe. He believed that if that were destroyed the automaton would stop. As it had done before, the automaton charged back towards him. That showed that the controlling machine was still responsible for the thing's movements, thought Gordon, as he hacked desperately. Then the thing was upon him and he fled, dropping the battle-axe beside the machine.

And as if imbued with a mind the automaton followed him. Its speed was terrible. Its terrible face seemed the embodiment of the devil himself. Again and again Gordon dodged the thing, avoiding it by sheer speed and skill. He sprang to the machine again and swung the battle-axe. He thought of the scientist; his thoughts were short and disconnected: "A wonderful machine"—"if he built this he can build another—"

With a last swing he dropped the weapon and slipped under the arm of the Terror. But this time he was not quite quick enough. The hand holding the broken sword-hilt struck him a glancing blow and he staggered. In an instant the other arm was crushing him against the metal figure.

There was no sound; there had been no sound all along except the scuffing of feet, the crash of overturned furniture now and then and a slight sizzling sound from the controlling machine.

And silently, frenziedly, Gordon fought against the metal monster that gripped him. With all of his incredible strength he fought. And slowly he was being crushed.

And then suddenly the arm relaxed and Gordon slipped to the floor.

Wonderingly he rose and watched the Terror go blundering across the room, its arms now hanging at its sides. It went slowly. As he had known, the destruction of the controlling machine had stopped the automaton. Evidently he had done more with the battle-axe than he had thought. The Iron Terror stopped.

"*Gordon, The American*"

(untitled and unfinished)

Gordon, the American whom the Arabs call El Borak, possessed, together with a vast knowledge of the Orient and the ways of the Orient, certain preferences to certain tribes and races. Also certain strong dislikes to other races. Gurkhas, Sikhs and Zulus shared his preference and Turks, Kurds and Tauregs shared his enmity.

As he sat upon a camel, rifle in hand, close to an oasis at the edge of a certain African desert, his enmity toward the Tauregs was increased by the sight of several mounted warriors of that tribe. They were galloping off across the desert. They showed no intention of attacking him, although Gordon would have been rather pleased than otherwise if they had attacked.

The sight of a white man, alone in the desert of the Sudan, would have been surprizing if the man had been any other than Frank Gordon. It was his custom to wander off into deserts and other unmapped places of the world, alone or with only one companion, although on occasion he had raised and led small armies composed of friends and companions.

Somewhere to the northwest of the Bagirmi, a large safari was making its way leisurely in the direction Gordon was headed, but Gordon was unaccompanied.

The country through which Gordon's route lay was the land of many Taureg tribes, most of them hostile to Europeans. Their hostility bothered Gordon very little. If there were too many to fight he could always flee, and the camel he rode was the fleetest in the Sudan, possibly in all Africa. It had been bred in another desert in another continent, and was of a breed which owned no superior. It was a Bikanir camel, from the desert of Rajputana, in India. The swiftest Bishareen camel was inferior to it. Gordon had a number of such camels and they were the envy of every Arab and Taureg who saw them.

Gordon dismounted and refilled his canteen, letting the camel drink. He looked about him. To the northwest the desert stretched away beyond the horizon. Some distance away, to the south, veering toward the east, was what seemed to be a good-sized forest. Gordon reflected that so far as he knew, such a forest was not shown on any map of the Sudan. He was pleased by the thought that he was probably the first white man to explore the region.

He mounted again and rode toward the forest. The desert, nearing the forest, was no sandy waste such as it was further out. It more resembled the veldt of South Africa. Gordon wondered why even such desert people as the Tauregs preferred the wilder regions of the desert to those nearer the forest. Probably some wild tribe, hostile to the desert men dwelt in the forest, Gordon reflected. There are few tribes more warlike than the Tauregs and Gordon wondered what tribe could be powerful enough to drive them away. They ranged close to the forest, as he had seen, but only as raiders.

Presently he sighted a band of mounted warriors, galloping swiftly toward him from the desert. Tauregs, some thirty of them. Gordon drew a long- barreled rifle from its scabbard. An instant he gazed along the surprizingly well sighted long barrel, then he pulled the trigger. One of the warriors flung his arms into the air and tumbled from his saddle. Gordon levered another cartridge into the barrel and fired again. Another saddle was emptied.

The Tauregs were sweeping toward him in a long, curving line, that was meant to cut him off from the jungle and surround him. Gordon kicked his steed and the well-trained camel started forward in a long gallop that was surprizingly swift. After some distance, Gordon looked back. He was outside the half-circle of warriors and was leaving them behind. Two Tauregs were some distance ahead of the rest. He slowed his camel to a walk, shoved his rifle back into its scabbard and drew a long, curved saber of Indian steel. The foremost Taureg, screeching like a demon, swept past, standing up in his stirrups and slashing savagely with a long sword. Gordon leaned forward, warded the blow and cleft the Taureg's skull. Then he wrenched the saber free, turned a long spear in the hands of the other Taureg and ran the warrior through. Then he was again sweeping across the desert, bending low so as to offer as small a target as possible for the rifles of the pursuing Tauregs. They were not aiming at the camel, for they hoped to capture it. Even the swift desert horses could not keep the gait set by the Bikanir camel, and Gordon soon left his pursuers far behind. They galloped away across the desert.

The Coming of El Borak

(unfinished)

* * * * *

This tale was told to me in Delhi. The narrator was a hawkeyed Northern gentleman, an Afridi, one Khoda Khan.

* * * * *

Sahib, is it not strange that the British rule India when just beyond live such men as I?

Consider you and I for instance. I could slay you with one hand. What would you be among the mountains?

Yet your race rules the world.

No, it is not physical strength that counts in the struggles between nations. It is something else. Something unnamable, which the West has and the East has not.

Unity? Yes, but that is not all.

Consider the affair of mullah Hassan and memsahib Marion Sommerland.

The tale? Assuredly, sahib.

Among the mountains across the Border, miles from British territory, there is a village in a vale. The vale is the vale of Kadar and the village is the village of Kadar. That is my village, sahib, and it is one of the strongest of the Afridi tribe.

What is law to us there? Either the law of the British or the law of the Amir? We robbed caravans and raided into India and took women from the Hindus and from other tribes—before the coming of El Borak.

Our only law was the word of the mullah Hassan and the chief Kulam Khan who was a mighty swordsman.

So when I was a very young man, scarce attained to manhood, I and certain youths of the village went to the Border in hope of taking some rifles from the British.

There was I, and Yar Ali Khan who was the best swordsman of the tribe excepting Kulam Khan, and Abdullah Din and Mahommed Ali and Yar Hyder who was the oldest of the four, though Abdullah Din was nearly as old. Yar Ali Khan, Mahommed Ali and I were young men.

So as we were scouting just within British territory we saw a young British memsahib riding alone. What possessed the woman to ride alone among the hills I know not, but the women of the British are ever fearless and reckless.

"Soho!" quoth Yar Hyder. "She should bring good ransom, for I have seen her in Peshawur and she is the daughter of the colonel sahib Sommerland." So we hid ourselves in an ambush and as she rode past we sprung upon her. Yar Ali and Abdullah Din and Yar Hyder seized the horse. I caught the girl about the waist and lifted her out of the saddle. Mahommed Ali helped me and well for us that she was not stronger for she fought like a young leopard!

However, we bound her hands and gagged her and then placed her on her horse, tying her feet in the stirrups. Then we took to the hills.

After we had gone a distance we removed the gag for she was young and soft and pretty and we did not wish to hurt her.

She asked us where we were taking her and Yar Hyder who could speak English better than the rest of us, told her that she was to be held for ransom.

She bade us take her back instantly, threatening us with the British army, at which we laughed. Then she said her father would not pay the ransom.

"Then we will cast lots for you," quoth Abdullah Din with an evil smile.

Yar Ali cursed him and bade him be silent. Abdullah Din was older than he and a mighty fighter, but Yar Ali was afraid of nothing.

After we had covered halfway to Kadar we stopped under the shade of a cliff wall, upon another cliff, to rest and eat. I lifted the girl off her horse and she gave me such a look that I would fain have dropped her and fled to the mountains but for shame of my comrades.

We untied her and gave her food and drink and she was so slight and helpless we took compassion on her, all except Abdullah Din. He was a strong man and an evil one and he suggested that we cast lots for her. We refused.

"No, by Allah," said Mahommed Ali. "We are all partners in this and we will share the ransom equally."

"Children," jeered Abdullah Din, "I am a man. I take what I will."

And he laid hands on the girl. She struck him in the face and he struck her to the earth.

"Coward!" quoth Yar Ali Khan, smiting him across the face with his open hand. "Lay hands upon a man, not a weak girl."

So Yar Ali Khan and Abdullah Din fought there and Yar Ali slew Abdullah Din and hurled him over the cliff.

"Take warning," quoth Yar Ali, wiping his tulwar. "Let no man lay hand on the memsahib."

But none of us wished to, even had Yar Ali said nothing.

The girl had not been hurt, but she was frightened and for the first time she wept a little and begged us to take her home. And we pitied her and hated to see her weep, but we thought of the gold that her father would give for ransom. So at last we came to the village of Kadar.

The people rushed out to see what we brought and when they saw the girl they yelled as a wolf pack yells when the valleys are hid with snow and the packs range close to the villages.

But we forced them back and allowed no one to offer rudeness to her. That is not the way of the Afridis? Perhaps not, sahib, but we had both pity and admiration for the memsahib and we were her friends, though she would not believe it.

Then came the chief, Khumail Khan, striding along like a man of might, scowling under his brows, the people scattering before him.

He looked on the girl as a tiger looks on a young fawn.

"We were fools to bring the girl here," whispered Mahommed Ali to me and I knew it was so, for we could not withstand the chief.

"Where got ye the girl?" asked Khumail Khan.

"Just this side the Border," answered Yar Ali shortly.

The chief let his eye wander over us.

"Where is Abdullah Din?" spoke he.

"I slew him," Yar Ali replied. "I slew him with the Khyber knife and hurled him over a cliff."

"For what reason?"

"For that he laid hands on the girl and would have taken her for himself," and Yar Ali dropped his hand to his knife and looked Khumail Khan straight in the eyes. I thought the chief would have drawn his tulwar and smote Ali to the ground but he said nothing. His eyes sought the girl again and she shrank back under his gaze.

"Take her to my hut," he ordered, but we made no move to obey.

"Have ye ears?" said Khumail Khan savagely, laying his hand on his tulwar.

"Aye, and knives also," answered Yar Ali, and I reached for my cheray. I feared Khumail Khan but not so much that I would not have stabbed him in the back.

But just as it seemed the chief and Yar Ali would draw steel and leap at each other, the mullah Hassan came forward.

"Peace, peace!" he ordered, and the chief stepped back. Even he feared the mullah who could call down the Koran curse on any that offended him. But Yar Ali stood glaring nor gave back so much as a foot.

"There must be no war in the village of Kadar," ruled the mullah.

No one spoke and he went on.

"This woman must not cause strife, so I will take her to the temple and seek to convert her," and I saw the same look in his eyes that had been in the eyes of Abdullah Din and the eyes of Khumail Khan.

None of us spoke but Yar Ali.

"Well played, priest," he jeered. "Aye, thou wouldst like to 'convert' the memsahib. Aye! By this hand, this girl belongs to me and to Yar Hyder and to Khoda Khan and to Mahommed Ali. And we be men!"

The mullah hesitated. Yar Ali Khan feared not man or devil and I believe Hassan feared him. So we stood. The chief dared not seize the girl because he feared the mullah and the mullah dared not seize her for fear of Yar Ali Khan.

But the mullah was crafty.

"Let the matter rest," quoth he. "Let no harm come to the girl and presently we will decide at the council what shall be done with her."

"We need no council to decide that," spoke Ali. "The girl shall be well-treated until the ransom arrives and then returned unharmed to the British. And the ransom shall be divided between we four—I and Khoda Khan and Yar Hyder and Mahommed Ali."

"Enough," said the chief impatiently, and he strode away.

We turned to the girl who had sat on her horse during the discussion, not understanding what it was all about but frightened just the same. However, she sought not to show her fear and we admired her.

"You have brought me here, now what are you going to do with me?" she asked.

"You shall be well-treated until the ransom arrives, memsahib," Yar Hyder made answer. "You shall be kept in my house and watched over by my wives."

"Very well," she said, wearily. "Please take me there now because I am tired."

Yar Hyder was the only one of the four who was married, so we put the memsahib in the charge of his wives and Yar Ali made horrible threats as to what he would do if she was mistreated.

Then Mahommed Ali took a message to the fort where her father was, saying that the girl had been taken by raiders and that she would be returned unharmed for the sum of five thousand rupees and four rifles and five hundred rounds of ammunition. The message (it was written by Yar Hyder who could write both Pushtu and Urdu) also said that if Mahommed Ali was not back to the tribe by a certain time the girl would be slain. Mahommed went boldly to the fort and delivered the message to the colonel. They dared not detain him for fear of what would happen to the girl and he would answer no questions.

Then the colonel waxed furious with his stubborn British pride.

"Not one rupee will I pay!" he swore. "But if Marion is not returned to me unharmed I will sweep the mountains and wipe your tribe out of existence."

"Aye," Mahommed mocked, "ye know so well where my tribe and my village is!"

And the colonel cursed at that, for no Englishman knew where was Kadar.

"If the girl is not returned in such-and-such a time," said the colonel, "I will lead an army into the hills."

"And if the ransom is not at such-and-such a place within the same time," answered Mahommed Ali, "my tribesmen will fling the girl over a thousand-foot precipice."

The colonel was wild with rage but he could do nothing. When Mahommed returned certain scouts sought to follow him, but he was mountain-bred and he laughed at them and eluded them.

Now Khumail Khan was chief in Kadar, but there were others who wished for the chieftainship. There was Kulam Khan and Darza Shah and Yar Hyder. Of course there were many others, but those three were the most powerful, besides the mullah and Khumail Khan, in Kadar.

Of those three, Kulam Khan had the most powerful following, but even so he dared not openly strike for the chieftainship—yet. Then of course the other two were jealous and any two of the three would have united with Khumail Khan against the third; that being the way of the East, especially in Afghanistan.

So it was the day after we captured the girl that Kulam Khan came to me where I sat in my hut and said: "Thou and Yar Ali and the others have earned the hatred of Khumail Khan and the mullah."

"So it would seem," I answered grimly.

"Khumail Khan desires her and so does Hassan," he went on. "They desire the ransom also, but the girl they lust for more. Khumail Khan sits in his hut and curses the mullah but he dares not seize her for fear of mullah Hassan. And the mullah fears the vengeance of Yar Ali and the British. Also, he fears to push Khumail Khan too far. So he plots. There be much plotting in Kadar."

"Aye," I answered. "And where does this plotting lead to?"

"To the slaying of men," Kulam Khan answered, looking into my eyes. "To the rape of a girl. To the seizing of the chieftainship."

"So," I mused gazing upon him.

For a moment neither of us spoke. Then I said, "Yar Hyder is my friend."

"A chief needs a right-hand man," answered Kulam Khan.

"Speak plainly," I requested.

"This then," he looked about to see that no one spied upon us, "aid me when I strike for the chieftainship of Kadar and I swear that the girl will be unharmed and no one will question your right to all the ransom. And I will raise you high in council and war. All this will I do if thou and Yar Ali aid me."

"And Yar Hyder?" I asked.

"If he will aid me, I promise him the same. And also Mahommed Ali. But speak nothing to Yar Hyder as yet, lest he betray me to Khumail Khan."

I was silent for a while.

"Think on what I said," spoke Kulam Khan, rising. "I trust thee, Khoda Khan, for you have no love for Khumail Khan, and besides, you seem to lack treachery. Which is strange in an Afridi. Speak also to Yar Ali."

So he strode away and I watched him as he went. Tall and proudly straight he was, wearing his tulwar like a man of valour. It was said he was of Durani blood and I believed it. Kadar might do worse than have Kulam Khan for her chief.

Soon I sought Yar Ali where he sat in his hut and I told him all that Kulam Khan had told me.

"We had better aid him," I said. "For the chief will seize the girl, else. Or the mullah will take her or perhaps if Kulam Khan gains the chieftainship without our help, he may take the girl or the ransom."

"By Allah!" swore Yar Ali, driving his Khyber knife into the floor of the hut as was his want when wrathful. "The girl I will keep and the ransom I will have in spite of Khumail Khan, Kulam Khan, the mullah, and the devil himself. Why should I aid Kulam Khan? Why should I aid any Afridi? By Allah and by Allah! I want but the ransom which will enable me to leave these cursed mountains and see some of the outer world. Go ye to Kulam Khan and tell him that I slay Khumail Khan when I wish and no sooner. And when I have slain him, Kulam or Darza or Shaitan may take the chieftainship and the devil fly away with them all!"

I left him sitting in his hut, scowling and driving his knife again and again into the floor. A strange man, Yar Ali Khan.

I dared not take his words to Kulam Khan for fear that if we were seen talking together too much the chief would suspect something.

Nor did I speak to Yar Hyder for he too wished the chieftainship and he would hardly stand aside and see Kulam Khan take it.

But Mahommed Ali I talked to, and he said he would aid Kulam Khan.

"I would aid even Darza Shah against Khumail Khan."

Came the day for the ransom. British troops had scouted among the mountains but Kadar they could not find, and we believed that the colonel sahib had given in and brought the ransom.

The idea was that Yar Ali and I should go stealthily to the place where the ransom was to be left and spy upon they that were there. Then we would return to Kadar and if all seemed well, the four of us, Yar Ali, Yar Hyder, Mahommed Ali and I, were to take the girl to the place of the ransom.

"And by Allah!" said Yar Ali to the people of Kadar. "If the girl is harmed I will raze Kadar to the earth! I will burn and massacre. I will slay every man, woman and child in Kadar!"

So we left the village.

Why a band of Zakka Khel raiders should range so far afield I know not, nor why they should be bold enough to venture into Afridi country, but the first thing we knew of them was when a Tonc jezail spoke from the mountainside and the bullet whizzed close to my face.

We leaped behind boulders and returned their fire. For awhile this duel lasted, neither of us doing any damage to the others, but there were some ten of the Zakka Khels and they worked nearer and nearer, crouching and leaping from boulder to boulder, firing as they came.

Presently one was indiscreet and his turban showed for a moment above a boulder. Thereafter there were but nine Zakka Khels.

Yar Ali and I began to retreat, slipping from boulder to boulder as the raiders did.

Then as I rounded a huge boulder I came face to face with a Zakka Khel who had stolen around to take us from behind.

I had my tulwar unsheathed in my hand and I struck before he could draw or raise his rifle.

Then with savage yells the Zakka Khels rushed in. As they broke cover Yar Ali's rifle spoke and one of them dropped. The rest closed in. I saw Yar Ali strike down three of them with three blows of his tulwar and then I had no time to look, for I was fighting with a great Zakka Khel who was a ferocious swordsman. I had thought there was but ten but either I was mistaken or others had joined them.

By Allah, they set on us like wolves on a tiger!

I had much ado to defend myself and at last the Zakka Khel laughed sneeringly and swung up his tulwar to deliver the blow that would hurl me into Iblis.

But as his arm went up, high on the mountainside a rifle rang out and the Zakka Khel spun around and dropped.

Yar Ali had his back against a boulder, fighting for his life, his garments in tatters, his Khyber knife red to the hilt. Four Zakka Khels lay at his feet.

As they swarmed in upon him the rifle spoke again and a Zakka Khel pitched forward on his face.

The warriors whirled about, and as they did one of them crumpled to the earth.

Then upon the mountain I saw a strange sight. Down the steep mountainside a man was coming, a white man, dressed in a riding suit and helmet, such as Englishmen wear when riding. And he was not picking his way but was coming swiftly, leaping down from ledge to boulder, from boulder to ledge as does a mountain goat.

The Zakka Khels saw him, too. They stopped short and watched and then, wonder of wonders, they turned and fled as though the devil were after them!

The white man came on down the mountain. Silently we watched him. He was not a large man. He was of medium height, slim and wiry. His hair was black and so were his eyes. On his face was a smile.

Khoda Khan's Tale

(unfinished)

The American Gordon, whom the Moslems call El Borak, came into the mountains of Afghanistan again, and with him came Yar Ali Khan, who had gone away with him, some time before, when El Borak had come into the mountains and had rescued the memsahib Marion Sommerland from Khumail Khan. El Borak came to the village of Kadar and Kulam Khan made him welcome, for Kulam Khan owed his chieftainship to El Borak.

El Borak was older than he had been when he first entered the village of Kadar, but he was still little more than a youth.

Yar Ali Khan was clothed and armed like a chieftain and he was loud in the praises of the courage, skill and wisdom of El Borak in war and peace.

El Borak stayed awhile in the village of Kadar and presently he made it known that he wished some warriors to accompany him to a far country on a raid. Whereupon there was much arguing and discussion, some wishing to go with El Borak, some arguing against it. Chief among the men opposing El Borak was Darza Shah, who aspired to be chief, and who was forever causing quarrels and disputes.

Yar Ali Khan cursed them for fools who did not leap at the chance to gain fame and gold by following El Borak.

"I have followed him," said Yar Ali, "and behold my possessions." And he showed us his turban and his garments of the finest cloth, his costly Bokahariot belt, his pistols, his American-made rifle, his gold-mounted Khyber knife and cheray.

"And I have gold, also," quoth Yar Ali Khan, "though I brought it not into the mountains, knowing my tribesmen as I do."

Darza Shah opposed El Borak, as I said, making many objections. But El Borak did not argue. He said that he had sent word among the tribes that no warriors should attack the village of Kadar until he should return, and that if any tribe attacked Kadar, they should reckon with him, El Borak. And the tribes heeded, for already El Borak was known all over India and Central Asia.

El Borak said he would take only men who were unmarried, that he would arm them and that they would all share equally in any loot captured.

And El Borak said that, as the people of Kadar were his friends, he had given them the first chance, but that it mattered little to him whether they accompanied him or not. There were a thousand villages that would gladly furnish him with men.

So it came about that when El Borak left Kadar, nineteen Afridi warriors, including Yar Ali Khan, went with him. And among them I, Khoda Khan.

We marched through the Khyber Pass and at Jamrud we met five other men of El Borak's, a Sikh, an Orakzai, and three Afghans, and a Gurkha.

The Sikh was a skilled swordsman, named Lal Singh. The Orakzai was a savage warrior; his name was Ormuzd Shah, but we Afridis usually spoke of him as the Orakzai.

One of the Afghans was a tall, slim man, a lesser chief, one Bagheela Khan. Bagheela means panther and the name did not belie the man. He was an Afridi also but his tribe lived far to the north and west of Afghanistan.

The other two Afghans were north-Afridis, men of Bagheela Khan's village.

The Gurkha was a short man, not so tall as El Borak, and not heavy of build. His name was Ghur Shan.

We twenty Asians, led by Gordon, went down into India and across country by various ways to Bombay. And you may guess what manner of man El Borak was when I say that not once did British officials stop and question us and not one Indian man was slain nor one Indian woman outraged by any of our band. Nay, not one of our band was even thrown in jail.

At Bombay, Gordon had a ship awaiting us and we slipped aboard secretly at night and the ship sailed before the British learned of our departure. There was much talk and objection at going aboard but now that we were started, no man would turn back.

The ship was what is called a trading schooner and was owned and captained by a white man, an American like Gordon and a friend of Gordon likewise. The schooner sailed southward and though the rocking of the ship upon the waves bothered us at first and made too many to wish they were on land again, we soon became used to it and enjoyed the voyage. The crew of the ship were black men from the islands and they laughed and jeered at us much at first because we could not keep our feet when the ship lurched with the waves. And there would have been slaying on that account, had not Gordon interposed. After awhile the black men and we became friends of a sort and they told us of the sea and the lands from which they came and the lands they had seen and many strange tales, which were doubtless lies.

So we sailed across the ocean until we came to a place called Madagascar, a great island, big as all Afghanistan. From there we sailed to a bay called Delagoa and there we landed. Before we landed El Borak went ashore and bribed various officials, Portuguese, like those of Goa. Then we all went ashore, bearing many large bags and boxes, at which the Portuguese made no comment, having received Gordon's rupees. Gordon there hired various black men, called porters, to carry the luggage, at which we were relieved for we had thought that he might wish us to carry it. Then we marched into the jungle, which was all about and was very great and very dense.

When we made camp the first day, Gordon gave us our knives and tulwars which he had taken from us when we went aboard ship at Bombay. Also, he gave each man a high-powered repeating rifle, a revolver, cartridge belts, a hundred rounds of ammunition, and a canteen.

We marched through the jungle for some days and saw many sights. We saw many great beasts which were like huge cats—lions, El Borak called them—and they were greater than the tigers of India.

We saw crocodiles also, and leopards and many monkeys. El Borak gave orders not to shoot anything, except in self-defense and we, remembering how the wolves of the Himalayas had obeyed him, did as he said. And we saw many strange beasts, like unto a hog, with a body nearly as big as an elephant and with very short legs. These creatures swam about in the rivers and made a prodigious splashing and the crocodiles molested them not. They were doubtless some demon of the river, though El Borak said they were only beasts called hippopotamus.

El Borak and the Gurkha, Ghur Shan, who grew up in the jungles of Nepal, did the hunting and brought down only enough game to furnish us provision, but sometimes El Borak would give various of us permission to hunt, providing we went two, three or four together and strayed not far from the camp, for we were not used to the jungle.

I was hunting with Mahommed Ali and Ahmed Kulal some distance from the camp and we had slain a small bush-antelope. I was skinning it so that we might divide the weight equally among us when we carried it to camp, and the other two had walked on further into the jungle. Presently I heard a number of yells and Mahommed Ali and Ahmed Kulal returned with great swiftness, calling on the prophet Mohammed.

"Flee, Khoda Khan!" shouted Mahommed Ali. "A demon comes! Aye, an ifreet comes."

And I was aware of a crashing in the bush as though an elephant was charging through.

"Hark!" exclaimed Ahmed Kulal. "'Tis the ifreet!" And forthwith he fled with great energy. Mahommed Ali tarried awhile for he and I were friends.

"Flee! Khoda Khan," urged he. "'Tis a very demon. Huge and mighty is he, and resembling a hog except that he has a horn and that on his nose!"

"Now," thought I, "they are drunk, for surely no such thing with such a horn ever existed."

"Come!" urged he.

"Nay," quoth I, "I have a wish to see this strange ifreet."

Whereupon Mahommed Ali turned and fled away into the jungle toward the camp, with surprizing speed.

Then out of the jungle rushed a huge form and by the beard of the Prophet, it was even as Mahommed had said!

I fired wildly once and may I change to a pig if the bullet did not glance off the thing's hide!

He was coming with amazing swiftness for all his huge bulk but he would have had to race far more swiftly had he caught me. I would have outrun him entirely had I not presently leaped over what seemed to be a many-colored log. The thing rose up and threw itself upon me and I saw that it was a gigantic snake, a python such as are in the jungles of India. It wrapped about and would have crushed me to devour, had I not severed it in twain with my tulwar. Then as I leaped away, the monster that was like an elephant was upon me. I bounded away and as he charged past me, I swung my tulwar and smote off his horn. That did not seem to bother him at all for he rushed on into the jungle and disappeared. So I took the horn, which was some two feet or more long, curved, pointed and heavy, and went back to camp.

As I entered camp I saw all the warriors gathered before El Borak's tent where Ahmed Kulal and Mahommed Ali were telling of their adventure.

"Where is Khoda Khan?" asked El Borak, then he saw me approaching. He said naught, gave no sign that he saw me, save that he smiled faintly.

But they did not notice.

"Khoda Khan is devoured by an ifreet," said Ahmed Kulal. "He was a terrible monster, bigger than the biggest elephant. His eyes flamed fire. His claws were like curved scimitars. On his nose, which was ten feet long, he carried a horn which towered to the treetops! We fought like very tigers but he overpowered us and seizing Khoda Khan, devoured him at one gulp!"

Whereat the warriors were much frightened and looked to their rifles, when I stepped forward and called loudly, "Ahmed Kulal!"

Ahmed gave a screech and dived headfirst into El Borak's tent and Mahommed Ali turned pale.

"After you fled," quoth I, "I fought with the ifreet and presently he vanished in a blaze of flame and brimstone, leaving his horn in my grasp."

Whereat they had naught to say. But El Borak, when I had told him, laughed long and loud. Which was a thing that pleased me for I knew that he thought well of me. Not often did El Borak laugh from mirth. And all the Afghans and the blacks looked on me with respect as one of much skill and valor.

We marched on through the jungle for some days. There were many wild beasts in the jungle and we saw elephants and many more of the things with horns on their noses. Those El Borak called rhinoceroses.

Ghur Shan desired El Borak to slay some of the elephants and take the ivory but El Borak refused. There were also many leopards, lions and great snakes.

A leopard leaped on Bagheela Khan from the trees, but Bagheela Khan slew it with his saber before Gordon could shoot it and before it could injure him.

Then a lion rushed the camp leaping over the thorn boma we erected about each camp, and seized one of the black porters. Gordon beat the lion away from its prey with the butt of his rifle, which few men could do, and it escaped in the darkness. The porter was not badly hurt.

Then we met another safari, a band of negroes and Arabs, a vile crowd, the Arabs and armed blacks, called askaris, always beating the black porters and insulting them shamefully. They were led by an Arab named Hassan ibn Zaroud.

He and El Borak talked together in El Borak's tent and I, having beaten one of the black men for seeking to eavesdrop, listened and heard most of the conversation, because I did not trust the Arab.

They spoke in Arabic which I had learned.

"If you will throw in with me, we will become rich," quoth ibn Zaroud.

"Doubtless," answered El Borak.

"Now here is my plan," quoth ibn Zaroud, "and you may see if it be good. With my askaris and your men we will have a force large enough to quell any chief who might oppose our way. We will go up beyond Nyassa, to Tanganyika. We will take many slaves and ivory. We will seize the ivory the natives have hoarded up and we will shoot elephants for their ivory."

"And what then?" asked El Borak.

"We will sell the slaves at Dar-es-Salaam," said ibn Zaroud. "And there are men at Zanzibar who will buy our ivory and ask no questions."

"Aye, very good," said El Borak, dryly. "I hear that there is much ivory in the jungles at Nyassa. Also the natives would doubtless make good slaves."

For a moment nothing was said and then El Borak spoke, "But ibn Zaroud, I wonder if I would share the profits on the slaves and the ivory at Zanzibar?"

"What mean you, El Borak?" quoth ibn Zaroud, scowling.

Gordon laughed. "When I had slain the elephants for you and conquered the chiefs for you what then?"

"What then?" quoth ibn Zaroud.

"A spear from the jungle," said Gordon, "or a dagger in the night. Then all the slaves and the ivory would be yours."

The Arab scowled. "By the Prophet, sahib, you call me an assassin?"

"I call you nothing, Hassan ibn Zaroud," answered Gordon, "but it is well if we understand each other, if we go into any enterprise together."

"Ah," exclaimed ibn Zaroud, "you will do it?"

"Nay, I have not said so," answered Gordon. "How do I know all you say is truth?"

"It is plain that you are new to Africa," said the Arab. "Anyone knows that there are many natives for slaves and much ivory between Nyassa and Tanganyika."

"But that is not all," said Gordon.

The Arab hesitated, looked at Gordon. "What do you mean?" said he.

"Slaves and ivory do not interest me over much," said El Borak. "No, ibn Zaroud, I do not think we can join safaris."

"What would interest you then?" asked ibn Zaroud.

"Gold," answered El Borak.

The Arab gazed at him as if trying to read his mind.

"Listen," quoth he, "if I tell you that I can lead you to great stores of gold, will you join me?"

El Borak laughed, "Verily, ibn Zaroud, a liar is no friend of mine."

"I am not lying," said the Arab, angrily. "I can show where is more gold than a hundred men can carry away."

"Yours is a pleasing tale, ibn Zaroud," laughed El Borak.

For Gordon was very crafty.

The Arab cursed, "I tell you I speak truth," he said.

"Admitting that you do," said El Borak, "it is too great a distance to go even for gold."

"It is not as far as you have already come from India," said the Arab.

Gordon laughed again, "Why do you lie, ibn Zaroud; do you think I know nothing of Africa. There is no gold nearer than Kumassi."

"You know nothing," scoffed the Arab.

"You are a fool," said El Borak. "The British would never let us take gold out of Johannesburg."

The Arab gazed at Gordon as a fox gazes on a fat fowl. He was thinking how simple Gordon was and how easily he could dupe him at any time.

"Kumassi and Johannesburg," said he scornfully, "that is what you know. The British will have nothing to do with it."

"Better the British than the French," said El Borak. "I cannot go in French territory. There is a small trifle of an incident that occurred in French Indo-China, you understand?"

The Arab grinned. "You need not fear the French, sahib. We will go nowhere near them."

"But I was thinking of going southward into the Transvaal," objected El Borak. "My men are mountain men and they weary of the jungle."

"They will indeed weary of the jungle if they go with me," admitted the Arab. "But perchance they will find other mountains."

El Borak arose, "No, I think we cannot join safaris," said he. The Arab leaped to his feet, murder blazing from his black eyes.

"You tricked me!" he hissed.

"You tricked yourself," said Gordon. "I did not say I would go in with you."

For a moment the Arab glared. Then, for he was a very crafty man, he shrugged his shoulders and seemed to forget his anger.

"You are a shrewd man, sahib," quoth he. "There are few men who can trick ibn Zaroud. Come, let us be friends. Have you any good wines or rum?"

And thus he caught El Borak almost off his guard. Remember, El Borak was still little more than a youth. Gordon turned toward his wines, quick as a jungle-cat, the Arab snatched out a heavy revolver and smote El Borak across the head. Wolf though he was, Gordon reeled, then with a pantherish leap he was on ibn Zaroud, one hand wrenching away the pistol, the other driving a yataghan at the Arab's breast. Ibn Zaroud caught Gordon by the wrist and then as they struggled I leaped within the tent, jerked the Arab headlong to the floor of the tent and stooped above him, my tulwar bared for slaying.

"Shall I kill?" I asked El Borak.

El Borak shook his head, sheathing his dagger and I saw what incredible control he had over himself, for if ever the lust for killing gleamed in a man's eyes, it was in El Borak's.

He motioned me to let ibn Zaroud up, which I did, but holding my tulwar ready.

"Ibn Zaroud," said Gordon with a thin smile, "why should you assume that every man you meet is as great a fool as yourself? I am obliged to you for giving me the information I wanted, but outside of that I do not care for you. You annoy me. You disgust me. You are no gentleman. Khoda Khan, kindly throw him out."

I did as Gordon asked me, also landing a most noble kick while ibn Zaroud was in the air.

"How much of our conversation did you overhear, Khoda Khan?" asked Gordon.

"Why, all," quoth I, somewhat taken aback.

"You will oblige me if you make no mention of it," said El Borak.

"I will do as the sahib bids," quoth I.

"It will be greatly to your advantage," said El Borak and for an instant his eyes glittered as he gazed into mine and my flesh crawled.

"In another instant," said El Borak, "I would have—" then he stopped. I knew that he was about to say that in another instant he would have slain the Arab and had changed his mind, lest I think him boastful and that he offend me.

"You did well, Khoda Khan," he went on. "And as a reward you may keep the Arab's pistol which you have in your shirt. You have my leave to go."

And by the Prophet, I could have sworn that he did not see me when I stole the pistol!

The other men had seen the Arab thrown from the tent and they asked me many questions. I told them of the fight, but said nothing of what passed between Gordon and ibn Zaroud.

Yar Ali Khan was very jealous that another man than he should aid El Borak in a fight and was nearly ready to pick a quarrel with me for he considered himself Gordon's right-hand man.

The Arab had gone back to his camp and some of the warriors, Bagheela Khan and Lal Singh and Yar Ali foremost, wished to go and attack the Arab camp, but Gordon refused and presently the other safari broke camp and marched away.

We marched also, in a different direction, and presently we came upon a native village in the jungle. It was a cluster of huts made of grass and mud surrounded by a wall of the same stuff. The people, who were black men and very ugly, brought us fruit and goat-flesh and milk in great gourds. They, the black men, were ugly and dirty and wore only loincloths. There were women too, but Gordon did not need forbid the men to have aught to do with them, for they were uglier than the men and wore great rings in their noses.

After leaving their village we came to a river which Gordon called the Limpopo. This we crossed by means of native boats and found another village on the other bank, where we hired more porters, our others having desired to return to their homes on the coast.

We presently quit the jungle and came out upon wide plains, covered with very high grass, which Gordon called the veldt. There were lions there, and buffaloes and deer and many baboons upon small hills, which Gordon called kopjes.

We camped upon the veldt and El Borak and Bagheela Khan and Lal Singh and Ghur Shan and Yar Ali Khan held council in El Borak's tent.

Then El Borak spoke to us saying, "So far you have followed me well and faithfully, knowing nothing of my plans, trusting that I would lead you to good loot. Now you shall know my plans. In Central Africa there is a strange people, who have great store of gold and jewels. It is an ancient empire, that has been there since beyond all memory of man. I have heard much of it but did not know the exact part of Africa until recently."

"And how far is it to that country?" asked Ormuzd Shah.

"Near a thousand miles to the northward by westward," said El Borak. Thereat we were discontented.

"Ho," quoth Yar Ali Khan, "they must be men who follow El Borak. Why, why grumble ye? You have come already twice that far from Afghanistan."

Then El Borak spoke again and he told us of the ancient grandeur of that old empire and of all the gold and jewels we should get. And, truly, El Borak had the gift of language, for when he had spoken, not one of us would have turned back.

"And are you certain the Arab gave you the clue?" Bagheela Khan asked El Borak, not at that time but afterwards, and Abdullah Ghulab overheard.

"Certain," El Borak answered. "He was so sure of his craftiness that he gave no thought that I was seeking to learn all he knew. It is not on British territory, nor French, so it is certainly located in the Belgian Congo. Hassan ibn Zaroud thought that I was a fool."

"So did Khumail Khan, also," quoth Yar Ali, grimly.

Marching across the veldt, Gordon gave us permission to hunt, so among others, Mahommed Ali and I set out across the veldt and, having rounded a kopje, came upon a native. He was no such native as we had seen in the jungle. He was a tall man, young and well-built, clad in a loincloth and bearing in his hand a heavy stick some three feet long, having a large knob on one end. He was muscular and lithe as a black panther, and his features were not negroid but straight as a European's.

This black we accosted, but he could not understand our language and his was not like that of our porters, of which we had some scant knowledge.

"Let us take him prisoner," quoth Mahommed Ali, "and take him before El Borak."

I agreed and we rushed upon him simultaneously, intending to beat him with our rifle-butts if he resisted. But he stood his ground and smote me right heartily over the head with his knob-stick, and well for me that my turban was thick. Mahommed Ali, seeing that, drew his tulwar, but the black man avoided the blow and knocked Mahommed Ali sprawling.

Then Lal Singh came around the kopje and intervened, for he could speak the language of the black man, Gordon having taught him many languages.

"Ye be two fools," quoth the Sikh in great scorn. "This is one of a tribe of whom Gordon wishes to make allies." And he went back to camp, the black man accompanying him and we following, somewhat crestfallen.

Gordon and the black man talked together. The black's name was Unalanga and he was of a tribe called Zulus.

He guided us to his village which he called a kraal. As we approached, a band of armed men came out to meet us. They were tall, big men, with shields and short, heavy spears, battle-axes and knob-sticks. They were dressed in loincloths and many had rings of black rubber worked into their hair.

Gordon and Unalanga having spoken with them, they made us welcome, and it would seem that they had heard of Gordon, as indeed, who in all the East has not?

We camped outside the kraal and El Borak forbade the men to make free with the Zulu women, as well as telling us that the Zulus would slay any man who did so. Thereat the men grumbled some-what, for the women of the kraal were not like those of the jungle and were comely to look upon, and, truth to tell, I doubt much if Gordon's command was obeyed by all, for many Zulu girls found occasion to come to the camp and did not look on us with disfavor.

Gordon talked much with the chief of the kraal and the chief gave consent for twenty of his young warriors to accompany us. Gordon gave him presents of beads, bright-colored cloth, rum and a trade musket with ammunition. As in Kadar, he selected only young, unmarried warriors. Among these was Unalanga, who commanded them.

These, Gordon, half in jest, called his impi, which is the same in their language as laskar, and Unalanga the induna, meaning general.

We marched northwestward after leaving the kraal, marching far around a place called Bulawayo. Presently we were intercepted by a British officer with a squad of mounted black soldiers.

The Englishman scowled and seemed very angry and, having dismounted, enquired of Gordon what he meant by bringing a band of armed men on British territory and from whence he came.

Gordon smiled and invited him to have a drink. What passed between them Yar Ali Khan heard and told some of us afterwards, Gordon having given him permission to.

The Britisher was very angry and spoke of prisons and firing squads and Gordon smiled.

"Were you not in Tunis at a certain time?" asked El Borak.

The officer started and admitted that he was.

"So I thought," said El Borak, smiling. "I never forget faces. The beautiful wife of"—here he spoke too low for Yar Ali to hear—"is quite a charming woman, is she not, lieutenant?"

The officer's face turned red, then pale.

"What do you mean?" he exclaimed.

El Borak smiled blandly. "That little incident at the embassy, sir. It is unnecessary for me to speak more plainly, as well as distasteful."

For a moment the two men gazed at each other, the Britisher striving to read El Borak's mind.

"You devil!" he muttered. "What is your price?"

"Why speak of price among friends?" quoth El Borak smoothly. "But if my expedition were to be stopped or reported to the British government, it would inconvenience me."

"You will not be interfered with," answered the Englishman.

"Thank you," said El Borak. "I assure you that my expedition will remain on British land no longer than necessary. Allow me to refill your glass, lieutenant, the champagne is of the finest."

The Zulus were much impressed when the Britisher and his soldiers rode away without seeking to obstruct our march.

"Aye," boasted Yar Ali Khan, "ye will see greater wonders than that if ye follow El Borak as long as I have."

Then he narrated a long tale of how he and El Borak slew a terrible dragon of the Gobi desert which was a hundred feet long and weighed a thousand pounds and had talons like elephants' tusks, which was probably a lie.

Having marched across the veldt for some days, we came to a part of the veldt inhabited by a tribe called the Matabeles, a people akin to the Zulus, who were very war-like. Unalanga distrusted them and Gordon gave orders to avoid all kraals and to have nothing to do with the natives. We doubled our sentries and marched in close order, none of us straying. We saw natives watching us at a distance and several times we saw rather large bands. Once, when we were camped not far from a kraal, various Matabele girls came amongst the Zulus and sought to entice several warriors away to the kraal. But

Unalanga, who was a wise man though a young one, caused those girls to be seized and whipped soundly and driven from the camp.

Every night we could hear the native drums thudding in all directions and we expected attacks, but for awhile they did not come against us, although Ormuzd Shah slew with his bare hands a Matabele who slipped up upon him and sought to stab him as he was doing sentry duty.

Once, at dawn, a band rushed the camp but were driven back by our rifle fire without doing any damage.

Then one day we saw a large band of warriors some miles ahead of us. Gordon climbed upon a kopje and gazed about with his field glasses.

"There are some one hundred and fifty men, or rather less," said he. "And I notice a kraal which is about half, or rather more, the distance between us and the warriors. It is deserted except for the old men, women and children. Very good. We can reach the kraal, set it ablaze and get back to the knoll before the Matabeles can reach the kopje."

We heard him in amazement. The warriors were ahead of us, and the kraal of which Gordon was speaking lay off to the right. The warriors were, as he had said, about twice as far as the kraal. It was El Borak's plan to take the Zulus and race to the kraal, leaving the Afghans entrenched on the kopje with the camp servants and the baggage. There they would fire the kraal and return. Of course, many objections were raised, but Gordon said he would reply to them after we had routed the Matabeles. And in a very short time he and the Zulus were racing at full speed across the veldt toward the kraal. With them went Yar Ali Khan and Lal Singh. The rest of us piled boulders upon the slopes of the kopje near the top and made ready for battle. The Matabeles were puzzled, for they had expected us to continue on our march until we nearly reached them, as we had done on other occasions. And they were puzzled at Gordon leading his men against the kraal. But that was ever El Borak's way, to successfully attempt the most daring feats and to strike a foe as he least expected. Gordon never did as his foes expected him to and therein lies his success.

Presently the Matabeles came racing across the veldt, yelling their war cries, shields clashing, spears flashing.

We could hear faintly the yells of our Zulus, mingled with the clash of spears, an occasional rifle shot, and the screams of women. On came the Matabeles. Just as they were almost halfway to the kopje from whence we had first seen them, we saw flames leap up from the kraal and from the racing warriors came a savage yell of rage. Sounds of battle still came from the kraal and then they ceased and we saw men spring from the kraal and start swiftly across the veldt. It was Gordon and his warriors, but I knew the Matabeles would reach the kopje before they would. Then the Matabeles were within rifle range and our rifles began to crack. Such fighting was much easier than it is in the mountains and we did not often miss. Still, on they came, frenzied with the lust for slaughter. Some streamed out across the veldt in a long, straggling line to intercept Gordon and his Zulus. The rest swarmed up the slope. Then we were firing pointblank in their savage faces, and then we too went raging with the battle-lust and we leaped over our barricade of boulders and flung ourselves upon them with dagger, tulwar, the rifle-stock. The first force of our rush carried all of us, Afghan and Matabele, down the slopes to the foot of the kopje, and there they closed in on us. They far outnumbered us and we saw that we should have stayed behind the barricade. They were armed with stabbing-assegais, knob-sticks, and battle-axes and they had shields. We had some of us seen the Tibetans use axes and had thought them clumsy weapons, but where the Tibetans used great, long-shafted, unwieldy weapons and only swung right and left, the Matabeles, like the Zulus, used comparatively short-handled axes with curved, very wide edges, and they wielded them with as much skill as a Sikh wields a saber. Ali bin Razeel smote a Matabele's head from his shoulders and went down, cleft to his bearded chin by a battle-ax in the hands of a huge warrior. We were surrounded. I saw Ormuzd Shah swinging right and left with a battle-ax he had seized. Ghur Shan was leaping here and there, grinning like a monkey, warding spears and axes with the small round shield he carried and thrusting, hewing, smiting, his kukrie red to the hilt. Bagheela Khan was battling like the panther he was, and yelling commands for us to break away and retreat back up the kopje; the two north-Afridis fighting like two wolves beside him.

It seemed as if we would all go down beneath that flashing horde of spears when a new chorus of yells rang above the battle din and a new sound was heard, the clashing of ax on shield and the slither of spear against spear. Gordon and his Zulus it was, who, smashing through the line of Matabeles who had intercepted them, smote the Matabeles from the rear. I caught a glimpse of Gordon, raging though the battle, his dark face white and eyes glittering with the battle-joy, a pistol flaming in one hand, an Indian saber whirling in the other. For a moment the black men fought savagely and then the Zulus crashed through their ranks and the battle became a riot. The Matabeles fled over the veldt in all directions and most of them escaped, for we had no desire to pursue them.

El Borak looked about him. "You fools," said he. "Why did you not stay behind the barricade of the kopje?"

Bagheela Khan strode up to him, his garments tattered and bloodstained, his turban awry, one arm limp from a spear-thrust in the shoulder.

"Mine was the fault," said he, proudly. "I take the blame."

"There is no blame, Bagheela Khan," said El Borak. "Who can control wolves?"

"None but you, sahib," answered Bagheela Khan.

El Borak looked to the wounded. Ali bin Razeel and three more Afghans had been slain in the battle; one, like Ali bin Razeel, by a battle-axe, the other two by the Matabele assegais. Also, one of the Zulus had been slain.

Bagheela Khan had a spear wound in the right shoulder, Ahmed Kulal had a spear-thrust in the thigh, Yussef Hyder had been knocked senseless and one of the north-Afridis had a broken arm from a swing of a knob-kerrie, and there was not a man of the whole band who did not have bruises and slight wounds. Had not Gordon's Zulus arrived when they did, we should have been wiped out. El Borak and Lal Singh and one of the Zulus bandaged the wounded and set the arms and wrists that had been broken and dislocated.

Then, at El Borak's orders, the Zulus slew all the wounded Matabeles except one, whom they brought before El Borak.

"Take my talk to your inkosi and his indunas," said El Borak. "I am El Borak, I am Inginyama, I am the Wolf. I go through your country and I harm you not. Molest me not and I will not molest you. But you have seen how I strike my foes. Tell your king"—here Gordon leaned forward and his eyes glittered so that the Matabele shrank back from their gaze—"that if he sends another impi against me, I will raid his kraal and slay until my warriors wade ankle-deep in Kafir blood, and I will bind him and burn him in the flames of his palace."

The Kafir warrior drew back. "The king will slay me if I bear him such words," said he.

"And I will slay you if you do not," said El Borak. "Tell him, moreover, that if he slays you, I will slay him some time."

So the Matabele was given his weapons and set out across the veldt.

Gordon said the kraal they had burned was deserted except for the women, children and old men and a few warriors. Those warriors had to be routed before they could fire the kraal and return, but neither women, old men nor children had been harmed, for El Borak forbade it. Nearly all the warriors had left the kraal, as they had the other kraals nearby, some, the younger warriors, those we had fought, to march around and head us off, the others to join the impis the king of the Matabeles was getting together. The main horde of Matabeles were far behind us, and the warriors of the different kraals had orders to obstruct our march until the impis could come up with us. All that Gordon had learned from prisoners taken at the kraal.

So we took up our march with great speed, and at the next kraal we came upon, we raided it and seized many oxen. The Kafir train oxen to ride as other peoples do horses and we seized some sixty of them. The camp servants, being jungle people, and the Afghans had difficulty in learning to ride those oxen, but the Zulus rode them easily, for they were akin to the Matabeles and had many of the same customs.

So, upon those oxen we marched very swiftly indeed, for we seized fresh oxen at each village, and the impis of the Matabeles never got close enough to us for their scouts to catch sight of us. Sometimes armed bands of warriors tried to stop us, but as we were mounted and they were not, for it is seldom that they ride to war, we would ride around them and frequently raid their kraal and be gone before they could reach the village.

Presently we came upon kraals of a tribe different from the Matabeles. They were not Kafirs as are the Matabeles and Zulus, but a tribe akin to the Bechuanas and called Makolalas. They are not as warlike as the Matabeles and are a higher type of savages than are the Bechuanas.

They were friendly towards us and El Borak made them presents of the oxen which we had taken from the Matabeles, for he said we would soon take to the jungle where they would only be in our way. The jungle negroes who were our porters wished to return to their homes on the Limpopo River and Gordon gave them their pay in beads and cloth and rum. They started back, in spite of the Matabeles, and El Borak hired other porters from the villages of the Makolalas. They were tall, strongly built, but not over-large men, of good nature, and somewhat like overgrown children, forever laughing and shouting and quarreling and dancing.

After leaving the village where we hired the porters, we went on, the veldt becoming like a forest, great rolling parklands. Here there were many Makolala villages, for those tribes had inhabited all that country far to the south until the Matabeles came north from the Transvaal and drove them out. Here and there we saw several Hottentot villages whose people had hundreds of years ago come from some other land and driven out the tribes who dwelt there, so no man knows who those tribes were. Then the Makolalas had come into the land and conquered and enslaved the Hottentots, and had been in turn driven out by the Matabeles.

The Hottentots were a very low grade of savage, not an ebony black like the Makolalas nor a bronze black like the Kafirs, but of a dingy yellow. They lived in small, squalid grass huts and went entirely naked, both the women and the men. Then there were Bushmen who were even lower than the Hottentots, and who had hardly a human speech. There were not so many of them or the Hottentots either as there were further south, Gordon said, for they lived in deserts and swamps, the stronger tribes having seized the more desirable lands. The Bushmen were perhaps the descendants of those tribes the Hottentots conquered, and certainly, they hated the Hottentots enough to justify that opinion.

We were marching though a country, which, as I said, was like a great parkland, with great baobab trees that towered over a hundred feet high.

Our scouts, who were Zulus, returned with the news that a band of warriors were on the march, advancing swiftly towards us: a large band of warriors who were strange to them.

There were nearly two hundred of them, so the scouts said.

"They are of a strange tribe, inkosi," said Umbelazi, one of the scouts. "We never saw any of them before. They have their teeth filed to points like the Gronqounqo."

"Cannibals," said El Borak. He made us build a barricade around the camp, which we did by chopping down small trees and making a wall of them all about the camp, the Makolalas doing most of the work.

We were camped about a great baobab tree and Gordon had Abdullah Ghulab, Shah Abdhur, Abdul Khan and Yar Ullah go up into the branches of the tree with their rifles and conceal themselves among the foliage.

Then, leaving Bagheela Khan and Unalanga in charge of the camp, Gordon took Yar Ali, Lal Singh, Ghur Shan and two of the Zulus, Umbelazi and Sakatra, and slipped into the forest. There the forest had begun to resemble the jungle somewhat, for it was denser and thicker, though not true jungle.

After a while, some two hundred warriors emerged from the forest and halted at the sight of our barricade. We held our fire at Bagheela's command, although they were within range. Then instantly they took to cover behind trees and in the long grass, sending a hail of arrows at the barricade. One of them, a tall, hideous warrior, leaped erect and fired a trade-musket at the camp. In the same instant a rifle spat, not from the barricade, but from somewhere in the forest, and the cannibal plunged headlong. Then we opened fire, wasting no ammunition but firing at every movement of the bush, knowing we would not hit Gordon nor his men for they were further back in the forest. The cannibals answered our fire with arrows, throwing spears and firing trade muskets. They had surrounded us and were creeping nearer and nearer through the bush. But there was a clear space all about the camp for some hundred or more yards. The sharpshooters in the trees were at a great advantage, for they could see any negro who was not well hidden. The Zulus, having no guns, were impatient and wished to charge the cannibals, but Unalanga forbade them. Presently from the forest came the screech of a leopard, twice repeated, and Bagheela Khan gave orders to stop firing and not to fire at anything unless we saw for certain that it was a cannibal.

Then, fierce, wild and savagely exultant rose the yell of a wolf and we knew El Borak had made a kill. The cannibals stopped firing for an instant, then began again. Then suddenly a clump of grass higher than a man's head was shaken as if two men were struggling among it. Then for an instant the grinning face of the Gurkha, Ghur Shan, was seen and he tossed a black man's head into the open. The next instant the grass clump was the target for some two hundred arrows and musket bullets but we knew that Ghur Shan had darted away into the forest. Such swift and silent murder was beginning to shake the cannibals' nerves, as was shown by their wild firing and savage yells. I doubted not that Yar Ali and Lal Singh had done some slaying, and, as for the two Zulus—just then the bushes thrashed and two black men staggered into the open, clinched in a savage fight. A moment they swayed, then one broke from the other and with a savage thrust, bore his foeman down and pinned him to the ground with his spear. Then wrenching it forth, waved it high in the air with an exultant yell and leaped into the bush. And from the Zulus behind the barricade went up a fierce shout of triumph, for the slayer was Umbelazi.

For a short time more the cannibals kept up their fire and then suddenly they broke cover and charged down upon the barricade, yelling like fiends. They were tall, skinny men, most of them, hideous, with their teeth filed to points, naked, and armed with bows, long spears and shields. Their charge brought them almost to the barricade and then they broke before our rifle fire and fled back to the forest. They were no such fighters as the Matabeles. Not a man of us had gotten a scratch except Lal Singh, who had a slight spear cut on his arm, made by a cannibal whom he slew with his saber in the forest. We counted the slain and, including those killed by Gordon and those with him, they numbered forty cannibals. The Zulus were dissatisfied, all except Umbelazi and Sakatra. For Unalanga had not even allowed them to pursue the cannibals after they were routed and, as they had no rifles, they had had no part in the battle. Gordon said the cannibals were doubtless some Zambesi river tribe on a raiding expedition or one that had been driven away by a stronger tribe. He said they did not often roam so far south. We did not see their village, if they had one near, and we did not search for it, though the Zulus wished to seek for it and set it afire. We continued on our way and the cannibals did not molest us further, although we could hear their tom-toms booming away off in the bush.

We marched on through the jungle and across a plain, and one day as we were building the boma we erected about each camp, a man walked into camp. He was the Matabele whom Gordon had sent to the Kafir king after the battle with the Matabeles. He had traveled far, for what few garments he wore were tattered and dusty. He carried no weapons except a spear and a shield. We took away his weapons and brought him before Gordon.

"You bore my words to the inkosi?" said El Borak.

"Aye," answered the native. "And the king was very angry and he had me imprisoned, meaning to slay me for daring to bring him such talk. But I escaped, and since then I have followed your safari, inkosi, but you have travelled so fast that I have been unable to catch up with you."

"And what now?" asked El Borak.

"I wish to follow you, inkosi," said the Kafir. "I might have remained in my country, but if the king had ever captured me, he would have slain me. You are a mighty warrior, inkosi, and a wise leader. I wish to follow you."

"I have ever a welcome for brave men," said El Borak, "but my safari goes into the Congo country and beyond."

"No matter," said the Matabele. "When a warrior of the Matabele follows a chief, he follows him in all things and without question."

"You are a man of valor," said El Borak. "You shall have equal standing with the warriors of Unalanga, under whose command you will be."

"Good," said the Matabele. "They are brave warriors, the Zulus. And Unalanga is a chief of whom even a warrior of the Matabeles may be proud to fight under."

"Good," said El Borak. "When we have returned from this trek, ye will all rank as keshlas. You have my leave to go."

The Afghans looked upon the Matabele, whose name was Umgazi, with suspicion.

Yar Ali Khan especially eyed him suspiciously, for he was always jealous of any man to whom El Borak showed the slightest favor, and I always wondered why he did not murder Lal Singh.

"That black Shaitan tricked El Borak," he grumbled. "He joined our safari in order to assassinate El Borak. But though he befools El Borak he cannot befool me, by the beard of the Prophet! Let him make one suspicious move and I will hew him into a hundred pieces and scatter them over the jungle."

Whereat we jeered greatly, at Yar Ali hinting that he was superior to El Borak in craft, well-knowing that if any other man had laid claim to such in Yar Ali's hearing, he would have had a war on his hands.

As for the Zulus, they accepted Umgazi with no question. As I said, Zulu and Matabele are both Kafir and speak much the same language, though our Zulus came from south of the Transvaal and the Matabele came from northern Rhodesia.

We came upon villages, most of small tribes but some of them Makolalas, who seemed to be scattered all over that part of Africa. Those villages would welcome us as great curiosities and the natives would give provisions freely. At each village our Makolalas would mingle with those of the village and dance and feast with them. Sometimes there would be quarrels and fights, but there was always great laughing and shouting and talking, for without doubt the Makolalas are the noisiest people in all Africa. The Peshawur serai is nothing to one of their villages.

Gordon gave orders about the native women again, but was not as well obeyed as he would have liked. The Zulus made no bother, for they scorned the Makolalas and would pay no attention to their women. Some of the Afghans secretly went against Gordon's commands, but they were careful to keep it secret, as well from Yar Ali and Lal Singh as from Gordon and Bagheela Khan. Yar Ali Khan cared nothing for women, much less Makolala girls, but it always enraged him to have Gordon's commands disobeyed. Lal Singh said that the sins of followers discredited a leader and he had no intention of allowing anyone to disgrace El Borak. As he said that with his hand on a pistol, no one disagreed.

But it was the Makolala porters who disobeyed El Borak mostly. However, at the villages of other tribes they gave no bother.

We were now in the jungle and it was very dense. There were many wild beasts and serpents, and the trees were close together so that it was very hot in the jungle. Many tribes lived in the jungle, some of them very warlike, so El Borak took from the luggage twenty Martini rifles and gave them to the Zulus, at which they were very pleased. Cartridge belts and thirty rounds of ammunition was given to each warrior. They were instructed to practice at targets every day, for few of them had ever handled any gun at all, none any but trade muskets which were cheap muzzle-loaders.

Also, El Borak had we, the Afghans, to instruct them on the art of shooting, and he had them teach us the use of spear, shield and knob-stick. I forgot to say that after the battle with the Matabeles, El Borak had us to take fifty of their shields. Those shields were oblong and made of oxen-hide, dried and hardened and stretched on a very hardwood frame. They would turn spears and arrows and stop battle-axes and musket bullets.

El Borak taught us to use them, so we learned to fight with shield and tulwar, like the warriors of old. At first they seemed very cumbersome, but when we learned to use them we found that they were of great advantage. We were all well-armed, there were extra rifles and a great store of ammunition.

The natives we met were friendly, most of them, and the warlike ones were not powerful enough to attack us. Gordon treated all the negroes fairly and would not allow any of them to be imposed upon in any way.

Many of them had never seen a white man, for we had on the whole journey avoided the trade route and the slave trails, for Gordon wished the expedition to be kept as secret as possible, especially from the various governments. Presently we came upon a river, much larger than the Limpopo, which El Borak said was the Zambesi. Native tribes called the Batoka lived on the banks, and they carried us across in long, unwieldy boats, made by hollowing out a great tree trunk. These Batokas grease their limbs and bodies and go naked, not even wearing a loincloth. They are not a warlike people and they make their living by cultivation. They smoke very strong native tobacco, both men and women, which they grow themselves. The women cut their hair short and the men allow it to grow long and plait it into a cone.

They have an absurd custom of welcoming a guest, such as a chief or a white man. They lay upon their backs and wave their legs in the air, slapping their thighs and shouting, "Kina bomba!"

They are not especially warlike, but are usually embroiled in some quarrel with the Makolalas, many of whom live on the Zambesi.

After crossing the Zambesi, we proceeded northwestward. Beyond the Zambesi Gordon did not know the languages of the tribes, nor did our Makolalas, so he had persuaded a Batoka to come along with us as interpreter.

The jungle became thicker and denser. In some places we had to chop our way through. Treacherous tribes, the Banyai, lived there. We could hear their drums booming in the bush from all directions. They made several attacks on us but each time we repulsed them. After we had marched for days, El Borak said we were no longer in British territory, but in the Belgian Congo.

We had made a few marches in the Congo, and Ormuzd Shah, one of the Zulus, Sumundra, and I were scouting ahead of the rest. We heard a crashing in the branches of the jungle trees and paused. Then the sounds ceased and from the bushes stepped a thing that I thought was Shaitan of Iblis himself, by the beard of the Prophet!

It walked on its hind feet like a man, but no such man ever lived. It was covered with long, coarse reddish hair, its great arms swung below its knees, and its face was that of a devil.

For a moment we stood, unable to speak or move because of amazement and wonder, then with a hideous scream the thing rushed upon us. For all of its bulk it was amazingly swift. The Orakzai jerked up his rifle, but before he could fire the monster had torn the gun from his grasp. And by the Prophet, the thing twisted that rifle between his huge hands and broke off the stock and bent the barrel double as easily as I could crush a straw! Then it closed with Ormuzd Shah and for all the Orakzai's great strength it would have crushed him like a babe had not Sumundra driven his assegai through the monster. With a fiendish shriek it released Ormuzd Shah and turned on the Zulu, but as it did I struck with my tulwar and even then was forced to smite twice.

We carried the monster back to show to Gordon and the others and it required the full strength of all three of us.

There was nearly a stampede when we brought it in, but Gordon said it was only a giant ape, called a gorilla. He said there were many of them in the jungles of the Congo. And as we marched further into the jungle we saw more of them but they did not again attack us.

It was very dense and hot in the jungle, the smell of decaying vegetation filling the air, the trees towering high and their branches entangled so that little sunlight filtered through, great creepers swinging to the ground, strips of marsh where crocodiles wallowed and snakes slithered. It was not a place for hillmen, though everyone in the safari remained healthy, perhaps on account of certain herbs which El Borak distributed among us and bade us chew. What those herbs were, I know not, but El Borak, though no hakim, knows of many things unknown to anyone else, for there is scarce a part of the world where he has not been exploring.

The natives who lived in the jungle were of a low order, naked, sullen and fierce, many of them cannibals. Once they laid an ambush for us but our scouts informed us of it, so we marched around the ambush and fell upon the cannibals from the rear, slaying many.

None of us liked the jungle, neither the Afghans, who had been raised in the lofty mountains of the Himalayas, nor the Zulus, whose homeland was on the veldt.

El Borak avoided the denser parts of the jungle all he could and indeed in some places it would have been necessary to chop a road even for one or two men. We saw elephants, not in very great numbers but with fine tusks, but Gordon would not hunt them.

"We will not burden ourselves with ivory," said he, "for we will want to carry as much gold as we can."

We camped close to a large village and the natives came out to view us. They were like those we had seen, filed-tooth cannibals. But they seemed more arrogant than others and the Batoka interpreter told us that they were of a powerful tribe who had defeated or enslaved all the other tribes of that region. The king presently came forth, attended by warriors with spears and shields, and dressed in parrot feathers and monkey skins.

He was haughty and arrogant and very fat from dissipation. He boasted of his wisdom and courage and of the prowess of his warriors and of the great store of ivory he had and of his wives, of whom he had two hundred and forty.

Then he commanded El Borak to give him twenty rifles and ammunition and rum.

El Borak laughed at him.

"You are here to steal my ivory," said the king with great anger. "I will kill you all and eat you."

Then all his warriors rushed upon us, but they broke and fled back to the village at our first fusillade and Gordon leaped upon the king and took him prisoner. Then Yar Ali and Bagheela Khan wished to slay the king and throw his head into the village, but Gordon would not allow it. So we kept the king for a hostage and the cannibals did not attack us again although war drums boomed in the village and we could hear the warriors dancing and yelling all night.

The next morning we took the king with us a short distance so the warriors would not attack us on the march. Then we let him go, the Makolalas first stripping him and beating him soundly and pulling his hair. For all of his fatness, he fled back to the cannibal village as if all the lions of the Congo were pursuing him. We came upon other villages but they were either not so warlike or not so powerful.

We came upon a river in the jungle, and none of the safari knew what river it was. So we called it Changaan, for it was a Zulu by that name who first saw it. It was a fair-sized river and flowed north by west, toward the Congo. There were river tribes living on the banks and from them El Borak bought three boats. They were war canoes, forty feet long, riding low in the water, though nearly flat of bottom and very strongly built.

El Borak apportioned the men and the luggage equally and the Makolala porters became rowers. The river was muddy and there were many hippos, crocodiles and mosquitoes. On either bank the jungle ran down to the water's edge.

We rowed on steadily, day and night, only pausing to kill fresh game. The deer and wild hogs would come down to the river's edge and Gordon would shoot them. Then we would take them aboard and skin and cut them up there. We made a sort of platform in the bows of each canoe, on which was a shallow, round, dishlike affair in which we cooked. So we did not have to go ashore for anything, except for fresh water. The water of the river was too muddy to drink.

We began to see natives in canoes, some fishing, and native villages. Some of those villages were built on the banks of the river, some on stilts set in the river itself.

Gordon stopped at one of the villages and purchased thirty shields of rhinoceros hide. They were very hard and strong and were superior to the shields of the Zulus, though so heavy that they were unwieldy.

Those shields, and the shields which we had taken from the Matabeles, El Borak had us fasten to gunwales of the canoes, from stern to prow. This made a barricade behind which we would be sheltered from spears and other missiles, and as they were spaced properly, it did not interfere with the oars.

We saw the wisdom of this, for one day a number of war canoes put out from a village to intercept us. We kept straight on until we were within rifle range. The natives, who were cannibals, were brandishing their spears and yelling their war cries. Presently their arrows began to spat against the shield-barricade and Gordon gave the order to open fire. Our three boats had abandoned the single-file formation and had drawn up parallel to each other. The Makolalas rowed straight ahead and every Asian and Zulu crouched behind the shields and poured a perfect storm of bullets into the cannibal canoes.

Some of their canoes were riddled and sank, the warriors in them being seized by crocodiles. The rest turned and rowed back to their village.

At the next village, which happened to be friendly, Gordon purchased a light, two-man canoe and thereafter he and another man would stay some distance ahead of the boats, scouting as it were. Sometimes he would take Yar Ali, sometimes Lal Singh, sometimes Umgazi.

Umgazi was with him as we came upon a bend of the river, and their canoe had disappeared around the bend before the three boats got to it. And when we rounded the bend there was no canoe in sight. The river flowed away for miles to disappear around another bend. A few hippos splashed near the bank, a crocodile was swimming to shore. There was nothing else in sight.

"By the Prophet!" swore Yar Ali. "Here is something strange."

"Perhaps they went ashore," suggested Abdhur Shah.

"Then they would have pulled the canoe up on the bank," said Lal Singh.

We fired several shots but got no reply. It was as if the jungle had swallowed El Borak and Umgazi. Some thought perhaps a hippo or crocodile had sunk the canoe, or the canoe had struck a sunken object and sunk, and the two had been devoured by crocodiles. But we found no trace of any such thing.

One canoe rowed down midstream and the other two close to either bank. And presently those in the boat on the east bank gave a shout and we rowed over to them. They had found the canoe, half-sunk in the river close to the bank. We dragged it up on the bank. It was hacked in places as though by spears and there were evidences of a terrific battle on the gunwale and thwarts, where great splashes of blood stained the wood of the canoe.

"By the Prophet!" swore Yar Ali. "That black Shaitan of a Matabele has murdered El Borak."

And that thought had come into the mind of each of us. But there were objections.

"How could a single man overcome El Borak?" asked Lal Singh.

"He might have taken him by surprize," said Yar Ali. "I have never trusted that Matabele. He joined our safari for the single purpose of murdering El Borak. Even now he doubtless is hurrying back to Matabeleland—with El Borak's head."

At those words a savage mutter rose from the boats, and the rustle of tulwars loosed in their scabbards.

"Perhaps they slew each other," said Bagheela Khan. "And were both eaten by the crocodiles."

Some of us went ashore, but outside of some grass being broken down, which might have been done by a crocodile crawling out on the bank, there was no sign, either of struggle or flight. The mud at the water's edge showed no tracks.

Lal Singh took command. I glanced at his dark, sardonic face and saw that it was grimly set.

"If I am at any time slain or captured, Lal Singh will lead you," El Borak had said, and the Afghans had harkened. But Lal Singh knew that there was but one man in all Africa who could control those wolves and that was El Borak.

"Umbelazi, Ghur Shan and Sakatra will go ashore and search the bank for a spoor," said Lal Singh. "Search back up the river first and we will await you here."

After awhile the Gurkha and the Zulus came back with word that there was no trace either of Gordon or anyone else.

"Follow the river downstream," instructed Lal Singh. "The boats will drift downstream and keep even with you."

So we did so, and we had not gone far when we heard a shout from the bank ahead of us. The boat in which was Lal Singh and I, and in which Yar Ali had gotten so they could discuss the mystery, put inshore. When we were some distance from the bank, a man waded into the water and climbed aboard. It was Umgazi. He was bloodstained from head to foot. There was a cut on his cheek and another on his forehead. His loincloth was in tatters and the knobstick, which was the only weapon he bore, was stained and clotted to the handgrip.

"Where is El Borak?" demanded Yar Ali, clutching his Khyber knife.

This is the tale the Matabele told: Gordon and he paddled around the bend and were out of sight of the boats, when a black man shouted to them from the bank. They saw a few negroes standing on the bank, making signs of friendship. El Borak made Umgazi row inshore and he stood up in the bows of the canoe, his rifle ready.

As the canoe approached, the black men saw Gordon's rifle and laid their own weapons down, advancing closer to the water's edge.

The jungle, as we had seen, ran down to the river and the bank was low, sloping into the water. El Borak could not understand their language and had the Matabele row closer in. The natives seemed frightened and Gordon, after scanning the jungle behind them and seeing nothing, lowered his rifle, taking his hand from the trigger. Umgazi rowed closer in than he intended, and then while the black men were talking to Gordon by means of signs, from the jungle behind them a heavy knob-stick had flown, striking El Borak full in the forehead and knocking him senseless. The next instant the negroes, snatching up their weapons, had leaped into the canoe, and out of the jungle came others. Umgazi had only time to snatch up his spear and knob-stick when they were upon him. He fought like a devil, slaying one with his spear and another with his knob-kerrie, but they overbore him and bound him hand and foot, as well as Gordon, who was still senseless. Then, leaving the canoe where it had sunk during the battle, and carefully effacing their footprints in the mud, the warriors had taken to the trees which grew so tall and thick along the riverbank. They traveled like apes, leaping from bough to bough, and the trees were so large and their branches so entangled that it was easily done. After they had gone some distance, they descended to the ground and paused a few minutes for rest, for in spite of his bonds the Matabele had fought and struggled every step of the way, and why they had not slain him he did not know. There El Borak came to his senses and he told Umgazi that he would free him and for him to escape and bring the wolves to his rescue.

"For," said El Borak, "if you seek to take me with you, we will both be slain, and if you escape you can return with the warriors."

The natives had cast them down together and Umgazi rolled over so his back was to El Borak, for his hands were bound behind him. El Borak's wrists were bound together but he worked Umgazi's bonds loose with his fingers, before the black men saw what he was doing. Then, as they rushed upon him, Umgazi freed his feet, leaped up, seized his knob-stick from a warrior who held it, slew a black man with it and leaped away, escaping.

When the Matabele had told his tale, we said nothing for a space. We did not know whether to believe him or not.

"You lie, black man," said Yar Ali Khan. "No native could so befool El Borak."

"Where were those natives going?" asked Lal Singh.

"Upstream," said Umgazi. "They must be of a river tribe for they kept close to the bank."

Yar Ali Khan leaped to his feet. "You lie, Matabele!" he shouted. "You murdered El Borak yourself!" And he whipped out his long Khyber knife.

The Matabele cast one swift glance about him, read suspicion in every face, then, quick as a leopard, he warded Yar Ali's thrust, knocked the Afghan staggering, and leaped overboard.

Instantly a dozen rifles were leveled upon him, but at Lal Singh's quick command the warriors held their fire. All except Yar Ali. With a swoop he snatched up a rifle and fired from the hip. The bullet went wild and before he could fire again, Lal Singh leaped on him and, using all his strength, wrenched the rifle from his grasp. Then it took ten of us to prevent the Afghan from leaping into the river and swimming after Umgazi, and he nearly upset the boat, struggling and raging in savage fury. The Matabele swam swiftly ashore in spite of the crocodiles, and disappeared in the jungle. Yar Ali turned on Lal Singh.

"And if the Matabele slew El Borak, I will slay thee, also, Lal Singh," said the Afghan in a voice that was like the snarl of a blood-hungry wolf.

"I give you leave, Yar Ali," said Lal Singh quietly.

I saw that perhaps of all of us, Lal Singh was prone to believe Umgazi's tale. He recalled the two Zulus and the Gurkha and then he told us his plans.

"I will take Ghur Shan and eight other men," said Lal Singh, "and we will track the Matabele. The boats will proceed up the river until we wish to come aboard. Does that coincide with your plans?"—that to Bagheela Khan, Yar Ali and Unalanga. They agreed and Lal Singh selected the men he wished to take. He took Ghur

Shan, Abdul Khan, Mahommed Ali and I, and Umbelazi, Sakatra, Maleesa, Umlingaan, and Undaya.

Yar Ali was angered because Lal Singh had not chosen him to accompany us, but the Sikh explained to him that he should stay on the boats and aid Bagheela Khan and Unalanga in keeping the wolves in control. So Yar Ali agreed, but with no very good grace.

Ghur Shan and Umbelazi followed the Matabele's spoor with no great difficulty, and it soon became apparent that the black man was deliberately leaving a clear trail.

"He knew we would trail him," said Lal Singh. It began to look as if the Matabele had spoken truth.

"He may be leading us into a trap," said Abdul Khan.

So we went warily. We came to a place where the vegetation was trampled as if by a struggle and here were tracks of many men.

Ghur Shan looked the place over carefully. "The Matabele spoke the truth at least partly," quoth he. "Here men descended from the trees and here two men lay." And he showed us the impressions in the soft earth.

From there we followed the trail of the men, who were on the march, and we could see that they were carrying some weight, for the tracks of some were deeper than others.

"They carry El Borak," said Ghur Shan. "He is either slain or a prisoner."

"Bound hand and foot," said Umbelazi. "For if they had released even his feet to make him walk, he would have contrived a way to escape."

The Matabele's spoor was above that of the black warriors, so we knew he was somewhere ahead of us. Lal Singh believed that the Matabele would seek to rescue El Borak alone; Abdul Khan thought that he merely feared us and was hastening to join the band who had taken El Borak prisoner.

The trail led along the river bank as Umgazi had said, and at times we could see the river through the jungle. Umbelazi was scouting ahead and he presently returned with word that a band of warriors were coming down the trail.

We turned aside into the jungle and hid, crouching in the tall jungle grass. We could see the trail we had been following and which had begun to take on the appearance of a native trail, winding among the trees.

The warriors had not come in sight—when the tall grass was parted and a savage black face, surmounted by a headgear of ostrich feathers, looked down upon us. Evidently the natives had their scouts as well as we. Back went a long spear but before he could use it, Ghur Shan leaped erect and cleft the black man's skull with a swing of his kukrie. The native slumped down and was hidden in the jungle grass.

Just then a band of warriors came in sight, the band Umbelazi had reported. They were following the winding jungle trail.

"If they go up the river they will see our tracks," whispered Lal Singh. "If they go straight on we must ambush them, odds or no."

On came the warriors, some thirty of them. Our rifles were raised, our fingers on the triggers—then, just before they came even with our hiding place they turned off at right angles into the jungle, going south by east and disappeared in the jungle.

"A close shave," said Lal Singh as we took up the trail again. And it was, for them as well as us.

Following the trail, we came upon the bank of the river. And there we stood, amazed.

The river was wide at the point and we were on the northwest curve of the second bend. The three boats were just rounding the bend and they backed oars and stopped.

Out in the middle of the river there stood an island. It was long and narrow and rose some twenty feet on sheer cliffs above the water. I should judge that it was some two-thirds of a mile long and nearly a quarter-mile wide. The river split and rushed past it swiftly on both sides.

It lay as the river ran, south by east and northwest. There was a village in the center and another at the south end. The village in the center had very many large huts in it, for we could see the thatch tops above the high stockade that surrounded it.

The village at the south end had no stockade. It was merely a great many huts clustered together. There were several large huts built over the river, on timbers set in the river. They were level with the island and there were bridges running from it to each of the huts. And in the water beneath those huts were canoes. Scores of them, hundreds of them. A regular fleet. We saw many natives on the island and knew that it was a strong tribe.

The boats had stopped at the bends and the wolves seemed uncertain what to do next. Lal Singh led us back around the bend, attracting the attention of the men in the boats, and motioning them to do likewise.

We then went aboard.

"There is the tribe who have taken El Borak prisoner," said Lal Singh. "And they are strongly fortified."

Many plans were discussed. Yar Ali was for charging down on the island with torch and sword, but Lal Singh told him that would be folly. We would be pitted against hundreds of warriors, and at a disadvantage.

Ormuzd Shah suggested that we avoid the island, go on downstream and there throw a dam across the river and overflow the island. But it was evident that that would be too great a task. So some said one thing and some another and no one could suggest anything that seemed to be the best.

Lal Singh said we would row back around the bend again, and have a look at the island. That would aid us in laying our plans.

So we did so, and as we came in sight of the island, we saw some two hundred canoes put out to head us off.

That was what we wanted, so we rowed straight for them. The natives were standing up in the canoes, waving their spears and axes and screeching like fiends. Lal Singh commanded the three boats to draw up parallel and for us to hold our fire until he gave the word. On came the war canoes. We could see the savage expressions of the black men and their spears began to crash against our shield barricade. They were giants of men, clothed gorgeously in gaudy cloth, monkey hides and ostrich feathers and armed with battle-axes, long spears, bows and great war clubs. Many had trade muskets.

When they were within pistol range, Lal Singh gave the word to fire. Every rifle on the three boats flamed. At that range, and the canoes massed so close, it was not necessary to aim. We merely blazed away pointblank. Lal Singh stood up in the bows of the boat and hurled sticks of dynamite and hand grenades of gun-cotton.

That battle was brief. In a few moments the remnant of the cannibal fleet was racing back to their village. We had riddled, shattered and sunk nearly half of their canoes. The river swarmed with crocodiles who seized everyone who fell in the water. When the canoes began to retreat, Yar Ali's boat leaped forward in pursuit. When the blacks saw the boat draw out ahead of the others, two of their canoes turned back and closed in on it. That suited Yar Ali. He and his warriors leaped upon the negroes like devils. There was no shooting. The fighting was too close and swift for that. The spears and war clubs of the cannibals flashed and whirled and above and among and through them flickered and leaped the tulwars of the Afghans and the assegais of the Zulus. The Makolala rowers were doing their best with oars and weapons snatched at random.

Before our boats could arrive there, the battle was fought and won. Yar Ali was plunging recklessly forward for more to conquer, but at Lal Singh's shouted command, he reluctantly gave orders to turn and row back. Abdullah bin Sikander was slain, three spears through him, and N'Moto and one of the Makolala rowers were wounded, though not badly, but of the two canoe crews of black men, not one warrior remained.

"I wish you had taken a prisoner," said Lal Singh.

"It would have been better," agreed Yar Ali. "But when the killing lust is upon me, I have no thought but to slay, slay, slay."

And in truth he had slain. He wished to carry on our attack to the island.

Lal Singh pointed out that there were several hundred warriors on the island and that even if we reached it we would be unable to climb up the steep banks, which, as I said, were some twenty feet high.

Lal Singh took El Borak's field glasses and gazed at the island and then he ordered two boats to retreat to the bend and to drop overboard heavy weights of iron for anchors. Thus the boats would not drift downstream and no black men could ambush us from the jungle.

Then we made our plans for attacking the island. The Batoka interpreter said the islanders were a strong tribe who had held the island for as long as anyone could remember. Even in his land they had heard tales of them. They were pirates of the river and every canoe that passed the island they forced to pay tribute or else they slaughtered everyone. He thought they were of a Manyeuma tribe for they were cannibals.

Lal Singh said, "The center village is the larger and it must be where the king's palace is. The south village seems to be a naval base. Now I will tell you my plan. They will slay El Borak if it seems that we are winning, so we must smite them swiftly and fiercely. I will take one boat and go downstream in the cover of night and we will contrive to climb the cliffs at the northwest end. Then, when I give the signal, which will be a fusillade of shots, the other two boats must swoop down on the huts which are built over the river. If you capture them, you can easily destroy the village on the bank. Then we can attack the main village from both directions and force them to surrender."

"What if they have slain El Borak?" said Unalanga.

"Then we will wipe them out, men, women and children," said Lal Singh.

"It is good," said Bagheela Khan and we all agreed.

We expected the Manyeuma to send another fleet of war canoes against us, but they did not; neither did they throw a cordon of canoes across the river to prevent us from continuing our journey.

When the thick African night had fallen over river and jungle, Lal Singh gave the word and the boat started downstream. He took with him Unalanga and nine of his Zulus, as well as Ormuzd

Shah, Ghur Shan, Yussef el Hassan, Mahommed Ali and I, and five Makolalas. Lal Singh had armed all the Makolalas with very good trade muskets of which we carried a store, and spears and battle-axes which we had taken from the natives. Rowing as silently as possible, we slipped past the cannibal island, and indeed, the current was so swift that little rowing was needed, except to guide the boat.

We could hear the Manyeuma shouting and yelling, native fashion, in both villages. Their tom-toms were booming and from the campfires all over the island, we saw that they were expecting a night raid from us. We were so close to the island that we could see the black warriors dancing about their fires, looking like naked, black devils.

There were canoes patrolling the river close to the island, but fortune was with us and by chance we slipped past them unobserved, though sometimes so close that the oars nearly touched. Had it not been a dark night, they would have seen us.

The current was swift as I said, but we managed to bring the boat close up to the bank at the northwest end. There we spent most of the night, expecting any minute to be discovered. If the black warriors had discovered us, they could have wiped us all out of existence by hurling down spears.

As dawn began to touch the sky above the jungle to the east, we prepared to land on the island. Our boat had been made fast to the bank. Lal Singh left his rifle and saber in the boat and took off his boots. There was among the Zulus a black giant called Incubu, which means elephant, and he was the strongest man of our band. He and Ormuzd Shah stood shoulder to shoulder, gripping arms. Unalanga climbed upon their shoulders and stood upright, gripping the face of the cliff as well as he might. Then, and few warriors could have done it, Lal Singh climbed to Unalanga's shoulders, stood upright and leaped upward. Unalanga became unbalanced and toppled off into the boat, but Lal Singh caught the edge of the cliff and drew himself over.

There were no trees near the bank but Lal Singh let down the rope ladder he had carried up and Ghur Shan climbed up it, Lal

Singh gripping the other end of the ladder and bracing his feet. Then he and the Gurkha held it while Unalanga climbed, and so on until we were all upon the island.

Then we slipped toward the village, through the trees and tall grass which grew there as in the jungle.

Sabanda was ahead, when out of the bush in front of him rose a dozen warriors. We who were behind did not see them. Sabanda shouted the Zulu war cry, pinned a Manyeuma to the earth with his assegai and went down, a dozen spears through him.

The next instant we were upon them. "No shots," shouted Lal Singh, "or Yar Ali will think it is the signal and attack too soon."

That fight was a brief, whirling play of swords and spears. A battle-axe in the hands of a Manyeuma slew one of the Makolalas but not one Manyeuma was left when we ceased fighting.

Then we pressed on swiftly, for though the battle had been short, yet it was almost certain that it had been heard.

We avoided other bands of warriors, and daylight, which came swiftly as it does in Africa, found us concealed in a clump of trees close to the main village. We hastily hewed down trees and made a barricade all around us. The Manyeuma were yelling and making much noise in the village, and we saw warriors creeping through the long grass toward us.

Then Lal Singh gave the word to fire and we turned a fusillade on the village. We had brought along much extra ammunition and we fired rapidly. The cannibals replied with bows and muskets, but we were out of arrow range, almost, and the barricade sheltered us from the bullets.

Presently the Manyeuma made a charge from the village and from the bush where many were concealed.

Lal Singh told us to attend to those charging from the bush and he would rout the warriors rushing from the village. So we directed our fire on the cannibals he said, and what were left fled back to the bush. As for Lal Singh, he let the others get so close that they were hurling their spears and then he hurled dynamite into the horde where they were massed thickest.

"If the Manyeuma would keep on charging us," said Lal Singh, "we could destroy the tribe."

But the warriors did not charge. They would not come in reach of the dynamite.

Then there came a fusillade of rifle fire from the other end of the island and a great din of shouting and yelling.

"Yar Ali and Bagheela Khan have attacked!" exclaimed Lal Singh. And many of the natives who were firing at us set off for the other end of the island.

When Bagheela Khan and his men had heard the firing they knew it was the signal, so they rowed as swiftly as they could for the south end of the island.

Several canoes put out to attack them, but Bagheela Khan threw hand grenades among them, and those that were not sunk in that way, or riddled by rifle bullets, put back to the island.

But more canoes came and those closed in on the two war boats and there was much hand-to-hand fighting. So the Afghans and Zulus fought their way through, and some of them were wounded and one of the Zulus slain. But they fought through and the natives in the canoes fled to the huts in the river and swarmed up into them.

There was one great hut built out some distance from the others and Bagheela Khan bade them row for it. As they nearly reached it, from around the island came a great war canoe, larger than any of the others. There was a platform on the front of the large hut and as the warriors looked at it, El Borak was shoved out upon it, bound hand and foot, and a great warrior stood behind him with a battle-axe. Then the wolves paused, not knowing what to do next, for although they were almost beneath the hut, yet the Manyeuma would slay Gordon if they attacked, and meanwhile the great war canoe was swooping down upon them.

Then suddenly El Borak broke the bonds on his arms and threw himself upon the warrior with the battle-axe. For a moment they struggled, and then Gordon whirled the Manyeuma off his feet and hurled him amongst the Afghans below, who hacked him to pieces and flung his head into the oncoming canoe. Yar Ali also flung a bomb into the canoe, which sank it. The Manyeuma had hauled El Borak back into the hut and from the sounds of battle which issued therefrom, they were retying his arms. Meanwhile the Makolalas were spearing the cannibals who had been left in the water when their canoe was sunk, and some of the wolves were scaling the bamboo poles which the huts rested on, while others kept up a rifle-fire at every Manyeuma who appeared.

Yar Ali went what Gordon calls "berserk." He climbed one of the bamboos and leaped into the hut. Presently a Manyeuma warrior came flying through the hut door into the river. Then Yar Ali came through and landed on his shoulders on the platform in front of the hut. He sprang up and rushed in again and by that time other Afghans and Zulus had climbed the hut and they followed Yar Ali in. The Manyeuma fled, leaping into canoes and into the river, so many escaped.

The wolves rushed into the hut and, there in the center of the one room, they saw El Borak. He was lying on the hut floor, bound hand and foot, and two great Manyeumas were rushing at him with lifted spears.

They would have reached Gordon before the wolves could have, and every gun was empty. Then from somewhere leaped a figure who smote two blows, right and left, with a red-stained knob-stick. It was the Matabele.

They freed El Borak and told him all that had occurred since he had been made prisoner.

"It is good," said Gordon.

"And now what, El Borak?" asked Bagheela Khan.

"Now we will smash these Manyeuma," said El Borak. "I have seen much of them, and I do not like their ways. Besides being cannibals and slavers, neither of which I have any especial objection to, they have many customs and characteristics which no race should possess and be proud of, as they are."

Yar Ali went up to Umgazi.

"Umgazi," said he, "you are a man. I was a fool. An Afridi of Kadar asks your pardon."

"It is freely given, Yar Ali Khan," answered the Matabele. "You also are a man."

Gordon gave orders for all the warriors to conceal themselves in the huts and direct their fire on the huts on the bank. The boats had been made fast to the bamboo poles. The Manyeuma in the huts returned the fire for awhile with arrows and bullets, and one or two attempts were made to chop away the bridges which connected the huts in the river with the island. But every time a negro showed himself there was a rifle watching for him, and presently the Manyuemas deserted the huts on the bank and fled, men, women and children, to the village in the center of the island. There were not many women and children, mostly warriors, for the village on the bank was about what Lal Singh had guessed, a kind of naval base. Most of the warriors dwelt there.

Then Gordon and his men went upon the island and fired at long range at the main village, from the huts nearest it.

Meanwhile, at the other end of the village, we had defeated another charge of the cannibals, and Lal Singh told us that he would show us a trick of war, which El Borak had taught him and which had been used by the red Indians of Gordon's country.

Lal Singh had taken a bow and some arrows from a slain cannibal, and he tied some small pieces of cloth and dry bark to the arrows and set them on fire and shot them into the village. Some of the arrows were extinguished by the rush of the arrow through the air, but some of them struck in the thatch roofs and the huts caught afire. Soon that whole end of the cannibal village was blazing and the cannibals were yelling like fiends. Those in the bush tried another rush but we drove them back.

All of the Manyeumas were on the island by that time, and Gordon sent Bagheela Khan with two of the Makolalas to go all around the island and destroy all the canoes he could find, except a few, which he was to tow to the east bank of the river with our boats and wait there for more orders. There were many canoes so that it took him some time.

Gordon and his men constructed a huge shield out of pieces of canoes and huts, and holding this before them, ran forward and barricaded themselves within a short distance from the main village.

Then Gordon, taking with him Yar Ali, Umgazi and Sakatra, and telling the warriors who remained behind the barricade to keep up a fusillade on the village, left the barricade and slipped into the bush.

About the same time, Lal Singh had the same idea and he let Ghur Shan and Umbelazi take to the bush.

Then the warriors in both barricades poured their rifle fire on the village, and Gordon and his warriors in the bush crept like panthers upon the Manyeumas lurking there and slew them.

They excelled the cannibals in jungle craft, for Gordon had roamed jungles the world over and he was like a wolf. Yar Ali had learned from him and as for Ghur Shan and the Kafirs, they grew up accustomed to jungles and they were superior to the cannibals in wit and cunning.

So they matched cunning with cunning and savagery against savagery and presently many Manyeumas began to quit the bush and flee into the village. We fired at them and slew many but many got in the village.

No tall grass grew very close to the village wall, so there was a rather wide clear space all about the village, but Ghur Shan got close enough to fling three cannibal heads into the village and Gordon crept close and emptied his pistols into the village stockade, making the cannibals think that a band was attacking them from that direction.

Then the warriors in the village charged both barricades simultaneously. We were better barricaded than Unalanga's men and we beat them back, but they were leaping up on the other barricade before the charge broke.

The Manyeumas had put out the fire but it had burned several huts. If we had not been so well armed and barricaded we would have been overpowered by sheer force of numbers, for there were hundreds of warriors in the village.

We did not care to storm it, for that would have put us at the same disadvantage that the cannibals had, and would have given them our advantage.

So we crouched behind our barricades and fired at every black man who showed himself.

Sounds of combat came occasionally from the bush, where Gordon, Ghur Shan, Yar Ali, and the Zulus were lurking.

Presently all the warriors in the bush began to flee, some to the banks of the river, some to the village. Many sought to escape in canoes, but Bagheela Khan had destroyed most of them and the others he had over at the east bank of the mainland. And the river swarmed with crocodiles, so none could escape by swimming. So the warriors turned and fled into the village.

Presently a warrior shouted to us from the village. The Batoka interpreted. The Manyeumas had had enough of war and wished to know on what terms they could surrender. Gordon bade the Batoka tell them that if they would throw down their arms and open the gates of the stockade, that he would treat them with as much leniency as possible, and if they did not, he would burn the village to the ground and slay every man, woman and child in it.

Presently the warriors opened the stockade gates and Gordon ordered them to send out the king for hostages, but they answered that the king and some warriors had occupied the king's hut, palace they called it, and refused to surrender. But they sent out five of their lesser chiefs instead. So we marched into the village from both directions. We half-expected treachery, but the warriors had thrown all their weapons in the open space in the center of the village. Their submission was complete. Yar Ali wished Gordon to order a massacre of all the natives, but El Borak would not do it. He called on the king to surrender but the only answer was a flight of arrows and bullets from the great hut that was the king's palace. So we set fire to the hut and as the warriors ran out we slew those that would not surrender, except the king and the war chief and the priest, whom we captured.

As I said, it was a large village, with several hundred huts. The ruling population were Manyeuma. There were many slaves. There were especially many women slaves, for the Manyeuma had levied a tribute of women and ivory on all the surrounding tribes, and every time a native canoe passed the island they stopped it, and if there were young women in it they took them. There were Congo women and Batoka women and Bakubwa women and Bambarri women and Wavuma women. Women of every tribe of the Congo almost.

The Manyeuma women were all fat and well clothed, for native women. They did no work, none of the Manyeumas worked. The slaves did all the work. All the women slaves were young and handsome, as the black men judge beauty, for the Manyeumas took only that kind and when the women slaves became old and ugly they ate them.

The Manyeumas were ever a cruel race, and those of the island seemed especially so. The slaves, girls and men, were subjected to cruel and outrageous treatment all the time. The men did all the work that was to be done on the island and the girls were forced into the harems of the warriors and did the work of the Manyeuma women. They were all naked, and many of them had welts and weals of whippings on their shoulders and thighs. If a slave tried to escape or resisted a Manyeuma, he or she was killed, beaten or tortured as it might fit their ruler's fancy. The slaves that were killed were either thrown to the crocodiles or eaten.

The Manyeumas worshipped the crocodile as some peoples worship the snake. They had no witch-man as other tribes do, but priests. Those priests selected the crocodile's feast, who was usually a slave, or a Manyeuma who had something the priest coveted or against whom the priest had a grudge. The king was a savage monster, sensual and cruel. He had three hundred women in his harem. The priest was a grasping, cruel fanatic and the war chief was equal to the king in cruelty. They levied tribute of women, ivory and warriors on the other tribes. The warriors they burned in the open space in the center of the village. El Borak looked at the king, the priest and the war chief.

"You shall be slain," said he. "Not for fighting against me. That is no crime. But such fiends as you have no place in the world."

Then he told us to take the king and the priest and the war chief and strike off their hands and feet and throw them to the crocodiles. That was done and Yar Ali grumbled much. For, said he, El Borak was too soft toward his enemies.

El Borak had us search all the huts for weapons and all we found we placed in a hut and two Makolalas were placed to watch it so that no cannibal might steal a weapon. But there was no sign of revolt among the Manyeumas.

Gordon learned the history of the tribe. The main Manyeuma race lives far to the eastward, on the shores of Lake Tanganyika. Nearly a hundred years before, one of the Manyeuma chiefs had rebelled against the king. His warriors had been defeated and he had fled to the jungle, with hundreds of his warriors and their women and children. They had come upon the island in their wanderings. It had then been inhabited by an unwarlike tribe who fished and traded. The Manyeumas had enslaved those people and had seized the island. They had seen the strategic advantage of the island and had built them a great fleet of canoes. The surrounding tribes made war on them but the Manyeumas defeated and then conquered them. The river tribes traded much up and down the river and at first the Manyeumas would seize every canoe, but later they saw it would be more advantageous to them to allow the trading to go on and to levy tribute on each canoe.

So for nearly a century the wealth of half the Congo had flowed into the hands of the island kings.

And by the Prophet, the village bore out the tale!

In every village we found ivory, ostrich feathers, rubber, feathers of rare birds, weapons of every kind, besides beads, wire ornaments, gay-colored cloth, and such stuff as white traders sell to the tribes.

Much ivory and some native gold and silver and uncut gems were also found. Ivory was so plentiful among the Manyeumas that they did not merely store it like other tribes. They became skilled workers in ivory. The commonest warrior had ornaments of it and nearly all of their knife hilts, battle-ax handles and the knobs on their war clubs and spear shafts were of ivory.

"Now," said Bagheela Khan to El Borak, "we have enough to make us all rich. Is there more gold than this, in the place where we are going?"

El Borak laughed and dismissed the ivory with a careless wave of his hand.

"I will announce the terms of surrender," said he.

The lesser chiefs were brought before him and he spoke.

"First, you will stop the custom of eating other men. You will eat neither slaves nor captives of war. Slaves you may have, but they must be used well. Girl slaves cannot be forced into harems against their will and men slaves cannot be slain on any pretext. You will throw no more to the crocodiles.

"No more wars of extermination are to be waged. Women captured in war may be kept, for that is the custom of all Africa. In the same way, you may take men slaves, but if any slave tries to escape he cannot be killed. Slaves must be well-clothed and well-fed and they cannot be beaten with whips of hippopotamus hide. Treat them as ye would children.

"You will levy tributes of ivory and rubber and suchlike upon the tribes, but not women. The tribute you levy on canoes will be lighter. You will trade as well as capture.

"You will give to me the amount I shall name of ivory, ostrich-feathers, and other things, and you will furnish me with a number of warriors as askaris. Also, out of the total of the tribute you levy each year, you will set aside one-fourth, which is mine. Now these are my commands and if you disobey them," he leaped to his feet and the chiefs prostrated themselves in terror before the blood-hungry glitter of his eyes, "if ye disobey—"

He made no threat with words but the chiefs understood.

"We will obey, oh, king!" they answered.

"See that ye do," said El Borak. "For I will come again. And if any tribe attack you I will come to your aid."

We stayed several days on the island for many of the warriors were wounded, though none of them very badly. Gordon spent much of his time in learning the Manyeuma language, some of which he had picked up in the short time he was captive. And indeed, he knew more languages than any other man I ever saw, for he learned wonderfully fast.

Such of the slaves that wished greatly to return to their lands he allowed to go, in canoes or overland, with provisions and weapons. But since things had changed on the island and the slaves were not oppressed as they had been, many were content to stay. For that is the way of the black race.

The Manyeuma set to work to rebuild their canoe fleet and Gordon aided them, though there was little he could teach them about canoe building, for they were a river tribe in the truest sense. He studied their canoes and their ways of paddling and rowing, for Gordon was ever eager to acquire knowledge in any way. He also showed them how to fortify the island, for it was probable, since we had destroyed their war fleet of canoes, that other tribes would attack them.

Also, Gordon asked them of the tribes of the Congo and they said they had never heard of an ancient empire there.

"And what now, El Borak?" asked Bagheela Khan.

"Overland," answered El Borak. "This river, the Changaan, runs into the Lomani River, nearly a hundred miles to the northwest. The reason that this river, the Changaan, is practically unknown, is because the islanders have wiped out every Arab expedition that has come upon the river, and the white men have not yet come this far into the Congo. I have read and studied many ancient maps and old books, and I know that the land we seek is somewhere in this region of the Congo. Hassan ibn Zaroud knows too, though where he learned I do not know. I first learned of it in some very ancient Phoenician books which were in the possession of the Brahmins at Benares. The books related a tale of some Carthaginian traders and mariners whose ship was wrecked on the west coast of Africa, somewhere south of where Loando now is. They set out to return overland to Carthage, and in their wanderings they came upon an empire which was more ancient than Carthage. Gold was as plentiful there as copper was in Carthage, more plentiful. The people who inhabited the empire were white, fair skinned and fair haired, and the name of the empire was Valooze."

"And what manner of land was the country?" asked Lal Singh.

"An island," answered El Borak. "A great island in the center of a mighty lake."

"An island!" exclaimed Bagheela Khan. "Perhaps this is the island?"

"This island is not large enough by a great deal," answered Gordon. "And that island was in a lake, not a river. Also, there is no sign that any but tribes of black men ever inhabited this island. There are no ruins of city or palace such as the Phoenicians saw. The black men never leave ruins of buildings, for they never build anything that will last."

"What became of the Phoenicians?" asked Ghur Shan.

"Many perished in the jungle," answered El Borak. "But some got back to Carthage after much wandering. The tale of their explorations was put in books. When Rome destroyed Carthage, a Greek in the Roman army secured many Carthaginian books, that book among others. Eventually it found its way into India."

Ormuzd Shah was rather skeptical.

"How do you know the book was not a lying book of the Hindus?" said the Orakzai. "How could the book get to Benares from Rome?"

"I traced it by other old books," answered El Borak. "When the northern barbarians conquered Rome, many Greek teachers and philosophers who lived there went to the Eastern Empire, Constantinople. Later, many of them went to the Persian court. In that way the old Carthaginian book got into Asia. And so it went on to India."

We gave our boats to the Manyeumas and set out overland, west by north. We took a quantity of ivory and ostrich feathers, also, forty armed Manyeuma warriors went with us as askaris. As at

Kadar and in Zululand, Gordon selected the young warriors who were unmarried.

We now had a strong fighting force. There were fifty of our original force, twenty Asians, sixteen Zulus and the Matabele, twelve Makolalas and the Batoka. The forty Manyeumas made ninety warriors for El Borak to lead.

We marched through the jungle, though it was not so thick and dense as it was on the bank of the Changaan. There were cannibal tribes in the jungle but the sight of our Manyeumas was enough to deter them from attacking us.

There were many wild beasts in the jungle. There were elephants and hippopotamuses and rhinos. There were also many lions and leopards. There were monkeys and gorillas, many of them. The gorillas would not attack anyone if they were let alone and El Borak gave orders that they were not to be molested. The Manyeumas were very much afraid of the gorillas. They called them sokas.

Also there were many great serpents which were like to the pythons of the Indian jungles. We killed several of them, for they were bold enough to come to our camp and seek to attack men. The Makolalas were as much afraid of the snakes as they were of the apes.

Africa is indeed a land of strange wonders.

We came upon a tribe of men in the jungle who were not over three feet high! The Manyeumas called them pygmies and were afraid of them. They were black and kinky-haired and went entirely naked, both men and women. Some of them had beards, but not all. They were armed with spears and bows and some had tubes to shoot darts and arrows through. Some of the bows were made of hippopotamus hide, dried and hardened.

They were wild, like monkeys, and had a very primitive language. The other tribes were afraid of them. El Borak showed that he was friendly towards them and they came into our camp. They were much like monkeys. Gordon got some of them to guide us through the jungle, for the Manyeumas did not know much about the country away from the river. The pygmies guided us to a certain place and then turned back, for other pygmies lived beyond that place who were hostile to the first pygmies we had met. Strange, is it not, that the smallest, lowest, peoples have their wars and quarrels as well as the higher and stronger?

We saw signs of the dwarfs but they themselves kept concealed and out of our sight, which looked as though they meant to fight us.

We were marching past a village when Gordon, who was leading the safari, suddenly jerked up his rifle and something thudded against the stock. Gordon shouted for us to get into the huts, swiftly. We did so, without knowing why he ordered it, and the next instant a flight of arrows flew from the jungle. If we had not been in the huts, at least a dozen warriors would have fallen. The village was deserted. It was a village of regular black men whom the pygmies had driven out. For there were many such villages in that part of the Congo. There was no stockade, merely a cluster of huts. Gordon showed us his rifle. There was a pygmy arrow sticking in the stock. We watched the trees for the dwarfs and fired at them when we saw them. They were like monkeys and there were hundreds of them. They were hidden in the bush and up in the jungle trees and they kept shooting arrows at us. Their arrows slew one of the Manyeumas.

They were difficult to hit for they kept well-hidden and moved quickly from one tree to another. El Borak told us to stop firing. We did and the pygmies drew closer to the huts, in swarms like monkeys. Still we did not fire and they grew bolder. Perhaps they thought we were out of ammunition. They swarmed out of the jungle and surrounded the huts. Then, as a leopard leaps among a band of monkeys, El Borak leaped amongst the pygmies. He scattered them right and left, knocked their king senseless with the hilt of his saber, snatched him up and sprang back into the hut. Then the pygmies rushed the huts, but we fired on them at close range and drove them back. One of the Manyeumas could speak Bakuba and some of the dwarfs understood that language, so Gordon had the Manyeuma to shout to them and tell them that if they did not cease attacking us, we would slay the king. So presently the arrows ceased flying and the dwarfs shouted to the Manyeuma that they had ceased fighting and to let the king go. But El Borak said we would take the king with us until we were out of their country and then we would let him go. So they agreed and we came out of the huts and took up our march. The king was bound hand and foot and Ormuzd Shah carried him under one arm as if he were no more than a babe. And, indeed, he was not four feet tall. The pygmies came out of the jungle by the hundreds but they did not offer to attack us, but we went with our rifles ready. They were wild looking people and were very fierce. Some of the men and most of the women wore strings of beads around their necks and around their waists, but that was all any of them wore in the way of ornaments or clothing.

Some of them came into camp but they tried no treachery, and El Borak set to work to learn their language. It was not very hard for the pygmies' language is a small one, only a few words. They talk mostly by means of signs. They live like monkeys, on fruits and insects and small game, but they often hunt larger game and sometimes many of them hunt together and bring down elephants and hippopotamuses. For such small folk, they are very warlike and brave. Gordon learned their language and asked them much about the region of the Congo where they roamed. Certainly the pygmies knew about it if anyone did, for they wandered all through the jungle. They did not settle in large villages like the tribes did but wandered over large sections of country. They were jungle nomads.

They said that the jungle spread over hundreds of miles of territory and was inhabited by tribes of cannibals and the pygmies. They said there were many elephants and lions and gorillas and other wild beasts. They told Gordon of rivers and lakes that the white men and Arabs knew nothing of. The Arabs seldom came into the jungle of that region for they were afraid of the pygmies. They did not know anything about a race of white people who lived in a city anywhere in the Congo.

The only white men they had ever seen were Arabs, after slaves and ivory. They always fought those Arabs and drove them away.

The pygmies were not like the Bushmen of South Africa. The Bushmen did not fight, except among each other. They had been enslaved by Hottentots and Makolalas and Kaffirs for so many centuries that they knew nothing else. The pygmies were different from the Bushmen. They were wild and they were free. No one had ever enslaved them. There were thousands of them and though they fought amongst themselves, they always fought together against an enemy such as cannibals and Arabs. They did not keep slaves nor did they steal one another's women. In some ways the cannibals could learn from the pygmies.

They offered to trade ivory for weapons and beads. Elephants were numerous and they said that they had many tusks. Gordon would not trade, for we did not want the ivory, but he made them presents of such things as natives like. They became friendly to us and showed no desire to attack us, but El Borak kept the king prisoner.

The Manyuemas were distrustful of the dwarfs, but that was because they were afraid of them.

As I said, Gordon asked them of the ancient empire, but although they themselves are a very ancient race, they knew nothing about any such empire. Congo empires, the pygmies told Gordon of. Great empires that rose and flourished perhaps a hundred years and then were conquered by some other tribe. But most of that Gordon already knew, nor did the tales of the pygmies run back very far into the centuries, for they have no written languages and are not overly interested in the history of the land, anyway.

All the empires they told of were empires of black men. They knew nothing of a land of white men.

However, Gordon conversed much with them, learning their speech and their ways of war and hunting and their customs. For as I said, Gordon always sought to acquire knowledge of all kinds.

We marched on through the jungle and the pygmies guided us and showed us the best places to camp, and the best springs and streams, and they brought us fruit and game. And that shows what manner of man is El Borak, who contrived to make friends of the pygmies, one of the wildest races in the world, while holding their king prisoner. And Gordon did what no other man has done, marched an armed band through the land of the pygmies without having to fight his way through.

There was one of the dwarfs, a youth named Kubo, who seemed to have a great admiration for Gordon. He was always bringing in small bush deer and ripe jungle fruit and presenting them to Gordon. Several times Gordon's Makolala tent-boy chased him away from Gordon's tent, thinking he meant to steal something. But it soon became apparent that Kubo did not want to steal, but to watch Gordon's tent so no one else could steal anything. Presently he boldly asked Gordon if he could accompany him wherever he went. Gordon told him he might and asked him if he wished him to ask the king's permission. Kubo replied that it was none of the king's affair. When a child of the pygmies became strong enough to hunt for himself he quitted his family or was chased away by them. His comings and goings were his own affair. Neither his family nor the king made any attempt to rule him in that way.

So Kubo came with the safari. We saw other tribes and villages of the pygmies and they did not try to attack us. It seemed that the king ruled all the pygmies of that region of the Congo, though his rule was not very clearly defined. All these nations of pygmies are called Wambuttos.

The jungle was not as dense as it had been. The trees were very tall and gigantic, but as there was not much undergrowth, the safari made good time on march. There were few cannibal villages, for most natives feared the pygmies too much to dwell in their jungle.

So we came to a place where there was a ledge of rock rising out of the jungle two hundred feet into the air and there were steps cut into it to the top. Then Gordon said we were not more than two hundred miles from the lake where the old Phoenicians found the ancient empire, for the ledge was mentioned in the book they wrote of their explorations. And they mentioned the pygmies, also, Gordon said, so it was proven the pygmies were a very ancient race.

Bagheela Khan was somewhat skeptical. For, said he, if the pygmies were in the Congo at the time the white race dwelt there, why did they not have legends of them? El Borak pointed out that the pygmies had no way to keep history except by word of mouth, that none of their legends went back over a few hundred years and that they had few legends of any kind.

We climbed the rock and found that it had been used for centuries by the pygmies as a fort. No pygmies were camped there then, but the top of the rock was covered by the ruins of their grass-thatch and wicker huts.

El Borak said that there was a garrison of the white race on the rock when the Phoenicians passed.

After we left the rock-castle, we met other Wambuttos. They told us that nearly a hundred miles to the northwest was a great swamp that was many miles long and many miles wide. They told us of various lakes in the jungle, but they were only small ones. They did not know if there was a great lake in that part of the Congo.

We arrived at the swamp and it was a great swamp. Pygmies dwelt at its edges and they told us that it was a vast and mighty expanse of quagmires and small, stagnant lakes. They said nothing lived there except snakes and crocodiles. They had never crossed it, for why should they? They could go around, if they wished to go on the other side of the swamp. The jungle surrounded it all around, they said. They had no way of expressing distances and size, but we understood that the swamp was surprizingly large.

Gordon was puzzled.

"Close to here is where the lake should be," said he. "Yet here is a swamp. And there was a temple built of stone on the shores of the lake."

"What sort of a temple, sahib?" asked Bagheela Khan.

"A temple erected to the elephant," said El Borak. "The people of Valooze worshipped the elephant, according to the Carthaginians, and the temple was erected to him. There were many carved images of the elephant in it."

We camped in the jungle, back from the swamp and Mahom-med Ali, Abdul Khan and I, with Kubo, went to the edge of the swamp, partly hunting, partly to view the swamp and the land about it.

"We have traversed lands where ivory in abundance was to be had for the seizing," quoth Abdul Khan, "and we took no notice of it. Now we see that El Borak's tale of an empire of gold is an illusion. What now?"

"We do not know that it is an illusion," I answered. "We found the ledge of rock as the Carthaginians described it in the old book."

"But where is the lake?" asked Abdul Khan. "Where is the island? Where is the temple on the lakeshore?"

We were passing by a large clump of swamp trees, where the ground was higher than it was in other places, and Kubo sheered away from it. He had learned a few words of the Manyeuma language, which most of us had learned to speak, and Mahommed Ali asked him why he avoided the clump of trees.

He answered that the Wambuttos thereabouts had told him that many great snakes concealed themselves among the trees and devoured everyone who entered.

"Let us slay those snakes," said Abdul Khan, and we agreed. So we Afridis entered the clump, and Kubo remained outside for he would not accompany us. Abdul Khan and I entered first, Mahommed Ali coming behind, so that nothing should let us pass and then spring upon our backs. It was rather dark inside the clump of trees, for they were very tall and their branches were entangled. There seemed to be a regular wall of undergrowth, with an open space, where the ground was worn smooth.

"Here the serpents enter and leave," said Abdul Khan. The disgusting smell of pythons was all about.

None of us cared to be the first to step through that opening in the undergrowth, but no serpent came out, so I stepped into the opening, my tulwar held out before me, the others close behind me. We seemed to be walking through a kind of hallway, with walls on either hand. I supposed that the undergrowth was grown very thick and that I was merely following a trail made by the pythons. I would probably step into a lair of the monsters, which was not an overly pleasant thought.

Abdul Khan said we seemed to be walking on a stone flooring. So we groped on in the darkness until the darkness changed to a vague, half-light. Until I saw a hideous, reptile head swaying before me and smote it off, heard a rustle and sliding, felt myself wrapped about by a great, slimy, reptile body. I am no craven but I shrieked with pure, loathing, horror and Abdul Khan, striking blindly in the darkness, clove the snake in twain and it fell away from about me. Then we seemed to step into a kind of open space and saw at least a dozen frightful heads swaying on long, hideous necks, to and fro, to and fro, a dozen forked tongues flickering in and out.

The next were moments which were some of the most gruesome I ever knew. From all directions the great snakes swarmed upon us, great, scaly, grisly monsters, vaguely seen in the gray half-light that filtered through the mighty treetops into that grisly den.

We were surrounded, hemmed in, half-covered by the writhing, horrible forms. We riddled them with our pistols and hewed them in pieces with our tulwars and still they came and still we smote, smote, smote, until we could hardly raise our sword arms for weariness.

Then, when it seemed we could not smite again, the serpents came no more and we stood ankle deep in a mess of severed heads and pieces that still writhed horribly.

"Mahommed hu akbar!" said Abdul Khan. "Let us get out of this place."

"Nay," said Mahommed Ali. "We came to slay the serpents. Let us make it complete."

So we looked about for other pythons and found a strange thing. We had supposed the place was merely an open space in the undergrowth, with thick, dense walls of undergrowth and trees. But the walls we thought were undergrowth were of stone. They were some nine feet high and enclosed a space some twenty feet one way and forty the other. There was a stone flooring, but if there had ever been a roof, it had decayed and fallen away long ago. There was an opening in the wall, the opening by which we had entered.

"It was a corridor through which we came," quoth Mahommed Ali. "What manner of place is this? The Wambuttos never built it."

"Here is a kind of great door," said Abdul Khan, "that seems to lead into a kind of great clearing, like this, only larger."

So we entered, warily, and found the place a kind of eight-sided room, floored with stone and surrounded by a stone wall, some twelve feet high and no roof. It was, as I said, octagon shaped, and perhaps forty-five feet across, each way.

"Look!" exclaimed Abdul Khan, shrinking back, pointing. It was lighter than in the outer place, and we saw a vast, shadowy form near the wall opposite from the opening through which we came. We hesitated and then, having reloaded our pistols, we went forward, warily. The thing did not move and we saw that it was a great stone image.

"An elephant," said Mahommed Ali, and so it was. It was skillfully done. The trunk was uplifted and drawn back, the great tusks jutted straight out and curved slightly upward. The tusks were almost out of proportion to the form of the image, for the elephant was hardly ten feet high and eleven feet long, and the tusks were a good ten feet in length, and large. Abdul Khan looked closely at the tusks.

"Look," said he. The tusks were sharp at the points and there were dark stains upon them.

"Those are very ancient bloodstains," said Abdul Khan.

"How could that be?" asked Mahommed Ali.

"In an old temple in the jungle close to Delhi," said Abdul Khan, "there was the image of a tiger. And it was said that at certain times the tiger would leave the temple and range the jungle like a real tiger, slaying all whom he met."

"A lie of the Hindus," said Mahommed Ali, but not with overmuch certainty.

"It might be," answered Abdul Khan. "Yet, if a stone tiger can slay, why not a stone elephant? Imagery is the doing of ifreets of evil. Did not the Prophet Mohammed, on whom peace, forbid the making of images, either of men or of beasts?"

We looked askance at the image, half-expecting for it to charge us. I glanced about the walls. There were no snakes there, for if any had ever been there they had come out to attack us. I saw many carvings of elephants along the walls and suddenly I thought of something.

"A temple with many carvings of the elephant in it," Gordon had said.

"Mohammed hu Akbar!" I exclaimed. "This is the temple of which Gordon spoke!"

"How can that be?" asked Abdul Khan. "That temple stood on the shores of a lake."

"However," said I, "this is the temple. Did not El Borak say it was a temple of the elephant? He spoke of no other temple."

"Then if this is the temple," said Mahommed Ali, "by the beard of the Prophet, this is the work of ifreets or magicians, for then it stood on the shores of a lake and now it stands at the edge of a swamp. Let us hence."

Then a kind of fright took hold of us, so we rushed from the place, and if we had found the snakes grown together again and waiting to attack us we would not have been surprized, and we looked back over our shoulders as we fled, expecting to see the stone elephant pursuing us. We came out of the temple into the jungle and it seemed very good after the serpent-haunted den where we had been. Kubo was awaiting us, though he said he had hardly expected us to come out. We asked him if he had known there was a temple there and he said no one had known anything about the place, for whoever went near it was devoured by the serpents.

So we went back to camp, desiring to wash the scent and feel of serpent off us.

Gordon was seated in his camp chair, talking to some of the dwarfs who dwelt close to the swamp.

"And no one knows anything of the great swamp?" he asked as we came up.

The Wambuttos answered that none of them had ever crossed the swamp, but a few had gone some miles into it and said there seemed a kind of flat mountain in the midst of it.

Gordon seemed puzzled and he sat meditating a moment. Then suddenly he threw back his head and laughed. Laughed long and loud, while the dwarfs and all of us stared at him, and at each other, not understanding.

He sprang up. "A flat mountain!" said he. "Scatter, ye wolves, and search for the temple of the elephant, for unless I have lost my wits, it is not far from here."

"Aye," said Abdul Khan, "for we have found it."

Then we told El Borak of finding the temple and slaying the snakes.

"Ye have done well," said El Borak, "both in discovering the temple and in slaying the serpents. Had it not been for the pythons, the Wambuttos would have known of the temple."

"But if the temple was by the lake," said Ormuzd Shah, "how could it now be by a swamp?"

"Manu and Ganesha!" exclaimed Lal Singh. "The lake has become a swamp!"

Gordon laughed. "I wondered how long it would be before ye saw," said he. "The land has changed since the Carthaginians came and went. Nearly three thousand years have passed since they saw the lake and the island in the lake. There was an earthquake, a river changed its course, and the lake became a swamp."

"And the island?" asked Yar Ali.

"The island is in the midst of the swamp as it was in the midst of the lake," answered Gordon. "The Island is evidently what the Wambuttos saw and which they tell of as a great, flat mountain."

"But how can we cross the swamp and get to the island?" asked Ghur Shan.

"We shall see," said El Borak. "Anyway, we will cross it."

He asked the Wambuttos how they went into the swamp, and they said that for many miles the trees grew very large and tall and the branches were so close to each other that they traveled by swinging and leaping from branch to branch and from tree to tree, after the fashion of monkeys. That was easy for the dwarfs, for they spend much of their time in trees, where the lions and other beasts cannot get at them.

But they said that many miles from the edge of the swamp that no large trees grew, and there were only quagmires and small, stagnant lakes, with small islands of firm land. They said there were many crocodiles and some pythons, but that there were waterbirds of some kind in the swamp that ate reptiles, so there were not many snakes. They said the dwarfs who had ventured into the swamp had gone only as far as the great trees grew in the swamp and then had returned. They had never gone close enough to the mountain that was in the swamp to see it plainly, but it seemed to be high and flat, with very steep cliffs. There seemed to be trees on top of it.

"Did there seem to be buildings on the mountain?" Gordon asked them.

They said they did not know. That they were a great distance from the mountain and they could not see if there were buildings or not. They were not sure if there were trees.

Gordon asked them if they explored any of the small islands they saw. The dwarfs said the islands were all beyond where the swamp-jungle ran and they did not go on any of them. They said they were most of them covered with trees and jungle undergrowth.

"The Carthaginians mentioned the fact that there were several small islands on the lake as well as the main island, mostly not inhabited," said Gordon. Yar Ali said it seemed that if there were any men on the island that they would find their way through the swamp to the mainland.

"Perhaps there are no people on the island," answered Gordon. "And if there are, perhaps they either have no way of crossing the swamp, or do not even know that there is a world outside the swamp. The human mind is narrow. But we shall see."

We made our luggage into bulks as small as possible. Most of it consisted of ammunition and provisions. We arranged it so each porter could carry a minimum amount, tied with rope to his shoulders. So that each porter would not be too heavily loaded, some of the Manyeumas carried some of the luggage.

We released the king of the pygmies there, and he ordered five Wambuttos to accompany us for guides.

Then we set out across the swamp, traveling, as the dwarfs traveled, through the trees.

The trees were mostly mangroves and were fairly easy to travel through. We had many long ropes, some of native manufacture of long grass and some places we stretched them from tree to tree, making swinging bridges such as may be found in Afghanistan.

The marsh under the trees was dank and little but quagmire. There were snakes, though not in great numbers, and many crocodiles. Gordon distributed a kind of stuff among us. The Wambutto pygmies made it and it was a liquid which we put upon our clothes and it kept away the mosquitoes and tsetse flies, if there were any. They would not come near us.

The mangroves were hundreds of years old and were giants of trees. Many tall, slim bamboos grew in the swamp also, but scarcely any other kind of tree.

We traveled through the trees until we came to an expanse of swamp where no trees grew. It was a wide plain of quagmires and stagnant lakes, bare of vegetation except for the dingy swamp grass that grew scantily. Small clumps of trees and bamboos grew upon what seemed to be the islands the dwarfs had told us of. Gordon had us cut down the bamboos that grew in abundance.

Gordon gave the Wambuttos gifts of beads and muskets and they returned to their tribe.

The bamboos that grew in the swamp were tall, some of them growing a hundred feet and more in height. They were strong and light and we cut them and made rafts, making them fast together. The rafts were fifteen and twenty feet long, and four or five feet wide, each carrying five men and an amount of luggage.

Gordon wished each raft to be as light as possible. They were propelled by long poles, the men on the rafts shoving them along, over the marsh. That was sometimes rather difficult, for the swampland gave when the poles were shoved against it, but the rafts, being fairly broad and flat and light, would not sink into the marsh.

For many miles before we emerged from among the trees into the marshy plain, we could see the flat mountain the Wambuttos had told us of, and the view urged us on, for we lusted for the gold that Gordon said was there.

And it did not much resemble a mountain, but more an upland that had once been an island, as Gordon said it had.

It seemed to be flat on top, as the Wambuttos had said, rising straight up out of the marsh about. It seemed some hundreds of feet high and, if it were a mountain, it was a gigantic one, that is by wideness.

Gordon gazed at it through his field glasses and said that there were trees upon it, though there did not seem to be a jungle.

There were many crocodiles in the swamp but not many snakes, for there was a kind of waterfowl that destroyed the snakes. We had noticed many of them among the trees of the swamp-jungle and they were in great quantities on the marsh. There were hundreds of them. They were built something like herons, with long legs and long, snake-like necks. They were of a brown color, flecked with white and they made a very rasping, screeching cry. Their feet were webbed and they could run across the quagmires or swim in the lake with equal swiftness. They could fly, also, and their beaks were very long and pointed. They would even attack a large python. They destroyed the young of the crocodiles. Gordon and Kubo captured several of the birds. They were tied to the rafts by one leg and they destroyed any snake that came near.

Gordon and Kubo always went ahead of the other rafts on a small raft which was light and easily propelled. The other rafts followed their trail.

We had constructed the rafts so they would float in water, and when we came to one of the small lakes we floated across, using the propelling-poles for oars.

We laid our course so as to have the advantage of as many lakes as possible, for it was much easier to float across them than to pole across the marsh.

There were many crocodiles in the lakes and sometimes they would swim near us and occasionally they would attack us and seek to overturn the rafts. We slew many with spears and battle-axes.

The crocodiles fought and devoured each other and the marsh fowls destroyed the crocodile eggs and devoured the young crocodiles, but even so there were hundreds of crocodiles; thousands of them.

We landed upon some of the small islands. They were merely marshy uplands, like large hummocks. Mangroves and bamboos grew so thickly upon them that anyone could hardly get through them. The marsh-fowls nested upon them by the thousands, and on some crocodiles sunned.

Gordon said the islands were probably those spoken of by the ancient Carthaginian explorers. He said the Carthaginians found most of the islands uninhabited. They were probably used as a sort of naval bases, for El Borak said that the people of the island empire had a fair-sized fleet of boats and canoes, for war and for commerce. He said they traded with the pygmies of that age and with the tribes that dwelt on the shores of the lake and with other tribes further back in the jungle.

He said that the Carthaginians had remarked upon the fact that the island people greatly desired great stores of ivory. They hunted the elephant themselves and ivory was the main commodity for which they traded with other tribes. Gay furs and feathers came next in trade value. The Carthaginians, said Gordon, had not said from where the white race had come. Perhaps they had not learned. The empire might have been so ancient that they themselves did not know.

He said the race must have been as old, or even older, than the Sumerians, a race that settled in Mesopotamia so many centuries ago that no man knew whence they came.

"And where got they the gold?" Yar Ali wondered.

"I do not know, unless they mined it on the island," Gordon answered. "But gold there was, great quantities of gold."

"So I can get my hands among it," said Yar Ali. "I care little from whence it came."

We came upon an island in the midst of one of the small, marshy lakes. It was a rather large island, and higher above the marsh than most of the islands. We landed there and Kubo wandered inshore; presently, he returned and told El Borak that there was some sort of a building in the jungle on the island.

The bamboos grew so thick and dense that we hewed our way with axes, some places. At about the center of the island we came upon the ruins of an old temple. The jungle had grown about it and it was almost hidden.

It consisted merely of a stone wall, round in shape, with an opening at one place. It had no roof. In the center there was a great, carved serpent of stone, coiled on a stone pedestal which was decorated by carvings of other, smaller serpents. The stone wall was also decorated by snake carvings.

Gordon went over the ruins carefully. He seemed very much interested and slightly puzzled.

"The Carthaginians did not mention another race," said he. "Yet the race that erected this snake temple did not erect the elephant temple we found at the edge of the swamp. They represent two distinct forms of architecture, so distinct that it is scarcely possible that the same race erected both temples. In the elephant temple, the art itself was crude. The elephant carvings were out of proportion. The lines of architecture were strong, but crude. The whole plan of the temple of the elephant shows crude, primitive strength and freedom of expression. The carvings of the snake temple are much superior in art, but they lack the strength of expression of the other.

"The styles of the two temples are altogether different. The wearing of the centuries seemed to have done little to the walls of the elephant temple. But the temple of the snake is almost in ruins."

"Could not the snake temple have been built later by the same race?" asked Lal Singh.

"It might be," answered El Borak. "Yet it seems scarcely probable that a race, while gaining the higher knowledge of art, should entirely forget the earlier virtues of strong, natural expression and lasting architecture. And I believe that the temple of the snake was built before the temple of the elephant."

"Before?" said Lal Singh.

"Yes, before," answered El Borak. "There were unmistakable signs of the use of metal implements upon the walls and the elephant image in the other temple. But the snake temple was evidently constructed, even the carvings, by the use of stone implements alone."

"But could such carvings as are here on the walls have been done by implements made of obsidian or some such stone?" asked Lal Singh.

"Yes," replied El Borak. "The men of the Neolithic Age attained a perfection of the art of making stone weapons and implements, to the highest degree, although their art held about the same relation to the art of the Paleolithic men that the art of the snake temple holds to that of the elephant temple."

"Why were there bloodstains upon the tusks of the elephant image, do you suppose?" asked Abdul Khan.

"I do not know," answered El Borak. "I would have thought there would have been some sort of an altar in each temple, for most primitive peoples offered up human victims, especially the snake. Perhaps the victims were slain on the tusks of the elephant image."

"If there were two tribes, perhaps one tribe was black men," said Yar Ali.

"Not probable," said El Borak. "The black men never made any advances in art."

After we started back to the rafts, I approached El Borak.

"Sahib," said I, "not for me to say to those base-born that you do not posses all knowledge of the ancients. But I found this in the ruins of the temple of the snake."

And I handed him the copper ax which I had found. It was a light, long weapon, with the "eye" at the end instead of the middle, and turned at right angles to the blade. A handle, to fit the "eye" would have had to be bent. The blade had a narrow, very much curved cutting edge.

"A very ancient form of weapon," said Gordon. "I still believe that the carvings in the snake temple were done with stone implements. Perhaps the builders learned the use of metal later, or perhaps tribes using metal implements came into the islands. It must be that there was a race of white men of an earlier age here before the white men came whom the Carthaginians saw. Keep the ax, Khoda Khan. When we reach civilization again you can sell it to some British museum."

After we set out from the island, we were crossing a very marshy place when a crocodile made an attempt to overturn one of the rafts. A swarm of them attacked some of the rafts. One had indeed climbed onto the rafts, when Unalanga pinned the scaly reptile to the raft with his assegai. The other warriors took battle-axes and knob-sticks and beat the other crocodiles off.

Gordon returned in his small raft with Kubo to tell us that we would soon reach the island.

"Good," said Bagheela Khan. "I am tired of this swamp."

Gordon nodded. He looked about at the wide marsh that stretched away like a plain, at the crocodiles bellowing and wallowing in the slime, at the great cliffs of the island and the mangroves flinging aloft their great branches like grotesque arms in the distance, at the stagnant, slimy lakes, at the hordes of marsh-fowls swimming upon the lakes and wheeling, screeching harshly, in the air.

"Dante should have seen this place for inspiration," said Gordon.

"It is a place of ifreets," said Yar Ali. And of the ninety men that were upon the rafts with Gordon, there was scarce one who did not at least half-agree with Yar Ali, that the swamp was a place of ifreets.

Yar Ali suggested tying crocodiles to the rafts and pricking them with long spears to make them swim fast.

"Thus," said he, "we will not have to work poling and rowing the rafts and will go much faster."

We were all willing to try it, if Yar Ali would capture the crocodiles. He said he would do so and would select those that should help him capture them. The Manyeumas objected for they said that if we annoyed the crocodiles, they would come aboard and devour us all.

The warriors whom Yar Ali had selected to help him capture the crocodiles declared that they were not interested in the idea, so we did not try his plan.

We were crossing a rather wide strip of water when Umlingaan, sitting near the tip of one of the rafts, looked over his shoulder and saw a crocodile just behind him. The huge reptile had climbed upon the raft without being heard and its gigantic jaws gaped to seize the Zulu. Umlingaan gave a shriek and dived overboard and the rest of the warriors stampeded for the other end of the raft, nearly upsetting it. The crocodile was approaching them, and they were preparing to defend themselves with swords and spears, their rifles being at the center of the raft, made fast to the bamboos, when Umlingaan, who had swam the whole length of the raft under water, climbed up behind the warriors, seizing Abdhur Shah by the leg to help him in climbing. Abdhur Shah, thinking himself seized by a crocodile, gave a yell and bounded into the air and the other warriors rushed to the center of the raft, straight toward the crocodile, who, startled, turned and flopped back into the lake and swam away.

Yar Ali, who was on another raft, was indignant.

"There was a crocodile," said he, "practically captured. Why did you not bind him, tie him to the raft and fling him overboard, guiding him with your spear? By the beard of the Prophet Mohammed! They who follow El Borak and Yar Ali should be bold and quick of wit." So Yar Ali went on relating incidents to prove that he possessed all the virtues and abilities a follower of El Borak should possess.

When we reached the island we were pleased to find that for perhaps a half-mile all about it the ground was more or less firm. It was bare of vegetation and sloped somewhat steeply from the swamp to the cliffs.

The cliffs themselves were straight and were about two hundred feet high. In some places they were taller. They ran for miles in each direction.

"Unless the island has changed greatly," said Gordon, "the cliffs run in an unbroken line all around the island. Rather, the island does not slope. We must climb the cliffs to get on the island and this place is as good as any. We might explore the cliff, but I think it will be no great difficulty to climb them."

While we were pitching camp close to the great cliffs, one of the lookouts gave a shout, and from around a bulge of the cliff came a large, straggling band of men. It was the safari of the Arab, Hassan ibn Zaroud!

Instantly all the wolves and the Manyeumas formed in battle-order behind El Borak. But the Arab called out that he came in peace.

If El Borak was surprized, he did not show it. He walked forward toward the Arab.

"Greetings, ibn Zaroud," said he. "It would seem that we had met again."

The Arab scowled. "I see that you have strengthened your forces," said he. "You must be an ifreet in human form, El Borak."

"You flatter me," said El Borak. "But I had thought I made a quick march, yet here you are, almost as soon as I."

"I marched straight northwest while you were still in Rhodesia," answered the Arab. "But let us go to your tent and I will relate my travels."

"Why go to the tent?" asked El Borak. "Here is open air and a splendid view. Let us sit down here upon camp chairs which my tent-boy will bring."

"Very well," the Arab scowled. They sat down and we stood within hearing, watch-

[. . .]

El Borak

(unfinished)

Chapter 1.

Were you ever stranded in a strange land, broke, hungry and without a way of raising the necessary cash? Well, it's a mean feeling. I've been in that fix several times but I believe it was worse when I was in Aden for the first time. I'd shipped as an A. B. seaman on the merchantman *Aerial*, bound for Calcutta by way of the Suez and the Red Sea, and when we were making port in Aden, I had a row with the bucko mate and laid him out with a handspike. The captain butted in and I did the same by him. Then I took a header over the rail and swam ashore with the bullets from the second mate's six-shooter knocking up the water on each side of me and a flock of sharks heading my way with wishful looks. I dodged the bullets and outswam the sharks by a hair.

So there I was. I couldn't speak their heathen lingo and if there were white men in town I couldn't find them. Moreover I had to lay close for awhile for the crew of the *Aerial* was scattered around the town and I didn't have any friends in that gang. I spent my last coin for a supper and a place to sleep in a squalid native inn and, having spent most of the night fighting off the bugs and insects that overran the place, I arose and went to the wharf to watch the *Aerial* weigh anchor and sail away. As she disappeared over the horizon I almost wished I was aboard. Consider; there I was, alone and unarmed, in a town, which was then extremely hostile to whites, possessing nothing but the clothes on my back and a big pocketknife, not able to understand the inhabitants or to make them understand me, flat broke, and, apparently, the only white man in the city. I might have sold my knife for a meal or a few coins but I didn't want to do that, as it could be used as a weapon, and, judging from the scowls and ugly looks cast my way by the natives I had an idea I might need a weapon in the near future.

I roamed the town over trying to find a white man but nothing doing. I was ready to call the guy a liar that said there were Englishmen all over the world. I tried to make several Arab merchants understand that I wanted a job but they couldn't or wouldn't understand me, so near sundown I was standing by a well in the middle of a big square, wondering what to do. I was tired, hungry, and getting pretty desperate. And when a man gets desperate with hunger and lack of money, something's going to happen; especially if the man has been a rustler and a road agent. Copper and silver coins seemed everywhere. Dancing girls wore them in their hair. They were piled high on money changers' counters. The very slaves wore garments spangled with them. Sheiks rode by, with leathern bags at their saddlebows, which, as the horses trotted gave forth a musical jingle. Which noise, was, to my ears, as the sight of water is to a famishing desert traveler. Some chance I had of getting any, though! Sheiks and officers of the pasha riding by, eyed me in cold, haughty contempt. Many a lean, brown hand curled longingly around a saber hilt. Slaves coming to the well for water glowered at me with sullen distrust.

One of these, a huge black, deliberately jostled me, growling some insult in his own tongue, whereupon I felled him with a cobblestone. Although it did not kill him or even knock him unconscious, it seemed to instill some respect in the other negroes and they confined their hostilities to scowls and mutterings.

It was growing dusk when a richly dressed, portly Arab rode by on a donkey, accompanied by a big, husky Arab servant, on foot and armed with a scimitar and a long musket. The fat Arab, (I took him to be a merchant) seemed nervous and in a hurry so I judged that he had some money on him. Here was my chance! I followed some distance behind until I saw that they seemed to be heading toward a certain alley. A short cut home, I supposed. I ducked down another alley on the same side and emerged on another street running as near parallel to the one I had just left as those twisting, winding Arab streets can run. I had an idea I could find the alley I wanted for I had become somewhat familiar with that part of the city in my hunt for a job or a European.

I found the alley I sought and entered it stealthily. It was a long, winding, narrow place, dark as Erebus. I followed it until I could see the starlit sky at the other end. Then I drew back against the wall and waited. Nor did I have to wait long. Scarcely had I taken my position when two shapes appeared against the sky. Evidently there were no tall houses across the street from the alley. Perhaps none at all for the building arrangement in Aden is irregular and rather fantastic. So the figures were outlined against the sky and I saw they were the merchant, his donkey and his servant. I flattened myself against the side of the alley, poising a heavy cobblestone in my hand.

The servant came first, groping ahead with the long barrel of his musket. As he came within reach I brought the cobblestone crashing down on his head. He dropped, stunned, and before the merchant could flee or cry out, I was on him with a panther leap. Stifling his screech for help, I dragged him from his mount and knelt on him, pressing the keen edge of my knife against his throat.

"Move and die!" I whispered, and though it is doubtful if he understood the words, he understood the feel of cold steel and lay still.

I was about to ransack him when a cool, amused voice spoke out of the darkness behind me.

"Oh, sahib, why do you waste your time with that fat fool when there is gold, aye, and women too, to be had for the picking?"

"I don't know who you are," I growled. "But if you make a false move I'll slash this guy's throat and then—"

"Pah! Think you I care for that fat Jew fool? Slay him if you will, but do what thou wilt quickly and then come with me for I have work for a man such as thou art and will pay well."

"A paying job, eh? All right then, I'll let this guy go. But," I added softly, "if you're double-crossing me you'll never live to tell of it."

"No fear of that, sahib," was the answer. "Follow me."

I rose and followed him as he led the way down the alley in the direction from which I had come. My eyes had become accustomed to the dark by this time and I could make out a moving blotch which I knew was my would-be employer. I walked warily, my knife ready, but he made no treacherous move and presently we emerged on the street, now dimly lighted by crude lanterns set far apart. One such lantern hung close to the alley mouth and I got my first look at my unknown friend.

He was a tall, lithe man, dressed in plain but costly native clothes. His features were hidden by a burnous but I knew he was of high class, probably some sheik or noble of the Pasha's court. The erect form, proudly held head proclaimed him an Oriental chief as well as the jeweled hilt of the saber that protruded from his robes. Without a word he started up the street beckoning me to follow. But I had been thinking fast. I knew that no Arab sheik would hire an unbeliever for any honest purpose; doubtless he wanted some enemy of his put out of the way. Perhaps even, he was in disgrace with his ruler and wanted the ruler assassinated. I was not very familiar with the East, but I had an idea that if an Oriental noble wanted his sovereign put out of the way he would choose just such a fellow as I to do the job. Killing a king was a little out of my line; I had no desire to mix in world politics. So I stopped and said, "My English-speaking friend, with all due gratitude for your kind offer, I must hear the whole details before I follow you anywhere."

He turned and came back. "You must realize that it is impossible for me to give you 'details' here on the street," he said impatiently.

"So!" I replied. "Just as I thought. You want me to do dirty work for you. You want me to murder some man or carry off some girl for you. Well, nothing doing. I'll go back and collect the tax off that fat merchant."

"Wait, wait!" he exclaimed, seizing my arm. "If you rob the merchant you will have but a few wretched coins to pay you for your exertions while if you will follow me you shall have thousands of gold-pieces and as many beautiful girls as you can carry off."

Thousands! Why, I had risked my life many a time, yes and killed too, for a few hundred dollars.

"You can keep your beautiful girls," I answered. "But a few thousand gold pieces sounds good to me."

"You made two good guesses as the Americans would say. Suppose I told you I wanted you to steal a certain maiden for me?"

"I'd tell you to go to the devil," I snapped. "I tell you I won't be mixed up in anything that has a woman in it."

"Ah, indeed. And suppose," he lowered his voice, "I told you that I had a friend, or rather an enemy, that I wanted removed? A man."

"Well," I reflected, "that would depend on two things. Who the man was and the price offered."

"The price will suit you," he responded. "And as for the identity of the man—you are a stranger here and that should not bother you."

"Well," I murmured as I followed him down the street, "if the price is high enough it don't matter much who the man is; even the king."

At the words he whirled on me like a tiger, one hand outstretched to seize me, the other leaping to his saber.

"What devil put those words in your mouth?" he hissed. "Who are you?"

"Easy, stranger," I warned, backing away, my knife glittering in my hand. "If you try to draw that sword you'll never get it clear of the sheath."

"Are you in Mustapha el Hamid's pay?" he asked menacingly.

"Never heard of him," I responded, watching him warily.

He hesitated, looking at me uncertainly. I could see his eyes glitter above the burnous. Finally he said,

"I believe you. You would not dare—Come, we will go to my house and discuss things further."

As we walked down the dimly lighted street, I suddenly had the feeling that we were being followed. That instinct comes to a man who hunts men and is hunted in turn. I cast my eyes around. There were no booths or bazaars on that street and so it was deserted. At least that was my first impression, but presently I caught a glimpse of two vague shadowy figures stealing along at some distance behind us, on the opposite side of the street. I mentioned the fact to my companion who had not spoken since he had bade me follow him.

"They are my men." He answered without looking about.

I'm not going to describe that journey because I can't. I only know that I walked along beside my silent guide who led the way down dark, winding streets, through black alleys, across silent, deserted courtyards, turning and doubling in that bewildering maze of streets, cross-streets and alleys until I had lost my sense of direction entirely and couldn't have told which way we were going to save me life.

At last we emerged from the maze and came into the suburbs where the nobles, rich merchants and sheiks have their palaces and mansions. There were some fine-looking buildings and terraces there, but I had no chance for a good look at them because of the darkness and my companion's hurry. As we entered the suburbs he began to walk faster and faster and at last we were fairly flying down the way, keeping to the shadows and dodging places lighted by artificial lights or by the moon. Once I looked back and caught a vague sight of our two shadows scooting along behind us.

"Say!" I protested. "What's all the rush? I haven't eaten anything today and I ain't feeling fit for a cross-country run. I thought you were hiring me to do a few assorted murders, not run foot races with you."

"Be silent," he muttered.

We flitted along for a few hundred yards further, shying away from an especially elegant mansion. I didn't know why he did it, but I was following him and when he went nearly half-a-mile out of the way to go, I pulled in my belt another notch, and followed.

When we got past that villa he slowed up, for which I was devoutly thankful. We walked for perhaps a mile, swinging toward the bay, and at last we came to a large building, a regular palace set in the midst of wide rolling terraces, surrounded by a high stone wall.

We went through a small door in the wall and my guide carefully locked the door behind us.

"Ain't you going to let the shadows in?" I asked.

"Shadows?"

"Your men, I mean. The guys that were chaperoning us."

"They will take care of themselves," he answered, impatiently. "You ask too many questions. You annoy me."

I started to retort but changed my mind. The terraces were bathed in the soft light of the Arabian moon, gently rolling, dotted here and there with beautiful fountains and plots of dainty shrubbery; they were friendly and inviting while in startling contrast the great building situated in their center was dark and repelling.

I gazed in wonder and some apprehension at the mansion. Not a light showed, not a sound issued from it. Dark, sinister, forbidding, the great pile of architecture loomed against the star-scattered sky. My silent guide led the way up the terraces toward the house, and as I followed the short hairs of my scalp prickling for in some mysterious, occult way, in a way I cannot describe or explain, it seemed to me that for an instant the veil of the future had been rent and I had peered through at dark and bloody deeds yet in the maw of Eternity. I shuddered and glanced nervously at my guide as dark forebodings began to assail me. Who was this man who spoke and looked like a prince, spoke better English than I, kept his face concealed, maintained his strange silence, was followed by a bodyguard, and came through the night to hire a white man to do a deed of darkness? An Arab? A European who had become mixed up in Oriental politics? And who was this man whom he wanted slain? I had no way of knowing. I could form no theory, could make no plan. It was for me to walk warily and watch my step. I opened the knife I had put away and slipped it up my sleeve, then followed my companion who strode up the terraces until he came to a wing of the building. He opened a door and stood aside for me to enter. The hall, room or whatever it was, was dark as an alley. I hesitated and then stepped inside. The door clicked shut behind me and the next instant I *felt* the man step past me.

"Come, this way, sahib," he said in a low voice. I tried to follow him but it was so dark I couldn't see him, and I couldn't hear him for at every step our feet sank deep in costly Oriental rugs that effectually muffled any sounds. So I had not taken a dozen steps until I was as bewildered and turned around as I had been in the city a short time back. I stopped and addressed my invisible guide.

"How in thunder do you expect me to walk your trail when I can't see, feel, or hear you? Maybe you expect me to locate you by the sense of smell, hey? What's the idea, anyhow? Why can't we have some lights?" I added somewhat irritably, for truth to tell, the darkness and silence had begun to get on my nerves.

Something touched my arm and I jerked back instinctively.

"It is only I, sahib," a voice said. "Take my hand. It is necessary that we have no lights."

I didn't believe him, but I took his hand and he led me through darkened rooms, over rugs and carpets that I could not see but sank ankle deep in the fabric. And all this time not a sound, not a sight, not a feel, except the carpets under foot and the man's hand by which he was leading me. And I felt like a darn fool.

After we had trod the carpets for what seemed to me an interminable time and had climbed at least one winding staircase, (it had carpets on it too), he let go of my hand and left me standing like a lost calf. Suddenly a flood of light blinded me and when my eyes had become accustomed to the sudden change I saw my employer standing before me.

With a sweep he threw aside the burnous and I saw that he was an Arab. But an Arab such as I had never seen before. Here was no fat, greedy merchant, no fawning court noble. With lean, firm molded chin, thin lips, thin-bridged hawk nose and high, intellectual forehead, his was the face of a man among men, the features of a conqueror, an empire builder. He was lighter than the average Arab and extremely handsome. His eyes were dark and lustrous telling of a keen brain and a driving willpower behind them. He was, as I have said, tall and lithe. His movements reminded me of a panther. He was slim enough for litheness and heavy enough for strength.

I have seen few men who could equal him in appearance. He was one of the most perfectly built men I have ever seen. He waved a hand toward a divan.

"Pray, be seated."

I sat down and looked about me. The luxury and richness of the room and its furnishings made me gasp. The floor was covered with rich rugs of Bokhara and China, the walls were hung with gorgeously worked tapestry of silk, velvet and cloth-of-gold, the furniture which consisted of divans and an ebony-wood table were richly decorated, the table with gold and ivory and the divans with the same costly material to which was added beautifully worked silk and gold cloth. The walls themselves were graced with gold and ivory ornaments. The room, which was a large one, seemed illuminated by light that poured in through parallel slits in the wall close to the ceiling. Close by, beyond some curtains I heard a clear musical tinkle that I knew was made by a fountain.

"Say," I said, "I believe we've gotten into the pasha's palace by mistake." Then, as a sudden hair-raising thought struck me, "Say! Are *you* the pasha?"

"Not yet," he laughed, seating himself on a divan just opposite me. I was slightly surprized at his sitting down like a white man. I expected him to sit, tailor fashion on a cushion on the floor.

"I believe you said you had not dined?" he asked.

"I have neither dined, supped or breakfasted," I answered. "And furthermore," I hinted broadly, "I am one of those queer guys who cannot transact business on an empty stomach."

He clapped his hands and a black slave appeared with a suddenness that made me think of the "Arabian Nights." He said something to the slave in soft, slurring Arabic, and the slave salaamed and backed through the curtains.

"Forgive me," my host apologized, "that I begin asking questions relating to the business at hand, before you have eaten, but truth to tell, I am in something of a hurry."

"Go ahead," I answered, settling myself comfortably.

"In the first place, I believe your name is Allison?"

"Yes, it is," I replied, trying not to show my surprize, "Stephen Angus Allison."

"And you are a deserter from the English merchantman *Aerial?*"

"I am."

"You are an American?"

"Yes."

"From what state?"

"Texas. Born and raised on the Mexican Border."

He eyed me contemplatively. "You are younger than I thought."

"I'll be twenty my next birthday," I answered, "but what of that? I'm a man in experience."

"What has been your occupation?"

"Cowpuncher, horse-wrangler, rustler, brand-blotcher, road agent and sailor—at which I wasn't a success."

His brow puckered in thought. "Your American slang is hard for me to grasp. Am I correct in understanding you to have said that you have been a cattle herder, a horse thief and a highwayman?"

"You are," I answered without argument, for just then the slave came back with a big tray loaded with dishes of food and vessels of drink. He set it before me on a small table and salaamed himself out. I'm not going to try to describe that meal because most of the dishes were unfamiliar to me, but there was lots of it and it was cooked wonderfully. The vessels were filled with wine and sherbets cooled with snow brought from the Lord knows where.

"Aren't you going to join me?" I asked my host. He apologized for not joining me, having already eaten, but he needn't have. I felt perfectly able to do away with that meal without any assistance. So I waded into it and got another surprize. Silver knives, forks and spoons were on the tray. I wondered where he got them. Arabs, like most Orientals, eat with their fingers and do not know the use of table implements. My host watched me a while in silence and then said,

"I have travelled a little in the Western United States, that is why I am familiar with the jargon. There are many interesting characters there. One of the most interesting, to me, is the character called a gunfighter." Here he paused and watched me with narrowed eyes.

I devoured a piece of roasted meat in a noncommittal manner.

"I found the gunfighter *very* interesting," he repeated.

"Indeed?" I commented politely, pouring myself a glass of very rare Medoc wine. I wondered how it got to Arabia.

"By an odd coincidence, the man I have hired you to deal with is one of that trade," he went on.

I sat down my glass, "A gunfighter? And a Spaniard?"

"Yes, and one of the swiftest and surest of gunmen."

"Well!" I reflected. "A gunfighter in Arabia!"

"He is a marvelous marksman," the Arab continued, "and his speed and skill are incredible."

I did not reply. I sat silent, feeling once more that fierce, driving power within me that had driven me time and again into a gunfight. My fingertips tingled and the muscles of my hands twitched with the force of that strange urge.

The Arab watched me closely. "Perhaps you dare not go against this man?" he suggested. "Even now you may refuse—"

I merely laughed. "I have answered all your questions," I told him. "Now perhaps you will answer some of mine."

"With pleasure."

"Well, who are you?"

"You may call me El Bahr."

"And how did you know my name?"

"I talked with the captain of the *Aerial*. What he told me showed me that you were a man of determination and courage. I was searching for a man to do the deed of which you know when I saw you following the merchant. If you had not been so intent on him you might have seen me stalking you. But it was to your interest that I did so. The incident with the merchant showed me that you were a man of little wealth, skill in stalking and banditry and—few scruples. Such a man I may afford to pay high wages."

"And who is this man you want me to kill?"

"He is a Spaniard and his name is" (here it seemed to me the Arab hesitated and his eye wandered from me) "Diego Valdez," he said.

"Any relation to the original?" I asked innocently.

"Original?" He darted a quick glance at me.

"And in the face of Fortune and lost in mazed disdain,
I made Diego Valdez, High Admiral of Spain."

I quoted. In that brief instant of hesitation before the name it had seemed to me that his wandering glance had rested on a book on the table and that book bore the name of "Kipling" on its vellum binding.

"Ah," he said, perfectly at ease. "You refer to Kipling's poem? It is quite a coincidence. Perhaps it is an assumed name, yes? We have no way of knowing and he has not long been out of Spain."

"Spain," I mused. "A gunfighter from Spain in Arabia! Well, tell me why you want him murdered."

El Bahr paused a moment and then began: "The Sultan of Oman has but little real power. Yet the people and the army are back of him and he who is the sultan's favorite is the ruler of Oman. The position of favorite is rightfully mine and I have but one rival. A prince named Mustapha el Hamid. His was a losing cause until Diego Valdez came to Oman. He became Mustapha's ally and together they have worked to bring about my downfall. I have tried time and again to have Valdez removed but he is a terrible fighter, fierce as a wolf and cunning as a fox and he has a band of outlaws from India, bandits and murderers. I am not without power, yet until Mustapha's power with the sultan declines, I dare not have him assassinated; and his power will not decline as long as Diego Valdez is his ally. Here is my proposition: kill Diego Valdez in a fair fight or in any way you choose and I will give you a thousand pieces of gold, assure you of protection from his Indians and Mustapha's Arabs and give you passage back to America."

I was silent.

After a pause the Arab went on, "You can still draw back. I warn you that this man is a magician with a gun. The Arabs call him "El

Borak" on account of his speed and sureness. Better men than you have not dared meet this Spaniard."

I laughed. "I accept the position. But I kill this man fair, in a public gunfight. But you'll have to get me a gun."

He clapped his hands and the slave entered, bearing an armful of revolvers and holsters. He laid them on the divan before me. I ran over them with an experienced eye. There was quite a collection: Webleys, Brownings, Lugers and a Colt or two. There was one that I selected at once. It was a heavy-calibered, single-action Colt with a stiff leather holster.

I tried the action of the gun, did the double-roll and the road-agent's spin. The balance was perfect.

"I procured that gun in the United States," remarked El Bahr. "It is yours."

"Thanks. Now about the details of the meeting with Valdez."

"That will be arranged later," replied the Arab, signalling the slave to take away the other weapons.

"What kind of a man is he?" I wanted to know.

"A man of about your size. Middle height, light and wiry. A lean strong face, dark eyes and black hair, blacker than mine, blacker than yours. Always smooth-shaven. He wears sometimes European clothes, sometimes the dress of an Arab."

For a while there was silence as I sat meditating, balancing the gun on my palm.

Suddenly there was a light rustle of silk, the curtains parted and a girl tripped into the room. She was a slender, beautiful young thing, unveiled, her soft, sheer garments modeling the contour of her lovely form. She stopped short at the sight of me, evidently having not known that El Bahr was not alone. She started to retreat, but the Arab rose, strode forward and caught her by the arm. There was an angry scowl on his face and the girl appeared to be frightened. I could not understand their conversation, of course, but I knew that he was threatening her and that she was pleading with him. Her large, fawn-like eyes were soft with tears. Suddenly he dragged her over to the wall. I did not understand what he meant to do until he took from the wall a riding whip. Still I could not believe he meant to whip her till he raised the whip and the shrinking girl closed her eyes in anticipation of the lash. I leaped across the room and caught the descending whip across my arms. Then I wrenched it from his hands. I was furious and it was all I could do to refrain from laying his face open with his own whip but something told me that it wouldn't do. However, I told him what I thought of him.

"You cowardly, dirty, horse-thieving, woman-whipping, yellow imitation of a Siwash Indian!" I told him. "You can't try anything like that around me." He was angry at my interference of course, but to my wonder, he seemed more surprized than anything else.

"You dare to interfere with me?" he asked, wonderingly, as if he could hardly believe it himself.

I laughed. "Dare interfere with you! Why, it's all I can do to keep from pinning you to the wall, you cowardly jackal."

His eyes glittered but he asked quietly, "And how have I incurred your displeasure, may I ask?"

"How?" I was dumbfounded. "Do you mean to say you don't know? Let go of that girl."

He laughed unpleasantly. "Oh, I had forgotten that the Feringi do not like to see women corrected. So that is why you are angry. That is a small affair!"

"Small to whip a girl?"

"Certainly. One of my slaves disobeys me; it is no one's concern what I do to her—much less an Unbeliever. Give me that whip."

"She is a slave?" I asked in wonder. I was new to the East then.

"Yes, you fool. And whether she is a slave or not makes little difference. Give me that whip."

I stepped forward. "You may not know it," I said between my teeth, "but you are trifling with death. You are right; it makes no difference whether she is a slave or not."

For a moment we looked each other in the eyes; then he shrugged his shoulders. "After all," he said, "this is a trifling matter to quarrel about."

He released the girl with a shove. She darted away through the curtains.

"Does that satisfy you?" he asked, ironically.

"It does not," I responded. "Swear on the Koran that you will not harm that girl or you can find someone else to fight Diego Valdez."

"Very well," he answered. "I swear on the Koran and by the beard of the Prophet. Does that satisfy you?"

"Yes," I answered; but his eyes were glittering and I knew that he was furious and that I must be on my guard.

"Perhaps you are weary," he suggested. "I will show you to your bed."

He led the way through the curtains on one side of the room and made his way down a large hallway, finally entering a small room. It was as luxuriously furnished as the room we had just left and I perceived that I was to sleep on a kind of Oriental couch or divan. The room was lighted with richly ornamented Arabian lamps.

I sat down on the divan and El Bahr stood a moment in the doorway.

"Do you desire that dancing-girls be sent to lull you to sleep?" he asked.

"I do not!" I replied emphatically. "And by the way, El Bahr, I am a very light sleeper."

"You shall not be disturbed," he replied. "May you have pleasant dreams, Sahib."

After he left the room I still sat on the divan, going over my day's adventure. To tell the truth, I was somewhat bewildered. It seemed that I had torn a page from the "Arabian Nights"; here were mysteries, intriguing princes, beautiful maidens as slaves and here was I, a more or less unsophisticated American youth put down in the midst of the confusion. Then my thoughts wandered to the Spaniard, Diego Valdez, whom El Bahr had hired me to kill. Who was this strong man who mixed in Oriental intrigues and Eastern politics? Some ambitious soldier-statesman with a dream of carving out an Empire for himself or some wandering adventurer such as I was?

I mused awhile on such thoughts and finally lay down, dressed completely except for my shoes. I laid my open knife on the divan beside me and put the gun on the other side. It was not loaded but a gun is as good as a blackjack in a hand-to-hand fight. Then I composed myself for sleep, lulled by the soft Oriental music that filled the air.

I awoke the next morning rather early and was arranging my clothes when a Nubian slave entered with many salaams, escorted me down the corridor and into a room that was furnished much like a European breakfast room. El Bahr was there before me.

"Good morning, sahib," he greeted. "I hope you rested well."

I sat down to a sumptuous breakfast. I was fast falling under the lure of Oriental luxury. For weeks I had been accustomed to the plain fare and hard toil of a "windjammer" merchant ship and now, dropped as it were into "the lap of luxury" I felt the comparison strongly. Would it not be well to accept constant employment under El Bahr? That was my thought as I listened to my employer talk. He was evidently highly educated and extensively travelled. I later learned that he was a graduate from a famous European college and had travelled practically all over the world.

When we had finished breakfast El Bahr remarked, "Perhaps you would like to get a birds-eye view of Muscat?"

I assented and he led the way out into a corridor (the castle seemed to be a maze of endless corridors), and started down in. I followed when suddenly I stopped short, the short hairs of my scalp prickling. Through the whole castle, rising higher and higher until it broke at the highest note, rang a piercing shriek! And I knew that it was human, that it was the shriek of a man in torture.

"Who is that?" I exclaimed whirling on El Bahr. He merely shrugged his shoulders and smiled. With a curse I sprang past him and leaped down the winding stairs. He shouted after me angrily but I paid no heed. I raced down another corridor, found and descended another stair and following the direction of the shriek, kept on going. It was mere chance that caused me to at last descend a flight of stairs that led into a dark, gloomy corridor. Down this I went, cautiously, my knife ready. At last I came to an open door through which shone a gleam of light. I stepped through and the sight that met my eyes completely astounded me; it carried me back to the Middle Ages.

It was a dungeon into which I stepped. The dim light of torches thrust into niches in the wall lit a scene which seemed more in keeping with the Spanish Inquisition than anything else I could think of.

There were about a dozen Arabs in the cell, and they were grouped about a strange contrivance. It consisted of a wooden frame, shaped like a V. It rested on the point of the V, secured and held upright by heavy timbers. The V frame was not one solid piece but each prong or side of the V was fastened together at the point of the V with some kind of a pivot arrangement that allowed the V to be opened like a fan. To each side of the V were secured strong ropes that were fastened at the other ends to a sort of windlass.

And between the prongs of the V lay a man, his hands bound fast to one prong, his feet to the other, his form stretched out between the prongs of the rack. For that was what it was—a rack.

The Arabs had looked up as I entered but now at a word from one of their number they bent over the windlasses again. The heavy timbers creaked as the V widened slightly. A groan burst from the man on the rack.

Furious, I leaped forward, to the nearest windlass, caught an Arab by the shoulder and swung him away. He cursed and as I caught the glint of a knife I struck, sending him sprawling to the floor. At that moment the voice of El Bahr hurled a sharp order and the Arabs paused in their rush at me.

El Bahr stepped forward and the men fell back and salaamed.

He strode up to me. "What do you mean coming here?" he asked sharply. It was evident that he was in a fine rage. But I had a rage to match his.

"Who is that man, you devil?" I asked, drawing my knife. "Tell your Oriental fiends to let that rack down." I stepped toward the rack.

"Stop!" ordered El Bahr peremptorily. "It is none of your business but that man is an Indian and a spy of El Borak."

The man on the rack spoke for the first time. He spoke English with a babu accent.

"Beg to differ. Never heard of El Borak. For Vishnu's sake, sahib, release me from present position, same being most embarrassing and humiliating to man of my high education. I swear I never heard of El Borak."

"It makes no difference to me," I replied. "El Bahr, are you going to give the order I told you?"

"You are a fool," he answered sneeringly. "Evidently you do not realize that I am absolute ruler here, that you are as completely in my power as you would be in the power of the Sultan were you in his dungeons."

"El Bahr," I said quietly but I knew that my eyes were glittering in the gloom like the eyes of a jungle cat, "are you going to give that order?"

"You fool! What is to prevent me from having you bound on the rack?"

"This!" and I drew. He did not see the gun until it was in my hand. A gasp went up from the Arabs and I saw El Bahr's expression change as he realized the speed of my draw.

But he only said, "Put that gun up, Allison. You know as well as I that it is empty."

I laughed gratingly. "You gave it to me empty. But, you fool, did it never occur to you that a man who has always carried a gun of this caliber might not have cartridges in his pockets?"

He looked undecided. "If you don't believe me," I said softly, "refuse to order that babu released."

Still he hesitated. The Arabs said something to him; he paused and then threw a curt order to them. They went forward, cut the ropes that bound the Indian and lifted him to the floor.

"As soon as you can walk," I told him, keeping my eyes on El Bahr, "go into the corridor and up the stairs. I will follow."

"Allison," El Bahr broke in, his voice full of suppressed rage, "you are going too far. I won't tolerate this."

"What are you going to do about it?" I asked. "If you try to stop us I'll kill you."

Suddenly El Bahr laughed and it was a laugh that made cold chills race up and down my back.

"Very well," he said, "I will let this Indian go, but I will remember."

He gave an order to the Arabs and they stepped aside to let us pass.

I backed toward the door, with the babu. "You'll come, too, El Bahr," I told him. He followed without a word. So did the Arabs.

The situation seemed to strike El Bahr's sardonic sense of humor. He not only made no protest but he led the way out of the castle and in a few minutes we were on the terraces.

"There is the gateway," he said, pointing. "Go, babu."

"Wait," I interrupted. "We'll accompany him to the gate."

As we walked along in the sunlight I got a good view of the babu. He was a typical Bengali, except that he was of a different build from most babus, being of middle height and rather slim and lithe. He had a pleasant face and I noted that he did not speak with such a babu accent or use such flowery language as most babus I had seen.

"What is your name?" I asked him.

"Ghopal Ramm, so please the sahib," he answered with a smirk. "B. A. degree, University of Calcutta."

"How is it you're a captive of this Arab?"

"Vishnu knows!" he replied. "If allowed to guess, would base supposition on fact that El Borak sahib (whoever he is) has a following of natives of India, no doubt budmashs and outcasts. Thus, Indian villains follow El Borak, this babu being Indian, consequently, he is in employ of El Borak sahib. Q. E. D. Such being no doubt conclusion reached by ignorant and thoughtless Arabs. So, thought being paternal parent to deed, next thing is to seize said babu and torture him, to make him reveal state secrets. Ignoring said babu's high intellectual standing and," with a smirk, "aristocratic lineage."

"What are you doing in Oman?"

"Savants of science," he replied glibly, "going all over the world regardless of expense and personal comfort in order to advance knowledge, I being one; many old ruins of castles and other marks of antiquity in Oman. Therefore, here I am!"

"Here's the gate," I said. "Now scoot. You better get out of Oman!"

"That is my only wish," he avowed. "Salaam, sahib!"

And he "scooted" out of the gate and fled down the road with amazing speed, his loose garments flapping behind him.

I turned to El Bahr who stood watching, a sardonical smile on his handsome face.

"You can take your gold and go to hell," I told him resentfully. "I wouldn't do no work of no kind for a gink like you."

"Indeed!" His aristocratic heavy eyebrows lifted. "You have forgotten that the Oman police are already on your trail for the attempted robbery of the merchant?"

I didn't even know that Oman boasted a police force.

"You are in my power," he went on. "If you try to leave my palace you will be slain by my Arabs. If you should escape them the Oman police will seize you and put you to torture. On the other hand, if you do as I say, you will leave Oman a rich man."

I hesitated.

"You have scruples about killing a European?" he continued. "The man is a scoundrel and a villain. A murderer and a ravisher of young girls."

I shrugged my shoulders.

"I gave my word," was all I said. "But don't try to get me to do anything else for you."

Chapter 2.

The bazaar was a sea of gaudy colors: robes, turbans and swarthy faces. As I followed El Bahr through the bazaar I paid little heed to the surroundings. I was too preoccupied with my thoughts. The bloodlust was burning in my veins. Yes, my eyes blazed and my hand twitched with the lust to kill a man whom I had never seen.

He was a gunman; I was another. That was enough.

Suddenly my pulse gave a bound as I saw ahead of me a man in European garments.

At the same instant El Bahr touched me on the shoulder and whispered, "Kill! It is El Borak," and vanished in the throng.

I strode forward and the crowd backed away on both sides, leaving a broad space clear between the Spaniard and me. Evidently they had seen El Bahr speak to me and had seen El Borak and had drawn their own conclusions.

My hand hovered, claw-like, just above my gun butt. I had greased the holster whose end was tied to my leg with a leather thong and hung low on my right hip. The pistol rested easily in it. I had carefully removed the trigger and had examined each cartridge.

And now I was gazing at El Borak. He was of medium height, of lithe, wiry, build. His eyes were black and so was his hair, for his sun-helmet was pushed back.

He was dressed in linens and riding boots. What hesitation or scruples I might have felt at killing a European in a strange land were swept away by the sight of the big pistol swinging low on his right hip. And with an experienced eye I noted that it was not tied down.

A big Oriental, evidently not an Arab, was walking at his side and he pointed me out to El Borak, apparently. The Spaniard nodded; he stepped forward and seemed on the point of calling to me when I saw his expression change. A gunman himself, he knew the signs of the bloodlust.

"El Borak!" I said, not loud but clearly. "Draw!"

And I went for my gun.

I put all my speed and skill in that draw and never before did I draw so swiftly. My intention was to fire from the hip, the instant the muzzle cleared the scabbard. I cocked the hammer as I drew the gun.

Yet even as the gun left the holster, before I could fire, there was a crashing report. I felt a stunning shock in my right arm and my gun spun from my hand, exploding harmlessly in the air.

I staggered back, cursing and gripping my right hand.

El Borak was standing as before, except that now he held a smoking gun in his hand.

There seemed to be a somewhat puzzled look on his dark face.

He strode toward me, stopping just in front of me.

"Well, why don't you shoot, damn you!" I exclaimed, wild with rage and the humiliation that comes to a gunfighter when he has met a greater one.

For answer he sheathed his gun.

"You are certainly fast," he commented without sarcasm, to my infinite amazement.

"Fast?" I was thrown off my track by this remark. "Fast? When you shot the gun out of my hand, before I could fire?"

"You had your gun out and cocked before I fired," he answered, and there was no vanity in the statement.

"My—!" I ejaculated in awe. "What kind of a guy are you?"

He picked up my gun and handed it to me. A certain wistful expression seemed to be present on his face.

"It's a pity that two Americans in a foreign land should try to kill each other."

"Americans! Are you an American?"

"Certainly. What did you think I was?"

"A Spaniard," I said slowly, "named Diego Valdez."

He laughed. "What other lies has El Bahr told you? I was born in Texas, just north of the Border and my name is Frank Gordon."

Texas! The Border! So El Bahr had sent me to murder an American. I stood staring. And then came the crash of a jezail rifle and the wind of a bullet fanned my cheek.

The shot was reechoed by the crash of Gordon's pistol and turning, I saw an Arab spin around and fall, his long rifle dropping from his hand.

"A message from your erstwhile employer," said Gordon, dryly.

I was bewildered. "But why, what—"

"Ahmed Habib has no use for one who has failed," he answered. "Oman is no longer safe for you. You'd better go home with me. Ali, go bring the coach."

The big Asian strode off without a word and Gordon said, "Suppose we go into this shop, Allison."

Feeling rather dazed I followed El Borak into a shop, whose proprietor, at a word from Gordon, salaamed us into a room at the back, piled with Oriental cushions.

Gordon motioned me toward a pile of cushions and sank down upon another pile himself.

I seated myself; surely not many men have had such a strange experience. Here was I, throwing in my lot, apparently, with a man whom I had tried to kill a few minutes before.

I scanned him curiously. As I said, he was of middle height and lithely built. Except for a certain pantherish quality in his movements, there was nothing unusual about him, nothing to indicate that he was the terrible fighter that El Bahr had avowed him to be. He had the narrow hips and straight, firm-built, rangy legs of a fighter but his square shoulders were not broader than usual and his chest was not especially large. His arms were longer than most but their muscles did not bulge or show signs of the extraordinary strength El Bahr had said he possessed. Speed, that was what he was built for, rather than strength, it seemed to me. His hands as well as his feet were rather slim and rather long, his fingers long and tapering; the fingers of a gambler or a musician or an artist.

I have said his eyes were black. They were, and different from any eyes I ever saw before or since. They were neither small, beady eyes nor large, soft eyes, such as is the case, one way or the other, with most black eyes. Gordon's eyes were of medium size, with extraordinary depth. Quiet, imperturbable, clear, and farseeing.

They were pure black and pure white. There was no hint of any other kind of color about them.

He looked anyone straight in the eyes, with no hint of mockery, no challenge. His eyes gave the impression that if he would, he could read your very soul, but refrained because of courtesy. And for some reason, this put anyone singularly at their ease.

That was my first impression.

His hair was black; the blackest I have ever seen. Straight but not coarse. There was no hint of Indian blood about him.

His features were rather aristocratic; there was something about his face that reminded me vaguely of El Bahr, although there was none of the Arab's arrogance.

Gordon was not handsome. His face was rather too lean, his lips rather too thin. Though when he turned his face a certain way he appeared almost handsome. His face was rather dark, though not as dark as is common for a man of his eyes and hair, and was tanned by the Arabian sun. He could have passed for an Arab easily in native garb.

His features were clean; there was absolutely nothing greedy, shifty or sensual about him. His straight nose was thin bridged, his jaw lean and rather long. His face was absolutely smooth.

He was slightly taller than I, as I had not reached my full height then. His height, I should say, was between five feet eight inches and five feet nine inches.

His build was deceptive and I was afterwards surprized to learn that he weighed close upon one hundred and forty-five pounds. I doubt if there were five ounces of surplus fat upon him. Such was my first view of El Borak, Frank Gordon.

"Have a smoke?" he asked, offering me cigarette papers and Turkish tobacco.

I am not an habitual smoker but I felt I needed something to steady my nerves. As I rolled a cigarette with no very steady hand, I noticed that he did not prepare himself a smoke.

"You'd better throw your lot in with me," he said without preliminaries. "As I said, Ahmed has no use for an employee who has failed. If you try to stay in Muscat (and you can't get away), his Arabs will get you sure."

"But what, how—" I began bewildered.

"I know Ahmed hired you to kill me," he went on, imperturbably, "but you didn't and he'll be after you now; anyway, two Americans ought not to be fighting each other in a strange land, as I said before. Throw in with me and I'll guarantee you a good time, if nothing else."

I hesitated. From what I had seen of El Bahr, whom Gordon called "Ahmed," I knew that he was right. Indeed, was it not I whom the Arab Gordon killed had aimed at?

But it was not fear of El Bahr that led me to make the decision I made.

I liked Gordon. Of course, he was a white man, but it wasn't that that caused my liking for him, alone. There was something about the man that attracted me.

I often act on impulse and I did then.

"Gordon," I said, "I don't know what your game is but I'm with you. If it's crooked politics, international robbery, empire building or what, I am with you just the same. I'm not particular."

A wonderful smile lighted his dark face. "Good," was all he said, but he held out his hand and we shook.

Just then in came the big Asian Gordon had sent for the coach. I took special note of him. He was a big, tall man, with a big turban that was not Arab, and a heavy black beard. He was big, no mistake. And he wore a strange kind of a garment, a wadded coat that I don't see how he stood on account of the heat. A heavy leather belt was around him, and through this was thrust a yard-long knife in an ornamented sheath.

"Mr. Allison," said Gordon, "this is one of my companions, Yar Ali Khan of Kadar, Afghanistan."

He spoke a few words in some strange tongue.

"Salaam, bahadur," rumbled the big Afghan. I seemed to detect a sarcastic note in the greeting.

"We will go to my place if you are ready," said Gordon. I followed him to the street where a crowd had gathered about a most unusual vehicle. It consisted of two seats mounted on four wheels. The front seat was between the front wheels, the back seat between the hind wheels, and both were connected by a floor. The seats seemed to be made of divans, shortened and provided with arms.

Two Arab horses were hitched to the vehicle by a complicated system of harness.

Yar Ali dispersed the crowd with a few kicks and a flourish of his long knife and mounted to the front seat. Gordon and I climbed into the back seat.

"This is Ali's own invention," Gordon explained. "He made the thing out of a rajah's chariot and the furnishings out of a rao's palace."

The inventive gentleman now started his invention in motion by the simple process of giving voice to a hair-raising screech and prodding the steeds with the point of his knife. We were off down the street at a speed that made my hair rise. Bump! bump! bump! Over the cobblestones and ruts of those abominable Oman streets. I was jerked and flung from side to side and only escaped being deposited in the street by an activity and skill at acrobatics not equaled by many.

Gordon seemed not to mind it. He swayed to every motion, never changing his position, never seeming disconvenienced.

How the Afghan kept his seat I don't know, but finally he stood up on the front seat and waved his knife and yelled and chanted some kind of heathen war song, stopping every now and then to curse the horses in seven different languages.

It was a wild ride, I want to say, and it was no wonder people stopped and stared after us. Of the three of us, Gordon was the only one who appeared to have any sense at all.

I have no idea how far we went but at last we came in sight of a castle on a small hill, quite a distance from any other houses.

A high wall surrounded the castle which loomed up more like a medieval European baron's castle.

Without slacking the pace we dashed straight up the slope and a pair of great iron gates swung wide. Through them we dashed—I had only time to note an armed Arab on each side of the gate—straight up to the castle doors—the hill was flat on top. Straight up to castle doors, whirling about in a giant curve that swung the coach around like a whip and deposited me on my head in the courtyard.

Yar Ali leaped out, hauled me to my feet, brushed me off with blows that would have knocked mules down, nearly, and bellowed what I took to be an order, since two or three young Arabs appeared and took charge of the horses.

"Welcome to our city," chuckled Gordon. "The accommodations are not of the finest but I trust you will make yourself at home, Steve. (If you will pardon me for calling you by your first name.)"

I glanced curiously around. There was quite a large space between the wall and the castle. It was not terraced, as was the estate of El Bahr. But there were fountains and trees and the whole was covered with grass and flowers.

The castle had on its front a large veranda, evidently a new addition. To this Gordon led the way. But we had not reached it when there came a screech of fear followed by a fierce yell and a perfect Babel of heated conversation. We turned to see Yar Ali striding toward us, dragging a man by the slack of his clothes with one hand and waving his knife in the other. The captive was speaking rapidly and with great feeling and Yar Ali was replying with, apparently, some quotations from the Scriptures.

"A babu," Gordon remarked with some surprize evident, which was a rather unusual thing for him.

And I saw it was Ghopal Ramm!

The Afghan dumped him down before Gordon and began an impassioned oration which I would love to have been able to have understood.

Gordon replied in the same tongue in a quiet voice and the Afghan stopped abruptly. Gordon put a question to the babu in Hindustani.

Ghopal climbed to his feet, arranged his clothing and replied in English:

"Most noble sahib, having escaped dungeons of Arab-in-power, owing to bravery and skill of yonder sahib," respectfully indicating me, "and finding Muscat no longer suitable for a man of my refined tastes, owing to hostility of aforesaid Arab, taking sahib's advice to seek Gordon sahib.

"Therefore, seeing sahibs careening through the streets, and being unable to attract attention by vocalizing 'Hi! hi!' this babu took the liberty of mounting rear part of vehicle. While resting after ride was discovered by this Himalayan chief who evidently suspects treachery. Suspicion quite unfounded, I assure you!"

"He is a spy of El Bahr's," rumbled Yar Ali Khan, thumbing his knife suggestively.

"He seems to know you?" Gordon turned to me.

"El Bahr was having him tortured in his dungeons," I replied. "I made El Bahr release him and told him he'd better come to you. I knew Oman wouldn't be safe for him with the Arab after him and I took a kind of liking to the man."

Gordon looked at the babu who wriggled beneath the gaze.

"Well," he decided, "you are a clever man or you couldn't have boarded and ridden that coach without my hearing you. You are either a spy of El Bahr or an ordinary wandering babu. In the first case you will be found out if you are a spy and in the second case you may be useful. At any rate, you can go or stay as you choose. If you throw in with me and become one of my men you will be treated the same as the rest. What is your name?"

"Ghopal Ramm, please your worship," smirked the Bengali, "B. A. degree, babu university, Calcutta. At present engaged in research work in Oman."

"What kind of research?"

"Exploring antique castles, most noble sahib."

"Very good. This castle may interest you."

The babu salaamed and smirked.

Gordon led us up on the veranda, Yar Ali and the babu following. The babu kept close to me and cast apprehensive glances toward Yar Ali.

"What kind of a place have we gotten into, sahib?" he whispered.

Gordon clapped his hands.

"Possibly you would like to meet some of my friends," he remarked.

Almost instantly the great doors swung back, revealing heavy velvet curtains screening the entrance.

What followed was dramatic, impressive. Whether it was staged to impress me or merely because of the Eastern love of dramatics, I have no idea.

Hardly had the doors swung open when a man stepped through the curtains.

He was slim and lithe, rather tall. He stepped with a catlike grace and was handsome in his way.

He was clothed with elegance. A rose-colored turban with a diamond brooch adorned him, and his clothes were of silk and satin. A wide silk sash supported a jewel hilted dagger. Pointed satin slippers were on his feet.

His dark, handsome face was adorned with a pointed beard.

"Mr. Allison, my friend Rustum Bey of Persia. Rustum Bey, Mr. Steve Allison and Ghopal Ramm of Calcutta."

The Persian saluted gracefully and stepped aside as another man came through the curtain. I knew him instantly for what he was. I had seen his tribe before, clad in the uniform of the British army or police force. Tall as Yar Ali Khan but rangier built, with plain white garments.

"Mr. Allison, my friend, Lal Singh of Lahore."

The Sikh lined up with the Persian, the introductions over and the curtains parted again.

A bronze image of a man appeared. Of medium height but with such broad shoulders and heavy chest as to appear stocky, the face of the Sphinx, skin the color of bronze, clad only in a loincloth—

I heard the babu gasp and step back. I recoiled, myself, as I saw the caste-mark on the man's brow. I had seen that mark before!

"Vishnu!" the babu gasped. "The mark of Kali! A Thag! Oh, my aunt!"

"—Juggnara Nath of Delhi," Gordon was saying. Fascinated, I gazed at the silken handkerchief in the Thag's girdle.

A tall, stately Arab came through the curtains.

"—sheikh Ahmed el Kadour—"

I nearly forgot my manners in my fascination. This was, in truth, a page from the "Arabian Nights"!

I looked with wonder. Gordon, in his European garb, the great, uncouth Afghan, the elegant, catlike Persian, the white-clad Sikh, the sinister, immobile Hindu, the stately Arab, the perspiring, apologetic babu—they formed a picture such as is the privilege of few men to see.

"A Paythan, a Sikh, a Thag and a babu," I remarked. "It seems that India has emigrated to Arabia."

Gordon smiled and spoke a few words in some language. With the exception of the Arab and the Afghan they vanished so quickly it made me dizzy and they took the babu with them.

The Arab seated himself in one of the chairs on the veranda and the Afghan retired to a distance, seated himself cross-legged on the floor and drew his knife, casting a significant glance at me. Evidently he still had suspicions.

Gordon clapped his hands again and a young Nubian brought a tray of liquors and placed them on a small table.

"What will you have?" Gordon asked. "Champagne? Brandy? Whisky? Wine? Cocktails?"

"Champagne," I decided. It was cold and delectable.

I noticed the Arab drank his share in spite of the Koran's forbidding the use of wine. Probably he argued that brandy isn't wine.

Gordon drank less than any of us. I think Ali waylaid the Nubian for I saw him making gestures with a long bottle of wine.

"I'm taking you on trust," Gordon said. "I can sometimes see a man's character."

And he could, too. He could read a man like a book.

"I'm going to start at the first," he went on. "I don't mean a story of my life or anything like that. That would take too long. I mean why I am in Oman.

"The tale starts in India. Owing to the fact that I have friends among the Thags, I am admitted into the temple of Siva and other places that no white man is ordinarily allowed to enter. In a temple in Delhi I found some old books. With the aid of a priest I translated them. Aside from many things which have no bearing on this tale, I found evidences of a great treasure hidden somewhere. The book was vague as to its exact whereabouts but stated definitely that the treasure was beneath the sands of a desert. What desert? My first thought was that it referred to the desert of Bikanir. But translating further I found this could not be the case. Translated roughly it stated the treasure lies: 'Between a sea and a sea and two narrow seas.' That could only mean Arabia. The 'sea and a sea' are the Mediterranean and Arabian Sea. The 'narrow seas' are the Persian Gulf and the Red Sea. But where in Arabia? I made a guess. The treasure was evidently Indian. Oman is closest to India. I guessed Oman. There was a page gone from the book. The priest declared the page was a map, locating the treasure. It had been torn from the book by a Frenchman who had gained admittance into the temple in disguise.

"Trying to escape through Afghanistan he was killed by bandits. I searched through Afghanistan for the map but found that it had been taken from the Afghans by a band of Turkoman raiders. The Afghans thought it had magic powers and this belief has evidently been shared by all other peoples, for there has been murder and tribal war to gain possession of it. With my friends I traced the map across half of Asia." (Here Rustum Bey appeared silently and sat down.) Gordon went on, "We traced the map from Delhi to Khabul, from Khabul to Pamir. Thence to Bokhara, then to Khiva. From Khiva the trail led to Teheran and from Teheran to Bagdad. From Bagdad the trail doubled back to Ispahan and from there it led straight to Shiraz. From Shiraz across the Persian Gulf to Muscat.

"When I arrived in Muscat my only thought was to secure the map and go after the treasure. But I found it harder than one would expect. I found it to be in the possession of sheikh Ahmed Habib Abd Ullah Saden. He whom men call El Bahr. I soon found myself mixed up in Arabian politics. For whom should I meet but Mustapha el Hamid, an old friend of mine. I knew he was of Oman but had no thought of meeting him here. He is a rival for power and the Sultan's favor is with Ahmed el Saden. They are the powers of Oman.

[. . .]

"I emptied my revolver..."

(untitled and unfinished)

I emptied my revolver and then went down before the charge of the Arabs. They swarmed over me hacking and stabbing, but as I fell I dragged an Arab down with me and held him as a shield against the other Arabs who danced about seeking to get in a blow with spear or sword. They were about to succeed when above their shouts and screeches there sounded a yell, "Allah il Allah! Akbar il Hyder! Hai! Yo-hai!" and like a great panther Yar Ali leaped among the Arabs swinging his long knife. Before the fury of that onset his foes gave back and back. And still he raged among them until the press was cleared and I threw aside my cursing captive and struggled to my feet. The Arabs had returned to the charge. They assailed the Afghan like wolves attacking a tiger. They swarmed about him striking and thrusting with scimitar and spear. But scimitar and spear seemed futile against the long Khyber knife that danced and flickered like a flame—and it seemed a man fell at each blow. Snatching up a spear, I sprang to the Afridi's aid. The Arabs had forgotten me and I was upon them and had my spear through an Arab's body before they knew I was there. Then before they could turn on me I had forced my way through the throng of attackers and was at Yar Ali's side.

He smiled grimly. "Back to back, sahib, and we will show these jackals of Arabia what real warriors are like!"

I snatched up a saber and took my position. Hardly had I done so when the Arabs hurled themselves upon us again. I could not describe that battle or begin to describe it. I only know that the enraged Arabs hurled charge after charge against us and again and again we beat them off. I remember that it seemed a sea of furious, swarthy faces swam before me and we were hemmed in by scores and scores of flashing, stabbing, hacking blades. And I parried and struck, struck and parried and warded, and five times I struck with the terrible Mameluke thrust that Gordon had taught me and saw a man go down before it. And once a man ran in under my guard and struck me in the shoulder with a jambazeh, and I stabbed with my dagger and he fell cursing. And still they came until my arm was so weary that I could hardly lift my blade. Then came a clatter of horses' hoofs, a crashing volley and the foes melted away like snow before the sun. Yar Ali and I stood alone. I had a vision of wild riders coursing the battlefield and cutting down the fleeing Arabs.

Yar Ali turned to me, a smile on his grim face. "It is El Borak."

[. . .]

The Land of Mystery

(unfinished)

Ancient of nations as the pyramid,
What mysteries lie vaguely hid,
Amid the ancient jungles and the plains,
Where, lichen-grown beneath the jungle rains,
Half-hid by trees that tower toward the sky,
The ruins of strange, ancient cities lie;
Cities that were forgot already when
Stonehenge and Karnak sheltered tribes of men.
Cities whose kings had gone to their last sleep,
Ere lost Atlantis sank into the deep.
Oh, land of ancient mystery's domains,
Dark as the tribes that roam thy ancient plains,
There you will find, as stayed Time's tracing hand,
Yesterday's ages in that ancient land, Thou, Africa.

Chapter 1.
"There are strange things in Africa."

Gordon was speaking. His listeners leaned forward eagerly, with the utmost interest.

"Not only my porters deserted, but my askaris also. I was left in the midst of a tropical jungle, the only white man for hundreds of miles, with a good supply of provisions, but armed only with a .577 double-barreled elephant rifle, my pistol, a yataghan and a heavy scimitar of Arab make. For the rifle I had perhaps eighty cartridges, and for the pistol some two hundred. The askaris and porters had managed to make off with most of the other luggage. I saw little use of trying to make it back to the coast. Indeed, I was so near to the interior that I had an idea that one coast was almost as near as another. At any rate, I plunged on into the jungle.

"There did not seem to be any natives. The jungle itself did not differ from other African jungles. Finally I emerged from the jungle and came upon a strip of desert. I could see what appeared to be mountains in the distance. That desert I crossed. The heat and desolation was ghastly. The sun beat down with a fierce heat which was cast back by the hard, barren soil. There were no oases, no springs. There were no mirages such as I have seen in other deserts. There was nothing but a barren waste of sand and rocky soil. But the desert was not wide. Presently I came into a strip of savanna country, level, rolling plains, with tall waving grass.

"There was much game there and there also lived tribes of black men. They were savage, warlike tribesmen, bowmen and horsemen, riding some of the finest horses I've ever seen.

"They were easy to elude. I came to one of their villages which was set on a kind of prominence above the plain, and had a tall, strong stockade. Unobserved, I slipped into the village and appearing suddenly before the tribe, created quite an impression. They had never seen a white man before and though they were hostile at first, I managed to show that I was a friend. They were tall, well-built people, with good-shaped features, and the women were not bad looking. They had few of the typical negroid features. They spoke a language that seemed to have come from a Bantu stock and I learned to speak it fairly well, although there were words and phrases entirely new and different from any language I ever heard. Their country was between the desert and a great jungle. It seemed that other tribes of black men inhabited the jungle and there was always war between them.

"The tribe in whose village I was, was called the Shansai. They were, as I said, splendid horsemen."

"Ha, good horsemen," said Lai Singh, leaning forward with new interest. "And good fighters?"

"Some of the best I ever saw," Gordon answered. "The tribes were always fighting among themselves as well as against the jungle-negroes.

"Their country was bordered, as I said, by the jungle on the east. The negroes told me that the strip of savanna where they lived swung round the jungle to north and south, in a kind of great half-circle, finally running into the desert at the southeast and northeast. The jungle stopped before it verged into the desert, which, they said, seemed to be shut in at a distance both at northeast and southeast by a wild, desolate expanse of barren crags and foothills and mountains.

"The negroes of the plains had never crossed the desert and seldom ventured into the jungle unless it were to raid the jungle negroes whom they called Balingas.

"Beyond the jungle I could see, afar off, mighty mountains rearing up toward the sky with snow on the peaks. I spoke of them and found the Shansai unwilling to speak much about them. Investigating this strange reticence in regard to the mountains, I found the negroes to believe them haunted. They told me strange tales, little more than legends some of them were, of a strange, savage race who from time to time came from the jungle and raided the villages, slaughtering men and carrying off women, and who were neither of their own race nor Balingas. They dwelt in the mysterious mountains, said the Shansai, and were a terrible people. Apparently they were a race of negroes but of different stock from the Shansai. They showed me a dagger taken from the raiders. Here it is."

And Gordon laid a dagger on the table by which he sat.

Steve Allison took it up and the others crowded around him to see it.

The blade was long, straight and slim with two edges and of fine blue steel, on the surface of which were engraved faint lines of what seemed to be writing. There was a gold-inlaid steel guard and the hilt was of silver worked and inlaid with gold. Small stones that were undoubtedly diamonds and rubies were set in the hilt and a large one formed the pommel. On one side of the hilt was a small gold plate and on it was carved a lion with the most consummate skill. Tiny rubies were set for the lion's eyes.

"A wonderful piece of skilled workmanship," said Omar Bey. "I have never seen better."

Yar Ali Khan's eyes glittered as he handled the dagger.

"And how did you obtain the dagger, sahib?" he asked. "Slay three or four, belike, or take it by stealth?"

"Neither," Gordon laughed. "A priest of the Shansai had it in his possession and he traded it to me for a few tricks of sleight-of-hand and parlor magic that I taught him."

"And what did you do after you got the dagger?" asked Abdul el Kadour.

Gordon continued: "As you might guess, I began to have a desire to see the land where such costly daggers were made. I tried to persuade some Shansai to accompany me. But they refused and tried to dissuade me.

"'You will be slain by the Balingas or by some wild beast of the jungle,' the Shansai said. 'Or if you should make your way through the jungle (which you might do for you are a mighty fighter), you will be captured or slain by the savage people of the mountains. Better stay in the land of the Shansai and we will make you a chief.' For I had aided them in some of their battles with other tribes.

"So, finding the Shansai would not accompany me, I set out alone. Many of the warriors went with me to the edge of the great jungle but would go no further.

"That jungle was thick, with much underbrush and mighty trees which towered sometimes hundreds of feet into the air. Many of the trees were unfamiliar to me. For awhile I cut my way through the jungle with the scimitar, which was well-adapted to the work, being heavy, long, and of the best steel.

"Then I came upon narrow paths, which I judged to have been made by the Balingas. So I went warily. I took to the trees which were so huge and so close together that I could travel with ease along the branches from tree to tree. Presently, after several miles, the jungle became less tangled, with less underbrush, though the trees were still larger, their topmost branches entangled so as to shut out the sky and most of the sunlight except such as filtered through the branches. It was rather an uncanny place and I did not wonder that the Shansai and their tribesmen seldom came into the jungle.

"I had noticed tracks of lions, leopards and deer and as I swung through the trees, I suddenly come face to face with a huge gorilla. I was surprized to find a gorilla in that part of Africa and was more surprized when with a wild screech he leaped upon me, his great, hairy arms clutching for me. Story books to the contrary, it is very seldom that a gorilla will attack a man. He took me off my guard and nearly crushed me before I managed to stab him with my yataghan. And even as he released me and rolled from the branch where we fought, his small, piggish gray eyes glared at me so hideously malignant that I shuddered.

"I went on my way and when night fell, slept in the crotch of a great tree, a hundred feet from the ground.

"The next day I continued on my way through the jungle and presently came to a trail down which a party of Balingas were coming. There were ten of them and I concealed myself in a tree whose branches spread above the trail and watched them with interest. The Balingas were not as high a type of negro as the tribes of the plains. Not so tall as the Shansai, with more negroid features and somewhat receding foreheads, clad only in loincloths, they were far from prepossessing figures. They were armed with bows and long spears. They walked as lithely and noiselessly as leopards.

"And as they passed beneath the branches where I crouched, a branch broke and I tumbled into their midst, breaking my fall somewhat by snatching at branches as I fell. The Balingas gave back an instant in surprize and then charged me from all sides. For a few moments there was some quick and swift fighting, the long spears flashing and licking in and out like serpents' tongues and I using my scimitar with all my skill. I downed one Balinga with a Mameluke upper-thrust and cut another down. Then, snatching up the rifle I'd dropped in my fall, I dashed the butt into a Balinga's face and broke away, making for the trees. I reached them ahead of the negroes and swarmed up out of reach just as a flight of arrows whizzed up at me.

"It didn't seem to occur to the Balingas to follow me through the trees, I found out why afterward, and I soon distanced them."

"And the reason the negroes did not follow you?" asked Omar Bey.

"Gorillas," answered Gordon. "I never saw so many before or since. And they were different from any apes I ever saw. They travelled almost entirely in the higher branches of the tress and were as big as any I ever heard of. The full-grown males would have weighed between three hundred and five hundred pounds. And their ferocity was a thing to marvel at. As I said, a gorilla seldom attacks a human, but the gorillas of the Balinga jungle were perfect fiends. Every time one of the great apes caught sight of me, it charged me furiously with hideous shrieks and bellowings. I always managed to elude them, in spite of the fact that I was burdened with my weapons and what ammunition and provisions I carried.

"After roaming through the jungles for some days I came upon a large lake. About the shore I found deserted villages, similar to those I had seen back in the jungle occupied by the Balingas, but the villages by the lake had long been deserted and were falling into ruin. Which fact struck me as rather strange. Beyond the lake, which was dotted here and there with small islands, was the jungle and beyond that rose the mountains. On all sides the jungle ran down to within perhaps a mile from the lakeshore.

"I constructed a kind of crude raft with a sail made of bamboo leaves pinned together with thorns and managed to float across the lake on it. The lake abounded in fish of many varieties, including what seemed to be a kind of small, fresh-water shark, exceedingly savage and voracious.

"Having sailed across the lake I plunged once more into the jungle of the Balingas. Occasionally I came upon a village, but the natives seemed scarcer than on the other side of the lake. Those that I saw were typical Balingas. The jungle, after some miles, had less underbrush than on the other side of the lake, which for lack of a better name, I called the Balinga Lake.

"Presently I emerged from the thick jungle into a kind of forest, with no underbrush whatever and gigantic trees hundreds of feet high. They were set rather far apart, as a rule, but so widespread were their branches that they shut out most of the sunlight. No Balingas lived in that forest; there was no sign of a village. There seemed to be nothing in the great forest except gorillas and even they did not seem so numerous as in the jungle. And, which struck me as being rather strange, the great apes were not so prone to attack on sight. The few gorillas I saw swung along through the trees, noiselessly and seemed somewhat in awe of something.

"I decided that if the forest was inhabited by something so terrible that even the monstrous gorillas feared it, I did not care to meet it, so I took to the trees once more.

"Tree-travelling in the forest was not so easy as in the jungle, but I managed it without very much difficulty.

"I climbed to the topmost branches of a great tree that towered above the others, and gazed about me.

"All about me, for numberless miles, was a sea of waving tree tops. To north and south the forest and jungle stretched away as far as I could see. To the west lay the great Balinga Lake and beyond the jungle I could see the savanna lands and beyond that, the desert."

"You could see all that?" exclaimed Steve Allison incredulously.

"Certainly," Gordon smiled. "I had a pair of field glasses.

"To the east the great forest stretched away to meet an upland that sloped up toward the mountains. Just beyond the forest, there was a tangled strip of jungle. The upland was something like the veldt and something like the steppes of north Asia.

"The mountains themselves did not seem to be so very steep and beyond the uplands, seemed to have something of a large forest on the lower slopes.

"As I said, there was snow on the peaks.

"Proceeding on my way, I came upon a great hollow tree. The hollow was some fifty feet from the ground and extended twenty-five feet up the tree, and was at least fifteen feet across. The tree was so huge that the trunk was not weakened in the least by the hollow and I decided to spend the night there.

"The great forest was an eerie place at night. There were no sounds except the night wind blowing through the great trees. The wind rustled the branches and leaves, making the forest seem full of weird whisperings. The branches were entangled and formed a lofty roof, through which no moonlight nor starlight shone through. The forest was so blackly dark that even my jungle-trained eyes could make out no object.

"Sometime in the night I was wakened with the knowledge that something, some monstrous thing, was prowling in the night close to the tree where I was. Rifle in hand, I peered out of the hollow of the great tree but could see nothing in the darkness under the gigantic trees. There was a faint reptilian odor in the air, but there was no sound. Presently I sensed that the thing, whatever it was, had moved away into the forest.

"Next morning, under and about the great tree, I found, here and there, the tracks of the creature. They were huge and wide-spreading and something like the claws of a monstrous bird. But they were not the tracks of a bird, I knew, and I was amazed, not because I did not know what they were, but because I knew. I had seen such tracks, in slabs of rocks and in great stones in museums, in the Bad Lands of the Dakotas and upon the steppes of Mongolia.

"The creatures who had left such tracks were evidently the 'devils' of whom I had heard vague legends among the Shansai."

"They were devils, undoubtedly," rumbled Yar Ali Khan.

"I did not attempt to trail the thing that left the tracks," Gordon continued, "because I was sure that I would meet similar creatures before I got out of the jungle.

"I went on through the trees for some distance and was presently aware of some monster coming through the forest. I climbed to the ground and waited. And presently, through the mighty trees, there came a weird, monstrous, shape, on silent feet.

"Although I had known, almost exactly what would appear, still I could hardly credit my sight.

"There among the huge trees the monster stood, at least twenty feet high, standing upright like a monstrous kangaroo, evil, reptilian, a great dinosaur!"

"A dinosaur!" exclaimed Steve Allison.

"A dinosaur," replied Gordon. "In that instant I seemed to be transported back a million years into the old Stone Age.

"There the monster stood, amid the uncanny silence and gloom of the mighty forest trees, as ancient as the age it represented. Primeval silence reigned. It was a setting wondrous strange for the modern age and I had an uncanny feeling that by some means I had been carried back into ancient days. I even glanced at my rifle, half-wondering whether I would find myself clutching, not a modern cordite rifle, but a crude stone hatchet. It was with difficulty that I rid myself of the feeling of unreality, and convinced myself that I had merely come into some strange land, rather than having stepped into a long-past age.

"The great dinosaur stood glaring evilly with its small, hideous eyes and then charged, covering the distance in great bounds, like a kangaroo.

"I threw my rifle to my shoulder and fired twice and the gigantic reptile plunged to the earth. I doubt if a lesser rifle than the cordite .577 would have stopped it. I cut a talon from the monster that had come out of the gloom of the ages. Here it is."

And Gordon laid upon the table a great curving claw. Nearly a foot long it was, curved, sharp and like steel.

Steve Allison vizuallized the reptile that had worn the talon and shrugged his shoulders as he realized that his imagination could scarcely picture the monster.

Yar Ali Khan swore wonderingly in his beard.

"A devil, without a doubt," he said. "It was an ifreet, sahib, surely."

"It was monster enough for any demon," Gordon answered. "I found many signs of dinosaurs in the forest and I knew the reason that no Balingas lived in the forest, and why the great apes went swiftly and silently.

"I caught glimpses of other dinosaurs, but I did not come face to face with any more except one, and it I eluded by slipping behind a great tree and gilding silently away.

"Finally I came out of the forest and came upon a swamp. It was a ghastly swamp of quagmires and stagnant lakes, abounding in reptiles. But it was not very wide and I crossed it, partly in a crude pirogue, partly by leaping from hummock to hummock. At any rate, I crossed the swamp and came into the strip of jungle I had seen from the great tree.

"It was a jungle of thorn trees. The trees were large and grew close together and the thorns were nearly as strong as steel. I hacked my way through that jungle with my scimitar and it was no easy task.

"All the time I was wondering whence came the terrible black men whom the Shansai had told me about. I had found no trace of them in the jungle or forest of the Balingas, though of course I had traversed only an exceedingly small part, comparatively speaking, having travelled by a more or less straight route. Just the same, I did not believe that they inhabited the jungle. The Shansai had said that they lived in the mountains and I was inclined to that belief myself. But by what route they came when they raided the villages of jungle and plain, I had no idea. I found no traces to show that any human being had ever come that way. As far as I explored, the thorn-jungle was unbroken by path or trail.

"When I emerged from the jungle I came upon the sloping steppes I had seen. They were a strong contrast to the country I had been travelling through for days. Verdant grass grew tall and deer, gazelle, bison and antelope grazed there by the hundreds. Also many wild horses, fine as Kabuli or Arab steeds. The steppes sloped gradually upwards for miles and miles, to meet a great plateau, on which was a great forest. Beyond, to the east rose the mighty mountains.

"I fashioned a lariat out of plaited grasses and caught a wild horse. I half-tamed him, at least enough to ride. I was nearing the forest, where I intended releasing the horse and going on, on foot, when I saw some fifty horsemen coming at a run. I rode toward them. They were soon near enough for me to see that they were negroes and I was sure that they were of the race of whom the Shansai had spoken. They were giants in stature and perfectly built. They had even features, high, broad foreheads with almost no negro characteristic except color, and would have been handsome except for the expression of fiendish fury and cruelty they wore. They wore little except loincloths and a kind of feathered headdress and ornaments, consisting of armlets and anklets which seemed to be mostly gold, often set with costly gems. They were armed with long spears, bows, short swords and knives. Some of them carried small, round shields. The horses they rode were splendid steeds and were richly caparisoned, though the saddles were merely leather pads.

"Such were the warriors who were charging down upon me. They ignored my peace-sign and swooped in. Three or four were ahead of the rest and with wild war cries they swept in, wielding short swords. I saw that they had no mind for anything but battle. And I gave it to them. Using my scimitar I cut down four negroes and broke through the ranks that surrounded me, smiting right and left. They were close behind me as I raced for the forest, but the half-wild horse I was riding was a swift one, and I managed to get beyond bow range.

"From all sides the negroes came racing until my pursuers numbered some two hundred warriors.

"I tried my elephant rifle, knocking two negroes from their horses with long range shots, but it did not daunt the other warriors.

"As I neared the forest I saw another band of mounted black men ride out to intercept me. There was a clump of huge boulders close by and to them I headed. Reaching them, I sprang down and leaped for cover, turning the horse loose. He raced away over the steppes and the black men made no effort to recapture him, being too intent on me.

"The warriors raced around the boulders, much like Indians, sending flights of arrows. But I was sheltered by the boulders so that not an arrow touched me. In the meantime, I managed to drop two more negroes.

"Then the black warriors, finding that they could not reach me on horseback, dismounted and charged me. I have seen many furious battles and many fierce fighters. I have seen the Cossack fight and the Moro *juramentado* and the Ghazi and the Zulu. But those black warriors excelled them all in sheer savagery and reckless valor.

"Nothing daunted them. I emptied my elephant rifle twice and my pistol once before that charge swarmed over the boulders, and I did not miss. Yet the warriors never paused but leaped over the boulders and fell upon me with spears and swords. And among the rocks and boulders we fought, man to man and steel to steel."

"Would I had been there," muttered Yar Ali Khan, toying with the hilt of his tulwar.

"I slew with scimitar and yataghan," Gordon went on, "but they overcame me. I was surprized that they did not kill me, but they bound me hand and foot and threw me across a horse. They tied my weapons upon another steed, handling the firearms gingerly. Then the whole band set out, leaving the bodies of the slain negroes where they lay, having first taken their weapons.

"The black men headed in a direction somewhat southeast, skirting the forest. When night fell, they camped, leaving me upon the ground, loosing my feet but tying my hands behind me and binding them to a tree, with a huge warrior as jailer, watching me and my weapons which they laid close by, evidently believing them to posses some uncanny power. That night I managed to slip my bonds and escape, leaving behind me a negro, knocked unconscious with the shaft of his own spear.

"I took to the forest which was something like the forest of the Balingas. It was without underbrush, with tall and mighty trees, but lacked the uncanny silence and gloom of the Balinga forest.

"It was, as I said, on a great plateau. There were lions, leopards, apes and other wild things.

"I made my way through the forest, now and then sighting bands of black warriors, sometimes mounted, sometimes not, but they were not hard to elude. Besides individual characteristics and different styles of ornaments and headdresses, they were all of the type of those who had captured me.

"I went higher into the mountains, and found them something like the Himalayas, but not so great nor rugged, nor so barren."

"No mountains can equal the Himalaya," said Yar Ali Khan with conviction and satisfaction.

Gordon continued, "I came upon a ruined city among the mountains. It showed signs of being very ancient and was built of granite and stone resembling marble. The architecture was strange to me, having some of the solid stability of the Assyrian, some of the art of the ancient Greek, and yet in some ways reminding me of the Egyptian.

"It had been a great city, situated on a high-flung plateau, and with a strong, high wall about it, most of which was still standing.

"I entered through an ancient gate and began to explore the city with great interest. High in the mountains the creepers and lichens did not grow as they did in the jungle and the city was not hidden as one in the jungle would have been.

"There were lions and leopards prowling through the ancient streets and buildings, and I was very wary as I went. However, they showed no especial inclination to attack me.

"On one side of the city I saw a great building which seemed to me, as well as I could see at the distance, that it had had additions added, much newer than the rest of the building. Approaching it warily, I saw that it was a magnificent place, fit for a king's palace, and was set in an open space, with no other buildings very close to it. It was strongly built, reminding me strongly of the great pillars of Karnak.

"There was a mighty hallway in front, with gigantic arches upheld by mighty pillars, and a kind of lofty roof went around the entire building, held up by pillars almost as large as those that held up the arches. In that respect it was a great deal like the ancient Roman residences. I could see that it had been made into a fort. Blocks of stone had been built in between the pillars, forming a wall about ten feet high all about the building. There were loopholes at regular intervals in the wall, which seemed to be very strongly built.

"I scaled the wall with caution and dropped down on the other side. Just as I did so, I heard a clank of arms, and the sound of men marching, whose approach was hidden by the gigantic pillars. I darted behind some other pillars, and saw what seemed to be a doorway. I stepped within and found myself in a maze of rooms and corridors which seemed to run in all directions, without any plan, though that, I believe, was only due to the peculiar form of architecture of that country.

"Having crossed innumerable rooms and followed numberless corridors, I came to a winding stair. Up that I went. Many of the rooms and corridors I had traversed showed signs of being, or having been, occupied. That was especially true of the second floor.

"I came from the stair into a long corridor and followed it. Presently I came to a large doorway, which seemed as well as I could see, to open into a more elaborate room than most of the others I had explored. And I was aware that someone was in that room. I knew that people of some race occupied the great building. I heard several times the tread of feet and what seemed to be the clank of armor or weapons. But I had not caught a sight of the inhabitants.

"Listening carefully, I found that there was only one person in the room. Scimitar in hand, I stepped through the door. The person in the room was a woman. She sprang back with a frightened cry, and I stopped short in amazement. For the woman was white!"

"White!" exclaimed Abdul el Kadour.

"White and very fair," Gordon answered. "She was only a girl, a slender girl of medium height. Her hair was long, wavy and golden. Her eyes were a violet color. She was quite a pretty girl, with one of the best faces I have ever seen.

"A very pretty girl, with a merry face and eyes that sparkled with good humor. She had a face such as usually wears a happy smile. But there were traces of tears on her rosy cheeks and a bruise on her pretty, round arm, as if she had been roughly handled. She was dressed in a garment of soft, white material which was sleeveless and low-necked, belted at the waist with a plain cloth girdle. The skirt came just below her knees and her small, dainty feet were bare.

"She shrank back against the wall, her hands out before her as if to ward off a blow. Her face was full of terror.

"I thrust my scimitar back into its sheath and advanced a few steps, with both hands upraised, palms outward, in the universal peace sign.

"She seemed somewhat reassured and some of the fear faded from her pretty face. I spoke to her in several languages and dialects, but she could not understand any of them and motioned me to be quiet.

"Hesitatingly she came forward and timidly touched my hands, my face and my sword belt, with seemingly great interest. She reminded me of a child with a new toy and the resemblance was strengthened when she smiled.

"Then she paused and glanced around, rather nervously. She took me by the arm and drew me toward a door, not the one by which I had entered.

"But I held back. I was not sure of her intentions. Then she began to make signs. She pointed to me and then stood on her tiptoes, reaching up as high as she could, with her hand held flat and bent at the wrist, as though indicating the height of something. Then she pointed to my scimitar and made a gesture as of drawing a sword and striking.

"I believed that she was telling me that a big man with a sword would come kill me if I stayed. Then she urged me toward the door again. But I was interested. I had a desire to see the man she described and I did not particularly favor the idea of being hidden by a woman.

"And presently I heard the sound of someone approaching over the marble floor. The girl started and her evident terror was pitiful. She caught my arm and tugged to draw me toward the door. I pushed her away as gently as possible and as I did a man entered the room. He was a big man. One of the largest I have ever seen. He was white and was dressed a great deal like the black warriors I had been captured by. He was dressed in a loincloth, a feathered headdress and wore barbaric ornaments of gold and silver on his arms and legs. On his feet were a kind of sandals and from his girdle swung a long straight sword in an ornamented scabbard.

"Thrust through his girdle, also, was a dagger in a golden sheath. Aside from the costly ornaments the man wore, I knew instantly that he was a chief. His face was rather handsome, but cruel. He carried himself like the barbarian chieftain he was, proud, arrogant, dominant. I hated him on sight.

"He paused in amazement and turning to the frightened girl, spoke to her in a language that I could not understand. She answered humbly and her shrinking, frightened look and attitude convinced me that my assumption was correct, that she was a slave or a captive.

"She came close to the chief, holding out her hands appealingly and apparently pleading. Begging for me, I believed, and it did not lessen my antipathy for the chieftain.

"He laughed sneeringly and swung her out of the way. Drawing his sword he strode forward, motioning me to throw down the yataghan I had drawn. Naturally I declined. He seemed rather pleased. With a cruel smile he stepped forward, rather leisurely, as a leopard plays with its prey.

"And as he raised his sword I was in, under his sword arm, and stabbed him three times with my yataghan.

"He flung up his arms and fell, his sword flying from his hand and ringing on the marble floor.

"I stood ready, listening, half-expecting to hear a rush of feet and a clash of weapons, but I heard nothing.

"I glanced at the girl. She was leaning forward, her lips parted, her eyes wide with wonder. She did not seem to be afraid and there was real relief in the gaze she cast at the body of the chieftain. She must have been his captive.

"I was examining his weapons with interest when she took my arm and motioned toward a door. I saw that she was urging me to come with her and I thought that perhaps I might aid her to escape, supposing she was a captive.

"Before I left I took the chief's dagger and handed it to the girl. She took it, somewhat gingerly it seemed, and slipped it into her girdle.

"The sword I took, noting that it was of blue steel with the hilt and guard of gold, set with diamonds and rubies, much like the dagger that I had gotten from the priest of the Shansai.

"The girl led the way out of the room into another and then into a maze of rooms and corridors such as I had traversed in coming to the room where I saw her.

"Several times we hid behind pillars or in hidden rooms, while warriors passed by, sometimes in bands, sometimes singly, sometimes marching in order, sometimes chatting as they marched along. They were of a type of the man I had killed, tall, large men, well built and powerfully muscled, some seeming to be of higher rank than others. But few of them seemed so arrogant or domineering as the chieftain.

"Presently we came to a long, wide corridor with a winding, narrow stairway and the girl started to lead the way when at one end of the corridor appeared a band of marching warriors. We turned toward the other end of the corridor, but they had seen us and in an instant the corridor was filled with armed warriors who rushed from almost every door at the shouts of those who had first seen us.

"There was but one way of escape; straight up the stairs, and up them we went. Before we were halfway to the top, warriors were swarming up after us, but a narrow, winding stair is not an easy place to take with a rush.

"The very force of their numbers forced me back and up the stair, but I piled that stairway with slain men. I broke three swords, each time snatching another from a foe. Still they came on, savagely, silently, slashing and thrusting with sword and dagger, clambering over the bodies of the warriors I had slain.

"At last I stood on the top of the stairs, the warriors massing for another rush, halfway down the stairway. I threw away a broken sword and drew my scimitar, intending to make a last stand, when the girl touched me on the arm. We were in a long corridor, similar to the one below. Other corridors led away from it, and toward one of those the girl went, motioning me to follow her.

[. . .]

The Shunned Castle

(unfinished)

The jungle. Thick, hot, the sunlight scarcely making its way through the branches of the great trees that crisscrossed for a hundred feet into the air.

Two horsemen were riding down the narrow trail. Neither of the men were large, but were wiry-built men of medium height and both had black hair. The eyes of the older were black, the eyes of the younger gray, long and rather narrow. There were rifles in saddle scabbards on each saddle and each of the men wore a heavy pistol swinging low at the right hip.

"We have come quite a distance not to have seen a tiger," remarked the older man. "Especially as they are quite numerous in the vicinity."

"Well, to tell you the truth, Frank," the younger man responded, "I'm not very much disappointed. I'm not to say 'burning' to meet any tiger."

Frank Gordon smiled. "It's nearly night. We won't try to reach the Grand Trunk Road until tomorrow."

"Meanin' we'll have to spend a night in the jungle? Nix, nix, friend Frank. I can see myself dozin' gently in the jungle while the tigers and crocodiles and elephants prowl around looking for dessert."

"I see a building through the trees," Gordon answered. "It's either a temple or an old castle. No matter. It will furnish us shelter for the night."

Steve Allison rose in his stirrups and gazed about him.

"You have some eyesight, Frank," he said. "I can't see a sign of any castle or any building."

"You'll see it presently," Gordon replied.

For awhile they rode on in silence.

"No other man but you, Gordon," Steve remarked, "would have started through the jungle with no guides or anything."

That was mostly true. Frank Gordon, the slim, dark man whom Arabs and Indians called "El Borak, the Swift," was as much at home in the wilds, whether jungle, desert or mountain, as any American Indian. His sense of direction was amazingly highly developed. No wolf or panther that ever roamed the wilds was ever more at home or more at ease than Frank Gordon.

His companion, Steve Allison, little more than a youth, was ahead of most people in wilderness-craft, thanks to the careful tutelage of Gordon, but was still far behind the older man in knowledge.

The companions rounded a bend in the trail and saw, something like a half-mile ahead, a massive pile of masonry rearing up gray and forbidding against the dark background of the jungle.

There came a sound from the jungle.

Gordon's hand whipped to his gun.

"A man," he said, quietly.

"How do you know—" Steve began, when out of the jungle a man sprang into the trail. He was a native Indian peasant, his scanty garments tattered, his turban awry, his eyes wild with fright.

The horses reared and swerved as the man came fleeing up the trail.

As he raced by, Gordon leaned from his saddle and caught the man by the shoulder of his garment.

"Make haste slowly," he instructed in the vocabulary of the region. "Why fleest thou?"

The man glared at him, wide eyed. "Oh, sahib," he gasped, "I am a woodcutter and I was cutting fagots."

"But what scared you?" Gordon asked.

"Go back, sahib, from whence you came!" the Indian gasped. "No man may pass through this jungle at night. The castle of Janir Khan—djinns—devils—Moslems—"

With a swift effort the Indian wrenched himself free of Gordon's grasp and fled down the trail with all speed.

Allison swung his horse about to pursue the man, but Gordon stopped him.

"He'd take to the jungle," Gordon said.

"What do you suppose was after him?" Allison wondered.

"Nothing," Gordon answered. "If there had been, it would have caught him."

"Not unless it was a record-breaking runner," Steve chuckled. "That Indian sure was making tracks."

"He was cutting wood near the castle," Gordon mused. "Something scared him. Janir Khan, Moslems. Um."

"Who was Janir Khan?" Allison demanded. "And I didn't know there were any Mohammedans in this jungle."

"Janir Khan was a Mohammedan chief," Gordon answered, absently.

They had been riding on down the trail and they were now close to the castle.

They reined up and scanned it. It was a tall, massive castle, evidently built for military as well as residential use.

There had been a tall wall about, and outside of that a deep moat. But the wall was mostly fallen in ruins and the moat was filled up.

Only an ancient drawbridge remained and the ruins of great gates, sagging on mighty pillars that had stood the test of time.

Much of the old castle itself was in ruins, the ancient lines of architecture almost lost in the crumbling but mighty piles of masonry.

Steve eyed the castle askance.

"Nope," he decided. "I prefer the jungle to that pile of loose cement, or whatever it is. Gimme tigers to ghosts, anytime."

For answer Gordon reined his horse toward the ancient drawbridge.

With a shrug of his shoulders, Allison followed.

As he came to the drawbridge, Gordon stopped and swung down from his saddle. Tossing the reins to Allison, he walked cautiously to the moat. For a moment he stood gazing down at the drawbridge and the moat beneath. Allison watched him, puzzled, for a moment; then with a startled curse he whirled in his saddle, his pistol leaping to his hand. Close by stood a tall, old man, an Indian, white of beard, with a hint of a mocking smile on his face.

"Say, Frank—" Steve began dubiously.

"Put up your gun, Steve," Frank answered without turning around. "I saw him when he came. Village patriarch, doubtless."

Steve shrugged his shoulders with helpless wonder. He shoved his gun back into its scabbard and shifted himself to a more comfortable position, watching the old man suspiciously.

Gordon finished his inspection of the moat and turned.

He took in the old man with a casual glance.

"Thy village is near?" Gordon queried, in a tone of polite inquiry.

"Mayhap, sahib," the old Indian agreed, drily.

"Then what do ye at the castle of Janir Khan?" asked Gordon. "The castle whom all men shun?"

"Who might the sahib be?" asked the old man, indirectly as is the way of the East.

"The Moslems call me 'El Borak' or sometimes 'Bagheela'," Gordon answered, watching the Indian narrowly.

"El Borak!" exclaimed the old man, his dark face lighting with interest. "Bagheela, the black panther! Aye, even in the jungle we have heard of thee, sahib."

"Then take these horses to thy village," Gordon commanded, signing Steve to dismount. Steve obeyed without question, but with a look of surprize.

"Take these horses to thy village," Gordon repeated, handing the Indian some coins. "Stable them and keep them well. Bring them here at sunup."

The Indian salaamed and took the reins.

"But you will not spend the night in the castle?" he protested.

"Certainly."

The old Indian hesitated and then said swiftly, "But sahib, it is not safe for men, white men, to go in that castle."

"And why?" Gordon demanded.

"Nay, that I know not," the Indian replied evasively and refusing to meet Gordon's eye. "But men have been slain and have disappeared in this jungle, close to the castle. Perhaps tigers took them but—"

"But what?"

"It is the old castle of Janir Khan, who—" the Indian began.

"All that I know," Gordon interrupted him. "Still, my friend and I will pass the night in the castle."

"As you will, sahib. Perhaps, being El Borak, you will succeed."

"And the horses are yours should the tigers carry us off in the night," Gordon said with a touch of sarcasm.

The old Indian salaamed and turned down the trail, leading the horses.

Steve Allison, who had said nothing, now turned upon Gordon with a desire for information.

"That looks like a fool play, on the surface Frank, but I know you never do anything without a reason," said Allison.

Gordon did not reply, but stood for an instant, scanning the jungle.

"How do you know that Indian guy will bring those horses back in the morning?" Steve demanded. "And if there are bandits in the jungle, how do you know they won't steal them?"

"The Indian will bring them back," Gordon answered. "If he does not, it will be no great matter to trail them. And the bandits, if there are any, will seek to dispose of us first."

Gordon strode toward the castle. Allison followed. When they came to the ancient drawbridge, Gordon stooped and pointed.

"Look."

Allison looked. Although ancient, the bridge seemed solid and stationary enough, but on closer inspection, Allison could see that the flooring sagged and barely rested on the heavy iron girders that seemed to support the ancient timbers. The bridge would fall if a heavy weight were placed on it. Probably would not even support a man walking across it.

The moat was filled with silt and weeds and fallen trees. Allison decided he could cross on some small trees which had apparently fallen into the moat and which were entangled with one another and with other vegetation.

But when Steve started to make his way across, Gordon stopped him.

"That stuff won't hold you up," he said. "And besides, it may be full of snakes."

"Then how are we goin' to get over?" Steve demanded. "We won't have time to drop a tree across for a bridge, before it's too dark."

"It's not wide," Gordon answered, and with a light bound he cleared the fifteen foot space that separated them from the opposite bank of the moat. Allison tossed the rifles over to him and measured the moat with his eye. He shook his head dubiously, but backed off several yards and with a short run, managed to leap across.

Then the two men walked toward the castle and Allison, at least, walked warily, glancing suspiciously from side to side, his rifle ready.

They came to the mighty gate, whose two great doors sagged on rusty hinges and Allison reached his hand toward the great handle on one of the doors. But Gordon, who had been scanning the great gate, drew him back.

"Let's climb over the wall," he suggested, leading the way.

Keeping a wary eye for snakes, they clambered over the crumbling wall into the ancient courtyard.

Then Gordon turned toward the ancient gate again. Approaching it cautiously, he pushed on the section Allison had started to open, and then leaped swiftly away. With a crash, the mighty iron door fell outward.

"My gosh!" Allison breathed awedly. "How did you know that would do that, Frank?"

Gordon shrugged his shoulders. "Intuition, perhaps," he suggested.

"Bosh!" Steve said, rudely. "You saw it would fall, or guessed it."

Gordon smiled. "Let's go in the castle."

[. . .]

The White Jade Ring

(unfinished)

"Five thousand rupees. Not a cent more," Allison's voice was rather impatient.

The Chinaman placed the tip of his long-nailed fingers together and gazed over them through slanted lids.

"But consider the antiquity, sir," he said smoothly in his perfect English. "That ring was made long ago, in the days of Jhengis Khan. The early emperors of the Ming dynasty wore it, used it as a seal, even. Look again, Mr. Allsion, and then ask yourself if it is worth ten thousand rupees."

Allison held the ring on his palm and eyed it closely. It was of heavy white jade, curiously carved with dragons and Chinese characters which were the names of emperors. It was set with a large ruby which glittered like a red star. It was a thing of antiquity and immense value.

"Five thousand rupees," Allison repeated.

"Ten," murmured the Chinaman.

"Seven, then."

The Chinaman bowed. "As you will, sir."

Allison paid in cash, bringing a look of polite surprize into the face of the Chinaman. "You dare to carry so much money about on your person?" he asked.

Allison shrugged his shoulders. "If anyone can take the money from me they are welcome to it."

There was no bravado or boasting in his voice. He merely stated a fact.

The Chinaman raised his eyebrows slightly. "And you will carry the ring with you?"

"Certainly."

"But consider, Mr. Allison," the Chinaman expostulated, "that piece of jewelry is priceless. There are a dozen governments and a score of individuals that would pay enormous sums to get possession of it. There are men who would commit murder for it. You are reckless to say the least, Mr. Allison."

Allison's eyes narrowed and he eyed the Chinaman suspiciously. Suddenly, with incredible speed, he flashed his hand in and out of his shirt. There was a glint of steel and the startled Chinaman found himself looking into the muzzle of a big revolver. Then the gun had vanished with no sign to show whence it had come; Allison's hand lay on his knee—empty.

"Are any of your stranglers, wrestlers or knife-throwers quicker than that?" he demanded. As before there was no hint of boastfulness in his voice. There was nothing of the bravado in his exhibition.

"You are swift," murmured the Chinaman. "But there are many and—the ring is priceless."

Again Allison shrugged his shoulders. He rose and slipped into an inside pocket the gold case containing the ring.

"If you have any more antiques, let me have the first chance at them," he requested, and turned to go.

"But you are not going?" the Chinaman protested. "Surely you will remain to tea—at least for a glass of wine."

"Thanks," Allison answered, "but I have business in another part of Canton."

From a window the Chinaman's eyes followed him down the street, cunningly, speculatively.

"But, Steve," Marlo protested, "you will not keep that ring in your possession. Why, do you know that that is the famous 'Ring of Emperors'? That there are scores of men who would murder you for that ring?"

"Li Fong told me all that. But I walked from his palace to your villa and no attempt was made on me."

"Of course not, you young fool," snorted Marlo. "In broad daylight, not even a tong would try to assassinate you in the streets of Canton."

"I don't know," Allison answered thoughtfully. "When Gordon and I were having our war with the Si-Fan, a gang of Chinese jumped me in the streets of Hong Kong."

"What did you do?" inquired Editha Marlo.

Allison moved uncomfortably. "Oh, nothing much," he answered, for he hated to do or say anything that might be construed as a "hero pose." "I just fought them off until Gordon arrived. Then they scattered—quick."

Editha gazed at Allison in admiration. Girls were usually attracted to Steve Allison. He was far from being a ladies' man, but something about him, his never-failing courtesy, his old-fashioned Southern chivalry, naturally drew girls to him. Many girls had fancied themselves in love with the young Southerner, but none of them thought so after seeing him in a fight.

"Where did Li Fong get the ring?" her father was demanding.

"I didn't ask," Allison answered. "I don't care."

"What will you do with it?"

"Send it to Gordon in Hong Kong."

"Gordon is known among the Chinese?" Marlo asked.

"Yes."

"And well hated, I presume, since he tracked down the Si Fan Society and the Priests of Erlik?" Marlo pursued.

"That's the truth," admitted Allison.

"And yet you did China a great good."

"People are ungrateful. The honest, hard-working Chinese and the progressive rulers, Manchus, most of them, like Gordon and are grateful to him, but the rest, tongs, priests, stranglers, Chinese politicians and such like trash are down on him—and me, too, for that matter."

"And knowing all this, the enmity of the Chinese toward you and the great value of the ring, you yet dare walk the streets of Canton alone with the ring on your person?"

"Yes."

Marlo shrugged his shoulders.

"When will you send the ring to Gordon?"

"As soon as possible."

"The import duty on it will be enormous."

"Doubtless," agreed Allison.

There was something in his tone which caused Marlo to look up quickly. But the expression of Allison's face did not change in the least. However, Marlo had a suspicion that the importing of "The Ring of the Emperors" would not add much to the country into which it would be imported. Marlo discreetly concluded to say no more on that subject.

Allison placed the ring in its gold case and slipped the case in his pocket as he rose to go. He took a step toward the table where his hat lay when suddenly he paused and his eyes narrowed to slits. Before the two could note the change in his expression, almost, he had whirled toward the opposite side of the room. They did not see him draw his gun, but there was a flash and a roar, filling the room with echoes. And from the curtain across the room lunged a Chinaman, his face contorted with hate, a high-flung arm grasping a knife by the point, lunging forward until he crashed to the floor, his knife flying from his hand and ringing against the floor.

Allison was standing where he had stood, his smoking gun held at his hip, his narrowed eyes watching, not the Chinaman on the floor, but the curtains beyond.

Marlo had sprung to his feet; Editha leaned back in her chair, pale with fright, but staring fascinated at Allison.

[. . .]

A Power Among the Islands

(unfinished)

The schooner, *Marquesas*, was riding smoothly beneath the moon of the tropic sea when the two passengers heard a woman scream in the captain's cabin. Steve Allison was out of the cabin he shared with Gordon and at the door of the other cabin before the frightened cry ceased to echo.

From within the cabin came a muttered curse and a sound of scuffling feet. There was no other sound except the soft sound of the waves breaking against the ship. The seaman at the helm turned his head toward the companionway and grinned evilly.

Steve Allison tried the door. It was locked. He wrenched at it savagely. Then he saw that Gordon was beside him.

"That—Herran," began Allison, "I'll bet it's that native girl—"

Gordon nodded. He drew Allison out of the way and then, with a quick, catlike movement threw himself against the door, striking the panel with his shoulder. The door crashed inward and Gordon, without seeming to even lose his balance momentarily, sprang into the room, closely followed by Allison.

The cabin was in disorder, chairs and the one table being broken and overturned. Over in one corner a native girl crouched, her single garment in tatters, wild fear in her eyes. Captain Herran turned, cursing vilely. He was a huge, hulking man of great strength, sincerely hated by all decent men.

He glared at the two men who dared to interfere with him and recognized the two passengers who had come aboard at Samoa. He saw two men of medium height, both rather slimly built. He sneered.

"Get out of my cabin," he ordered, with embellishments.

Gordon walked toward him. One might almost say he strolled casually.

Herran grinned contemptuously and suddenly lunged forward, great, gorilla arms reaching for the smaller man.

To the captain's surprise, Gordon did not attempt to evade the grasping hands. With a motion that seemed unhurried yet was as quick as a striking snake, Gordon stepped in, crouching beneath Herran's flailing arms. One lean brown hand caught Herran just beneath the chin and the other gripped the captain just above the right knee. Gordon jerked and pushed simultaneously. Herran's lunge aided him and the captain catapulted over Gordon's head and struck the cabin floor with a crash. Dazed by the fall and wild with rage, Herran snatched a pistol from his belt. With incredible swiftness, a Colt appeared in Allison's hand and spat flame simultaneously. The gun flew out of Herran's hand and went spinning across the cabin.

The captain shook his numbed hand, cursing bewilderedly.

"Oh, shut up," Allison said, dryly. "I probably saved your worthless hide by that trick. It ain't noways wise to draw on Wolf Gordon."

Herran started. "Are you 'Wolf' Gordon?" he asked.

Gordon nodded. "The girl has your permission to go?" he suggested politely, and no trace of irony. But Herran winced for all of that.

"Yes," he answered sullenly.

Gordon spoke to the shrinking girl in her own language and she sprang up and scurried through the door, to the stateroom she had occupied.

"Herran," Gordon said, "it is very impolite to misuse passengers, and when the passenger is the daughter of an island king, it is bad politics. I do not make a practice of giving advice, but I am asking that you leave the young lady alone, and that you put her ashore at the first opportunity. Do I make myself clear?"

"Yes," Herran answered sullenly.

Steve Allison chuckled. It was an increasing wonder to him the effect that the mere name of Gordon had on the wildest and most criminal men.

It was evident that Gordon was a power among the islands.

[. . .]

North of Khyber

(unfinished)

Chapter 1
"The Afridis are stirring up a row."

In an upper room of a great hotel a man lounged in an armchair and gazed through the wide window. Outside and below, the crowds swirled by and New York's traffic roared, but the man paid no attention. He seemed to be looking beyond the skyline, preoccupied by his own thoughts.

He was young, little more than a boy, but his face was strong and showed high intellect and character. He was of medium height, of a slim, wiry build, with black hair and long, narrow gray eyes.

He picked up a newspaper and began to scan it, presently throwing it down with an exclamation of annoyance.

Just then the door opened and another young man entered. He was of about the same age as the occupant of the room but was shorter in build with broader shoulders. His hair, too, was black and his eyes were gray, but they were different. They were a lighter gray and were somewhat wide.

The two men might have been taken for brothers, but in fact they were of no kin. In one respect they were alike, however, the forms and faces of both were of clean, strong lines that showed clean living and clean thinking. There was nothing greedy, shifty or sensual about the countenances of either.

The newcomer had a newspaper in his hand and he strode over to the discontented looking youth in the armchair.

"Still dreaming a daydream?" he asked with a chuckle. "The life of the idle rich don't suit you much."

The other waved his hand toward the papers he had discarded.

"I'm trying to find something interesting," he said, "but there's nothing happening in the whole world except divorce suits."

His friend laughed. "You're behind times," he chaffed. "I have a later edition than those."

He seated himself comfortably and opened the paper. "It says that Ecuador and Colombia are on the verge of war."

"They always are," answered the young man languidly.

"And the Bolsheviks are calling on the Balkan states for support."

"I should worry," yawned the ennui-ed one.

"And there were over a thousand divorces last month," pursued the other.

The languid young man sat up suddenly.

"Say!" he said with force. "You know such stuff don't interest me. You've got something up your sleeve. Spill it!"

The other shifted himself to a more comfortable position and eyed his friend speculatively.

Finally he asked, "Steve, were you ever in India?"

"Yes, I was there with Gordon a couple of years back."

"Um, I suppose you know all about the Afghans?"

"No, I've heard a great deal about them, but I've known only one personally. That was Yar Ali Khan, who was with Gordon in Arabia. I've never seen very many of them. You see, I never went north of Lucknow."

"Well, it says in this paper that the Afridis are stirring up a row. There's been looting and murder all along the Afghan border. Seems like there's a mullah, a descendant of the Prophet, who's preaching a jihad, a holy war. The British fear an invasion of India through the Khyber Pass."

Steve's eyes lighted with interest. "Indeed. Let me see that paper, please."

He read the article silently. Then he turned to his friend.

"Billy, run down and get tickets on the first ship while I pack up."

His friend grinned. "It's already been done. What's more, we make the straight trip. We're booked on the liner *Valencia*, sailing tomorrow for Bombay."

"Good work," Steve approved. "Now to pack up."

The task of packing trunks and travelling bags having been brought to a satisfactory conclusion, Steve said, "Buck, I'm going to leave the rest to you while I chase around and give my regards to my respected relatives. Meet me on board."

At a certain elegant mansion on Riverside Drive, a highly respectable family were dining. Only part of the family were present, two to be exact. These two were a stately, silver-haired lady and a beautiful, dark-haired girl.

And upon these people descended Steve. He entered with scant ceremony.

"Where are Uncle John, Teddy, Dorothy and the rest?" he demanded.

"Father is at the golf club," the girl answered. "The others have gone with a party to Delmonico. Did you want to see them?"

"Well, I rather hoped they would all be here," he admitted. "I wanted to give them all my respects as I am leaving on the next boat."

"Where are you going?"

"To India."

"India!" exclaimed middle-aged respectability.

"India!" echoed budding respectability.

"Well, of all the weird ideas!" chorused the two.

"Stephen," said his aunt, rather sternly, "I must really protest. This running about all over the world does you no good. This new whim of yours is simply preposterous."

He laughed. "Say," he said, almost rudely, "the opinion of you stay-at-homes doesn't matter in the least. You said I was silly to go to Yucatan—and I discovered a lost silver mine. You said that it was 'preposterous' for me to go to Arabia—and I came back with a fortune. So wish we luck, for I'm bound for the Orient."

"Oh, very well," sighed his aunt. "If you have made up your mind I suppose you will go, but I had hoped that you would stay longer in New York."

When the ensuing conversation was concluded, Steve kissed his aunt's hand with all the grace of a courtier and turned to go. His cousin followed him to the hallway.

"You are really going?" she asked wistfully. She was a beautiful young woman, no older than Steve, but as is usually the case, she appeared at all times more of the grown woman than he did of the grown man.

He regarded her with a brotherly affection, just as he did his sisters, but the feeling she had for him was something more than that. Steve, however, did not suspect it. He was no ladies' man, was Steve Allison.

"Are you going alone?"

"No, Billy Buckner is going with me."

"Why must you go?" she asked.

"Why, of course I don't have to," he laughed. "But you know me, Madge. I can't stay still long. I have the wanderlust, strong."

"Then why don't you go to some civilized country like France or England?"

"And moon around and go to teas and theaters? Hardly, my dear. I don't think," he laughed, "that I am scarcely civilized, myself."

"But you will stay in Bombay or some city?"

"No, we will go north to the Khyber Pass and perhaps beyond to Kabul and Herat."

"But I have heard that those mountain tribes are hostile."

"They are, sometimes."

"Aren't you afraid?" she asked curiously.

"Say," he protested uncomfortably, "you're making me talk like a melodrama hero. Yes, no doubt I shall be scared, but think of the fun I'll have."

She could not understand. Her idea of pleasure was idle luxury, dances, balls and an occasional tour of Europe. She could understand why anyone would wish to go to Paris or London, but to invade the wilds of Asia!

"Well, kiss me before you go," she said. "You might get assassinated by bandits."

He took her in his arms and kissed her as he would have his sister. She returned his kiss and then lay quiet in his arms, her eyes closed. He tenderly brushed back a stray lock of hair from her soft, white cheek and said, playfully, "I'll bring you back a rajah's crown jewels or would you prefer the rajah himself?"

She drew back from his embrace and stood erect. "I suppose you will have a harem, of course?" she said, banteringly.

He chuckled, "I've been to the Orient three times and have escaped so far. I don't think you need have any fears in that direction."

"Let us hope so," she said demurely.

"Well, give my respects to the rest of the folks and tell them I'll bring them each something from India."

Chapter 2.
"Moriarty's on this boat!"

Allison stood on the promenade deck of the *Valencia*, leaning on the rail and gazing eastward. Two days out of New York and the voyage seemed most promising as to time and weather.

Allison eyed the liner in admiration. He had tried his hand at sailoring, both steam and sail, and he knew a fine ship when he saw one.

"What a change!" he mused. "Here I'm bound for the same place Columbus was, he in a wooden tub, I in a floating palace and headed in exactly the opposite direction."

A quick step sounded behind him and Billy Buckner leaned on the rail beside him. Allison cast a quick glance at him and asked, "What's up, Buck?"

"Moriarty's on this boat!" was the answer in a low, quick tone. "I just saw him."

"Moriarty, eh?" Allison repeated softly.

"What had we better do?" demanded Buckner.

"Does he know you saw him?"

"I don't know. I don't think so."

"Listen, then. After dinner you go to his cabin. And manage it so that he knows you go. The door will be unlocked; open it and go in, then—well, you'll see. But be sure that Moriarty follows you."

On another part of the deck a large, genial looking man reclined in a deckchair and chuckled. Moriarty, corporation detective, had reason to feel well of himself. Some years before, Allison with the aid of Buckner had successfully staged a most daring robbery and gotten away with a vast sum of a large mining corporation's funds. The proofs were not sufficient to send Allison or any of the others to the penitentiary, yet the corporation felt there must be proofs somewhere and finally they put Moriarty on the trail. Moriarty was a keen, persistent detective, a bold man and something of a genius in his way. For months he had tirelessly followed Allison and members of the former road-agent band. But especially he had pursued Allison. But the young ex-road-agent had outwitted him at every turn.

Now, Moriarty felt that it was his turn. For here were Allison and Buckner on the same ship and so far as he knew, they were not aware of his presence aboard.

Moriarty believed that he would soon be collecting that two thousand dollar reward that the corporation had offered for the capture of the highwaymen, in addition to his regular wages which were considerable. This sum was highly desirable to Moriarty, but the zest of the game was more so. He really did not need either the salary or the reward to live comfortably, for he had been both a private detective and a Federal detective and had accumulated quite a tidy sum. But the joke of it was, that the two had taken passage on the same ship in which he had booked, intending to go to Lisbon and not aware that Allison was in New York! He chuckled and twirled his mustache.

Just then the dinner gong rang and he went to the salon. Buckner was there, but there was no sign of Allison.

Moriarty watched Buckner closely. He seemed to be nervous, glancing around occasionally in a furtive manner.

"I was wrong," thought Moriarty. "He knows I'm aboard."

Moriarty did not know what a perfect actor Buckner was.

Buckner finished his meal rather hurriedly and then hurried out of the salon.

Moriarty rose and strolled after him, unhurriedly. Walking with a lightness surprizing in so large a man, he followed Buckner across the deck and down the companionway.

"Oh, so it's my stateroom you're after calling on!" he murmured as Buckner stealthily approached the stateroom belonging to Moriarty. He fumbled with the door, opened it and stepped inside, leaving the door open. The room was dark, but the lights in the corridor illuminated it enough so that Moriarty could see Buckner step to the table and begin to go through the papers on it.

The detective drew his pistol and stepped noiselessly through the door, covering the young man.

"Put 'em up, Buckner. I've got you," he said sharply, and at that instant something pressed against the back of his neck and a soft voice remarked, "Please do the same, Mr. Moriarty." And simultaneously Buckner stepped aside, out of line with Moriarty's pistol.

Moriarty knew when he was caught. His hands went into the air; Buckner stepped forward and twitched the gun from his fingers and went over him skillfully in search of hidden weapons. He found a detective's badge and a pair of handcuffs, both of which he appropriated.

The man who had held up Moriarty had pushed the door to and turned on the lights. Now he locked the door and stepped in front of his prisoner.

"Allison, eh?" grunted Moriarty. "Well, I might have looked for it."

"Sit down," ordered Steve, motioning toward the berth. The detective went over and sat down.

"You were easy, Moriarty," commented Allison, sitting on the edge of the opposite berth and twirling his gun by the trigger-guard.

"You come lumbering in here, yelling 'Han's up!' and all I have to do is to step out from behind the door and tickle you with the muzzle of my gat. Buck didn't come down here to steal anything or to establish your identity; he knew you'd stalk him. That's what I like about you, Moriarty, you do just exactly as we think you will do."

Moriarty was boiling, but he smiled grimly. "Well, well, 'tis me old friends, 'Drag' Buckner and th' Sonora Kid. This is indade a pleasure."

"It is indade," they murmured politely.

"How well the two av yez will look in sthripes," mused Moriarty.

"Moriarty," said Allison, "you haven't got anything on us and never will. But you interfere with us. We are trying to go straight, but how can we with an idiotic detective following us from place to place, never giving us a minute's rest?"

"Oh, I'll get yez, me buckoes," promised Moriarty.

"If you were a gunfighter, I'd know how to manage it. But it would be murder to force you to a gunfight. However—Drag, what did you take off him?"

"The gat, handcuffs and a badge." He flipped up the badge, caught it and asked, "Don't it keep you broke most of the time, Moriarty?"

"What?"

"Buying badges, handcuffs and guns to replace the ones we take off of you."

Moriarty cursed soulfully.

His captors chuckled softly.

"What an orator you'd have made, Moriarty," said Allison admiringly.

"What do you want av me?" demanded Moriarty.

Allison was silent for a moment and than said, "It's like this, Moriarty. As I said, we're going straight. I don't mind telling you we're going to India. We're going to try to do the world a mighty good turn, if you only know it. What we want you to do is to get off at Lisbon as you intended. (Oh, yes, we even knew where you were going). We want you to promise us that you won't molest us, at least until we have completed our business in India."

"And do yez think I will make any such promises?" asked Moriarty.

Allison stood up and looked straight into the detective's eyes.

"You will promise or by heaven, I'll kill you," he said. "I'm going to India and no detective on earth shall stop me."

Moriarty was looking at Allison's eyes. They were mere slits and they flamed and glinted like daggers. Moriarty knew that the soul of a killer was looking out through them and he winced in spite of himself.

"Make your choice," Allison was saying. "Promise what we ask you and keep that promise and we will not molest you. Refuse, and we will kill you and throw you through the porthole. Choose."

Moriarty was a brave man. These threats were like melodrama but for the look in Allison's eyes. It is nothing to Moriarty's discredit that he answered as he did.

"And suppose I make this promise, what will prevent me breaking it?"

"Nothing," Allison replied. "But I don't think you'll break it, Moriarty. I've always found you a man of your word."

Allison had skillfully touched the right chord. Moriarty had always prided himself on keeping his promises, even to criminals.

He shrugged his shoulders and grinned.

"All roight. I promise yez that I will not molest yez in any way until you blaguards have finished your 'business' in India and also, that I will lave the ship at Lisbon as was me former intentions. Does that satisfy you, Kid and Drag, me cheerful road-agents?"

"It does," answered the Sonora Kid, replacing his gun in its hidden holster. "Give him back his stuff, Buck. Good. Now, Mr. Moriarty, unless you wish to talk of old times with us, we will wish you a pleasant good night."

"Good night," answered Moriarty, and a second later the state-room door closed behind his erstwhile captors.

"The young blaguards," muttered Moriarty. Then he grinned and a close observer might have drawn the conclusion that he did not dislike the two as much as he pretended.

Chapter 3.
"That's Bombay."

Straight across the Atlantic, stopping for a day in the Azores, then to Lisbon, swinging around Gibraltar, then straight across the blue Mediterranean. Through the Straits of Suez, down the Red Sea and around Aden into the Indian Ocean.

Buckner and Allison stood for'ard, in the bows of the liner. Buckner was eagerly scanning the eastern horizon, but Allison's gaze was turned westward, where the sandy, desert shore of Arabia was fading into the skyline. He was deep in thought. In Arabia he had first met his friend Gordon, and had had his first close experience with the Orient.

He was living over again the conspiracies and intrigues of an Eastern court: the fierce struggle for supremacy between the court nobles; the swift expedition into the desert; the pursuit; battles and running skirmishes; and finally the finding of the buried city and the fierce battle for the fortune discovered; then the victory in the swirling simoon and the flight across the desert to Aden.

Buckner's voice broke in on his thoughts. "We should be getting close to our destination, shouldn't we?"

Allison nodded.

Buckner's thoughts swerved to something else and he remarked, irrelevantly, "Moriarty's a pretty good scout after all. He got off at Lisbon just like he promised."

Steve grinned. "Yes, I thought he'd keep his word. There's nothing mean about Moriarty."

And then one morning Buckner gave a gasp of delight as he gazed on the spires and mosques and minarets of a great city, rising from the horizon, each detail leaping into clearness as the liner neared the shore.

Allison threw out his arm in a gesture that embraced both bay and city.

"That's Bombay," he said, "and beyond lies India."

And more wonders were in store for Buckner. As they rode through the streets to a European hotel, he wondered at the amazing blending of East and West; for Bombay is the cosmopolitan of the Eastern world.

Northward they rode, in first-class apartments on a train, and Buckner got his first views of India from the car windows.

At Delhi, Allison sought the office of a certain unobtrusive Government official, to whom he was not unknown, and asked certain questions.

And because he was not unknown to the Government, the official answered him.

Briefly, what he told Allison was: "We have heard only rumors. We know there is revolt and war in Afghanistan, but we can get no authentic news. We have heard rumors of a mullah preaching a holy war to drive the 'Giaours' into the sea, and establish the Amir of Afghanistan as ruler of all India. It is also known that the Amir looks with disfavor on the mullah and his schemes; he is friendly to the British Government, but is losing power fast with his people. We have sent several men into Afghanistan, but they never reached Kabul, being either murdered by the mountain tribes or driven back by them. There has been raiding, looting, raping, all along the Frontier. Whether the mullah is a mere fanatic, a man wishing to make himself an emperor, or whether he is in the pay of some European power, we do not know."

Allison was silent, but his eyes sparkled. He asked, "Is Frank Gordon in India now?"

"I do not know," the official answered. "It is probable."

"If you will give me a pass into Afghanistan, I and my friend will see what we can do, as regards to the Afghan situation," Allison said.

"What! You would go into the mountains?"

"Yes."

"Can you speak Pushto? Do you know anything of the country? Of the people?"

"Yes to all three questions. Give me the passes. Who, even Afghans, would molest two ambassadors from the United States of America?"

"Dare you impersonate ambassadors?"

"Why not? You said the Amir was for us; if we can get to Kabul, I'll do the rest. I have friends north of the Pass."

"And what are your plans?" the official was skeptical.

"Haven't any, so far," Allison laughed. "I want to be introduced to the mullah first. Maybe I'll join him and help him whip England."

The Englishman shrugged his shoulders, "Very well. I'll give you the passes. After all, you are an American."

Northward to Peshawur. That part of the journey first in a train and then on horseback. Allison was exultant. He hastened. He wanted to feel the mountains under his feet and the mountain breeze in his face.

As they travelled, Buckner asked many questions.

"What kind of people are Afghans?" he wanted to know.

"I pointed some out to you in Delhi," Allison replied.

"Yes, but I only saw them from a distance."

"Well," said Allison, "as I said, Yar Ali Khan was the only Afghan I ever knew intimately. He was a big, tall man with a big, black beard and he wore a wadded coat nearly all the time in spite of the heat of Arabia. He carried a Khyber knife a yard long and he could use it, too! He's an Afridi. Some fighter, even for an Afghan. In the desert, when the Wahabis captured him and I rescued him, he gave me a ring of Afghan make and said if I were ever north of the Khyber and needed friends, to show certain men that ring. He especially mentioned two: Yar Hyder and Khoda Khan, both chiefs of clans."

"And how are we going to go to Kabul?" was Buckner's next question.

"How do I know?" asked Allison. "Wait till we get to Peshawur."

Chapter 4.
"By Allah! It is the ring of Yar Ali!"

The Peshawur Serai. A riot of colors. A throng of shoving, crowding, haggling traders. A noise as of the Tower of Babel. A mingling of Moslem and Hindu; wild tribesmen and moneylenders; hawk-faced chieftains and smirking menials. And horses, horses, everywhere.

Allison and Buckner were bewildered by it all. It was Allison's intention to engage a kaflia as an escort and fortune favored them.

Soon after their arrival in Peshawur, as the two were walking down the bazaar, they passed a tall, stately Northerner, who strode majestically along as if India belonged to him. His face was strong and hawklike and his beard was graying. A tribesman saluted him with respect, "Greetings, Yar Hyder."

Allison jerked about. He stepped forward and accosted the chief, speaking in Pushto, which Yar Ali had taught him. The customary salutation, and then: "You are chief Yar Hyder?"

"And what if I were, sahib?" responded the Paythan, somewhat haughtily.

For answer Allison extended his hand. On one finger was a golden ring of curious make, set with a brilliant jade.

Yar Hyder started. "By Allah!" he exclaimed. "It is the ring of Yar Ali!"

[. . .]

Intrigue In Kurdistan

(unfinished)

The Turk gazed at the prisoner before him. In that gaze were anger and hate and some wonder. At least there was no contempt.

The prisoner met his gaze levelly. There was no fear in his black eyes. His arms were bound behind him and on each side stood an armed Turkish soldier.

Here and there about the great room soldiers stood and some civilians, all eyeing the prisoner with interest.

The Turk in the thronelike chair was a bold man but he found it difficult to meet those black eyes.

"He fought strongly, you say?" he asked.

"Aye, your Excellency," a Turkish officer answered. "He fought first with rifle and pistol and then with scimitar and dagger. When we finally took him, my lord, the dead men were piled high about him and in the taking he slew a man with his bare hands."

"Where is the Kurd that told you of him?"

"Here, my lord." An eagle-eyed, hook-nosed tribesman clothed in ragged robes was led forward.

"Tell your tale."

"My lord," the Kurd began, casting a rather apprehensive glance toward the prisoner, "this man came amongst us and in a short time gained influence over some of the tribes. Then he spoke of a united Kurdistan that should lead all Islam. He said he would lead us to victory against the Turks and—"

"Go on," as the man hesitated.

"He said he would build an empire on the ruins of Turkey, that if the Kurds would follow him and shatter the power of Turkey, he would make Kurdistan a great nation. But there be many who like him not, and I thought of the gold I might earn, so I came to the officer Hassan and told him and he took a troop of cavalry and captured the Feringi. But as yet I have not been paid."

"Is this true?" asked the Turk, turning to the officer.

"Yes, my lord. The Kurds fled our coming and would not aid the Feringi, but on the other hand they would not aid us, not even those we took with us."

"What are you? An Englishman?" asked the Turk, addressing the prisoner.

"An American," was the reply in faultless Turkish.

"What is your name?"

"Frank Gordon."

The Turk looked with new interest.

"It cannot be that—yet he is an American—. Are you he whom the Arabs call 'El Borak'?"

"Yes."

"It is truth, your Excellency," interposed the officer, Hassan. "That is what the Kurds said when they saw him."

The Turk's eyes narrowed. He seemed on the point of saying something and then changed his mind.

"You heard the Kurd's accusation," he said. "What have you to say?"

"Nothing against the charge," answered Gordon.

"You admit to having tried to stir up the tribes."

"Yes."

The Turk was puzzled.

"You know what to expect? Yet you make no defense."

"Yes, I know what to expect," the American answered, sardonically. "I know the Turk, Kemul Bey, and that is why I make no defense. I argue with Turks with steel, not with words."

Kemul Bey scowled.

"High words from a prisoner," he said, menacingly. "You are in no position to be haughty."

Gordon merely shrugged his shoulders.

"Why did you seek to lead the tribes against us?" asked the Turk, curiously. "Our countries are not at war."

"There is always war between the Turk and I," Gordon answered. "If you seek the cause, go to Armenia, to Palestine, to Greece. For burned cities, for murdered children, for unarmed men massacred, for the raping of girls and the enslaving of women, Turkey is my foe. And she or I shall fall."

The Turk listened silently to Gordon's speech, given in rather stilted Turkish.

"You rate yourself highly," he said, drily. "What do you hope to do against the great Turkish Empire? What is your power?"

"Ask the men of Oman," Gordon replied, rather indifferently. "Ask the Amir of Afghanistan. Ask this Kurd."

The Turk turned to the tribesman.

"Do you know this man well?"

"Fairly well, my lord."

"Had you seen him or heard of him before he came to Kurdistan?"

"Yes, my lord. Some years ago he led a band of raiders into Kurdistan. He smote many tribes and burned many villages, both in the mountains and on the plains."

"Raiders? Of what race?"

"They were Afghans, my lord."

"Afghans?" the Turk exclaimed incredulously. "It is a far cry from Afghanistan to Kurdistan."

"Aye, my lord, but El Borak can lead men around the world. He is a devil. No man can stand before him in battle and when he leads men, the devils enter into them so that they follow where e'er he leads and perform wonders at his word."

"But if Gordon has raided the Kurds, why did the Kurds receive him as a friend?"

"They did not receive him as a friend, my lord. They feared him, and—and—"

"Well?"

"There be some chiefs among the Kurds who lust for power and loot, and it is well known that men gain those things, who follow El Borak."

The Turk's gaze wandered back to Gordon.

"Place him in one of the strongest dungeons," he said.

The Turks stepped back and signed Gordon to walk ahead.

Out of the great room, into a corridor, up a winding stair and down another corridor, lined on each side by cells with steel or iron doors. One of these the Turks stopped before and opening the heavy iron door, drove Gordon into the cell. Then they locked and bolted the door and one of them stood before it, with his rifle.

Inside the cell, Gordon worked at his bonds and soon freed his hands.

Then he inspected his cell. Except for a rude iron bench there were no furnishings. The floor, walls and ceiling were of stone. Some ten feet above the floor there was a small window, heavily barred, and there was a still smaller window in the iron door.

Gordon stepped upon the bench and leaped lithely to the window above. Catching the bars with both hands and drawing himself up, he peered out. The cell was not on the top floor of the castle but it was high. From the window to the ground was a distance of fully fifty feet. The castle wall was straight up and down and afforded no holds for climbing, even if he could pry the window bars apart and climb through the window.

The building was an old castle, erected by some feudal Saracen lord of ancient times and was being used by the Turks as a fort.

There was a high stone wall around the massive building and outside of the wall a moat encircled both wall and castle. Turkish soldiers patrolled the wall.

"They think they have me this time," Gordon thought. Evidently if that was the belief of the Turks, Gordon did not agree, for he smiled as he looked about his prison. He had received a few sword cuts in the battle in which he had been captured but they were slight and did not trouble him.

He examined the iron bench. It was a massive affair, made so to prevent prisoners using it as a means to escape, for it was far beyond the power of an ordinary man to lift such a bench.

Gordon, however, was no ordinary man. He was of medium height and of wiry frame but his strength was astonishing.

He felt sure he could employ the bench to smash the door of the cell, but he did not wish to do that. Battering down an iron door with an iron bench would make a terrific din that would bring some two hundred Turkish soldiers to prevent his escape. He crossed the cell and came close to the window in the door. The soldier stood close to the door, his rifle in his hands. Gordon passed his arm between the bars. So noiselessly he moved that the first thing the Turk knew of his attack was when a slim but sinewy hand gripped him by the hair and jerked his head back against the wall. He sagged down, unconscious.

Holding the Turk up against the door with one hand, Gordon attempted to get his other hand through the window. Impossible; the window was too small and the bars too thick. Gordon desisted and looked into the corridor again. The soldier's rifle had fallen from his hand so that the stock rested on the floor and the muzzle against the door, held in that position by the body of the unconscious Turk. Gordon measured the distance with his eye and then released the Turk, snatching at the rifle as it fell. He managed to catch it with his fingertips and a second later drew it through the window.

Then he waited, watching the corridor. It was not long until a Turkish officer, making a round of inspection of the cells, came down the corridor.

He saw the unconscious Turk and stopped short, glancing about him.

Gordon called to him softly in Turkish.

The Turk glared in amazement as he saw Gordon gazing at him over the barrel of the rifle.

"Make no outcry," the American instructed him. "Come forward with your hands up."

The Turk did so. He was one of those who had captured Gordon and he had no wish to be the target of the prisoner's skill of marksmanship, which was almost uncanny.

The Turk stopped within a few feet from the rifle muzzle.

"Now take the keys from that soldier's pocket," Gordon ordered. "You can do it with one hand."

Keeping a wary eye on the rifle, the Turk did as Gordon ordered.

"Now unlock this door and when it swings open don't try to run or try to draw a gun."

According to Gordon's instructions, the Turk stepped back, first pulling the unconscious soldier out of the way. In an instant Gordon was out of the cell. He searched the soldier and the officer, taking from the latter a pistol of Turkish manufacture. Then he forced the officer to enter the cell.

"Is Kemul Bey in this castle?" he asked.

"Yes," the Turk replied sullenly, "he is judging several Kurds who plotted rebellion."

"Are there any European prisoners in this castle?"

"I do not know."

Gordon looked at the Turk speculatively. "I ought to kill you," he said. "You are an arrogant, cruel, scoundrel; in other words, a Turk. However, I'm going to lock you up in this cell and leave you."

As he spoke, Gordon swung his left fist suddenly to the Turk's jaw. The Turk dropped, stunned. The American then turned his attention to the soldier, who was recovering consciousness. He bound both Turks hand and foot and gagged them, using the ropes he had been bound with and the soldier's jacket which he tore in strips. Then locking the cell door he slipped down the corridor, as swift and noiseless as a wraith. He came to another flight of stairs leading upward and mounted them. He came into another corridor from which other corridors branched off bewilderingly. Gordon chuckled. The castle was undoubtedly one of the strangest forms of architecture he had ever seen. He ascribed it to the fact that the original building had been altered and changed by many conquerors to suit their needs.

Saracen, Seljuk, Crusader, Kurd and Turk had each in turn held sway, changing and adding to the castle.

A Turkish soldier, making the rounds of the cells, paused close to a dark side corridor to light a cigarette, leaning his rifle against the wall. And from the corridor leaped a vaguely seen form and struck with bare fist, once. No need to strike more.

Gordon leaned above the soldier, listening. No sound. With swift, dexterous hands he searched the Turk. He found keys and a quantity of money but he took only the keys and a wicked appearing Turkish knife that was thrust into the Turk's sash. The rifle he left leaning against the wall.

Traversing corridor after corridor he finally decided to try some of the keys he had taken, on a chance that he would discover a way of escape. Selecting a door at random he found a key to fit the lock and opened the door with some difficulty. Entering, he found himself in a cell that apparently had not been used for many years. There was a small window, opening upon the courtyard, and an iron bench, as in the other cells. The bench was riveted to the floor. That fact aroused Gordon's interest.

"That bench is too heavy for a man to lift," he mused. "Why then should it be fastened to the floor?"

Gripping one end of the bench he tugged. The bench moved slightly! Desisting for a moment, Gordon examined the floor. It seemed to be formed of long, even slabs of stone and the bench rested upon a single slab. Seizing the bench again, Gordon exerted all his strength. And the bench and the slab on which it rested, swung up until the bench rested on one end upon the floor. A staircase was revealed.

"Crafty, by Erlik!" Gordon exclaimed in admiration. "One end of the slab is fastened to the rest of the floor with hinges. Raising the bench lifts the slab like a trapdoor. Quite medieval, with a secret passage and hidden stairway." The cell door locked from the inside as well as from the outside. Gordon locked it and stepped onto the stairway, leaving the hidden door open. The stair went both up and down. Gordon went upward. After leaving the trapdoor, the stairway was quite dark and Gordon could feel the wall on both sides. He had known that both the outer and inner walls of the castle were very massive and thick, and he was sure the stairway had been built within a wall. Probably there were many secret ways in the castle.

Gordon wondered if Kemul Bey was aware of the hidden stairway. He doubted if any Turk knew of it. The dust was thick upon the steps and he knew it had not been used lately, probably not in many years.

Once or twice, feeling along the wall Gordon came upon what he believed were hidden doors of some sort, probably opening into some room or cell.

However, he made no attempt to open them.

Presently he came to what appeared to be the top of the stairs. It was dark but Gordon, standing erect, felt what seemed to be a stone roof. He pushed upward; felt it give slightly. He shoved with all his strength and the trap-door, for that was what it seemed to be, slid upward a few inches and then swung to one side, revealing a blue Asian sky. Springing up, Gordon caught the edge of the opening and drew himself out. He peered out cautiously. He was on the roof of the castle. No one was in sight so he climbed out onto the roof.

Turreted battlements surmounted the castle roof, which was composed of square stone slabs. The hidden door was a slab exactly like the other slabs on the surface. It was hung on sliding hinges and was opened by pushing from below. Shoved upward a few inches, it swung back on the hidden hinges like a trapdoor. Gordon did not see how it could be opened from the top until upon closer examination he saw that the door-stone was raised slightly above the level of the roof and had faint grooves on two sides. Having examined the door, Gordon turned his attention to the castle roof. The roof itself was flat and at regular intervals rose a narrow tower, some ten in all. These rose sheer from the battlements and in ancient times were used as forts from which the castle soldiers shot arrows and hurled missiles down upon besiegers. The Turks had mounted machine guns in the towers, which, levelled at an angle clearing the outer castle wall, could sweep the space beyond the moat on all sides. Gordon knew at least two Turks were stationed in each tower.

The door of the secret stair was cunningly situated in the angle the rounded tower made with the battlement so that unless someone approached close to the battlements from the opposite direction, anyone coming from the hidden door would be unseen.

Gordon was sure that Turkish soldiers patrolled the roof, however, so he was cautious.

He peered warily around the tower. He could hear the sibilant Turkish speech of the two soldiers stationed within the tower and he saw another Turk walking away. He carried a rifle and walked with measured stride, keeping close to the battlements. The Turkish sentry, making his rounds.

Gordon turned and looked over the battlements. The sun blazed down from a cloudless Asian sky. The small city huddled close to the great castle showed drab and unlovely. It was one of the furthest outposts of Turkish rule in Asia.

Gordon turned his eyes from the crooked, narrow streets, lined with shops, and the bazaar, and gazed out across the plain. To west and south the plain lay, level and bare, as far as eye could reach. But some miles to the north and the east the plain sloped up to meet the mountains that, bleak and gigantic, reared their mighty peaks to the sky.

Gordon gazed, meditatively. Among those mountains roamed tribes of savage warriors, mountain-Kurds, as fierce and cruel as the Afghans and nearly as warlike.

They had never acknowledged Turkish rule and it was against them that the old castle had been garrisoned and fortified. And Gordon had sought to unite those Kurds and hurl their full force against the Turks with torch and sword.

They imagined, the Kurds did, that Gordon desired to build an empire out of Kurdistan and make the Kurds supreme in Asia. Gordon smiled crookedly. His hatred of the Turks was equaled only by his hatred of the Kurds. All that he had desired was to cause the two nations, Turkey and Kurdistan, to go to war. With all the tribes of mountain-Kurds raiding the Turkish borders, together with their allies, the plains-Kurds, Turkey would be forced to send a large army into Kurdistan. Then, with the Turkish forces divided, if Gordon could convince some European nation, Turkey would be forced out of Europe and back into Asia.

Such was Gordon's dream, but it seemed to him that it had come to naught. Gordon had come into the Kurdish mountains, alone and fearing nothing. He had come among the Kurds, neither as a captive nor an enemy. They knew El Borak of old and they feared and respected him. And he had begun at once to unite the chiefs and the tribes. The Kurds had distrusted him and some of the chiefs wished to murder him. But Gordon went his way, unperturbed, knowing that the Kurds would have slain him, had they dared. He had made no threats except once, when speaking in a council of chiefs, a Kurdish chieftain had threatened his life in veiled words.

"Aye," Gordon had said, standing erect and fearless, his eyes sweeping the rows of chieftans, "slay me and Afghan raiders will drench the mountains in Kurdish blood."

And the chiefs whose eyes had met his, had lowered their gaze sullenly. Gordon was a power in Afghanistan and they knew it.

And then the Kurd had carried information to the Turks and Gordon had been captured.

Gordon shrugged his shoulders. "Ungrateful skates," he murmured whimsically and with mild sarcasm. He felt no especial enmity toward the Kurd who had been the cause of his capture. Treachery was a dominant characteristic of all Orientals, he knew; especially the Kurds.

He turned and let himself down upon the hidden stairway, lowering the stone door into place with some difficulty, as he did so.

He descended the stair until, feeling along the walls, he came to what he believed was a secret door. He could hear a murmur of voices on the other side of the wall. Feeling in the dark he came upon a narrow strip of metal that seemed movable. It was rusted, but Gordon tugged at it and it slid back in a groove, revealing a narrow slit in the hidden door, if such was what it was.

Gordon peered out. He was looking into a cell, in which sat two Kurds, arguing. They were two chiefs who had been arrested by the Turks as plotters. Gordon knew them both. One was quite a powerful chief, who had been prominent in opposing Gordon's plans of a united Kurdistan. His name was Abdullah Hassan and he was as cruel as he was bold. An arrogant, fiendishly cruel bandit chief whose murders and ravishings were numberless.

Gordon began to work noiselessly at the hidden door and presently found a rusted spring. A pressure upon the spring and he believed the door would open.

The Kurds had risen and were striding about the cell, arguing with some heat. Abdullah Hassan stopped close to the door behind which Gordon stood. The other Kurd turned and gazed through the bars of the cell door into the corridor.

Gordon pressed the spring. Silently the hidden door swung inward. The light that filtered through the bars of the cell glittered on Gordon's knife as he struck once. And Abdullah Hassan flung up his hands, swayed and pitched forward on his face without a sound.

The other Kurd turned at the sound of the fall; he saw a blank cell wall and a cell empty except for himself and Abdullah Hassan, who lay, face down, a rent in the cloth of the burnoose between his wide shoulders.

The Turk patrolling the cells was startled by a commotion in one of the cells. Hurrying there he found a Kurd kicking and beating on the cell door and on the bars and calling lustily on Allah and the Turkish soldiers and old heathen idols in the same breath. He was scared half out of his wits and desired to be placed in another cell.

"Why?" the Turk wanted to know.

"Why?" yelled the Kurd. "There lies Abdullah Hassan on the cell floor, slain by a knife-thrust and no one in the cell but he and I! Mahommed akbar!"

The Turk glanced through the bars, saw the slain Kurd, and set off down the corridor at a swift pace, pursued by the maledictions of the other Kurd who called down upon him all the curses of Allah for leaving him in that place of devils.

The soldier soon returned with some more soldiers and an officer.

"It is quite plain," the Turkish officer said. "The men quarreled and Abdullah Hassan was slain by this other Kurd."

The Kurd cursed. "Fool!" he said heatedly. "Have I a knife? And even if I had, could I overcome Abdullah Hassan, the curse of Allah upon him."

The Turkish officer ordered him seized and stripped but no weapon was either upon him or upon the body of Abdullah Hassan. Nor was any weapon found concealed in the cell. Nor was the hidden door discovered.

Gordon, meanwhile, was exploring the castle.

He discovered narrow corridors branching off from the stairway, now and then, and he followed one of them. After traversing it for a time, he again heard a murmur of voices, hunted and found a slot and drawing aside the sliding metal slip, found himself looking into the great room in which he had faced Kemul Bey. There were two great arches in the room, huge and massive, but entirely for ornamental purposes, it seemed. The hidden passageway in which Gordon was in one of the arches. Halfway across the room was the thronelike chair where Kemul Bey sat. The Turk was sitting there even then, Gordon saw. Also there were a few Turkish soldiers about the room.

The American could hear their conversation plainly. Just then a Turkish officer entered to report that the Kurdish chief, Abdullah Hassan, had been murdered in his cell. The other Kurd, who had occupied the same cell, was brought before Kemul Bey, who questioned him. The Kurd swore it was the work of ifreets.

And then came another Turk to report that a soldier had been found murdered in the upper corridors.

A Turkish surgeon was brought who informed Kemul Bey that the soldier had evidently been slain by a blow from a bare fist.

Kemul Bey mused upon the statement.

"By Allah," said the Turk, "I know of no man who could slay such a man as that soldier with his bare hands—except Gordon, whom they call El Borak."

A soldier rushed into the room.

"Your Excellency!" he shouted. "El Borak has escaped!"

Kemul Bey leaped from his throne.

"What! Ho! Mirza Sulieman, take fifty soldiers and search the castle. Throw a cordon about the walls and let no one leave the castle until Gordon is recaptured or slain."

Then to the soldier, "How did he escape?"

"Your Excellency," the soldier answered, "El Borak overpowered the sentry and, taking his rifle from him, with it forced officer Nureddin to unlock the cell door. Soldiers coming to relieve the sentry found both the officer and sentry bound and gagged on the floor of the cell."

Kemul Bey rose and picked up his fez. The report of a pistol sent the echoes flying from walls to ceiling and the fez flew out of Kemul Bey's hand.

With a curse the Turk leaped back, snatching out a pistol. The soldiers started at the shot and raised their rifles. But they paused, uncertainly. There was nothing to tell them from whence the shot came. They stood, looking fearfully about the great castle room.

"Gordon is in the castle somewhere," said Kemul Bey, somewhat recovering his poise. "Search the castle. Capture El Borak or slay him."

Gordon smiled as he slid the metal slide back in place. He was beginning to enjoy the game. To conceal himself in the very stronghold of his enemies, to match cunning with cunning and war with war, to deal swift death to his foes and to match his life against theirs, that was a game that gave Gordon the thrills he wished. And his foes were Turks and that pleased him also.

Coming to another hidden door, he opened it cautiously. It opened into a room so pitch dark that even Gordon's eyes could not penetrate the darkness. Presently he made out the faint outline of a door across the room. He stepped forward noiselessly and then crouched back against the wall, as he heard a slight sound in front of him. Then silence. Gordon crouched close to the wall, his knife bared, waiting, listening.

A faint rustle of garments and Gordon leaped swift and noiseless as a panther, slashing savagely.

His knife touched something and someone cried out in a low voice. And Gordon jerked back in amazement. For the voice was that of a woman.

"Oh, spare me!" the words were in imperfect Turkish and full of fright and piteous appeal. "Oh, please! Would you murder me?"

Gordon groped in the dark and his hand touched a soft arm. He drew the woman toward him and felt her shudder with terror.

"Don't be afraid," he said softly. "I won't hurt you." He drew her toward the doorway. Some Kurdish woman, he imagined, or Armenian, either imprisoned because of breaking some Turkish law or because she was the property of some officer. Even in the dark he could tell that she was young.

He stepped through the doorway into a room or cell dimly lighted by a barred window. Then he turned to look at his captive.

And Gordon dropped her arm and stared. For the woman was little more than a girl and she was white!

In spite of her tattered garments and white, terrified face, on which were traces of weeping, she was a very pretty girl, one of the prettiest Gordon had ever seen, with golden hair and soft, gray eyes.

When Gordon released her she shrank back, her arm thrown out as if to ward off a blow. But now as her eyes became accustomed to the light and she saw Gordon's European clothing and features, she started forward.

Her eyes were wide and a glad cry was on her lips.

"Oh, are you a European?" she cried in the language of Gordon's own land.

"I am an American, miss," he answered, "and I hope I can help you."

She threw herself into his arms and clung tightly to him, her slim body pressed close to his and her golden hair falling about his shoulders. Her slender body shook with sobs.

And Gordon held her to him, soothing her as one would soothe a little child. Presently her sobs ceased and she looked up, smiling through her tears.

"I'm a silly, hysterical goose," she said, half laughing, half crying. "But I've been so frightened."

"You poor child," Gordon said with some tenderness. "What are you doing in Kurdistan?"

[. . .]

*Lal Singh
Oriental Gentleman*

The Sword of Lal Singh

(original draft untitled)

Men I have slain with naked steel,
Mahratta, Afghan, Jat and Bhil,
And German too, though they were white,
I've smote and slain in many a fight.
The Turk and Arab too, I've slain
Upon Arabia's level plain.
And still the British sahibs say,
"Come, draw thy sword, Lal Singh, and slay!
"The foes press in on every hand
"And only thou canst save the land."

Why should I sail beyond the sea
To slay the men of Arabee?
To do this but at the command
Of people of a foreign land?
They say, "The King hath need of thee."
What is the British king to me?
The Afghan and the Afreed band,
Foes of my race and of my land
A pleasure, 'twas, such men to kill,
I let my saber drink its fill.

Of Moslem life, that sword drank deep,
Afghans a score, it's sent to sleep;
It's sang and whirred with speed of wind
In all the countries of the Hind.

The Tale of the Rajah's Ring

Truly, sahib, the men of Hind are great liars, especially those of Delhi, yet I am not one of those. I am a Marwari of the Punjab and a Sikh. By the hilt of my tulwar I am a true man!

It came about in this manner: I was visiting with my father's brother in Meerut. He is a rich goldsmith there.

I? I am a warrior, sahib!

Well, one day my uncle came to me and said, "One day the rajah sent to me much gold and a great ruby. 'Fashion,' said he, 'a ring of the finest. Here are one hundred rupees and thou shalt have as many more if the ring pleases me.' Now, the ring is made, and it is in my mind that thieves have gotten wind of it and I dare not go to the rajah with it. Now, Lal Singh, you are a man of valor and much cunning and you have a sword. Take this ring to the rajah, I pray you."

Then, I, knowing what he would say, made answer, "Why should I do this thing?"

Whereupon he replied, "I am thy father's brother and thy host. Thou should do this because of respect and loyalty to me."

"And so I will," I answered, "but it is far to the rajah's palace and perchance I may thirst on the way."

"Here are ten rupees," he said, "and may a curse light on you if you deliver not the ring to the rajah."

So saying, he took from his robes a ring, and it was of carven gold set with a great ruby which sparkled wondrously.

"Take it at once," said he, "to the palace of the rajah. Loiter not and if you get drunk on the way, never set foot in my house again."

So, concealing the ring in my girdle, I set out. As I passed the bazaar of Ghulab Singh, a man accosted me. He was a Mahratta of Delhi, a small man with a face like to a rat.

"Ho, thou Sikh!" he said. "Where goest thou?"

"And what is that to thee, oh detestable descendent of unspeakable ancestors?" I made answer, courteously.

"Dost thou wish to earn much gold?" he asked me straightly. "Thou art a man without a trade and I have gold—"

"Out of my way, rat of Delhi!" I said, waxing wroth. "I am a warrior, by Kali, and am on the rajah's business!"

Thus in my anger and pride giving away the secret which my uncle had entrusted to me.

"Fair words are better than abuses," quoth the Mahratta, "and even a Sikh knows that in the rajah's service there are more bowstrings than rupees. Now, I will show you how to gain many rupees."

"Show me," quoth I.

"Follow me," he answered, and I followed him through the streets until we came to a certain house by the side of the river. Into this he went and I followed but warily, with my hand on my saber hilt.

He led me up a stair that wound up and up and stopped at last at a hallway. I began to be suspicious for the house seemed to be deserted. He led the way into a room which overlooked the river.

Then he turned to me and spoke hurriedly, as a man in much haste, glancing now and then nervously toward the door which he had shut.

"Give me now," sayeth he, "the ring of the rajah, for I am his messenger."

I laughed. "Think you to trick me so easily?"

"Make haste," he said, "and jest not."

"If thou art indeed his messenger," I countered, "why didst thou speak of the rajah's bowstrings? And where is the royal seal?"

"I spoke in that manner so as to throw dust in the eyes of any thieves who might hear. As for the seal, I dared not bring it."

I laughed. "Am I a fool?"

"I speak the truth!" he exclaimed. "I am the rajah's man!"

"Trust a snake before a harlot, a harlot before a priest, and a priest before a Mahratta!" I jeered.

"Fool!" he cursed, white with rage. "I tell you I am the rajah's spy!"

Then I, waxing cunning, said, "If thou art the man to take the ring, then surely thou hast the money wherewith to pay for it?"

"Now I see that even a Sikh may possess some scant mind," said he, drawing a purse from his girdle. "Here is the money—rupees fifty."

"The price was two hundred rupees," I told him, and then, sahib, the door was flung open and a dozen men of all nations rushed in. Before the Mahratta could move I leapt upon him, even as Shere Khan leaps, and whirling him high in the air, I hurled him through the window.

The others were upon me before I could draw, but one I smote in the countenance so that he fell backward and one I caught by the throat and girdle and, lifting him, cast him into the faces of the others. Then as they gave back, I drew my sword and placed my back against the wall, waiting.

For a moment the thieves hesitated, and then one, a Wahabi, rushed in, stabbing upward. I thrust straight, running him through and a second later avoided a blow from a hide-bound staff in the hands of a Jat and cleft the wielder's skull. Then a big, tall man, an Afghan of Allahabad, sprang forward, and thrust with a Khyber knife. I turned the blade and struck once.

Then as he fell, I sprang over him and with the cursing bandits at my heels I bounded across the room and leaped from the window!

By the hilt of my tulwar, sahib, that was a strange experience! Down I went, down and down, whirling over and over at first and seeing now the window from which I had sprung filled with savage faces, and now the river shimmering far below. And then I was falling straight and the river was rushing up to meet me. *Splash!* And I struck straight, cleaving the water with my arms and the sword I had not dropped in my fall. A Sikh never loses his sword, sahib!

Down, down I went and still down until I could see the ooze of the riverbed and a mugger who eyed me greedily. I was bursting for air and the water was deep below and above, but I struck upward with all my might. I am a good swimmer, sahib, and though it seemed ages, I was soon gasping on the surface. The mugger had followed me up and now he swam toward me, eyeing me evilly. I struck at him with my saber and he kept away as I swam to land. No one was in sight when I climbed out on the bank, and the current had swept me clear out of sight of the house where I had so nearly been trapped, so I sat down and looked to see if the rajah's ring was safe. It was, and so was the purse I had snatched from the Mahratta just before I hurled him from the window. It had in it one hundred and fifty rupees, seventy-five annas.

A good haul, indeed, sahib! I laughed to myself, "A thief to catch a thief and a Sikh to catch them both!" I placed in the purse the ten rupees my uncle had given me and went my way toward the rajah's palace.

As I neared the palace, while I was yet among the houses of the nobles, a babu stopped me and said, "Oh, handsome and most honored Sikh, are you a man of war?"

"Can you ask a Sikh that?" I asked him.

"Then give me attention," he said. "Most highly remunerative position to be obtained." He was a short, plump man, a university babu of Calcutta.

"If ever thou needest employment, come to me. A man who can outwit Marendra Mukerji is a man of wisdom." So he paid me and I departed.

At last I came to the palace of the rajah and was admitted by the sentries when I told them of my business there. I was showed to an inner chamber where presently there came to me a fat councilor or steward of the rajah. Saying naught of my adventures, I told him I had brought the rajah's ring, and he desired me to give it to him. But I demanded first the pay, five hundred rupees. He swore that the price was seventy-five rupees and would not give me more. And I, on my part, refused to give up the ring. So we wrangled until he rose in wrath. "The rajah shall hear of this," he swore, and went from the room.

I sat there thinking, "Have I hawked at too high an eagle?"

And then the curtains swung wide and who should enter but the rajah himself, escorted by several nobles of the court.

There was the steward, too. I salaamed. Did I prostrate myself? What, I a Sikh of Lahore, humble myself before a North Province rajah?

"This Sikh—" began the steward wrathfully, but I interrupted.

"Hold thy tongue, steward, wouldst thou cheat thy lord and then falsely accuse his guest?" Then, to the rajah who was smiling at my boldness, "Ah, great and mighty lord, this man, thy steward, is deserving of a bowstring. My uncle, the goldsmith, hath made thee a noble ring and this steward, out of greed and envy, refuseth to pay, thinking to keep for himself the money put aside for the payment—five hundred rupees. We are poor folk, ah, great lord, but shall it be said that the Rajah of Meerut was balked of his ring by a badmash steward? Here, therefore, is the ring without fee." And with a deep salaam I handed the ring to one of the nobles who handed it to the rajah.

The rajah placed it upon his finger and gazed with admiration. And the nobles murmured with wonder.

Then the rajah turned on the steward, "What!" he thundered, "shall it be noised abroad that the rajah of Meerut is too niggardly to pay for his rings? And because of a thieving steward? Thou shalt die for this."

The steward gave a screech of fear and flung himself at the rajah's feet, begging for his life.

The rajah said, "This time I shall forgive, but another—Bring out thy money chests." And the steward did so, white with fear.

"Count out five hundred rupees," commanded the rajah, "and of thine own store thou shalt give this Sikh fifty."

And the steward obeyed. Then as the rajah turned to me to thank me anew for the ring, into the room burst a man, his clothing awry and dripping wet. And, lo, it was the Mahratta whom I had hurled into the Gunga!

He rushed straightway to the rajah and began to speak rapidly, "Oh, great and mighty lord, I have fallen among thieves and the ring is gone!"

Then he stopped short as he saw the ring on the rajah's finger. He stared and then his gaze swept over the room. When his eyes fell upon me, they blazed, and snatching a dagger from his robes, he would have sprung at me had not the rajah interposed.

"Hold, Ananda Lal, what means this?"

"That Sikh is a badmash," the Mahratta screeched. "He stole the ring!"

"Nay, he brought it here," the rajah answered, doubtfully.

"Now harken to what I say," exclaimed the Mahratta. "Thou knowest I was sent to take the ring. I looked out for a Sikh and I thought this was he with the ring. Fearing spies, I spake of other things, pretending to wish to hire him; he answering in such a wise that I was sure he was whom I sought. I led him to the house of Ramma Baksh and there demanded the ring of him. He denied it, ensnaring me into drawing out my purse. Then a great mob of men burst the door down and rushed in upon us and the Sikh leaped upon me before I could draw my dagger, tore the purse from my hand and hurled me through the window. I came near drowning and the current carried me far to the bounds of the city so I am only now returning. I was dazed with bewilderment."

"Who art thou?" I asked the Mahratta.

"I am Ananda Lal, Sikh," he answered. "The prime minister of the rajah."

"Then why didst thou seek to steal the ring from him?" I asked dryly.

"I!" he swore furiously. "I! What meanst thou, Sikh?"

"I mean that you lured me to that house to entrap me and rob me," I answered straightly. "Those men who burst in upon us, they were men of thine."

"Of mine!" he shrieked. "Why—"

"Peace," said the rajah, "Ananda Lal is my loyal councilor. It is out of the question that *he* sought to steal the ring. But what of thou, Lal Singh? What hast thou to say?"

"Why," I replied, bewildered, "he speaks truth in part. I *did* follow him to the house, but there I thought him a thief and when those others rushed in upon us, I hurled the Mahratta from the window and then I fought the others, slaying three of them, knowing that they were dacoits and sought to steal the rajah's ring. Then I leaped from the window and escaped."

The rajah was silent for a moment. "Thou art in truth the nephew of the goldsmith?" he asked.

"In very truth I am," I answered.

Then he said musingly, "If thou acted in good faith, thou hast done nobly and well and deserveth of reward. And yet—"

At that a noble broke in, "Doubtless he lies, oh, rajah," he said harshly. "He is a traitor and deserving of a bowstring."

Then I recognized the lord, "Ha, speakest *thou* of traitors," quoth I. "What of Marendra Mujerki, sahib?"

"I know not what thou meanest," he made answer, changing color.

"Is thy memory so short, oh great Thakur?" I asked sarcastically. "Now if this were in Lahore—"

He stood staring at me, the color quite gone from his face.

"And the price is seven hundred rupees," I purred.

"What means this?" asked the rajah.

The noble turned to him. "Oh, mighty and great king," he said. "This Sikh and I are old friends. All that he says is true. It is impossible that *he* should seek to rob the rajah. He is in truth the nephew of the goldsmith and a true man."

The face of the rajah cleared. "It is well," he said.

"But what of my purse?" screeched the Mahratta. "Seize him and search him for the purse he snatched from me!"

Then I, remembering the other monies I had put into his purse, cursed inwardly. But Thakur said, "It is out of the question that Lal Singh robbed this man. Doubtless he lost the purse in the river."

And when the Mahratta, speechless with rage, would have interrupted, the rajah spoke, "Peace. Lal Singh is a man of value and shall be rewarded. If thou, Ananda Lal, lost money, thou shalt be reimbursed ten times."

Then he bade the steward to give me three hundred rupees, saying, "These be for the three bandits thou slew in defense of thy rajah's gold."

Then I salaamed and, thanking him greatly, withdrew. Thakur followed me out.

Outside the palace he accosted me. "Who art thou?" he asked.

"I am Lal Singh," I told him, looking him in the eye. "The nephew of the goldsmith and a man of Lahore."

He looked me over. "I think thou hast cast thy net for a minnow and caught a swordfish," he said meaningly.

I shrugged my shoulders. "Mayhap. Yet it is in my mind that though I am removed, that still the secret is known. There is Marendra Mukerji."

"Thou art right," he said. "I cannot touch thee. But here are a hundred rupees. Leave Meerut at once."

"Two hundred," I said.

He cursed, but gave me the amount I asked. I did as he said, sahib, and left Meerut, pausing only to return to my uncle, the goldsmith, to give him his share of the rupees.

By Vishnu, sahib, I came to Meerut a penniless wanderer, owning only my sword, and I left Meerut riding my own horse with servants to attend and my purse bulging with gold.

Finis
(till next time)

The Further Adventures of Lal Singh

(unfinished)

Now after I had left Meerut, bearing with me, it seemed, a third of the wealth of the city, I went to Delhi, for *there* is the place to spend money; but there I met a Rao of Rajputana whom I had had the best of in a matter of smuggled jewelry some years before, so I went from thence to Bombay.

Bombay is the greatest city of India. I had been there before and had friends there. And then, there is money to be had from the rich Parsee merchants and moneylenders.

So to Bombay I went and put up in a great hotel, like a sahib.

The rates were high and I kept a servant and horses and a coach so my money went fast, but I had hopes of making more soon.

One day as I was driving down the streets in my coach I saw a man walking along the sidewalk and he saw me and hailed me. I bade my servant stop the coach and the man came alongside.

And behold! it was Marendra Mukerji, the babu I had tricked in Meerut!

"Here is a pretty situation!" he said, clambering into the coach. "Ordinary Sikh vagabond riding in coach while highly educated babu must walk. Drive down by the quays," he ordered the coachman as if he owned the outfit. The driver obeyed, dumbfounded. The babu gave a sigh of comfort and mopped the sweat from his face with a silk handkerchief. I watched him, wondering. Presently he said abruptly, "How much money have you?"

Thinking he meant to blackmail me, I answered, "What is it to thee? Moreover, I have a sword."

"Tut!" said he. "Noble Sikh is a fool to talk about swords. I have proposition to make."

"Well?"

"Well, noble Sikh left Meerut with vast store of gold, large amount of which being this babu's. Of course, being Sikh, comes to Bombay. Purpose, to spend money, including babu's. Naturally, being Sikh, and spending money most highly developed talent, money goes fast—including babu's. Same old tale: wine, women and song."

"No women," I told him.

"Of course not!" he agreed smoothly. "Now it is quite unlikely that friend Sikh is averse to procuring more rupees?"

"Gold is gold," I answered.

"Quite so. And in hands of a Sikh it is wine, women and song. Ah, pardon me. No women. Same being quite unusual.

"However, to return to original proposition. As I said before, I have high admiration for noble Sikh's qualities. Any man, woman or child who can get best of Marendra Mukerji deserving of high regard and most worshipful admiration. Now, you still have some money and—can coachman be trusted?"

"He is my servant," I answered; he was a low caste Hindu of Delhi and would do anything for me.

"Very well. Now listen. I have money also. What I propose is this: we go into partnership as Europeans say. You furnish money and muscles; *I* furnish some money and brains. Thus we grow rich."

I pondered. "You will trick me—if you can," I said bluntly.

"Now I swear by Vishnu," he said. "I will keep faith with you." And if ever a man's eyes showed sincerity, it was that babu's.

"By Ganesha," said I; I believed him in spite of myself.

"Very well," I said, "we shall see. What are your plans?"

"Now you begin to speak with wisdom," the Bengali answered. "Now listen. There are many Parsee merchants in Bombay—many and greedy."

[. . .]

Lal Singh, Oriental Gentleman

The crowd surged through the bazaar. It was headed for the ghats and all types of the Orient were represented there. There a group of Hindu pilgrims forced their way forward, their faces gleaming with fanatical exultation; there a huge Jat strode through the press, which gave way before him, for Jats are proverbially quarrelsome and quick to use the seven-foot, iron-bound, bamboo lathi which they usually carry; there a wild-eyed, long-haired Akali hastened; there a Moslem made his way through the throng, drawing his garments aside to prevent them touching a Hindu, a sneer of scorn on his thin, hawklike face; near the river the crowd swirled aside where a faquir sat motionless, meditating; here the crowd divided as a rock divides a stream, closing again beyond him, the people dropping coins or other offerings before him. Already his begging cup was full, for none but a Moslem would steal from a faquir, and not even a Moslem would dare now, for this is Benares in the season of the pilgrimage.

To one side of the crowd might have been seen a character which was different from any other so far seen. It was a Sikh, who watched the throng with speculative eyes. He was tall with the lean build and broad shoulders of his race. His face was lean and strong, with the broad, high forehead which designates the thinker; his nose was thin and rather high bridged, his lips were likewise thin and straight and his jaw was lean, well-shaped, the outlines of which could easily be seen as, contrary to the customs of his race, his face was beardless, adorned only by a small mustache, of the style favored by Europeans and Americans.

He was dressed in plain garments and a heavy saber swung at his side. One would naturally seek for the motives that brought him to Benares. Certainly he had not come on the pilgrimage, for his caste is exceptionally cleanly, and prefer keeping their sins to the doubtful task of washing them away in the water of the Ganges simultaneously with several thousand people of all kinds and castes. It was not likely he had come merely to see the sights, although, indeed, that was a minor reason. The main reason that brought Lal Singh to Benares in the season of pilgrims was this: the people of India do not take kindly to banks. They keep their money hidden and when they make the pilgrimage to Benares many of them take it with them. No Indian would admit that he possessed an anna but it is there, just the same. Therefore it follows that there must be good pickings in Benares for a shrewd man who has a certain amount of courage and a knowledge of the people. And Lal Singh knew his people, none better. As for those other qualities, no man can be a Sikh and not possess them.

There were people in Benares for the same reason, low caste Hindus and Moslems, mostly, with a goodly number of Thags. But these traveled, almost exclusively, in bands of from three to a score. Lal Singh was a lone wolf. He had but one confidant, a babu, a genial rascal in the employ of the Raj. They were partners, in the Western sense. At present babu Marendra Mukerji was engaged in some moneymaking fraud in Delhi, so Lal Singh was playing a lone hand in Benares.

Up to this time Lal Singh had not been very successful in his efforts to accumulate money. This was not due so much to lack of opportunities as to the Sikh's unwillingness to exert himself for small prizes. Others might rob dancing girls of their ornaments and murder Hindus for a few rupees, but not Lal Singh. He set his net for larger fish. There was nothing small about Lal Singh.

So when there passed a band of men he knew to be thieves, he watched them with carefully veiled interest and presently followed, unobtrusively. He knew that they had a great store of rupees somewhere for they had been working systematically for weeks. He had been waiting and carefully watching their movements, as the tiger waits for the deer to grow fatter before he springs. Let them glean as much money as possible by theft and robbery and stealthy murder;

then Lal Singh would swoop down on them, precisely as the frigate bird swoops down on a fishing hawk bearing a juicy fish. The risk attached and the spice of the game, the matching of wits, appealed to Lal Singh almost as much as the thought of the rupees. The Sikh strolled along, seemingly aimlessly, in reality shadowing the thieves. They went toward the interior of the city, traversing the crooked, seemingly aimless alleys with a confidence that showed them to be familiar with the city. And the Sikh followed, flitting from corner to corner, taking advantage of every cover, as the jungli stalks the tiger.

Presently they passed through an arched opening, which resembled a magnified doorway, and went down a particularly tortuous alley, which turned and doubled until Lal Singh felt slightly bewildered. At last the band passed out of his sight and, hurrying rather incautiously after, he came upon a small courtyard—and came face to face with the band he had been following! They stood on each side of the courtyard, seven men and a woman. Lal Singh cast a swift look about him as they closed in on him, slowly. The courtyard was completely enclosed by tall buildings; a call for help would not be heard by any except the bandits, and, besides, the people of Benares are not over-quick to respond to such a call. At any rate, Lal Singh was not used to calling for help.

He glanced at his assailants, who, sure of their prey, were taking their time. The men were mostly strong and well built, but their only weapons appeared to be daggers and cudgels.

Lal Singh put his back to the wall and drew his sword. At that the dacoits paused; they had not looked for resistance. They hesitated and seemed to look to one of their number, a big man with the caste-mark of Kali upon his brow.

He smiled grimly and seemed inclined to parley. "What dost thou here, Sikh?" he asked.

"I am new to Benares," answered Lal Singh, glibly, "and I lost my way—and fell among thieves," he added, grimly humorous.

The chief gazed at him keenly; the others gathered behind him, holding a whispered council. Lal Singh, watching warily and listening with all his might, heard fragments: "He is a fool—" "Nay, a liar—" "Vishnu! Why all this talk? Slay him and—" "No, no, one may see that he is a swordsman of might and surely some of us would fall—" "Aye, and there are other Sikhs in Benares, Akalis as well—"

The leader stopped the discussion by peremptorily commanding "Chup!" Then he began, "Friend Sikh, thou doest us an injustice, who are but peaceful pilgrims, come to be freed of our sins—"

As he spoke, he came nearer the Sikh and seemingly unconscious of the act, drew a silk handkerchief from his girdle.

The Sikh recoiled. "Stand back, priest of Kali!" he warned, "or by Ananda, this sword shall free you of your sins more completely than ever Ganges did."

The Thag stopped short, a crooked smile on his lips. He was thinking rapidly. He was in something of a quandary. He was not sure of the Sikh's purpose there. He might be speaking the truth, but the Thag doubted it. Yet it was incredible to suppose that any one man would deliberately track such a band as that to its hiding place. It would simplify matters a great deal to slay the Sikh and hurl him into the Ganges, but the bandit chief did not particularly relish the task. He looked at the Sikh's saber; it was long and razor sharp and the owner looked as if he could wield it with great efficiency. He looked at Lal Singh's eyes; and he knew that here was a man absolutely without fear; one that would fight as long as a drop of blood remained in his veins, as long as his hand could lift sword or dagger. Then he was not sure that the intruder was alone. For all the Thag knew, there were a score of armed Sikhs lurking within call. It was this last consideration which led him to adopt the plan that he did in regard to Lal Singh.

"Shall we refuse courtesy to the stranger within our gates?" he asked smoothly. "If thou wilt not accept our hospitality we can but set thee aright. Thou and thou," indicating two of his followers, "go with the sahib that he may not lose his way."

As Lal Singh strode back down the alley, accompanied by the two dacoits, a quick glance over his shoulder showed the rest of the band entering one of the houses that enclosed the courtyard.

The Sikh had sheathed his saber, but his hand still gripped the hilt and his other hand was thrust into his girdle, clutching the concealed dagger. He took good care that neither of his escorts came too near him or got behind him. He had already thought out a plan and the moment they were out of sight of the courtyard, he put it into execution. With a sudden movement he thrust one of the Hindus against his comrade, and while they were struggling to disentangle themselves, he set off down the alley at a full run. And after him they came, robes flying, daggers glinting, eyes glittering with the bloodlust.

He easily distanced them, running fleetly until he came to the arch. A swift look backward told that his pursuers were not in sight; without pausing in his stride he raced for the arch, leaped high, caught the framework and swung himself up. As is usual with Hindu architecture, the arch was highly ornamented with carving and inlay. Perhaps, hundreds of years ago possibly, that arch had been the entrance to some temple. For Benares is a strange city and was old when Menes built the first pyramid. To the carvings above the arch Lal Singh clung and watched his pursuers come down the alley at full speed, rush through the arch and disappear down another alley.

The next moment the Sikh was racing back up the alley as swiftly as he had fled down it a few seconds before. Casting caution to the winds, he darted into the courtyard, springing for the house into which the robbers had disappeared, ran, catlike, straight up the sheer wall for at least ten feet until he could catch hold of the antique drain pipe which came from the roof. The rest was easy, for Lal Singh was as skilled as a Thag in the art of climbing. He went silently across the roofs, listening intently for a sound that would betray the whereabouts of the dacoit band, providing they were in an upper room. Presently, doubling back toward the courtyard, he seemed to hear a low murmur of voices. The next moment he was flat on the roof, seeking for a crack to see through. He found one and, cautiously enlarging it with his dagger, he peered into the room. He had guessed right. Below him was the whole band, excepting the two Hindus who had followed him.

Two more had joined the band since he had seen it, so that it was the original number, seven men and a woman.

One of the men was the big Thag who seemed to be the chief. Only one other of the men displayed the mark of Kali, and he had features which showed him to be of the chief's kin. His nephew, although Lal Singh did not know it. One of the others was a Jat, a huge, surly fellow. Two of the others were evil-visaged, low-caste Hindus, similar to the two who had pursued the Sikh. The other two were of a different type. One was undoubtedly a Moslem, a Turki from Haiderybad, the other a bold-eyed young Rajput; a person unusual to find among a band of thieves and brigands. The woman was young and had a certain lissome, sensuous beauty. She seemed to follow the young Rajput and seemed to have more assurance than most ordinary dancing girls. Lal Singh knew that she was the lure to draw the victims of the dacoits. He knew, too, that he had found the hiding place of the thieves. He listened closely. There seemed to be some discussion.

The Thag leader was speaking, "No, no, I tell you it shall be as I say. Already the British Raj is hearing rumors of us. We have left a wide spoor and it may be that we can be traced more easily than we think. We have remained long enough at Benares. We must move on."

"But the money?" asked the girl.

The Thag turned to the wall and pressed his hand against it. A door opened, worked by some hidden spring. From the safe thus discovered he drew a leather bag. It bulged and when he threw it upon a table it emitted a jingle which was music to the ears of Lal Singh.

"It is all there," said the Thag. "Three thousand rupees."

"Divide it," quoth the Jat, licking his lips. "Give me my share."

"We are not all here," answered the Thag.

At that instant the door was flung open and two men rushed in, hot and breathless. They were Lal Singh's escort.

"What of the Sikh?" asked the Thag.

"He fled," one of the men answered, "and we pursued him until we lost him in the crowd of the bazaar. He was afraid; he will not return."

Up on the roof, Lal Singh grinned in sardonic humor.

"We were fools to let him go," said the Jat savagely.

"I did not see *you* rushing to do battle with him," the Moslem remarked pointedly; the Jat scowled and muttered in his beard.

"Enough," ordered the Thag. "We have come here to speak of the money, not of wandering Sikhs. We have three thousand rupees and—"

"My share!" interrupted the Jat. "Give me my share!"

The Thag ignored him. "Some," he went on, "wish to divide the money and scatter. Some, to remain with the band until more plunder is gotten."

"We are tired of thee, my lover and I," announced the girl. "Give us our share and let us go."

The Jat said nothing but sat gazing upon the bag of gold, pulled both ways by avarice. The Turki shrugged his shoulders.

"I stay with the band," he announced. "Three thousand rupees is not so much divided between ten."

"Let us take our share and go," whispered the girl to the Rajput, who made no sign.

"Listen!" said the Thag, commandingly. "Ghulab Rass, thou art right. Three thousand rupees, shared amongst ten, is no great sum."

"Need it be among ten?" muttered the Jat, fingering his lathi.

The Thag flipped out his silken handkerchief, the same Lal Singh had seen. "I will slay the man who causes strife," he said, simply, and the Jat looked away, sullenly.

"Hear ye my plan," the Thag continued. "We stay in Benares until we have five thousand rupees. This, shared between us, will give each five hundred rupees."

The others made no reply but sat gazing at the pile of gold which the Thag had spilled out on the table. There were coins of gold, silver and copper, some few bank notes and a quantity of jewelry of more or less value. The whole amount represented weeks of steady effort: thefts, robberies and murders.

One of the Hindus spoke the mind of them all: "It has taken us weeks to obtain these three thousand rupees. I think we will be here longer than thou wishest if we must get two thousand more."

"I have thought of that," answered the Thag. "Now the richer class of pilgrims are begun to come into Benares; wealthy landowners and moneylenders of Dacca and the southern provinces and Meerut. We came too early; the constables begin to look upon us with suspicion. We must move on, but first we shall dip into the money bags of these pilgrims. It should not take long to get two thousand rupees."

A murmur of assent answered him. The Thag watched them narrowly. "I have no doubt some of ye have some small sum about you, as it was thought that we would share and scatter this day. Place it, I pray, with the rest," he said dryly.

Every one of them placed something on the table, coins, banknotes or jewelry; the Jat sullenly and reluctantly, the Turki with a crooked grin, the Rajput with a careless gesture, and the rest with looks and gestures showing each individual's characteristics.

The Thag placed the whole amount in the bag, tied it up and replaced it in the safe.

"There has been much talk in the band," he said coldly, "and some are not to be trusted. Therefore, Ghulab Rass and Jala Nosh," indicating his nephew, "shall stay here, day and night, and watch the gold. The rest will work our trade, as before, and it would not be well for any man to withhold any money which should be shared among us all."

There was a loud assent. The Thag was skilled in leadership, knowing how to play the men off against each other.

"Now," said he, "we shall go forth to ply our trade; Ghulab Rass and Jala Nosh remaining with the loot as I have said."

That was enough for Lal Singh. The next moment he was in full flight across the housetops. Presently he returned to the street and walked slowly in the direction of the bazaar, thinking deeply. He had found what he wished, the rendezvous of the band and the hiding place of their loot, and his mind was busy with a plan. Presently he looked up, a grim smile on his lips. He had formed a plan, but to carry it out it was necessary to have help. For his plan included, not only getting away with the gold, but wiping out the entire dacoit band as well! As has been said before, there was nothing small or mean about Lal Singh. He did not want any thieves interfering with his enjoyment of the gold, and in his cool, deliberate way he began to plot the extermination of the whole band. He began to look about for a partner in the enterprise. This would mean sharing the loot, but Lal Singh thought he saw a way of preventing the partner from getting any more than his share. He wanted a man with some skill in the use of the sword and pistol and possessing iron nerves and dauntless courage. He preferred a Turkoman or Afghan, for most of them have the characteristics he desired, and besides he would not feel so many scruples in dealing with one of them as he would one of his own race. He wished for his friend Ali Beg, a Turkoman, but Ali Beg had gone to far Bokahara to buy rugs and horses for the Indian trade. However, Lal Singh had no thought but that he could find a man in Benares that would fit his purpose as well. There are many sorts of people in Benares. So presently he saw the man he wanted; a truculent, swaggering Afghan. Lal Singh approached him.

"Lord of a thousand—" he began in Pushtu. The Afghan, turning toward him, began to curse him for an impudent Hindu badmash, then ceased suddenly.

"Oh, a Sikh," he said, somewhat lamely. "Well, that is better than if it were a fool of Hind." It is not as well cursing a Sikh as a Hindu.

The Sikh shrugged his shoulders and seemed to lose interest in the Afghan. "Rupees a thousand," he murmured.

"Eh?" the Afghan looked up with great interest. "Rupees, sayest thou?"

The Sikh turned to him suddenly. "You are a swordsman?"

"A swordsman? By Allah, I am a prodigy! No man can stand before me. I smite them down! I hew them in pieces! By Allah—"

"Enough," interrupted Lal Singh drily. "I am convinced that you are a man of might. Now I have need of a man to share a certain adventure with me—also share the proceeds. Perhaps thou art the man."

"There is money?" suggested the Afghan.

"Aye. Great store of rupees and jewels."

The Afghan's eyes lighted with avarice.

"By Allah, show me where I may gain gold with steel and—"

"Come," directed the Sikh, turning into another street. "Follow me and I will tell you how you may gain gold."

He led the Afghan to a shop kept by a countryman of the Sikh and going to a room where he knew no one could listen unobserved, he unfolded his plan to the Afghan, Lutaf Abdullah.

"It is in this way. There is a band of robbers in Benares; badmashs, Thags. They have much money which they always carry with them lest if they hide it, one of their number steal it from the rest. Now this is my plan. Thou and I will go through the bazaar, speaking as foolish men of our gold. Then thou shalt go to a house which I will show thee. I will arrange so that part of the band will follow you there and the other part I will contrive to trick and rob. You will hold the others at bay until I arrive. Then together we will slay the bandits and share the treasure."

Lal Singh expounded in detail and Lutuf saw that the plan was good. Presently the inhabitants of Benares were edified by the sight of a Sikh and an Afghan swaggering down the streets, commenting and airing their views like men from out of town. A certain band of men also followed them persistently but unobtrusively.

Presently the Sikh turned to his companion and said in a voice which he did not appear to make loud but which, nevertheless, carried to a certain Hindu nearby: "Lutuf, go you to such-and-such a house and await me there. Take care no one robs thee. Two thousand rupees is a vast sum."

"Bah!" said Lutuf, arrogantly. "No Hindu could rob me."

The Sikh turned and vanished in the crowd and the Afghan strode away in another direction. If anyone noticed a band of Hindus following, no one spoke of it. The leader of the band had upon his forehead the caste-mark of Kali.

Lal Singh walked along hurriedly, until he came to the alley where the old temple arch was, then he cast a quick look about him and slipped down the alley keeping close to the wall. He came without incident to the courtyard and, having seen no one, climbed up the drainpipe as he had done before and gained the roof. Then he slipped silently along the roof until he came to the room where the dacoits stood guard over the money. He saw them, looking through the aperture in the roof, sitting in the room, smoking. He looked about until he discovered what he had found before, a trapdoor opening into the room. It was carefully concealed and Lal Singh did not believe the dacoits were aware of its presence, at least they did not use it, for the trapdoor was secured by a lock, much rusted. From his robes the Sikh drew out a small hacksaw and a tiny can of oil and set to work, sawing the lock in two and using the oil to prevent the saw squeaking. He worked swiftly, silently.

In the room below, the Thag refilled his hookah and remarked, "This is over-dull, waiting."

"That is the truth," answered the Moslem. "Well, mayhap our comrades will bring back a great store of rupees. Would they would bring a girl. Though these Hindu women are naught; now Moslem women are fair."

And then down upon them came Lal Singh!

Silently as a leopard and as swift and ferocious.

The Thag was down before he could touch a weapon and the next moment the Moslem was battling savagely against the glittering saber that danced in the Sikh's hand like a flame. But the Moslem had a sword too, and he was no weakling at swordplay. Back and forth across the room they reeled, fighting grimly, silently, no sound except the slither and rasp of the sabers as they met; and then the Moslem went down with Lal Singh's sword through him.

Lal Singh smiled grimly and stepped to the hidden safe. Another instant and the bag of rupees was in his hands.

In an unoccupied house in another part of Benares, Lutuf Abdullah fingered his tulwar and wondered when the Hindus who had followed him would attack. He was ready for them. He believed that he could easily best half the Hindu population of Benares.

He sat up suddenly and the next moment leaped to his feet as a young woman rushed in. Lal Singh had told him there was a woman in the dacoit band. This, no doubt, was she. Very well. He would claim her as part of his share of the loot. She ran to him and, throwing herself against him, clung to him and beseeched him to save her!

"From whom?" he asked drily.

"Thags!" she gasped. "They come! Oh, at the door!"

In spite of himself he turned toward the door, but in time whirled toward the girl again. In time to wrench a dagger from her. Then he seized her in his arms and began to drag her toward an inner room. She struggled savagely, striking him in the face. And at that, all the savagery of the Afghan blazed up and he stabbed with her own dagger. She shrieked once and at that the room was filled with armed men rushing for Lutuf. Seven of them. But they had an infuriated Afghan to deal with and an Afghan is a terrible fighter. With a single motion, it seemed almost, he cleft a Hindu's skull and ran another through. He leaped back against the wall as the young Rajput rushed in; for a moment their weapons clashed and then the Rajput was down and Lutuf set his foot on him and struck down another Hindu. At that moment one of the other Hindus leaped upon him from behind and stabbed savagely. But the blade caught in the folds of Lutuf's turban and the next moment Lutuf had hurled him forward over his head and knifed him. Almost simultaneously the lathi of the Jat descended on the Afghan's head, only his turban saving him from being knocked unconscious. Lutuf reeled, and struck blindly upward. Once was enough. But the Thag who had stood aside now leaped forward. He caught Lutuf's descending arm and wrenched the Khyber knife from his grasp. Then both unarmed, they swayed and rocked, locked in fierce conflict. Lutuf was a powerful man, but the Thag slowly overpowered him. And then the Rajput staggered to his feet and, picking up the Jat's lathi, struck at Lutuf with terrific force. The Afghan went down and, before he struck the floor, he felt the silken handkerchief around his throat. In vain he struggled; his life was swiftly being forced from him, the Thag was smiling cruelly.

Darkness was swimming before Lutuf's eyes when he saw, dimly, the expression on the face of the Thag change. The silken handkerchief relaxed and the Thag pitched forward and rolled over. Dazed, Lutuf watched Lal Singh recover his saber. The Rajput was lying beside the Jat, finished by the Sikh's saber.

The Afghan staggered to his feet, reeled to a table and sat upon it. He watched Lal Singh go over the bodies of the bandits and take such money and ornaments as he found. The Afghan noted, with a sneer, that he did not touch the girl. Lutuf rose, recovered his Khyber knife, and proceeded to plunder the girl, keeping an eye on Lal Singh meanwhile, to see that the Sikh did not hide money. This was not the Sikh's intention, however. He dumped the money and ornaments on the table.

"Some three hundred and fifty rupees worth here," he announced. "And we share even?"

"Nay, by Allah," answered the Afghan. "I slew these. What didst thou do? Two hundred and the girl's jewels for me, one hundred and fifty for thou." The Sikh shrugged his shoulders. He was willing that Lutuf take all the loot for he felt he had earned it, but had he acquiesced, the Afghan would have suspected him of having taken a great sum from the others. As it was—

"Nay, by the Prophet! Thou shalt have but one hundred rupees. And what of the others thou were to rob? Share what thou hadst from them."

"No, no," replied the Sikh, drily, "I had a small sum from those others, but since thou will not give me my rightful share, I will keep what I gained." The Afghan scowled; he was bested and he knew it.

The Sikh divided the loot as the Afghan had said.

"You are in truth a warrior," remarked the Sikh. "That was a great battle."

His glance wandered over the room until it rested with disapproval upon the form of the girl.

"Was that necessary?" he asked.

The Afghan grinned. "Not necessary, but a pleasure," he answered.

The Sikh shrugged his shoulders with distaste. The East does not trouble itself about its women overmuch, but there was a savagery about the killing of the girl that disgusted Lal Singh. He would not have been averse to picking a fight with Lutuf Abdullah.

The Afghan was fingering his Khyber knife and eyeing Lal Singh closely. He had been bested in the bargaining and he was angry. Also, his avarice prompted him to seize all the loot. And then he believed that Lal Singh had a large store of gold somewhere on his person. The fact that Lal Singh had just saved his life did not enter into his calculations. In fact, he believed Lal Singh to be something of a fearful weakling. His praising Lutuf's warring prowess, his disapproval of the slaying of the girl, all, to Lutuf, pointed to the fact that Lal Singh was no man—as Lutuf Abdullah judged men. All of which goes to show that Lutuf knew very little about Sikhs. Had he ever fought against the Sikhs there is little chance that he would have attempted what he did.

Lal Singh knew Afghans much better than the Afghan knew Sikhs. He knew an Afghan is no more than a savage and he kept his eye closely on Lutuf. The Afghan had fully regained his breath from the battle and now felt a match for any ten men of India. He had not replaced his Khyber knife in its scabbard and now he thumbed it, and said, "I slew all these. I should take all the loot. And I will!"

And without the slightest warning he leaped upon the Sikh. Lal Singh saved himself by a backward leap that would have shamed a panther for quickness. The Afghan's knife slit the Sikh's robes as he lunged upward. Then the air hummed as Lal Singh drew his saber, and in an instant the room rang with the clashing and rasp of tulwar and saber. Lal Singh was furious. The Sikh is no savage but a gentleman in every respect. But they are a race of warriors, and in the soul of every Sikh there lurks a latent ferocity which, on occasion, blazes forth more terrible than the savagery of Kurd or Afghan. The Afghans have learned this in many a Border raid; the British learned it at Lahore, the Germans learned it in Flanders and Lutuf Abdullah learned it now in a room in Benares. Almost instantly he was fighting on the defensive and Lal Singh's saber weaved a shimmering "fan" about him. Again and again he turned the sword aside barely enough to prevent it running him through or cleaving him. Back and forth, staggering over the forms of the bandits, slipping on the bloodstained floor, striking, guarding, thrusting, they fought. Finally, with his back to the wall, Lutuf gasped his surrender and Lal Singh lowered his saber. And then Lutuf leaped, striking savagely, the Sikh barely avoiding the blow; then, before the Afghan could strike again, Lal Singh struck upward with the up-curving stroke that drives a curved blade with as true a thrust as a straight one. The Khyber knife clattered to the floor and Lutuf Abdullah dropped beside it, wrenching the sword from the Sikh's hand as he fell.

Lal Singh recovered his sword and looked about him.

"Strange are the accomplishments of Karma," he mused. "Having, directly or indirectly, rid the world of ten dacoits and murderers, and a murderous Afghan, I leave Benares with something near four thousand rupees. Marendra Mukerji will be amused to hear this tale, so I go to Delhi."

*The Adventures of
Yar Ali Khan*

The Song of Yar Ali Khan

This is the song of Yar Ali Khan,
As he stands on a mountain peak
And hills below are veiled in snow
And above him the eagles shriek.

"These are the hills and the mountains,
And the forests of Yar Ali Khan,
Every man's hand is against me,
My hand is against every man!

Friends have I of my tribe only,
They follow me against my foe,
My foemen? Why, they are the peoples,
Above and beside and below.

English and Afghan and Russian,
And the swart Punjabi man,
All men are the foes of Yar Ali
Excepting Yar Ali's clan.

But Yar Ali is strong and his sword is long,
And his tribe are men of war
And the fame of Yar has reached afar,
From Sikhland to Candahar."

The Lion Gate

(unfinished)

"No place for a girl," I growled in my beard. Long residence in the hills of the Northwestern Border tends to make a man curt, even churlish with his own kind. My rudeness was unpardonable. But a woman north of the Khyber!

The man to whom I was speaking smiled, a dry, humorous smile.

"Admitting that you are right, my friend, I see no other way, than to let her accompany us. In spite of her looks she is a strong-minded young lady."

I shrugged my shoulders.

"Have it your own way. I'd send her back to Peshawar so quick that, but I'm only your guide." And I strode away to superintend the loading of the pack mules.

It was a wild, even insane, plan. And of the insane people there were five. There was the tall, lank Professor Berwick; his trim little niece, Alice; his assistant, John Ammiston, an athletic young American; and there was myself; and Ali Khan.

Berwick was a student of archaeology and his lust for knowledge therein was infinite. Like most real scholars, he was penniless. I have a suspicion that his brother financed the trip, and knowing nothing of the country into which he would go, induced him to take along the girl, Alice.

As for myself—Berwick had argued long.

"They told you," I sneered, "that if what you seek could be found, O'Brien, the crazy Irishman, could find it for you. Any why? Because I know the Punjab, because I have traversed Baluchistan, because the Zahka Khels and part of the Afridis do not slay me on sight, they think I can guide you through Hell and back."

"I will pay—" he began and I made a gesture of scorn.

"But listen," he said eagerly. "You are an archaeologist yourself. You have no idea of the wealth of knowledge among those far mountains. Why, man, Empires rose, flourished and fell there a thousand years before the armies of Macedon came through the passes. Now listen. Many years ago the British captured a Northern 'lifter'—a horse-thief—not far from the Dera Ismail. The fellow offered to bargain for his freedom, a strange tale of a wondrous unknown city, of great wealth. He said that only he knew the site of it and that in return for his liberty he would guide them to it. Of course, the British laughed at his tale and turned him over to the authorities. It is said that he escaped and fled back to the hills, breathing vengeance against the Raj; but no matter. But the story went the rounds and a resident, who was more than a little interested in the marvels of antiquity, went to the trouble of striving to trace the origin. The natives didn't know, or knowing would not talk. Everything was vague, illusive, pointing out the theory that the whole tale of the city was a product of the Afghan's imagination. But listen," the professor leaned forward, his gaunt, homely face lighting with an almost fanatical light, "that 'lifter' told of a Gate of Beasts, a great gate with strange beasts carved upon the pillars. He described them as best he knew, and though he did not know it, he described lions! How could he have been lying when he had never before seen a lion?"

I lit my pipe and smoked a moment, nodding. "The Lion Gates of Crete."

"Exactly!" he exclaimed. "Exactly! Now then, listen, you may possibly have read of the new discoveries in Crete, discoveries, sir, in which I had no small part. What was not given to the world was that I discovered a piece of parchment, yes, parchment! It took me a year to decipher the writing upon it. The gist of it was this: You know of course, how the great Cretan empire was at one time the ruler of the Aegean Sea, and the Mediterranean coasts, how the nation rose to its height and then decayed into a race of degenerates; how the Cretans imported thousands of negro slaves from Africa to do their labor and fight their battles; you know how the slaves finally rose and the Cretan empire went down in a flaming holocaust of slaughter and rapine.

The writing on the parchment begins abruptly, in this manner: 'So we put to sea and fire of the burning lit the sea like noonday and the smoke thereof was like a strong fog.' The parchment is torn and the tale goes on upon another fragment: 'So though we were sea-weary, we dared not put to land for fear of the Ionians. So we sailed on in an easterly direction, but great winds seized and tossed us about so that we knew not where we were, until after many days we sighted land and a great city near the shore. A ship put out to intercept us, but we saw that they were Trojans and clapped on all sail, bidding our slaves bend all their strength to the oars.'

"Here the ancient writer comments upon the hatred all the world seems to bear Cretans.

"'We believed ourselves to be near that strait of the sea, called by the Hellenes, the Straits of Helen, (or Hellespont). So presently we beach our galleys and found no city but a great desert. Presently came a trader of the Phoenicians who said that wild savages inhabited the desert, but that far to the east were many great mountains where such refugees as we might build a city and hold against all the ages.'

"And upon another fragment, 'Several galleys returned to the Empire Island, to bring off such of the people as yet remained.'

"And why not!" Berwick exclaimed. "Why should those Ancients have not won through to the high-flung reaches of the Himalayas and reared their city among the crags? Musty, century old parchment in a ruined temple in Crete, a hillsman's tale, galleys and Lion Gates—the fabric is complete!"

I nodded. "I have heard vague tales of this mythical city. Frankly, I never believed anything of it. Naturally, I knew nothing of the legend you have just told me. You are determined to go on this wild chase, I see. Since you are, I will guide you, but I warn you, we shall go into country where a white man has never before set foot."

"Fine!" he exclaimed with the enthusiasm of a boy.

"How did the parchment come to be in Crete?"

"The writer must have been one of those who returned to the island. Or else he sent the parchment back to the island as a guide for the others who might, and doubtless did, follow."

After our conversation, I had sought out Ali Khan. He was seated cross-legged upon a mat, smoking and staring out over the valley, on the crags above which our camp was pitched.

I sat down facing him and we smoked awhile in silence.

Presently, "Lion of the Durani," said I, "we go North."

He nodded. "Yesterday came these sahibs, seeking our camp among the crags. The tall one is crazed, even as thou, sahib. So it was in my mind that we went North."

I looked at him narrowly, but he returned my gaze imperturbably.

"Know ye what he seeks?"

"The bazaars have ears, aye, and tongues. The tall one has talked at Peshawar, at Jumrud. When the Raj gives a white man permission to cross the Khyber, kites have ears."

"Hast thou ever heard of a secret city?"

"I heard the breeze that whispered over the peaks of Jumgala at dawn. I caught a spice scent from a Herati caravan."

"How long ago?"

"The snow on Khyber's peak has melted thirty times."

"Why didst thou not speak to me of this?"

"Because thou, too, are possessed of an efrit and for lust of knowledge would have ventured forth where no white man may go."

"But I go now. What thinkest thou, that I am a fool?"

He grinned. "Aye, thou art a fool and I a greater, for if thou go, I go."

So it was that we were preparing to invade forbidden territory, and I was arguing with Berwick to send his niece back to semi-civilization, at least.

In a way, it was a new experience for me. Time and again I had gone up the Khyber or crossed the line elsewhere, but it had usually been secretly, with neither the knowledge or the sanction of the British government; and always alone or accompanied by Ali Khan. How Berwick obtained leave from the Raj I did not know, but I suspect that American gold and influence had much to do with it.

We had no servants or camp followers. What use, since any we could get would desert at the very first opportunity?

Five small pack mules carried our outfit and we rode small, shaggy Kabulis, not the higher breed, but very sturdy animals, adapted for mountain work.

The stars were out as we came into Afghan territory. Pausing a moment to look back, we saw the fires of Fort Ismail Khan glinting far down the Pass and heard the faint tinkle as picketed horses of a Kandahar trading caravan moved restlessly.

As I rode I pondered on the wildness of the scheme. The hills close to the Khyber I knew, and their wild inhabitants knew me. Whether their casual friendship would stand the temptation of loot and a pretty face, I doubted, but certainly a few days journey among those crags would take us among fierce tribes unhampered by any such sentiment.

The next day we pushed boldly into a small village, perched high upon a towering crag. The chief was a friend of Ali Khan's and though the villagers eyed the pack mules and the girl with desirous eyes, we were not molested. The chief offered us anything in the village.

[. . .]

The Sword of Yar Ali Khan

(originally untitled)

Now bright, now red, the sabers sped among the racing horde,
The Afghan knife reft Hindu life and leaped the Rajput sword.
Oh, red and blue, the keen swords flew where charged the
  hosts in whirls,
And as in dreams rang loud the screams of ravished
  Hindu girls.
And through the strife, where sword and knife clashed loud
  on spear and shield,
With sword in hand, Yar Ali Khan rode o'er the battle-field.
From heel to head the chief was red, the blood was not
  his own.
In crimson tide his sword was dyed that had so brightly shone.

"*When Yar Ali Khan crept*"

(untitled and unfinished)

When Yar Ali Khan crept into the camp of Zumal Khan, bandit and outlaw, and made a valiant attempt to knife the chieftain in his tent, the bandit was annoyed, to say the least. The Afridi's attempt was nearly successful.

Small things have changed the course of empires, it has been said. Which may or may not be accepted literally. At any rate, had it not been for a heavy Bokharian rug on the floor of Zumal Khan's tent, Yar Ali's knife would have struck as he intended and several million inhabitants of India would have felt extreme satisfaction.

As it was, Zumal Khan awakened as someone stumbled over the Bokharian rug, and saw, in the dim light that filtered into the tent from the moon that rode high above the Himalayas, the bearded face and gleaming knife of the Afridi.

Without rising from his pallet, Zumal Khan snatched a pistol and blazed away hastily. At the same instant Yar Ali whirled up his knife and flung it. The hilt knocked the pistol from the bandit's hand and before he could catch up another weapon Yar Ali had vanished, leaving only a long slit in the tent to show how he had come and gone.

The bandits came swarming in from all sides, roused by the noise but they did not intercept Yar Ali.

[. . .]

"Two men were standing"

(untitled and unfinished)

Two men were standing in the bazaar in Delhi. Tall, lean-built men they were, dressed in the costume of the land. They were not so heavily bearded as the average Asiatic and their faces were strong and hawklike, especially one. His thin, rather high-bridged nose and thin lips proclaimed the Afghan as plainly as the yard-long Khyber knife that hung at his girdle.

His companion was unmistakably a Sikh. He was armed with a long saber and this fact, together with his bearing, showed that he was a swordsman of no mean ability.

The Afghan looked up and down the bazaar and remarked impatiently, "Trust a babu for sloth. They should have been here by now."

The Sikh smiled. "They will arrive presently, Ali Khan. Doubtless our Bengal friend is engaged in preventing Ali Beg from squandering his rupees and pursuing every woman he sees, which is probably the reason they are not on time. Ah, here they come now."

Two men were making their way through the crowd in the bazaar. One was a portly young man, a Calcutta babu. The other was of a tribe seldom seen in Delhi or all India for that matter. He was a Northerner, but from a land much further North than the land of Ali Khan. He was a Turkoman. With a swaggering, rolling gait, a beard dyed red, a wide Bokhariot girdle with a yataghan thrust through it and a long, curved saber swinging from it, he was a conspicuous figure, and both Hindu and Moslem women turned to gaze at him. Which was quite pleasing to Ali Beg of Turkestan.

[. . .]

Steve Allison:
The Sonora Kid

The Sonora Kid—Cowhand

Ogallala Brent, foreman of the Double Z-U Ranch was rather irritable. It was hot and some unspeakable person had discovered his private store of liquor and used it as it should be used.

Therefore, he was in no mood for pleasantries when a young, lithe-built youth rode up, dismounted and strode up to the ranch house porch where Ogallala sat, in the absence of the owners.

"Greetings, fair one," spoke the youth airily.

The foreman gave a noncommittal grunt, eyeing him with suspicion. The young man returned his gaze innocently.

"Do you want to hire a good man?" he asked.

"Yeah," replied the foreman. "Bring him 'round."

The young man ignored the ponderous sarcasm. "We ought to get along well, then," he remarked sprightly. "You got a job, I want a job; you need a good man, hey?"

"Well?" glared Ogallala.

"I'm him!" announced the amazing youth, taking off his sombrero and sitting down on the veranda.

"Well, of all the unmitigated nerve!" the foreman swore. "Look-a-here, young feller, what do yuh want, where you from, what's your name and what can you do?"

The young man got up and faced Ogallala, hooking his thumbs into a belt from which swung a big gun.

"My name's Steve Allison," he announced. "It's none o' your business where I'm from, but I was born in the state of Texas; I want a job; I can lick any man on this ranch, ride anything on four hoofs, drink any man I ever saw off his feet and commit wholesale robbery at poker."

The foreman grinned. "I can see yore a man of some few accomplishments. Ain't they some other virtue you forgot to mention?"

"Yeah, they is, now you remind me of it," agreed Mr. Allison. "There's two: modesty and mindin' muh own business."

The foreman looked him over. "I'm goin' to take yuh at yore word." he announced. "Hey, Gunboat!" This last in a shout.

A bellow answered him and presently a small crowd of cowpunchers came around the house. In the lead was a burly, ugly-looking individual, so heavily built as to appear short. Yet he was above the average height. His jaw was prognathous and his eyes were small and piglike.

"Wotcher want?" inquired this interesting individual, in a deep, rumbling voice.

"This young feller is laboring under the illusion that he can lick any man on the ranch," explained Ogallala, indicating Allison.

"That runt!" gasped Gunboat. "Haw! Haw!"

"Haw! Haw!" echoed the cowpunchers.

"I done told him he could have a job if he could lick you and ride 'Cyclone,' and he's done accepted," went on the foreman smoothly.

"Him?" The astonishment was rather justified. Gunboat was some ten years older, eight inches taller and seventy-five pounds heavier. In fact, when Mr. Allison looked his opponent over, he wished he had not been so specific in stating his accomplishments and the job began to lose its attractions. But there was no backing out now.

"Name your weapons," Allison suggested. "Fists, knife or gun?"

"I ain't no gunfighter," Gunboat answered, "ner yet no Mex knifer. Fists is a gentleman's weepons."

Steve shrugged his shoulders. That was the answer he had expected.

"Let's adjourn to the back of the corral," suggested one of the cowboys, known as Skinny. "Yuh'd trample Miss Gladys's flowerbeds here and out there they's shade and th' spectators can sit on the corral."

At the back of the corral Gunboat removed his shirt with great deliberation and Allison did likewise, first taking off his gun-belt and handing it to Ogallala.

"Boy, what I'm goin' to do to you," opined Gunboat, knotting an enormous fist, "is a plumb shame."

"Gwan, yuh big boob," Steve retorted, fervently hoping no one would notice how profusely he was sweating. "I hate to demean muhself by killin' yuh with my bare hands, but yuh got yoreself to blame."

"The rules of this here combat," announced the foreman, from his vantage point on the corral fence, "is plumb rough-and-tumble. Yuh can hit, kick, gouge or whatever yuh want to do. Let's go!"

At the word, Gunboat lunged forward and launched a blow that would have demolished Mr. Allison had it landed. Owing to Mr. Allison's earnest efforts, it did not land, although it came so close that its breeze fanned the young man's face.

Followed a battle which, for pure, innocent primitive actions and cheerful ignoring of the Marquis of Queensberry rules, was a masterpiece.

A boxing enthusiast would have cursed soulfully and left in disgust, but ordinary mortals, like the cowboys on the fence, would have yelled as loud and felt as uplifted as they did.

Allison was about fifty times as quick on his feet as Gunboat and that was all that saved him from defeat. But it seemed he was unable to hurt Gunboat. Time and again, he got in a blow that would have laid out an ordinary man but which seemed to make no impression on Gunboat. It was like a bear and a wolf fighting; a big, surly, grizzly bear, at that.

Finally Gunboat's fist caught Allison on the shoulder and the very force of the blow knocked him down. Gunboat leaped into the air with the intention of coming down feetfirst on Allison's face. Allison rolled out of the way and kicked Gunboat's feet out from under him. Gunboat came down on his back, rolled over and grabbed Allison before the youth could get away. He dragged Steve to him and staggered to his feet, and with arms around him attempted to crush him against his chest.

Steve kicked him on the knee and then, getting his fingers at his eyes, made an earnest attempt to gouge. Gunboat had either to release Steve or lose an eye. He hurled Steve away from him and rushed after him. Allison made another effort to knock out his opponent and only succeeded in bruising his knuckles against Gunboat's unshaven jaw.

Then to the infinite astonishment and disgust of the watching cowpunchers, Steve turned and fled fleetly!

There was a tree close-by and Steve seemed to be running for it. Gunboat pursued as fleetly as possible for one of his bulk.

"He's goin' to climb the tree!" Skinny yelled excitedly. "Th' yellow coward!"

Indeed, it seemed that Skinny was right, for as Steve neared the tree he leaped high in the air and caught a low limb with both hands. The momentum of the leap caused him to swing far out, and to elude Gunboat's grasping hands.

Then, as the cowboys gasped in amazement, Steve swung back, with a heave of his lithe body and put terrific force to the kick he launched out.

Both heels hit Gunboat's jaw with a force that knocked the heel from one shoe and knocked Gunboat to the ground as if the man had been hit with a pile driver.

Allison dropped to the ground beside Gunboat and examined him. "His jaw ain't broke," he announced to the cowpunchers. "He'll be all right if you'll pour some water on him. He's just knocked out."

"My gosh!" Ogallala marveled. "Yore a fightin' wonder, boy!"

"Gimme my shirt," requested Steve.

Having donned it, he said, "Now lead me to yore wild cayuse."

"Cayuse nothin'," answered a puncher. "He's throwed every man on this ranch."

Cyclone was a weary looking steed of indifferent hue.

He slumbered while being saddled. However, Steve knew that the appearance was deceiving.

Mr. Allison mounted with care. The cowpunchers fled to the corral fence.

The noble steed still slumbered.

"Let's go," Mr. Allison requested.

The horse made no move to comply.

Steve tickled him gently with a spur.

The horse turned his head and gave Steve a long look of shocked surprize, but stood still.

"Well, of all the no-good nags!" Steve exclaimed disgustedly. "I'm goin' to get off if—"

He stopped suddenly. The horse turned his head again and gave Steve such a diabolical stare that he felt his hair rise.

And then abruptly the show started. The bronc bounded high in the air and changed ends repeatedly and with dizzy speed.

Mr. Allison lost his hat but he did not pull leather.

Then the horse tried straight bucking. Leaping high in the air and coming down stiff legged. Mr. Allison rocked with the jolts but he stayed.

The cowpunchers on the fence yelled delightedly.

Having tried all the regular pitching stunts without avail, the horse launched into a series of his own invention.

He appeared to turn himself from a horse to a whirlwind.

He danced. He pranced. He tangoed. He pirouetted gracefully on one leg. With a whoop of enjoyment he tried his favorite trick and then paused to see where Mr. Allison had landed. To his surprize and disgust, Mr. Allison was still in the saddle.

With a curse, the bronc hurled himself backward, but he landed only on an empty saddle, for Steve leaped off just in time.

He still held the reins, however, and when Cyclone regained his feet he was enraged to find his rider back in the saddle.

Cyclone felt sulky. After a few more lunges and an attempt to scrape his rider off against the corral fence—an attempt which was foiled by Mr. Allison's swinging half-out of the saddle on the opposite side—the horse walked out into the center of the corral and stood, sulking.

Steve dismounted and walked, somewhat unsteadily, to the corral fence.

"Do I get the job?" he asked the foreman.

"You do!" replied Ogallala, gazing at him with wonder.

The Sonora Kid's Winning Hand

(unfinished)

Dusk was gathering over the cattle town of _________. A horseman rode down the street, humming a cowboy song. As he neared the outskirts of the town he heard someone call his name. He turned toward a small house on one side of the street. A slim, girlish form was standing on the porch.

"Evening, Miss Marion," said the horseman, raising his hat.

"Do you know where Steve is?" the girl asked.

"He was at the Mountain Rose when I saw him," he answered, then, rather thoughtlessly, "He sure was stacking up the spondoolicks, too. Just before I left he scooped in two hundred dollars on a straight flush."

"Thank you, Billy," she answered, turning back into the house.

An elderly woman was preparing supper and Marion said to her, "I wish Steve would stay away from those awful saloons and gambling houses. He's there now, gambling."

"Is he winning?" asked her aunt.

"Billy Buckner said he had just won two hundred dollars."

"Well, goodness sakes!" exclaimed her aunt. "What are you grumbling about? If he was losing it would be different."

"But I don't want him to be with those gamblers and saloonmen. They are so rough."

Her aunt laughed. "That's silly. Steve is no angel himself. Besides, you shouldn't nag him about gambling; when he wins he spends most of the money on you."

The girl did not answer. She went to the door and looked down the street. Her eyes lighted as she saw a man coming down the street, his spurs jingling as he walked on the board sidewalk.

He was little more than a boy, a slim youth of medium height with clean-cut features, dressed in the ordinary attire of the cow-puncher, a heavy gun swinging low on his hip. He stepped up on the porch and greeted the girl cheerfully.

"Chow ready, sis?"

"Yes," she answered. "Where have you been?"

"Down at the Mountain Rose, relieving the honest gamblers of their hard-earned mazuma," he chuckled. "How about a new silk dress, kid?" and he slipped a banknote into her hand.

She hesitated, then pushed it back. "I can't take it, Steve."

"Why not?" he demanded.

"Oh, I just can't. It isn't honest, it isn't right. I wish you would stop gambling, Steve."

[. . .]

Red Curls and Bobbed Hair

The Allison family was at dinner. That is, all the family except the eldest son Frank, and the youngest daughter, Mildred.

Frank was in Arizona and as for Mildred—

She entered and sat down without remark—rather unusual for her. Presently she looked about her with more timidity than was usual for her. Some of the family noted this.

"Edith Burton had her hair bobbed," she returned casually.

The family received that startling information without enthusiasm.

"I wonder—" Mildred mused, avoiding the eyes of the family.

"You wonder what?" inquired her older sister Helen.

"If—if—if I had *my* hair bobbed—"

The family rose and fell on her, with one exception. She was surrounded, stormed and captured, verbally. Her feeble attempts at defense were smothered under by the words.

"Don't you dare to think of such a thing—" that was Mrs. Allison.

"You leave your hair alone, you little idiot—" that was Helen.

"You have such beautiful hair, Milly—" that was gentle Marion.

"Aw, you make me tired," cried the harassed girl. "Darn it, all the other girls are having their hair bobbed. Whose hair is it anyhow? What right have you to tell me whether to bob my hair or not?"

"You try it and see," warned Helen.

The exception was Steve, her brother. Throughout the argument he had remained calm, not speaking a word but eating industriously.

The feminine part of the family now turned to him.

"Don't you think it's perfectly awful for Mildred to want her hair bobbed?"

"Why?" he asked coolly. "It's her hair. Let the kid have it bobbed if she wants to. All the other girls of her set are doing it."

Mildred sent him a grateful glance.

But Steve was in the minority. Even Mr. Allison, who nearly always let his girls have their way, forbade Mildred bobbing her hair.

After dinner, Steve was taking his ease in an easy chair when a soft arm was slipped around his neck and a soft voice whispered, "Good old Steve." Mildred slipped into his lap; she nestled in his arms and kissed him. It was a perfect picture of sisterly love.

But Steve knew his sisters. He eyed Mildred suspiciously.

"What have you done now?" he demanded.

"I haven't done anything—"

"Well, what do you want then? I'm broke—"

"I don't want anything." She pouted; her lip quivered and there was a suggestion of tears in her dark violet eyes.

"I think it's horrid of you to suggest that I 'want something' when I only try to be nice," and she made as if to slip off his lap. He slipped an arm around her slim waist and held her.

"There, there, child," he soothed, caressing her gently. "Don't cry, little girl, I didn't mean to offend you."

"Well, you have," she responded indignantly.

"Don't be angry," he begged contritely.

"I'm not," she relented, nestling her face against his shoulder to hide the smile on her lips. Mildred was a wise little lady.

Presently she said, "Steve, do you think it would be a sin for me to bob my hair?"

There was a wistfulness in her voice that made Steve glance pityingly at her.

"Of course not."

"It makes me so furious," she sat up and her eyes flashed. "All the family pounces on me like a bunch of hawks after a poor little dove every time I mention bobbing my hair."

Steve gently pulled her back against his shoulder. He caressed her hair, running his fingers through the tresses. Her hair was black and glossy and curly and wavy. It was very beautiful.

"Your hair is beautiful," he said. "It does seem a shame."

"And now you—" she jerked away and glared.

"But of course it's your hair and might look better bobbed," he added hastily.

"I wish all the rest of the family were as sensible as you. They're tyrants and they treat me shamefully," said Mildred. "I've been to each in turn and they all *forbid* me to bob my own hair. And Helen said she'd spank me if I did," she added resentfully.

"She's quite capable of it," Steve chuckled.

"You all treat me as if I were a kid," Mildred exclaimed indignantly.

Steve discreetly hid a smile. "What do you want me to do?"

"You could persuade the family to let me," she informed him.

"I could not," he denied flatly.

"How do you know?"

"Because I've already tried it."

She was silent for a few moments and her eyes glittered. Finally she slipped out of her brother's lap and stood up. "My family had better beware," she said ominously. "I am a desperate woman when driven too far." And she turned and climbed the stairs in a dignified manner. Steve watched her in mirthful silence.

"Poor kid," he mused. "It's a shame she can't be in style.'"

Mildred did not reappear until nearly bedtime, when she came downstairs in her little nightie and went to Steve, carefully ignoring the rest of the family. She kissed him drowsily, and sleepily begged to be carried upstairs to bed. Steve objected.

"Please," she murmured, "you're the only one who is kind to me. Please."

Touched by this childish appeal, Steve lifted the slim, girlish form in his arms and carried her to her room. She was asleep when he reached it, so he tucked her into her bed as tenderly as a woman could have done. A moment he stood looking down at her as she lay with one white arm thrown back, a few curls resting on her rosy cheek. Then he kissed her gently and left the room.

If Mildred could have read his thoughts as he went downstairs she would have been shocked, for he was thinking, "What is the little devil up to now?"

The family was discussing Mildred as Steve reentered the drawing room. "The poor child thinks we are treating her shamefully, not letting her bob her hair," Mrs. Allison was saying. "And I hate to refuse her anything, too; she is so pretty and innocent."

"Oh, yes, very," agreed Steve, strolling from the room.

Some minutes later Mildred slid down a rope made of sheets tied together, from her window—into Steve's waiting arms.

Her startled shriek was muffled by his hand, her frantic struggles were promptly overpowered and a familiar voice hissed, "For goodness sake, be still, you little idiot; this isn't an abduction."

"Set me down," she ordered. "How could I know it was you?"

"Where were you going?" he demanded, as he complied with her request.

"None of your business," she answered sulkily.

"Don't get fresh," he reproved. "I suppose you were going to the Van Dorn ball?"

"Yes."

"Nice way for a girl of your age to act. Who were you going with?"

She stamped her little foot with vexation. "Will you lay off the subject of my age?" she cried angrily. "I'm going with Jack."

"You mean you were going with Jack," he corrected.

"How did you know I was going anywhere?" she asked resentfully.

"You're not in the habit of coming downstairs to kiss brother Steve goodnight," he answered. "You wanted an alibi. You wanted the family to know you went to bed. You're a quick worker, all right. I know you didn't have your clothes on under your nightie, but I reckon you had the sheet-ladder already prepared."

She was silent.

"That's a nice way to treat a fellow, isn't it?" his voice held an unaccustomed note of slight resentment. "Making me carry you upstairs and put you to bed so you could get the laugh on me. I feel like turning you over my knee."

"Go ahead," she said listlessly. "I'm never allowed to do things like other girls."

He smiled. "I just did this to let you know you can't put anything over on brother Steve. How were you going to get back in the house? You couldn't climb that ladder."

"I don't know," she confessed.

"You can come in through my room," he offered. "I'll leave the window open. But you stay with Jack and don't you dare let any boy kiss you, and if you're not back by twelve I'll wear out the butter paddle on you. Now run along and have a good time."

At about midnight a small, girlish form clambered through the window of Steve's bedroom.

"Take off your slippers," Steve said softly, "so you won't wake any of the family."

Steve always rose earlier than the rest of the Allison family, and next morning he mused as he dressed, "I guess I better wake Mildred up or she'll sleep late and the family may find out she was out late. I hope the little imp didn't kiss more than a dozen boys."

He went upstairs to Mildred's room. Evidently she was still asleep. He entered her room and stopped, astounded. On the pillow of the bed rested a mass of dark red hair! A quick step took him to the bed. He rubbed his eyes. What magic was this? Under that outlandish hair was his sister's face, but what was such hair doing there?

Just then Mildred opened her eyes and yawned. "Good morning, Steve," she said.

Sudden suspicion fell upon him. He caught a lock of hair and jerked. It came away! A wig! And underneath was Mildred's real hair—bobbed!

"So!" he exclaimed. "That was where you went! But why on earth didn't you get a black wig?"

Mildred was staring wildly at the wig. "Oh, goodness!" she wailed. "It's red!"

"Of course it is, what do you expect?"

"I didn't go to the ball," she said. "I went to the beauty shop and had my hair bobbed and—and I bought that wig."

"But why—"

"It looked black in the electric light," she wailed. "And Mrs. Dupaise said it was black. And it was pretty and wavy like mine! I was going to wear it at home. And now what am I going to do?" she asked piteously.

Steve sat down and laughed. "I don't know," he replied. "You've sure let yourself in for a row."

"And Helen will spank me, too, like she said," wailed Mildred. "But don't you think my hair looks nice?"

"I suppose it does," Steve commented dubiously, "but—"

"But what?"

"But the family may not think so," he added dexterously.

"But what will I do?" she wailed. "The family will delight in this opportunity. And I'll be lectured and scolded and spanked and shaken—I'm going to leave."

"If I had time I could run over to the beauty shop and get another wig, but as it is—"

"It's all your fault," she said resentfully. "If you hadn't let me go, I wouldn't have had my hair bobbed."

"Well, talk about gratitude," he gasped. He eyed the wig a moment and then grinned. "Let me have that wig," he ordered, "and you lock the door from the inside and don't let anyone in until I come back." He picked up the wig and left the room.

Somewhat later he entered, carrying a bundle. Mildred eyed it suspiciously, until he drew forth a wig. It was the same wig, but how different! Now it was a deep black, glossy and curly as before.

"How did you do it?" she wondered.

"My own invention," he answered proudly. "I've been experimenting with dyes in my laboratory and I dyed the wig and dried it, too, by a special process. Be still, now." He placed the wig over her real locks.

"Now you look natural and pretty," he complimented. She had dressed during his absence and now went to the mirror. She gazed dubiously.

"It's damp," she remarked.

"Of course. I couldn't dry it completely."

"It's too black, somehow."

"Well, for goodness sake," he exclaimed somewhat impatiently. "Quit finding fault with that wig and come downstairs. I hear mother calling you."

"All right."

As Steve turned toward the door, certain not-too-distant childhood memories caused her to say, "Steve!"

"Well?"

"While you are in the kitchen, hide the butter paddle, will you?"

Some moments later Mildred came downstairs, looking unusually demure. She breakfasted in silence—another unusual thing for her.

Helen remarked, "Your hair looks damp, Milly. What have you been putting on it?"

"If you won't let me bob my hair, it does look like you would let me put tonics on it without scolding me," Mildred replied reproachfully.

She looked so subdued that Helen felt pity for her and said in a gentle voice, "I'm not scolding you, child."

Mildred merely gave her a reproachful glance and continued her meal in silence. She seemed so quiet and subdued that the whole family wished that they had not scolded her the day before and wished to make amends. All of their approaches Mildred received in subdued silence, only casting reproachful glances that seemed to say, "So, you repent of your tyrannical treatment of me, do you? No matter, I am accustomed to such treatment." Which made the family wince and decide that Mildred was indeed a very badly used girl.

Suddenly Marion gave a gasp. All eyes were centered on her. She was leaning back in her chair, her soft gray eyes staring wildly, her finger pointing—at Mildred's hair!

"For heaven's sake!" exclaimed Mrs. Allison wildly. "What have you been doing to your hair, Mildred?"

Mildred turned pale and raised her hands to her curls. Steve leaned back in his chair and laughed hysterically. Mildred's hair was changing in color with incredible rapidity. It changed before the family's wildly glaring eyes, from black to sandy-color and then to auburn—and it didn't stop there, but changed to red, bright red, flaming red!

"She's on fire!" shrieked Mrs. Allison, snatching wildly at her daughter's hair. She nearly fainted when it came away in her hand. Then for a lone moment utter silence reigned. All eyes were turned toward the shrinking girl who sat in the same attitude, her hands clutching her locks, her cheeks white.

"So!" said Helen deliberately. Then the storm of words rose and descended on the small shoulders of the shrinking culprit. Mildred tried bravely to defend herself but it was futile. All the scoldings she had ever received were nothing to the one she received then. When talk of physical violence began to be cast about, she literally threw up her hands and fled to Steve for protection. She threw herself in his arms and clung to him like a terrified wild thing.

"It's all your fault," she hissed in his ear. "Now you've got to protect me."

Steve laughed and held the slender form close to his. The verbal storm raged about them. Mildred hid her face against his shoulder and refused to speak, trusting to him to defend her from the family's wrath. Which he did.

"But, Steve," Mrs. Allison was almost in tears, "to cut off her beautiful hair that way—"

"And after we had all expressly forbid her, too," Helen was toying with a switch. "Really, Steve, you ought to let us whip her for discipline's sake."

Mildred turned her head to make an angry retort, saw the switch, winced and hid her face again.

"I'm surprized," remarked Steve. "I sure am. You talk about spanking Milly like she was a kid of ten instead of a young lady. Just because she's the youngest of the family is no reason to treat her like a baby. It would be indecent, whipping a girl of her age. And you've scolded the kid enough. So stop it."

"But—" Helen began.

"You hush," Steve ordered. Helen bit her lip and was silent.

"As I said before, it's Milly's hair and she has a right to do with it what she wants to. She won't always be young, so let her have her fun. I took her to the beauty shop myself. So you let the child alone."

It seemed the family was ashamed of itself. It turned and went its way, except Mrs. Allison.

"I suppose you're right, Steve," she said rather wistfully. "But she had such beautiful hair." She gazed for a moment at the slight form in Steve's arms and then smiled and left the room.

Mildred raised her head and looked about. "Are they all gone?" she asked.

Steve laughed. "Yes."

"Thank goodness," she stood erect. "Steve, you're a good sport and I'm going to kiss you." And she did. "But what on earth made that silly old wig change color?"

Steve began to laugh. He laughed and laughed and laughed.

Mildred stood, her hands on her hips, and glared at him.

"Imperfect dyes," he gasped at last. "I dried it too quick. The dyes faded as they dried and made the hair redder than before. Oh, my! The expression on Marion's face when she saw your hair changing! Ha! ha! ha! 'She's on fire!' Haw! haw! And how funny you looked when you saw your wig!"

"Laugh if you want to," she replied haughtily, "but I think your mirth is very provoking. My hand fairly tingles to slap you, Steve."

"You better not," he chuckled. "If it hadn't been for me, you might be tingling somewhere else, just now."

She blushed. "Thank you for protecting me, Steve."

"You are welcome, Mildred."

"*Madge Meraldson*"

(untitled and unfinished)

Madge Meraldson sat her travelling bag on the station platform and glanced about for the buckboard that was to take her out to the Allison ranch.

A cowpuncher approached her, lifting his sombrero. He was a black-haired youth of medium height, lean and wiry of build.

"If yore Miss Meraldson," he said, flushing beneath his tan, "I'm to take yuh and the buckboard, I mean, I got the buckboard—aw." In evident confusion he picked up her travelling bag and led the way to the two-seated hack that stood close to the station, but far enough away to prevent the possible bolting of the wiry, half-wild range ponies that were hitched to it.

He tossed the bag into the back seat, helped the girl in the front, untied the horses, and got in.

"I suppose yuh had supper on the train?" he asked.

She answered that she had, and stole a glance at him. He seemed extremely capable and able to take care of himself, yet he flushed and stammered each time he spoke to her.

"You haven't introduced yourself," she reminded, smiling.

"Me? I'm Billy Buckner. 'Drag,' most folks call me."

"Drag? What does that mean?"

"Oh, nuthin' much," he squirmed. "Just foolishness."

"Where is Steve?" asked the girl.

"Roundin' up some mavericks," he answered.

[. . .]

"The Hades Saloon"

(untitled and unfinished)

The Hades Saloon and gambling hall, Buffalotown, Arizona, was in full swing when two sun-bronzed and dust-covered riders swung down in front of the saloon and strode through the doors.

They had hardly entered when they were recognized. And from the events which followed, it would seem that they did not crave recognition. Red McGaren, gunman of note, walked toward the two, something sinister in his catlike stride, his hands swinging lightly near the heavy guns that hung at either thigh.

He stopped directly in front of the two.

"In from a long ride?" he said in his sneering, menacing voice.

"Maybe," was the noncommittal reply.

"I figure the sheriff might be interested in you two birds," McGaren said cooly, half-crouching, his hands hovering close above his gun-butts, a sinister figure.

Silence fell over the saloon, the gamblers paused, the bartenders made ready for a swift duck behind the bar. Dancing girls and cowboys drew back against the wall. A few hard-looking individuals edged forward.

McGaren spoke, "There's a big reward out for the Sonora Kid and Drag Buckner, and I figure on collectin' it."

McGaren went down, riddled by the bullets of the Sonora Kid, his only shot striking the saloon wall. Then the Kid and Buckner proceeded to shoot up the saloon, which deed speaks for their nerve, for the Hades Saloon was well-named and was the rendezvous for the outcasts and ruffians of three states. The two outlaws escaped in the confusion, leaving behind them a raging mob.

Helen Channon came to the West on the invitation of a ranchgirl friend, and she came with little idea of the country or the people. She had always been skeptical in regard to the stories she had heard of the West.

[. . .]

"A blazing sun"

(untitled and unfinished)

A blazing sun in a blazing sky reflected from a blazing desert. Two horsemen riding slowly over the desert; no other sign of life except a Gila monster basking in the sun. Blazing heat, furious heat, desert heat.

The horses of the two men were tough, wiry cayuses, well adapted for desert travel. The riders were young, boys in fact. They dressed alike in wide-brimmed hats, plain, serviceable clothes, boots and spurs. Except for one thing they were no different from any of the other cowboys that rode the Arizona ranges. Low on the hip of each hung a heavy black Colt in a stiff black leather holster; and one of the youths wore two. Moreover, the end of each holster was tied to the leg of the wearer. The guns were big, single-action Colts and their stocks were polished from much use.

The riders themselves were both of a type: clean-built, wiry youths of medium height with black hair and gray eyes. They might have been mistaken for brothers, but in reality there was little real resemblance between them. The one with the two guns was slightly taller than his companion and of a somewhat slimmer build. His eyes, too, were different, being long and narrow and of a steely glint.

In the features of both could be read determination and courage, with a liberal amount of humor; one could see at a glance that here were two young men who lived clean and thought clean.

He with the two guns shifted in his saddle and gazed ahead at the mountains which flung up their jagged crests against the skyline.

"We'll be there presently," he remarked.

"Oh, yeah," replied his companion. "A few hundred more miles of this—desert and we'll have the privilege of climbin' those confounded mountains. This was a fool idea of yours, Steve."

"The urge of exploration, Buck," explained Steve Allison whimsically. "That everlastingly driveth the weary wayfarer onward to discover new worlds to conquer. The what-do-you-call-it of, well, you know what I mean."

"Oh, yeah!" Buckner answered sarcastically. "Quite so; very clear."

Steve grinned. "You know that yuh want to explore those old pueblos as much as I do."

Billy Buckner merely grunted. Ever since Steve had told him of the lost pueblos up in the mountains of the ________ range, Bill had looked forward eagerly to the rediscovering and exploring of them.

For a while they rode in silence, broken only by the creak of saddles or the clink of a hoof striking a stone.

"I betcha Miguel Gonzales is hidin' out in those mountains," opined Drag. "And furthermore, I betcha he sees us before we see him and ambushes us."

"He can try, if he wants to," Steve answered.

"He's some gun-fanner, for a Mex," mused Buckner. "Those two gamblers he drilled were pretty slick with a gun, themselves."

"They had no business framin' on him to roll him for his money," said Steve. "Cheap crooks, I call 'em."

"Yeah, that's right," agreed Drag.

Less than an hour's ride brought the two to the mountains. The range was wild, steep and rugged. They rode on, going higher and farther into the mountains, until they were forced to dismount and go on foot, after hobbling the horses and leaving them close to a mountain spring where there was water and mountain grass in abundance.

"Just right for Gonzales to grab a horse and make a slick getaway," Drag remarked.

"They wouldn't let a stranger come near them," Steve answered. Which was true, for Steve was always careful to train his horses in certain ways.

After something like an hour's climbing, they came to a ledge overlooking a wide valley. On all sides of the valley, high, steep cliffs stood. The valley seemed a barren waste; the soil was dry and appeared alkaline and was bare except for a scattering of mesquite and sagebrush.

"What's the idea of comin' here?" Buckner asked. "I don't see any place where the pueblos could be."

"The pueblos are in that valley," Steve stated.

"Huh? In that valley? Nix, Steve. There's nothing in that valley."

"Have you explored it?" Steve demanded.

"No."

"Has anybody ever explored it?"

"No, why should they? It's nothing but a desert, nothing growing, no springs, and besides there's no way of getting down into the valley. The cliffs at least a hundred and fifty feet high at this ledge and on the other sides the cliffs are higher. And they are straight up and down."

"Anyway," Steve said, "we're going into that valley."

"But say, Steve," Buckner protested, "we can see most of the valley from the ledge and if there were any pueblos we'd see them."

"They're there, all right," Steve replied imperturbably. "And I'm going into the valley, myself."

Buckner shrugged his shoulders. "All right, let's get started."

Steve chuckled. He turned to a rope that lay on the rocks and picked it up.

"Good hundred feet of hair-rope here," he announced. "That lariat I had you bring along is about forty feet long. Extra long lariat. We'll have to drop about ten feet, maybe not so far."

"I bet we get our hands burned goin' down," remarked Buckner. "And how are we going to get back up the cliff?"

"We can climb up easy, with knots in the rope," Allison replied. He tied the two ropes together carefully and made one end fast to a stunted oak several feet back from the edge of the cliff.

"I'll go first," Steve said, and wrapping the rope loosely about his waist he started down the cliff. The trip was none too easily accomplished, for though Steve was as active as an acrobat or a mountain-cat and the rope was knotted at intervals, at places the cliff bulged outward and the rope, not being fastened at the lower end, had a tendency to swing back and forth. Steve stopped frequently to rest and even then he was tired when he dropped the few feet from the rope to the floor of the valley.

Buckner, who had watched Steve's progress closely, and experienced much relief when he landed, then drew up the rope again. He tied the two rifles and the canteens to the rope and lowered them to Steve, who managed to reach them by standing on a boulder.

Then Buckner started down the rope with Steve bracing himself against the lower end to steady it.

He came down successfully and picked up his rifle and canteen.

"Now show me your pueblos," he demanded.

Steve looked up the cliff swiftly.

"Quick, duck into the sage!" he exclaimed, springing back into the scanty bushes. Buckner did likewise and as they did so the report of a high-powered rifle rang out and a bullet buzzed through the sagebrush close to Steve. Steve's own rifle spoke as he fired at a movement of the bushes at the top of the cliff.

Then the rope came sliding down the cliff.

"*Adios, señors!*" came a mocking voice from the cliff.

"Gonzales, _______ him!" swore Buckner, firing in the direction of the voice.

Allison swore softly. Then he rose cautiously.

"Hey!" exclaimed Buckner. "You boob! You wanta get drilled?"

"Gonzales has gone," Steve answered. He stood erect and walked to the foot of the cliff.

Buckner rose and came forward. Steve picked up the rope.

"He didn't even cut the rope," Steve remarked. "See, he untied it. I'm glad he did. It's a good hair rope."

"I'm glad he didn't cut the rope while I was coming down it," Buckner said.

"And now for the Indian pueblos," said Steve.

[. . .]

"The way it came about"

(untitled and unfinished)

The way it came about that Steve Allison, Timoleon Lycurgus Casanova de Quin and me came to be in the mountains of Thibet, was like this.

Steve and me went up there just for the fun of it and because Steve read where some scientist said that accordin' to his calculations and researches, the missing link was somewhere in the Himalaya Mountains, in Thibet. I didn't take much stock in that; I have seen lots of guys which easy pass for the missing link, but Steve said we'd make up an expedition and invade Thibet.

As for Timmy, which is Timoleon etc., he went along partly because he was studying botany and partly because Steve allowed the trip would make a man of him. Anyhow, Tim is wealthy and stood a lot of the expense.

So we rambled up the Himalayas, through northern India and Nepal and up into Thibet.

No use in describing the whole trip. I'll just start at the place where the guides scooted with most of the luggage and left us sitting on a mountain in central Thibet.

"This," remarked Steve, kicking over a camp chair, he was that peeved, "is some how-de-do. Why should those unmentionable coolies light out and leave us here?"

I'd been wondering about that myself.

"Maybe a hostile tribe of cannibals or somethin' is lurkin' about," I suggested. "Maybe the coolies got wind of it and blew."

"Cannibals? In Thibet?" Steve says. "But it may be something like that." He drew his gun and looked it over careful. Then he picked up his rifle and examined it.

"Anyhow," says he, "here we are, stranded in Thibet, and we gotta find our way out of these mountains, which is all Thibet is, anyway."

He looked all around at the high, snow-covered peaks.

"Some country, Thibet."

It is, too. It isn't all mountains, of course. It's more like a high, wide plateau, with tall peaks here and there. Mostly just desert-land. A bleak, barren country, but we were there in the summer, and it wasn't so bad. Cold enough, though.

Our camp was located on the top of a big, round mountain, as bare as the desert.

Our idea of camping so high up was so we could see anybody if they tried to raid the camp or anything, though Steve says the Thibetans were friendly and peaceable as a rule. He said the same thing, oncet, about some Sioux Indians that later tried to scalp him.

"Lookit here," says Steve, gettin' down on his hands and knees and drawin' a map on the ground with a stick. "Here's Thibet. We ain't far north enough to be anywhere near the Kuenlun or any of those other mountains. Moreover, we ain't nowheres near the borders of East Turkestan because there's not enough mountains and we haven't seen any Taghliks. East and south I know the country better. The way I figure it, we're in the nomad plateau of Thibet, somewhere north of Bogtsang-tsangpo."

"And havin' deducted that," says I, "what are you goin' to do?"

"Well," says he, "we had to have a startin' place, didn't we?"

"Why?" I want to know. "We're here, ain't we? And what does it matter what the name of the place is, so long as we're lost in it?"

"Well, you sap," says Steve, "how'd we know which way to start if we didn't know where we was?"

There's somethin' in that, come to think about it.

Just then we noticed Timoleon Casanova was missin'. He usually was when we was busy.

We looked around and saw him fussing around on the mountain slope with his fool magnifyin' glass and botanist outfit. We yelled at him and he came up to the camp.

"Lycurgus," says Steve plumb stern, "you gotta stick closer to camp and to us. This is a strange country and they is no tellin' what is lurkin' in the offing."

"Ah, yes," says Timoleon, blinking like a mild mannered mud-turtle. "I have been examining a specimen of the genus—" and he went off into a lot of botany names and words and such that maybe Steve understood, but not me.

"Well," says Steve, "try not to roam no further away from camp than you think is your bounden duty." Well knowin' Timoleon would be chasin' off the next minute, like as not. Butterflies was Timoleon's specialty. He knew more about them than Steve Allison did about guns, which is goin' some.

"Oh, yes," says Timoleon, "I nearly forgot. I found this." And he handed Steve what looked like a yellow pebble.

Steve took it and then gave a kind of a snort.

"Drag," says he, "look here!"

I looked. That "pebble" was as big as a goose-egg and it was solid gold!

"Gosh!" says I.

Steve pounced on Timoleon. "Where'd you find this?"

"Why, down the slope there, somewhere. I really do not remember exactly. I stumbled on it while pursuing the genus—"

Me and Steve was breakin' speed records down that mountain.

"Half an' half," says Steve, "or rather thirds."

Well, we searched that slope up and down but we didn't find any more gold.

Finally we sat down and rested.

"Funny about that nugget," I said. "You reckon somebody dropped it?"

"If they did and I can find 'em they'll drop some more," says Steve. "That gold is the real stuff. But there's gold somewhere in Thibet."

And just then we heard a noise and looked around to see ten big tribesmen covering us with rifles. Just like that.

That's the way. When a man gets after gold he can't see, feel or think of anything else. Ordinarily an Indian couldn't sneak up on Steve and me, but we were so busy gold-huntin' we hadn't noticed.

"Shall we put up a fight, Steve?" I asked, not putting my hand on my gun but getting ready to.

"No," said he, "these Thibetans are a peaceful people."

[. . .]

"The hot Arizona sun"

(untitled and unfinished)

The hot Arizona sun had not risen high enough to heat the clear, chill air of the morning. The shadows still lingered among the cliffs and the desert had just begun to shimmer in the sunlight. Along the cliffside a trail ran, skirted on one side by a sheer precipice and on the other by the cliff wall that grew lower and lower as the trail ascended, until at last it emerged upon a kind of high-flung plateau. This was the highest point of the trail; beyond, it dipped down into the lower levels.

Along this trail two horsemen rode. One of the riders was not what you would expect in a scene like this. It was a girl. She was a slim, lithe young thing, her rosy, untanned complexion proving her to be a newcomer, yet she rode with the ease that comes only with much riding and with a grace that proved her to be a Westerner. She possessed a fresh, vivacious beauty such as is seldom met with.

Her companion was a young man of medium size and a light, wiry build. He was dressed in ordinary cowboy outfit: Stetson hat, chaps, boots, and so on; a very commonplace figure except for two things. The first was his eyes; they drew the glance of one as a magnet draws metal. They were long, narrow eyes, of a grey that glinted like steel. Ordinarily they were perfectly inscrutable, but on occasion they blazed like flame or leaped like daggers. The other thing that drew the attention was the fact that, low on each hip, swung a heavy Colt in a black leather holster.

The girl and boy, (for he was little more) showed plainly some marks of kinship. There was a certain resemblance about the nose and the girl, too, had grey eyes, but there the resemblance ceased. There was no likeness between the lean, rather long jaw and thin lips of the youth and the soft, ruby lips and delicately molded, dimpled chin of the girl. Even the eyes differed, for hers were large and soft and gentle. But the main difference was in the hair, for while his was black and straight, hers was a silky, wavy, gold which cast back the beams of the sun most beautifully.

The pair rode up the trail until they were upon the summit of the plateau. There they stopped.

"Well, here you are," said the boy, casting his arm around in a gesture that embraced the whole landscape. "You wanted scenery so here it is; lots of it." The girl drew in her breath and clasped her hands ecstatically. To south and west the desert stretched away until it vanished in the blue haze of the horizon. To the north and the east, crags, cliffs and peaks were piled in magnificent chaos, as if hurled together by the hands of the Titans and then torn apart again in giant play. Man seemed to have no part in that colossal stage, yet the hand of man was there; high up on the cliffs, close under jutting rocks, on high flung crags, were the dwellings of prehistoric man, the Cliff Dwellers. There were the caves and pueblos that were deserted ruins countless ages before ever the man of Genoa dreamed his dream or the first mail-clad Conquistador turned his face to the West.

The boy had seen it all a score of times before, but it was all new and wonderful to the girl.

As she sat her horse, her soft eyes alight with wonder and joy and her silken hair, blown loose and whipping the air in the morning breeze, she made a picture that is but seldom equaled.

"Oh! I love it all!" she cried. "The mountains, the desert, everything! It's so big and grand and I've been shut in by city walls and people so long!"

The boy smiled at her enthusiasm and pointed with his quirt toward where a ribbon of silver wound its way among a scanty fringe of trees.

"The Rio Grande," he said.

"It looks near," she remarked.

"Twenty miles," he answered absently. He was gazing at the river with a faraway look in his gray eyes.

"Looks like a kriss blade," he murmured, half to himself. That was bringing up a train of thought. He forgot the girl at his side. He was hearing again the fanatical shriek, "Ai, hai, Allah il Allah! Allaho akbar!" and was seeing again the fleeing people, and the glittering blade flashing amid the press.

He shrugged his shoulders and turned to the girl. "When you're through admirin' the scenery, Helen," he remarked, "we'll start back for the ranch before it gets hot enough to ruin your complexion."

"I could look all day, and still not see enough," she responded, turning her horse toward the trail.

As they rode down it, there came the clip-clip of horse hoofs. Helen looked toward the turn of the trail and did not notice her companion lean forward in his saddle and drop a hand to a gun. A moment later he drew it away as a rider swept around the bend; a tall, broad-shouldered young man riding a magnificent black stallion. As he passed the two, his bold eyes sought the girl's face and he swept off his sombrero with a courtly gesture. Scarcely realizing what she did, Helen turned in her saddle and watched him until he vanished around a shoulder of the cliff. She was still gazing after him, a pleased smile on her lips, when her brother laid his hand on her shoulder and shook her gently.

"Tut, tut," he chided whimsically. "Is this the kind of manners they taught you in that Eastern college, gazing after strange gentlemen?"

She blushed and answered demurely, "What a splendid horse he was riding."

"Yes, wasn't it?" he asked, mildly sarcastic. "I'll bring him back and introduce you, if you like."

"Who, the horse?"

"No, the man."

"Why, who would think of such a thing!" she exclaimed, half-indignantly. "I do think you're the limit, Steve Allison."

[. . .]

"Steve Allison"

(untitled and unfinished)

Steve Allison settled himself down comfortably in a great armchair in the library of the Allisons' New York home. He drew towards him a massive, leather-bound volume entitled *Early Assyrian Art*, and settled himself for a quiet evening.

Thereafter the body of Steve Allison was sitting in the library in New York, but his mind was wandering among the temples and avenues of ancient Nineveh.

Presently he was aroused by the entrance of his young sister. She came over to where he was sitting, with the intention, apparently, of conversing with him.

With something of an effort, Steve brought himself out of his silent contemplation of the art of the ancient Assyrians, and gazed at the girl before him.

She made quite a pretty picture, he reflected, standing there, with her slim, graceful figure, her lips and cheeks rosy with a natural glow, her dark hair disarranged prettily.

Her skirt was a trifle too short, he decided, her clothing too prone to cling to her soft form; and her hair was not at its best advantage bobbed.

But if his sister wished to be a flapper, and it gave her any pleasure, Steve Allison was not one to stand in her way.

Nay, he took her part against the other members of the household and always shielded her if any of her escapades got her into any trouble.

Steve knew the girl was honest and virtuous and that whatever she did was either the passionate protest of a rebellious spirit against staid convention, or the mere expression of a joyful and jubilant child.

She sat upon the chair-arm and gave a sniff of disapproval.

"Fie on you, Steve," she scolded. "Why must you seclude yourself among old, dusty books, when there's all the great outdoors?"

Steve chuckled. "Your idea of outdoors is the riding park and suburban streets, where the scenery consists of signboards."

"It isn't," she defended, "but even that's outdoors and I can't stand to stay in, especially now in the summer."

"And you shouldn't," he answered promptly. "You are much like some wild bird, anyway; a mockingbird. Develop your body, child, and let your mind develop itself. A girl as pretty as you doesn't need any especial intellectual powers, anyway."

"Why, Steve!" exclaimed the girl, "I think you're just horrid and I'm not going to talk to you."

But when she would have slipped from the chair arm, Steve slipped his arm about her slim waist and held her.

"Don't fly away, little mockingbird," he said and drew her into his lap.

"Let me go," she ordered.

"Not until I wish," he answered, and the girl, seeing that he meant it, leaned her head against his shoulder and rested in his arms, quite contented.

Steve ran his fingers lightly through her soft, dark hair. He smiled as he remembered what a row there had been in the Allison family when Mildred bobbed her hair.

"Steve," Mildred said, "do you know a dark-complexioned woman with black eyes and black hair, oh, much blacker than mine, blacker than yours, even?"

"I couldn't say," Steve answered. "I've met so many people, in my travels. Why do you ask?"

"A woman like that was inquiring for you," Mildred said. "I was riding through the park to meet some friends, when a big limousine rolled up and stopped and a woman called to me from it. I rode back and she asked me if I was Steve Allison's sister and I said yes, and she invited me to take a ride in the limousine, but of course I had no one to leave the horse with. She asked if you were in New York, Steve, and said she was a friend of yours."

"What sort of looking woman was she?" Steve asked.

"She was dark, as I said," replied Mildred, "with very bold, black eyes and she had a way of looking at one with her eyes slanting. She was slender, but had a full, curvy figure and was rather beautiful in a bold way. But there was something rather coarse about her face, in spite of her beauty."

Steve was silent. His face betrayed none of his thoughts.

Mildred drew his arms from about her and sat up very straight upon his knee. "Steve," she said accusingly, "have you been mixed up with that woman somewhere?"

Where other men would have made vehement denial, Steve merely shook his head. That seemed to satisfy the girl.

"Did the woman strike you as being a foreigner?" Steve asked.

"Yes, she did," was the prompt reply. "She had a slight accent, different from any I ever heard before. And she looked foreign. She must have come from the Orient."

"Aye, from the Orient," Steve agreed, absently.

For awhile he sat silent. Then with a shrug of his shoulders he seemed to dismiss the woman from his mind.

As if she were a child, he drew his sister to him and kissed her rosy cheek and lifted her off his lap.

"Run along and play now, like a good little girl," he said, and the girl left the room, casting a rather puzzled glance at her brother, as she went.

Steve sat still for a moment and then rose quickly and with quick, silent strides, paced across the room and back. Then he threw himself into the great armchair and engaged in deep thought for some minutes. As usual, even when alone, Steve Allison's features gave no sign of his thoughts. His face was placid and expressionless, but once his eyes roamed to where two Arab scimitars hung on the wall, their blades crossed, and once his hand wandered to his left armpit.

Then he rose and, stepping across the room, scrutinized a large map that hung there. His eyes wandered across it and rested on Asia. Then his gaze centered on a dot in Turkestan, which was marked, "Yarkand."

Steve turned away from the map and paced the room for a few seconds. Then he turned swiftly toward the door and as he turned, from the large window thrown wide open for the hot summer night, a thing came singing through the air, a thing that flashed in the light, and thudded into the opposite wall.

Steve crouched back against the wall, a heavy pistol appearing in his hand, as if by magic.

The light button was close to his hand. With a swift motion he pressed it and stood motionless in the dark, his pistol poised, his thumb pressing down the hammer.

For some moments he stood so, then he switched the light on again, springing aside as he did so. The room was as empty as it had been before. Outside there was no sound except the passing of vehicles and the roar of the traffic in the business part of New York.

Alert and ready, Steve walked deliberately across the room. Nothing occurred. Then with a feeling of relief he turned his attention to the missile that had come through the window.

It was a knife of odd shape, driven inches into the wood. He drew it out and examined it. Hilt, blade and guard, were made of one piece of iron. The blade was long, slightly curved and furnished with double edges of fine steel. The haft and hilt were strangely and skillfully inlaid with gold.

He turned the knife idly in his hand and then seemed to come to a swift decision. Stepping to the telephone on a nearby table, he called a certain number and presently heard a familiar voice.

"Listen, Buck," he said rapidly, "don't ask questions."

He went on, speaking in a low tone and in the Pima Indian dialect. "Buck, meet me at Delmonico's as soon as you can get there."

"Sure," the other replied in the same language.

Steve hung up the receiver and turned toward the door, slipping the knife inside his shirt.

Presently, in an expensive limousine, he was speeding toward the famous cabaret in New York.

[. . .]

Brotherly Advice

(unfinished)

Piretto's Place was in full swing. A Greenwich combination cabaret and gambling house run on the style of _______________, Piretto's Place was a new sensation and the "fast livers" flocked there.

The dancing floor was crowded with couples doing the latest and frankest steps; the orchestra blared jazz music. Wine flowed freely, in contemptuous defiance of the Volstead Act.

But in the gambling room above, the excitement was greater, for a party of the "highbrows," dapper young men in dress suits and women in furs and jewels, were gathering around the roulette wheels and faro and poker tables and were squandering money in a way that made even the expressionless gamblers gasp.

At a certain table sat four young men, engaged in a game of poker. One of them was a quiet, rather pale-faced young man, a professional gambler, hired by the establishment. Two of the other three were of the type so common on Broadway, well-dressed, blasé young men, elegant and affected.

It was the fourth man that attracted attention. He seemed somewhat out of place there, yet he was perfectly at ease. His features were clean cut and rather lean, his eyes narrow and gray, his hair black.

There was nothing in common between him and the young men who patronized Piretto's. There was a certain something about him, undefinable, yet suggesting the gamblers of the place more than anyone else.

He was the youngest at the table, little more than a boy, yet the poker chips and money were stacked high in front of him. He accorded the gambler a certain amount of respect, but there seemed to be an amused sneer beneath his courteous manner toward the other two, even as he won their money.

Steve Allison had little liking for the young "highbrows" although at present he was accepted as one of their set.

Occasionally he cast a glance toward a roulette table, his eyes resting on a slim, black-haired little beauty, who was throwing money away by the handfuls. He shrugged his shoulders and set himself to win a sum equivalent to the amount she lost, which was not so difficult as it seems, for Steve had been a professional gambler himself, though his friends did not know that.

The girl was certainly enjoying herself and it was also certain that she was intoxicated by excitement and pleasure—and perhaps by a little champagne, likewise.

It was evident that she was a newcomer into the "fast set." Her cheeks were flushed, her laugh rang clear above the other noise of the gambling room. She was perfectly reckless; she lost money, laughed with pure enjoyment, tossed back her unruly curls and doubled her bet, again and again.

The young women watched her with a certain amount of fascination, and a certain amount of jealousy; the young men clustered about her, applauding her with the most frank admiration, some of them casting glances at her that made Steve curse beneath his breath.

By listening closely he could hear what was said, and he shamelessly proceeded to eavesdrop.

"Come," one of the young men coaxed, "just one spin of the roulette wheel for a wager."

"I'm broke," she laughed. "I'll have to get some money from Steve first."

"But I don't want you to wager money," he answered. "Don't interrupt Steve; he's winning."

"What, then?" she inquired.

"A hundred dollars against a kiss," he answered.

"All right!" she laughed. "Fair enough."

Without a word, Steve laid down his cards and rose. He was no prude; he wanted the girl to have a good time, but he had old-fashioned ideas about kissing and he did not care for his sister to cheapen herself by throwing kisses away. Especially to the man who made the wager. Steve knew him and felt that his very glance soiled the woman he looked on.

The patrons of the place flocked around the roulette table. Such bets were common enough, but it was the first time Mildred Allison had made such a one, and she was the "find" of the season.

"Prepare to be kissed, Milly!" laughed one of the women. "Kurt always gets what he wants."

Kurt Vanner smiled and bowed in acknowledgment of the compliment.

Just then Steve stepped up to the table and swept up the money Vanner had laid down. He placed it in the astonished man's hand.

"Bet's off," he announced.

"Why, what—" Kurt stammered, then flushed. "What do you mean by this?"

Steve stepped forward and gazed into Vanner's face.

"Do you want to argue the question with me?" he asked softly.

Vanner was larger, taller and heavier, than young Allison, but he had no desire to try conclusions with him.

Steve's slim form was deceptive, as Vanner knew, for he had seen him fight the New York light-weight champion to a bloody draw. A panther, that was what Vanner thought of when he looked at Steve Allison.

Kurt stepped back, bowing politely, with an apology that was intended to contrast his manners with Allison's and put the youth in an unfavorable light.

Steve ignored him and turned to his sister.

"Time to go home, Mildred."

Mildred didn't want to go home and she was angry at Steve; but his eyes were glinting and she knew that it wasn't well to argue with her brother when he had such an expression.

She rose and made apologies to the party; Steve escorted her to the street and hailed a taxi.

Mildred's indignation found vent in words, then. She was furious at Steve for breaking up her party. She scolded him and declared her intention of going back to the dancehall.

"You're a perfect tyrant," she declared, stamping her little foot. "I won't go home. I won't, I tell you."

However, she was mistaken. Steve, who could manhandle three men, was not to be resisted by a young girl who stood exactly five feet high and lacked several pounds of weighing a hundred pounds.

The taxi drew up to the curb just then and Steve picked his sister up and deposited her inside.

He gave the driver a certain number and stepped in also.

"Don't act like a baby, Milly," he admonished.

The girl overcame a desire to slap him. She sat in dignified silence until they reached their destination, a rather palatial residence on Riverside Drive.

"Everybody's gone to bed, I reckon," Steve remarked as he let them in at a side door.

"They are not," Mildred answered. "Madge is at a ball. She don't have any silly old brother to drag her away from everything," she added pointedly.

"Well, her brother ought to," Steve retorted.

Mildred's indignation at Steve had been increasing all the way home and now as they mounted the stairs to the floor where they each had a room, she became reckless in a desire to shock him.

"Anyone would think I was awfully bad, the way you haul me around," she began.

"Well, I don't want you kissing Kurt Vanner," he answered, "or anyone else."

"You're a tyrant."

"I'm not. But you don't know what kind of a man he is—and I do."

"Oh, you do?" sarcastically. "I suppose he's a villain."

"He is," was the imperturbable reply. "Also a cradle robber. That's why he selected you."

Mildred winced. Her age was a source of great dissatisfaction to her. She was the youngest of five and this gave the others a right to "boss" her around and "make her mind," or so it seemed to her.

Steve's remark served to make her angrier and more reckless.

"He's a gentleman and you're not," she retorted.

"I never pretended to be," was his unruffled reply.

They had entered a large drawing room, elegantly furnished and brightly lighted. Steve noted his sister's flushed cheeks.

He caught her by the shoulders, drew her close to him and sniffed her breath.

"Hades!" he said disgustedly. "Half-drunk, too."

"I'm not!" she protested indignantly, struggling to free herself. "I had only two glasses of champagne."

"One's enough for a kid like you," he answered.

"You needn't be so prudish," she retorted. "I'm just naturally bad."

He laughed. "You? A wild woman? You're nothing but a baby playing make-believe."

"Oh, I am, am I?" she said deliberately, exasperated beyond caution. "What about that bet I had with Jack Doorn?"

"What was that?" he asked.

"On a horse-race. He bet two hundred dollars against my stocking." Steve was eyeing her in a way she did not like, but she plunged on recklessly. "If he won he was to take off the stocking himself."

"You little devil!"

Steve's hair rose. He snatched his sister with one hand and a light riding whip with the other.

"I won!" Mildred fairly shrieked, striving desperately to wriggle off Steve's knee.

He hesitated, then deposited her on the floor, somewhat shaken and slightly pale. All desire to shock Steve had vanished. She had succeeded more than she wished. She didn't believe Steve would really have whipped her but still—

He was still toying with the whip.

"You stop making bets like that," he ordered.

"And what if I don't?" she retorted defiantly, getting back some of her courage.

"Then I'll give you a good whipping and send you back home," he responded promptly.

"You wouldn't dare!"

"Why wouldn't I?"

"You haven't any right to whip me."

"I haven't any legal right," he answered grimly, "but I've got the right of the stronger. Might's not right, but you disobey me and see what happens!"

"You have said you never could strike a woman," she accused.

"I wouldn't be striking a woman," he retorted. "I'd be spanking a naughty child."

"Oh, you—" words failed her in her exasperation.

"I don't want to seem like a tyrant, Milly," he continued in a milder voice, "and I want you to have a good time. But I can't let you cheapen yourself and have your name bandied about over wine cups. You don't know anything about the men you make these foolish bets with and the best men are not to be trusted with an innocent young girl. So you do as I say."

This advice was lost on Mildred who was furious at her brother for his self-imposed authority and she was humiliated in the extreme at the thought of having to submit to being spanked.

Her answer was prompt and unexpected. She slapped him soundly and fled to her room.

Desert Rendezvous

(unfinished)

The Allison family, at least the feminine part, were touring Egypt. The younger son of the family, Steve, who was the only man of the family with them, had left them at Alexandria with the avowed intention of seeing Khartoum. The family's leisurely progress was too slow for him.

Steve was to meet them in a certain time at Assuan.

Some weeks had elapsed since they had left Alexandria when Steve, leaner and tanned darkly by the African sun, rode into Assuan.

The first member of the family he met was his sister Marion.

That gentle person submitted to being kissed and immediately afterwards gave him some news that jolted him out of his habitual calm.

"You wouldn't think Helen was very romantic, would you?" was how she began the news. "But do you know what she has done?"

"What has she done?"

"Well, we met a very handsome man in Cairo; he was part Arab and part French, with some Spanish blood in him, I think, and he's some kind of a prince. He is a very gallant, handsome man, and all the women just flock after him and he's very wealthy, too. And what do you know! Helen fell in love with him! What did you say?"

"Go on," replied Steve between his teeth.

"He spent a lot of his time with her and he's in love with her, too. So yesterday, when I saw Helen talking to two Arabs through her window, she told me that they were the prince's men and that they had come to guide her to an oasis in the desert where he is. They had it all arranged in Cairo! She said he wanted it kept secret until after the marriage, and I promised not to tell, but I know she wouldn't care for you knowing. I wanted to go with her, but she wouldn't let me. So she rode off with the Arabs secretly this morning. Isn't that romantic?"

Steve laughed harshly. "What is this gentleman's name?"

"He is a gentleman," she answered. "If it were anyone else I wouldn't like the idea of Helen riding off to meet him, but he loves her wildly and is a perfect gentleman besides. His name is Sir Ahmed Narrudi. He's a lord."

"Ahmed Narrudi!" Steve turned toward the door.

"Where are you going, Steve?" she asked, surprized.

"After that little fool of a sister," he answered.

She sprang up, startled. "Do you mean—oh, you don't mean that—that Sir Ahmed isn't a good man?"

She was standing, a sudden fear in her eyes.

He laughed, gratingly. "If I am not back in a week you may notify the consul and the government," he answered. "Otherwise say nothing about this to anyone."

- - - - - - - - - -

Helen sat in the shelter of her tent and gazed dreamily out across the desert. The two Arabs were nowhere to be seen. They had taken the camels off to a wadi somewhere. She was alone.

Ahmed had not been there to meet her, but he would soon come and with him would come a priest or a minister. Soon she would be in his arms! She thrilled at the thought. He was an ardent lover, perhaps too ardent. Sometimes she had had difficulty in preventing herself being swept away by the tide of his passions.

He was different from Western suitors. His touch thrilled her. His avowals of love thrilled her. Yet, in spite of his Arab name, there could not be much Arab blood in him. He was too handsome. Then, too, she felt no racial aversion toward him, as surely would have been the case had he been an Arab. For she was a Southern girl and keenly racial-conscious.

She wondered what her people would say to her marriage.

Then she started up. Someone was riding at full speed across the desert. Was it Ahmed? It would be like him to come in that manner.

She shaded her eyes. No, it could not be Narrudi. The rider was coming from the direction she had come, following her trail it seemed, and Ahmed would come from the direction of Siut. Then, the rider was alone and was not large enough for Ahmed.

It was—surely it couldn't be! Yes, it was her brother Steve!

Steve it was who had ridden hard and fast, covering in a day and night what had taken Helen and her escort two days and a night, travelling in easy stages.

He had found out by inquiry what direction she had taken and then had ridden for the oasis, which he knew was her destination, there being no other within two hundred miles.

Born and raised on another desert, Steve Allison, known on the Mexican Border as the "Sonora Kid," found no difficulty in travelling and in marshalling the strength of his mount, a swift footed Bishareen camel.

As he rode he studied the problem of persuading his sister to return with him. That she would not go willingly he was sure and he shrank from the thought of using force with her. His natural chivalry was coupled with a respect and a slight amount of awe for his sister, who was a year older than he. Yet this feeling was not caused by the difference in age.

As he came in sight of the tent he saw that Helen was alone. So Ahmed had not arrived. He felt a mixture of relief and disappointment, relief because of the fact that Ahmed had not harmed Helen and disappointment because the Arab was not there for him to kill. For Allison was in a killing-rage about Narrudi. A dirty Arab trying to run off with a white girl! It had been done before.

Helen smiled as Steve rode up and dismounted. She was fond of Steve, but she was not afraid of him. Quite the contrary. In the few conflicts they had had, she had always come out victor.

She was aware of his awe of her and, woman-like, always took advantage of it. He would beg her to go back with him. She would laugh and invite him to stay to the wedding. She did not even consider the possibility that he might try to compel her to return.

"Hello, Steve," she greeted, as he strode up. "How did you find Khartoum?"

She was really majestic. She was only of medium height, and slender, but there was something queenly about her. She was the prettiest of the Allison girls, a real beauty, with wavy golden hair and large, dark-violet eyes.

"Helen," Steve began abruptly, "you can't intend to marry this Arab?"

"He isn't an Arab," she replied airily. "He took his mother's name. He's more French than anything."

"Will you answer my question?"

His tone annoyed her. "Yes, I will. I am going to marry him."

He laughed gratingly. "You little idiot, do you think he'll bring a priest with him? He's done this trick before."

The color rushed to her cheeks and she turned coldly away. He caught her hand.

"Wait!" he pleaded. "Helen, for heaven's sake, think what you are doing!"

"Let go my hand, please," was all she said.

He released her instantly.

"Helen, please go back with me," he begged.

She smiled. "You must stay to the wedding, Steve."

He felt helpless as he looked at her and the feeling put him in an ugly mood.

"I haven't time to argue with you, Helen," he warned. "You had better do as I say. I don't want to use violence, but you've got to go back with me."

"Violence!" she laughed scornfully; his slim, lithe form, except for the shoulders not much stronger built in proportion than hers, deceived her as it had deceived many men. She had never seen her brother exhibit his strength.

"Violence! You can't make me go. I think I am nearly as strong as you."

She was much mistaken. Steve's gray eyes glittered suddenly.

He stepped forward and caught her in his arms. She tried to resist and he swung her up against him, crushing her to him. She cried out in pain and fright. His arms felt like iron bands around her. She had never felt such strength. Resistance was perfectly futile. The world reeled before her terrified gaze. He was crushing her.

She writhed in his grasp. "Steve!" she screamed, "you're killing me!"

He made no answer. "Have mercy!" she gasped. "Oh, please, please! I'll—obey—you! Please put me down!"

Instantly the arms relaxed and she slipped to the ground. She felt terribly weak; her limbs would not support her. She sank to the sands and lay in a pitiful heap, sobbing from fright and weakness.

Steve bent over her and she shrank away, her arm raised as if to guard off a blow. Steve winced; his face was pale and he was sweating. He had never handled a girl so roughly in his life.

"Will you go back with me?" he asked, hating himself.

"Yes, yes!" she sobbed. "I'll do anything you want me to. Please don't hurt me, Steve."

He gathered her tenderly in his arms, kissed her, smoothed back her hair and arranged her dress.

"I hate to hurt or frighten you, child," he said, repentantly, "but I'd kill you before I'd leave you to that Arab. Now run along and put on your riding-suit, while I go get the camels."

For a moment he held her in his arms, gazing into her tear-wet eyes, then he set her down inside the tent and strode away across the desert.

She watched him. Her eyes widened with fear as she saw the two Arabs coming across the desert. They were coming swiftly, carrying long jezail rifles. Steve was advancing slowly toward them. Now one of the Arabs threw his gun to his shoulder and fired. Steve continued to advance. Now they were within pistol range and Steve stopped. The Arabs were firing wildly. Steve's hand flew to his hip. Two revolver reports rang out above the crackling of the rifle fire. One of the Arabs threw his hands high above his head and pitched forward. The other staggered, fired again, then as Steve's revolver spoke again, spun around and fell.

Helen leaned against the tent pole, white and weak. But she had seen men slain before, on the Border, and she did not faint.

Slowly she changed her costume, gazing wistfully at the pretty dress. She had put it on, hoping to please Ahmed.

She arranged her things for travel and had hardly finished when Steve returned.

He had selected the swiftest camel, the one she had ridden, and divided the load between it and his Bishareen.

While he was working with the loading of the camels, the girl noticed that his shirt on the right shoulder was wet with blood.

"Steve!" she cried, frightened. "You're hurt."

"A mere scratch," he answered. "A jezail bullet cut the skin. Those Arabs are very poor marksmen."

However, she insisted on binding his shoulder up. It was, as he had said, a mere scratch.

When he finished loading he made the camels kneel and turned to Helen.

She gazed at him wistfully.

"Are you going to take me to Assuan," she asked.

"Yes."

Suddenly she dropped to her knees before him. "Steve, please—" she began.

"Helen!" he exclaimed in a horrified voice, lifting her to her feet. She threw both arms about his neck and clung to him, gazing beseechingly into his face.

"Steve, please let me stay," she pleaded piteously. "Please!"

She used all the arts of a woman begging a favor. She kissed him. She clung to him, begging not to be taken away.

Steve only held her in his arms, his face white and haggard. Finally he lifted the weeping girl and placed her on her camel.

He spoke no word, but did all he could to make her comfortable.

[. . .]

The West Tower

(unfinished)

Helen Tranton was pleased and surprized, when, glancing across the lobby of a certain large hotel, she observed two figures whom she recognized.

"Steve Allison and Billy Buckner!" she exclaimed. "Who would have thought of seeing them in Berlin!"

"Ah, friends of yours, perhaps?" asked her companion, a blond young man with an upcurving mustache.

"Of course." She started across the lobby and her companion, raising his blond eyebrows slightly, followed.

"Steve! Billy!" The two young men turned quickly. In fact, they turned with a quickness that was surprizing, and their hands darted toward their coats, then fell away as they saw the girl.

"Miss Helen Tranton!" exclaimed Allison, taking the hand she offered him.

"This is indeed a pleasure," said Buckner, flushing to his hair.

"I'm certainly glad to see you," Helen said, introducing her companion, one Captain Ludvig von Schlieder. The captain placed a monocle to his eye and gazed at the two Americans almost superciliously.

"What are you doing in Germany?" asked Helen. "I thought you were going to Mexico."

"We did go to Mexico," answered Allison, "but the climate was too warm to suit us. We came to the land of the Mailed Fist as collectors."

"Collectors?" Helen asked. "Collectors of what?"

"Jewels, mostly," Allison replied. "We're working for a corporation that pays our expenses and gives us a rake-off on the jewels."

"That's nice," declared Helen. "I'd like to see more of you. You're staying in this hotel?"

Allison assented. "I suppose you're here for pleasure?"

"Yes," she laughed, "that's my only reason. I suppose I'm like a butterfly, always flitting from place to place and living for pleasure alone. I'm going to a big house-party soon, and I wish I could give you an invitation."

"Speaking for my friend, Erich Steindorf," spoke the captain, "I take the liberty of inviting you to the house party, mein herrein."

"Oh, that's so nice of you," exclaimed Helen.

"Any friend of Fraulein Tranton is welcome," answered the captain, bowing.

"You must come," said the girl. "We are going to have the house party in an old castle in the Black Forest. Think how thrilling and romantic."

"Certainly," answered Allison. "We'll be clean delighted."

Later on, up in their suite, Buckner looked at Allison with a disapproving eye.

"What's the game, Steve?" he asked. "You got a nerve, talkin' about collectin' jewels and acceptin' bids to house parties. Castle in the Black Forest, huh! We ain't done any scoutin' in Berlin, yet."

Steve Allison sat down and chuckled. "I didn't want to lie to Miss Helen about why we're in Germany. We are collecting jewels, aren't we?"

"Well," said Buckner, "yuh don't need to advertize it. I'm skittish enough, as it is. When Miss Helen yelled at us, I was as sure as —— that Moriarty had us by the collar. Why do you suppose the lager-swigger with the monocle invited us to the house party?"

"Well," answered Steve, "ginks that collect jewels, in the regular way, I mean, are very likely to carry a good deal of coin. When a duke or something sells his sparklers, he usually wants the cash, right there. Did you notice Captain Sckudlefuze's fingers? Long and slim and handy. Never did any work with them, you bet. A gambler, if I ever saw one."

Buckner nodded. Steve Allison, too, had hands of such a type.

"Captain Schooblebooze's idea is to get us into a friendly game and lift all our coin. All right, let him. But I had another idea in accepting. Miss Helen is a nice American girl and I know these lager-swiggers. Anyway, it's a good chance to see if there's anything worth collecting in the castle. We'll have plenty of time for Berlin."

"You was to a house party in England once, wasn't you, as a private detective?" asked Buckner.

A slight expression of distaste crossed Steve's face.

"Yes, I was," he replied. "I came as a private detective and found my sister Marion there, as a guest. One of the men was murdered in his room. I killed the thing that killed him. It was a —— big snake. A python. It had got away from a circus and denned up in a dungeon under the castle."

Buckner rose, walked over to a large window and stood looking out upon the busy streets of Berlin. An officer was swaggering down the street, the civilians scrambling to get out of his way.

"Steve," said Buckner, "there's a representative of a bigger snake than that python, the Prussian army. Some day it'll try to throw its coils around the world."

"Probably," answered Allison. "When it does it'll get cut in a great many pieces. Let's wander down the street and admire the goose-steppers."

The house party accepted the two Americans cordially enough, but to Steve it seemed that there was a rather thinly veiled contempt in the manner of some of them.

There was rather a large party, young men and women of the wealthy and noble houses, a few Britishers and a Russian. Helen Tranton was the only other American.

It was a huge, grim old castle, set amongst great old trees that flung out long, thick branches. It was on level ground; the forest surrounded it and ran close to the high wall that circled the whole castle. Around the wall ran a moat, long unused, but which had been cleared out and was used for a swimming pool. There was a drawbridge and great, iron-clad doors, as there had been in the Middle Ages.

The guests were delighted. The host, Erich Steindorf, was a tall, strongly built young man, with very blond hair and a very blond mustache, curving up in the Prussian officer style. He had a bluff, forceful way which passed for frank good nature. He was wealthy and popular in Berlin society, where, if there was money and forceful character to back it, arrogance and conceit were no objections.

The castle had been remodeled to suit modern tastes. The great hall, where the medieval lords of the castle had feasted and caroused, had been left unchanged except for various modern appliances. The rooms of the castle had been made into smoking rooms, cardrooms, breakfast rooms, bedchambers for the guests, and so on. The architectural lines of the old castle remained unchanged, for the most part. There were still the long corridors, the winding stairs, the towers at each corner of the castle, the dungeons beneath the castle.

"Select your rooms!" shouted Steindorf, flinging out his arms in a grandiloquent manner. "There are plenty of them. Go through the castle and choose your own rooms."

The guests scattered through the rooms and corridors, laughing, shouting and skylarking.

Helen Tranton, finding herself separated for a moment from the rest of the party, felt a slight touch on her arm and turned to see Billy Buckner.

"We've got the upper room of the east tower," he said in a low voice. "You take one near us." Then he was gone, leaving Helen somewhat puzzled.

Presently the guests, having selected their rooms, assembled again in the great hall. A luncheon was served, consisting largely of liquid refreshments, then a game of hide-and-seek was proposed, the great castle with so many nooks and alcoves naturally suggesting it.

The rooms and corridors were filled with merry shouts and laughter, the girls and young men scampering in all directions, hunting and searching and springing out suddenly from some recess to startle each other.

"For the love of mud!" commented Buckner. "Would yuh have thought grownups would cut up so?"

"Get into the game, yuh sap," Allison urged. "Listen," he whispered. Steve was a man who saw opportunities. Buckner joined the merrymakers.

Helen, seeking some good hiding place, opened a door and found herself in a large room that evidently had been left untouched when the workmen had remodeled the castle. Dust lay thick on the floors and, except for a few broken chairs, there was no furniture. There was another door in the opposite wall. She opened it and saw a flight of winding stairs leading up. To one of the towers, she supposed. The dust lay thick upon the stairs as upon the floor of the room. It was dark upon the stairs and she decided that she did not care for it as a hiding place. She shut the door and, turning, crossed the room to the door that opened into the corridor. As she did, she felt an uncanny feeling that someone or something was watching her, through the door of the stairway. Some of the guests, hiding there, she thought. She returned to the door, and called through it. There was no answer. She was about to open the door when a sudden and unaccountable panic assailed her. She turned and fled across the room, and did not stop until she was in the corridor. Then she laughed shamefacedly.

"I'm silly," she thought. "The silence and antiquity of this old castle must be getting on my nerves. I'm glad no one saw me act like a goose."

The guests tired of hide-and-seek and trooped down into the great hall, laughing and telling of their adventures.

Erich was called on to tell the history of the castle, which he did.

"It was originally the home of the Steindorfs," said he. "A long line of barons held it, who were virtually kings of the Black Forest. Their power was absolute and no one questioned them nor opposed them, unless they were very powerful. Some sixty years ago, however, the Steindorfs took up another castle on the Rhine. We retained this old castle, but no one occupied it and it was allowed to fall into disuse. Lately, however, I conceived the idea of making it into a pleasure castle."

He related tale after tale of the old barons who had ruled their domains with a hand of iron. Some of the tales were hardly the thing for ladies' ears, but Steindorf related them with a brutal directness that made nothing of modesty.

"Surely there must be ghosts!" exclaimed one of the guests, a vivacious young Englishwoman, Miss Elinor Winniston. "Such a grim old castle with such a bloody history certainly ought to be haunted."

"I certainly thought it was haunted," said Helen, and she related her adventure in the room of the winding stair.

"That is the stair that leads to the west tower," said Erich. "That tower is deserted and is reputed to be haunted."

"How delightful!" cried some of the guests. "Tell us about it."

"In the early part of the Fifteenth Century," said Erich, "the castle was held by a baron, Sir Otho Steindorf, a man noted for his great strength and dominance. One of his peculiarities was the hair which grew all over his body and limbs; in fact, he must have somewhat resembled an ape in that respect. He was a man who would own no power higher than his own. His soldiers and the other barons feared him, and as for his tenants, they scarcely dared to speak without his permission. There was among his tenants a handsome young maid whom he had his eye upon. He sent his soldiers to bring her before him, but she had fled with a young henchman of his. The couple were captured before they had gone far, and brought before him. What followed took place in the west tower. Otho killed the young man with his own hand and offered the girl her freedom, in return for a certain thing. The girl refused and Otho took by force what she would not give willingly. Then, infuriated by her opposing him, he hurled her from the tower. The next morning the henchmen found the baron Otho sprawled on the floor of the upper room of the west tower, a score of dagger wounds in his hairy breast, his bearded head severed from his shoulders. Who murdered him and how the murderer escaped from the castle, they did not know. Nor did they ever know, but at night it seemed to them that there was a rustling and a sound in the west tower as of a fiendish struggle. A knight who tried to spend a night in the room, leaped screaming from the window, and finally the west tower was closed and a great lock put upon the door. To this day the old legends persist, and one of my servants resigned and left the castle, swearing that a long, hairy arm clutched at him from a dark recess close to the west tower. I tried to get into the tower, but it would have required a charge of dynamite to shatter the great lock, and the hinges of the door are doubtless so rusted that the whole door would have to be demolished. As it is of the hardest material and nearly a foot thick, braced with iron, it would be no easy task. The west tower differs from the others in that it has but one door, that opening into the upper room. The lower room is evidently connected with the upper by a trapdoor and a flight of stairs. Some grim crimes must have been committed there."

"There must have been more murders?" asked one of the girls, eager for horrifying details.

"There were the usual numbers of medieval murders and assassinations," answered Erich, "but most of the crimes were of another sort. The old castle has heard more shrieks of girls than screams of murdered men. My ancestors," he went on, with a meaningful smile, "were ladies-men of a forceful sort. Their methods of courtship were effective, though sometimes rather violent. The women often objected, but it was seldom that they successfully opposed their passionate wooers. When one of the barons looked with favor upon a maiden, her willingness made little difference."

"Caveman stuff," laughed one of the young women.

"Rather rough on the girls, eh?" one of the Englishmen remarked.

"Oh, perhaps," Erich answered. "However, they belonged to their overlord, soul and body, hand and limb. What he chose to do with them was his affair."

"Strong, virile dominant males," said Helen Tranton. "I can't say that I admire the type."

"Yes, you would," laughed Erich. "All young women secretly wish for some man who would carry them off by force and rule them with a hand of iron. That is a girl's nature. They adore a strong, masterful man."

"I've met several of that type," remarked Steve Allison. "There was one, a big, domineering giant of a man, a Boer I met in Rhodesia. After playing the caveman with every black woman he met, he tried the same thing with a young British girl. We disagreed and I left Rhodesia."

"And the Boer?" asked one of the Britishers.

"He's there yet," Steve answered. "If the jackals left anything of him."

One of the British girls said, "Oh!" in a rather shocked voice.

"I take it that is your opinion of that type of men?" Erich asked, rather disagreeably.

Allison shrugged his shoulders.

"Perhaps some of us would find a game of cards agreeable?" broke in Captain von Schlieder. The suggestion was met with approval. Several of the guests went to the cardroom and several games were started.

"Perhaps Herr Allison would prefer American poker?" suggested the captain. "There are some of us who play it."

"Well, I'm partial to poker," Steve admitted. Six of them made up a game: Allison; the captain; the Russian, Zuranoff; two of the Englishmen; and a burly German, von Seigal.

The stakes were not large, and Allison was careful not to play anything but an ordinarily good game.

When he went up to his room in the east tower, Buckner was seated, gazing out over the forest.

Steve sat down and poured himself a glass of champagne.

"I managed to glance through all the rooms," said he, "and I looked into some of the alcoves and such. If Steindorf keeps any jewels or any large amount of money here, it's well hidden. Do you see any place where such stuff might be concealed?"

Buckner shook his head. "I didn't look very closely," he answered. "I went up a winding stair into an upper corridor. Hand me a glass of champagne."

Steve did so, also pouring out another glass of wine for himself.

"I went up into the upper corridor," Buckner continued, "where a lot of the guest rooms are. There were quite a few guests there, skylarking. I came onto another winding stair and went up it and came out into a big room. The room looked like it hadn't been used for a good many years, all dusty. There wasn't anything in it but a few suits of armor, like the knights wore in the medieval ages. The room looked out over the castle yard and there were several windows, pretty good sized, that had iron bars in them. I heard somebody coming up the corridor and I slipped into one of the nooks in the wall. There's lots of them in the castle, small spaces set back in the walls, for the baron to spy on his subjects, I reckon.

"I stepped into the nook and Erich Steindorf and that British girl, Dalia Sinclair, came in.

"Erich was talkin' to her right ardent. He picked up some armor and said, 'When men wore these, they were men indeed. They took what they wished and did not wait on a girl's whim.'

"Dalia laughed and said something I didn't hear.

"Erich said, 'Why should you resist me? I am a man and I am wealthy. What more do you want? Is it some other man? Am I not more of a superman than those simpering fools who are your countrymen? Or those American fools? Faugh! Some day Germany will arise in her might and crush the world. Then no one will oppose a German. The old barons, my ancestors, brooked no opposition and neither will I.'

"'Don't be silly,' said Dalia. They turned and walked toward the door. When they reached it, he stopped and wouldn't let her pass.

"'An old German custom, my dear,' said he. 'A kiss and I will let you through.'

"'Oh, a tollgate, eh?' she laughed. 'Very well, I suppose you are intent upon it.' She held up her pretty, rosy lips and he kissed her, several times.

"'A German custom modified to suit the modesty of the modern girl,' Erich said as they went out the door. 'I will tell you what the custom was in the early ages.'

"I heard her laugh as they went down the corridor."

Buckner paused and poured another glass of champagne.

"What then?" asked Allison.

"I wandered around amongst the upper corridors for awhile, but there isn't much there. It's mostly big rooms, bare and dusty. Erich evidently didn't do much remodeling on them. There's a cardroom or two, and two or three rooms that might do for a ladies' boudoir. I suspect that Erich has entertained feminine visitors before now."

"Sure. That was why he remodeled the castle," answered Allison. "In Berlin it's quite the fad to take old castles and make them into pleasure resorts. A lot of wealthy young Germans are doing it. And you know how Germans are about women."

"Well," Buckner said, "I went down a stair and came into a lower corner. There don't seem to be any well-defined stories to the castle. Some of the rooms and the corridors seem to be higher than others on the same floor. I went into a room where there were a lot of paintings on the wall. They showed men in armor and old-style clothing and were well painted, I suppose, but of all the mean looking galoots I ever saw. Arrogant, domineering, cruel, some with Kaiser-ish mustaches and some with long beards. I'd hate to have such fellows for my ancestors, but Erich seems proud of it. Because he's like them, I reckon. Sir Otho's picture wasn't there. I suppose the artists were afraid to come near him. There were several girls and men looking at the paintings, so I eased out of there. And, say, I saw that west tower he was talking about. It's like the other towers, rises from the ground up above the roof of the castle. I suppose there were two rooms, like there is in this tower, lower and upper, with doors opening into the corridors and an outer door in the lower room. But, like Erich said, there wasn't. I looked it over from foundation to roof and there was only that one door, to the upper room, and it fastened with a monster of a lock. There was a winding stair that led up from a corridor to a kind of a landing in front of the door and another stair ran down in another direction. It was rather dark on the other stair and I guessed it led to another part of the castle. Steve, it sure sounded to me like I heard something in that room. It</p>

could have been bats, but it sounded more like something big and heavy crossing the floor, walking with hardly any noise."

"Bosh!" snorted Steve. "Buck, those ghost stories the guests have been telling are getting on your nerves."

"No, sir," Buckner insisted. "Ghost yarns don't bother me and anyway that was before Erich and the others got to telling them. Maybe it was bats, but I bet it was something. Say, do you reckon that Steindorf has got maybe a girl shut up in that tower? Or somebody else that he's holding prisoner?"

"It might be," Allison answered, musing. "Or, say, the German government might have some inventor at work on some war machine. They'd want to keep it a secret, if they invented some new weapon."

"Or the inventor might be a prisoner," suggested Buckner.

Allison mused a while. "Well," said he, "we'll see what we can find out. What did you do after you thought you heard the noise?"

"I didn't hear anything else," Buckner answered. "I went down the other flight of stairs. It was rather dark and the stair was twisting and winding. I wouldn't like to try to charge up those stairs. I was nearly at the foot of them when somebody opened a door. I crouched back on the stairs and watched. It was Helen. She looked about but didn't see me, and closed the door. I came on down the stairs. There was a small opening in the door that can hardly be seen from the other side. I looked through it and saw the door opened into a big, bare, dusty room. Helen was just walking to the door. She stopped, came back, and started to open the door; then she got frightened or something and ran out of the room. I didn't like to scare her, but I didn't care to explain why I was prowling around in that part of the castle. I had an idea that Erich didn't want anyone exploring around the west tower. I went on down to the big hall where the other guests soon came."

"We'll scout about," Allison said in an absent way. He was musing about the mystery of the west tower.

He rose. "Let's go down to the hall. Most of the guests are there."

"Helen has her rooms just across the corridor," remarked Buckner.

Steve nodded. "Buck," said he, "you leave the hall early and pretend to go to the tower. Then you scout around. I'll tell some long tale to keep the attention of the guests. Don't let anybody see you."

Buckner did not reply. He was not particularly pleased with the thought of wandering up and down among those dark corridors.

"I can do the scouting," Allison went on.

"I'll do it," said Buckner, "but if anything jumps me, or anybody, I'm going to shoot first."

"All right," Allison said, "but don't harm any of the guests. Any that wouldn't be mixed up in any plot, I mean."

Buckner nodded.

A few card games were going on in the big hall and several couples were dancing.

Erich was playing the part of host-royal, stepping from one group to another, at his bluff gayest.

Presently some of the young women, their minds still on the ghost stories that had been told by members of the party, captured him and drew him away from the others. Others joined them and presently the party was matching tales of haunted castles and ancient crimes.

Allison, who had danced with Helen Tranton, presently strolled toward the storytelling group, glancing casually at Buckner, who was playing pinochle with the Russian, Captain von Schlieder, and one of the Englishmen.

Allison listened to a tale related by one of the German girls, which dwelt upon the naughtiness of a certain countess of medieval times, then he said, "I am an American and America has been the homeland for my race for over three hundred years. But the Allisons came from Scotland and some of the old legends have come down to this day.

"There is a tale of the time of the Border wars and Highland forays, during the rule of the first Scotch kings, when the Picts were still raiding, burning, slaughtering, from the wilds of Galloway.

"Fergus the Black, of the ancient Allison line, was a red-handed outlaw with a price on his head. He was wanted by the English and by the Scotch king and had a dozen feuds on his hands with Border chieftains and Highland clans."

As Allison talked, couples stopped dancing and card games ceased, the players and dancers gathering about the group of which Allison was the center. Allison could tell a tale when he would and the members of the house party listened and it seemed to them that they gazed upon the scenes he pictured. It was a tale of feud and raid and battle he told. There was no romance of the wooing of maidens, but the sheer, fierce struggle of men against men. The clashing of sword on sword ran through his narrative, oppression and rebellion, cruel injustice and savage vengeance and the ambition of a strong man. Bleak, wild mountains, barren heath and men, wild and grim as the land in which they lived. And from some of the scenes of the narrative leaped stark, wild savagery, the savagery of man of the early ages, from which some of the gay pleasure seekers shrank aghast. Allison noted that most of the members of the house party were there listening to him, and he made the narrative as lengthy as possible. He wished Buckner to have plenty of time to prowl through the castle and explore about the west tower.

When Allison ceased speaking, he rose.

"I ask your pardon for boring you with that long, tedious tale," said he. "And I will retire with your permission. I really am not used to late hours."

As he swung across the great hall with his easy, catlike stride, the others watched him.

"A strange chap," declared one of the Englishmen.

The Russian smiled in his beard, watching Allison with eyes that were slightly narrowed.

"I believe that he could be such a man as he pictured his ancient ancestor, Fergus, to be," remarked Dalia Sinclair. "Helen, are all your countrymen killers?"

"Certainly not," Helen laughed.

"Who knows any more good murder tales?" put in one of the young men.

"Not any tales of murderers," shuddered one of the young German women. "Herr Allison's story has me almost afraid to look behind me."

"Tales not dealing with murder then," said Erich. "About some jolly old baron such as bluff old Sir Ludwick Steindorf, whose favorite jest was in having the young women of the village stripped, forcing them to put masks on their faces, and then having the young men of the village to pick out their wives and lovers."

"The bally bounder," commented one of the Englishmen.

Erich laughed uproariously. "Not at all," said he. "The girls were not harmed, though they were probably very much ashamed. You British have false ideas of women's modesty."

Steindorf had been drinking. Zuranoff glanced at him and suggested that the dancing be renewed.

In the east tower Steve Allison rose from his chair with catlike quickness, a gun flashing into his hand, then slipping back into its concealed scabbard as he saw it was Buckner who had flung open the door.

Buckner turned and locked the door before he spoke. He was somewhat pale and his clothing was dusty and disarranged.

He poured himself a glass of wine and seated himself.

"Who saw you?" asked Allison.

"Nobody," answered Buckner, then after a pause, "and what was—strange, I didn't see anybody."

Allison said nothing, waiting for him to speak.

"I started toward the east tower," said Buckner, "then I sneaked around and made straight for the west tower. I went in the room where the winding stair is. I went up the stairs and before I got to the landing, something came plunging down the stairs and slammed into me. I didn't use my gun, because I thought it might be one of the guests or a castle servant. We bumped down the stairs in a clinch. The thing, whatever it was, didn't try to use its fists, just seemed to be trying to tear off my arms and legs. We hit the foot of the stairs with a bump and broke the clinch. I couldn't see where the thing was, but I swung at a guess with all my strength. I must have hit the thing in the face, if it had a face, but it didn't even jolt it. It was coming for me, head-on, and I jumped aside. The thing crashed into the stairs and went right on up them. Maybe it thought I had gone up the stairs. Well, I got out of that room as fast as I could leg it."

"What was it?" asked Steve.

"I don't know," Buckner hesitated, and looked at Allison. "Steve, you know Steindorf said that old Baron Otho was hairy all over? Well, the thing I fought, whether man or beast, was as hairy as a gorilla!"

Steve shrugged his shoulders. "You trying to make me believe it was Otho?"

"I don't know," Buckner answered, "but if it was a man, why didn't it use its fists or a weapon? And if it was an animal, why didn't it use its fangs and talons? It wasn't an animal. It had hands. Four or five, it felt like. And if there ever was a man any stronger, I never saw him."

[. . .]

Miscellanea

"Drag"

(unfinished)

Chapter 1.

It was a strange experience and I don't expect anybody to believe just for the simple reason that it don't seem possible. I wouldn't have believed it myself and, therefore, I'm not going to slam anybody that calls me a liar.

There was four of us in that adventure: Gordon, Steve Allison, Lal Singh, and me.

Maybe you've heard of Gordon, he that is quicker than any other man in the world on the draw and is a wonder in lots of other ways.

And Lal Singh, the Sikh, who is a marvel with a sword and knows a lot about Hindu magic.

And Steve Allison, who is something of a wonder himself in some ways.

Me? My name is William Buckner, usually known as "Drag." I was with Steve and Gordon in Afghanistan that time we captured the mullah and stopped a holy war, and before that I have helped Steve pull off some slick stunts down on the Border where Steve is known as "The Sonora Kid."

[. . .]

Under the Great Tiger

by Robert E. Howard & Tevis Clyde Smith
(unfinished)

Chapter 1

Some years ago I happened to be in Kabul on some business. What was that business? Wait and see!

I was seated at a table in one of the capitol's numerous inns when an Afghan chieftain and 12 of his men entered. Finding out that he was Yussef Ullah, an influential warrior, I decided that I must get acquainted with him.

So, half drunk, I arose from my chair and staggered to where Yussef Ullah was seated. Slapping him upon the back, I invited him to drink with me.

He looked as if he desired to knife me. But instead he followed me to my table. There we chatted and drank until he could stand it no longer. Then he arose from his chair.

"Accursed," he said, "you are a thief and a coward from a nation of such. You shall die!"

He jerked his sword from his scabbard and made a lunge at me. Stepping back to escape the blade, I tripped over a chair and went down.

And then, with him creeping upon me, I jerked my pistol from my pocket and fired into his face!

The bullet caught him clean between the eyes and he went down. Then I jumped to my feet and shot two more of the Afghans before they could reach me. Then one of the Moslems threw a long spear at me. Dodging this, I wrenched it from the floor and, using it for a vaulting pole, leaped over their heads and through the window beyond!

[. . .]

"A Cossack and a Turk"

(untitled)

309

A Cossack and a Turk met on the steppes of Sungar. The Cossack had a richly wrought scabbard but no sword. The Turk had a scimitar but no scabbard.

"I will gamble with you for your scabbard," said the Turk.

So they gambled and the Cossack won the Turk's scimitar. Whereupon, being armed, the Cossack took from the Turk his saddle, his steed and his turban eigret, and rode away.

Quoth the Turk, "He who puts a weapon in an enemy's hands is a fool."

Spears of the East

(unfinished)

"You will do as I say," said Ahmed Eb in Din. "The girl shall be mine. It matters not whether you give her to me or whether I carry her off from your burning village."

The old Arab winced. "She is so young, sahib, but a child."

"She is fifteen," answered the raider. His thin, bearded lips curled in a cruel smile.

"I give you a time to decide, Hadji, whether you will give the girl to me or whether I lead my horsemen over your mud walls and smite your tribe with sword and fire."

He turned and strode arrogantly away, mounted the horse that stood near and raced away over the desert.

The old Arab sat still, plucking his beard, uncertainly. That his people could hope to conquer the Bedouins he knew was improbable.

His people were "el Hadr," dwellers in walled cities, and they feared the wild "el Bedoo," who feared no man.

Yet to give his young daughter to the cruel and rapacious hands of the Bedouin chief! It was unthinkable.

"Hadji," spoke a tribesman, entering the tent, "a band of horsemen come from the west."

The old Arab mounted the low mud wall that surrounded his village as the horsemen drew up before it. They were strangers to him, some twenty lean, wild looking tribesmen, armed with swords, spears and repeating rifles. And they were led by a white man.

[. . .]

"…that is, the artistry"

(untitled and unfinished)

[. . .] that is, the artistry is but a symbol for the thought! Perhaps the writer of the book, the painter of the painting, the sculptor of the statue, did not have in mind any especial thought, yet the idea was there, vague and dim perhaps, only in the subconscious mind. Why, I ask you, is any great work attempted or successfully made, if for no purpose? No! There is a concrete idea or thought that must be expressed in visible form or at least in a form which can be grasped. Perhaps the ideal is abstract, yet the impulse is the same. So much for my beliefs.

I saw early that the priests and wise men of my race were blinded by their creed and prejudice. Wisdom, when they could recognize it, they did not seek its merits, did not investigate or explore. They only satisfied themselves on one point—if it were Moslem or other-wise. Since the days of Mohammed, how much has the world seen of Moslem wisdom?

And when the wisdom was that of Sikh, Hindu or Kaffir, the priests sought to destroy it and frequently destroyed themselves thereby, for I, who speak as one who knows, tell you that Hindu wisdom is not to be tampered with. Some call it magic, "black magic," but electricity and the telephone would have been called "black magic" two centuries ago.

It is no trickery, merely control over natural objects. However it is not for the good of man that he know all. Therefore, in this book I hold back much, for, not only would I be disbelieved, but the knowledge would fall into the hands of men, unscrupulous, such as was Iskaneder Akbar, and in a short time the peoples of the world would be slaves to that man, unless he destroyed himself in his attempt to use the wisdom he had learned.

The mullahs and the rulers, tools to the mullahs, thought to destroy Hindu wisdom by burning the books. Think you that if all the books on electricity, all the books on navigation and all the books on water power were destroyed that these three sciences would vanish from the earth? So it is with the wisdom of Hind. No, let no man tamper with Hindu knowledge. The men who burned the library at Alexandria—but enough of that.

I am of a noble house of Scindh, and a descendant of the Prophet. By that, my line should have been priests and mullahs, but we have always been warriors. From youth, indeed from early childhood, I was trained in the use of arms. To be a fine horseman came as a natural gift, for my line have always been riders! The lance and bow I was taught to use but it was in swordsmanship that I excelled. These things may seem to have little bearing on my tale, yet, were it not for my skill at arms it might be I had not lived to give my wisdom to the world.

Even in youth I knew some of the wisdom of India.

[. . .]

"Thure Khan gazed out"

(untitled and unfinished)

Thure Khan gazed out across the shifting vastness of the Dawn Desert with a preoccupied stare. His immobile features would have given an onlooker no clue as to his thoughts but they were many. And the majority of them had much to do with the long, straight sword that swung at his belt. That sword was one of Thure Khan's proudest possessions, and his highest ambition was to see, gleaming from its at present unadorned hilt of bronze, the jewels that would mark him Thul's foremost swordsman. He shrugged his shoulders.

Then, suddenly, there stood before him a youth, seemingly no older than himself. Thure Khan had not seen him until at that instant, but on the Desert of Dawn, that was no cause for wonder. The incessant changing and shifting of the thousand prismatic hues and reflections sometimes revealed objects miles away, on the one hand, while all about elsewhere, sight was completely veiled by the crimson, golden and yellow fogs.

The stranger was about Thure Khan's height, and like him, leanly and powerfully built, and his hair was the same dark hue. Also their eyes were alike, grey. But where Thure Khan's skin was bronze, the stranger was white, and hairless.

[. . .]

Blood of the Gods

(untitled synopsis)

First Night.
Midnight.
Gordon left el-Azem. Hawkston left el-Azem.
First Day.
Dawn.
Gordon was out on the desert. Hawkston was out on the desert.
Mid-day.
Gordon was on the desert. Hawkston was on the desert.
Dusk.
Gordon was on the desert. Hawkston reached the first well.
Second Night.
Gordon was on the desert. Hawkston was on the desert.
Second Day.
Sun-down.
Gordon's camel was shot. Hawkston was on the desert.
Third Night.
Gordon went on foot from the place his camel was shot to the Well of Amir Khan. Hawkston was on the desert.
Third Day.
Dawn.
Gordon reached the Well of Amir Khan which he should have reached before mid-night, had he not stopped to rest, as he would have been forced to for the camel. Hawkston reached the third well, and was attacked by the Ruweila tribesmen.
Mid-day.
Gordon was trudging on foot toward the Jebel El Khour, which he should have reached by mid-day. Hawkston was besieged at the well of Khosru by the Arabs.

Sun-down.

Gordon reached El Khour. Hawkston was besieged, at Khosru Well.

Fourth Night.

Gordon was at El Khour. Hawkston was riding from Khosru Well to El Khour.

Fourth Day.

Gordon was at El Khour. Hawkston arrived at el Khour, Shalan ibn Mansour following close behind.

Gordon, riding his camel, should have reached El Khour on the fourth day, at about sun-down, having ridden half a night, a day, a night, a day, a night, a day.

Gordon, riding his camel, should have reached El Khour on the sun-down of the third day, having ridden half a night, a day, another whole night, a day, a night and a day. He should have reached the Well of Amir Khan before midnight of the third night. But his camel was shot and he reached it at dawn of the third day. (His camel was shot on the evening of the second day.) He should have reached El Khour by mid-day of the third day. He reached it on foot just at sun-down, of the third day.

Hawkston should have reached the first well the dusk of the first day; the second well, the dusk of the second day; the third well the dusk of the third day; the fourth well, the fourth day, and turned off there and made it to El Khour in a day and half, a night, arriving there at about mid-night of the fifth day, but being attacked at Khosru Well, the morning of the fifth day, he spent the fifth day there, and it was nightfall before he left, arriving at el Khour at dawn, on the sixth day, or one night behind El Borak.

Hawkston should have reached the Well of Ahmed at dusk the first day; the Well of the Sultan at dusk of the second day; the Well of Suleyman the dusk of the third day; the Well of Khosru at dusk of the fourth day; the morning of the fifth day he would have turned off for El Khour, and by force marching reached El Khour sometime after night-fall; being attacked by Shalan at the Well of

Khosru at dawn of the fifth day, he lay there until dark, when he fled on a fast camel, and riding hard, reached El Khour at about sunrise of the sixth day, or one night later than El Borak.

Gordon should have reached El Khour on the night of the third day, or two days ahead of Hawkston; as it was, he reached it at sun-down of the fifth day, one night ahead of Hawkston. He had ridden from midnight to dawn; through the first day; through the second night; part of the second day; at midnight he should reach the Well of Amir Khan, or before midnight; but his camel was shot and he reached it at dawn of the third day. He rested there a few hours, and it was nearly mid-day when he started; he walked all day, all night, and part of the next day. He left Amit Khan at about mid-day of the third day; he walked through the rest of the third day; all the fourth night and arrived at about mid-day of the fourth day.

Gordon should have reached El Khour on the fourth night from el-Azem, having ridden half a night; the first day; the second night; the third day; the third night.

Gordon's camel was shot the afternoon of the second day; otherwise he would have reached Amir Khan before midnight; as it was it took him until dawn of the third day; with the camel he would have reached El Khour before mid-day of the third day; on foot he reached it at sundown, of that day, or rather mid-day of the fourth day.

Maps, Sketches and Lists

Possibly for "Blood of the Gods"

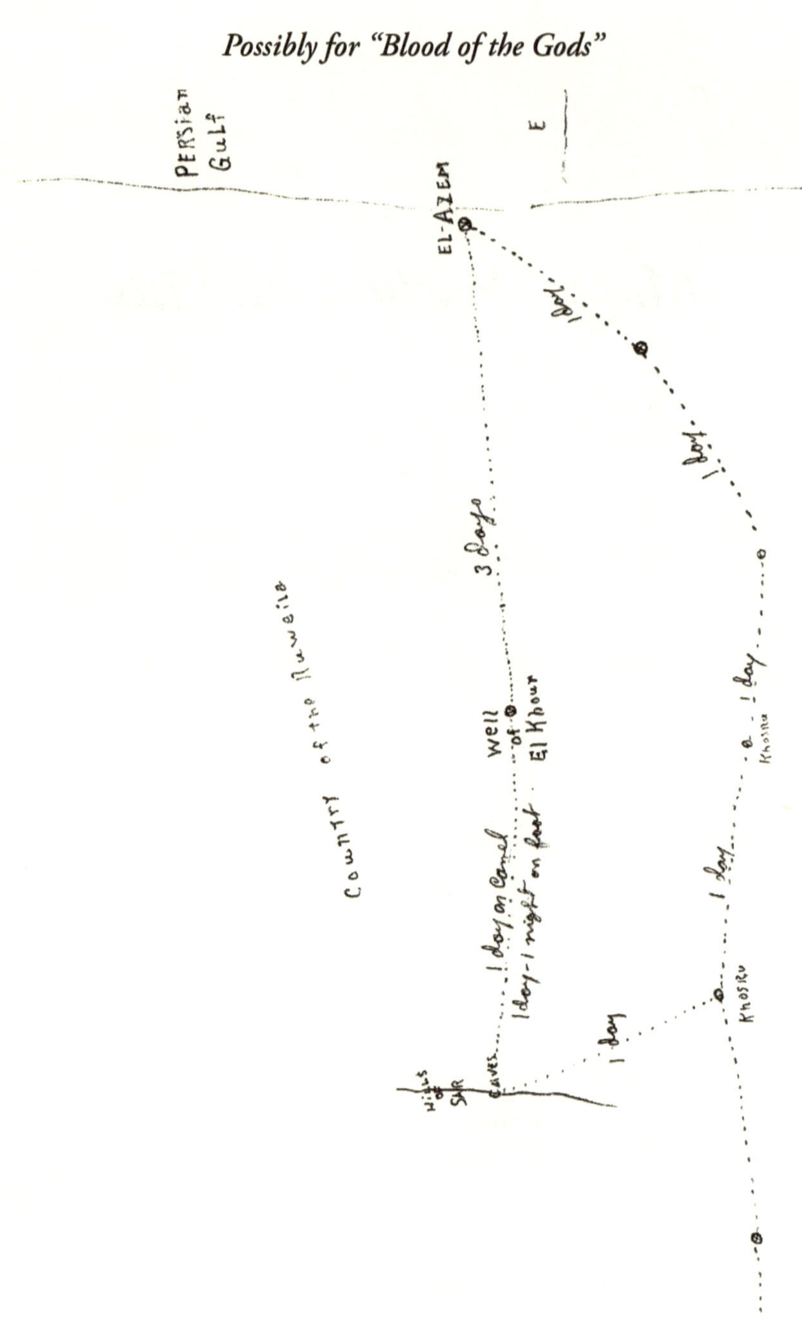

For an unidentified story

Found on the back of typescript pages for "Three-Bladed Doom"

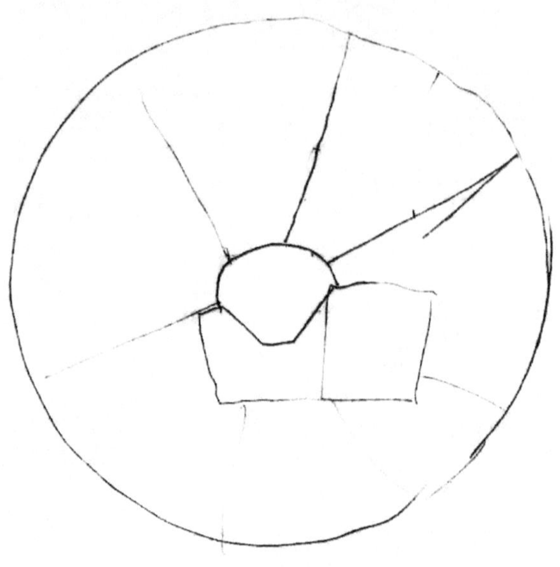

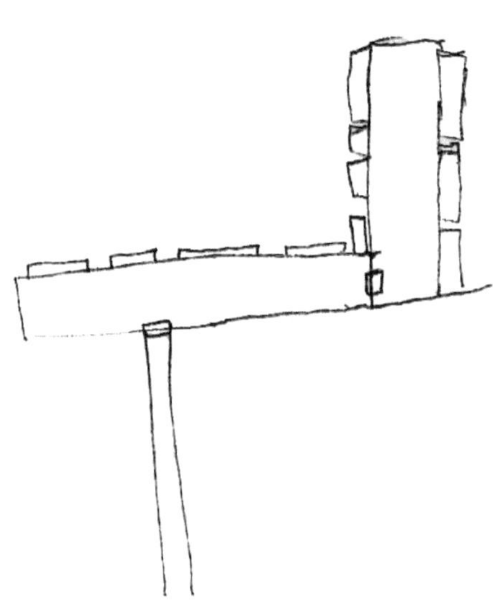

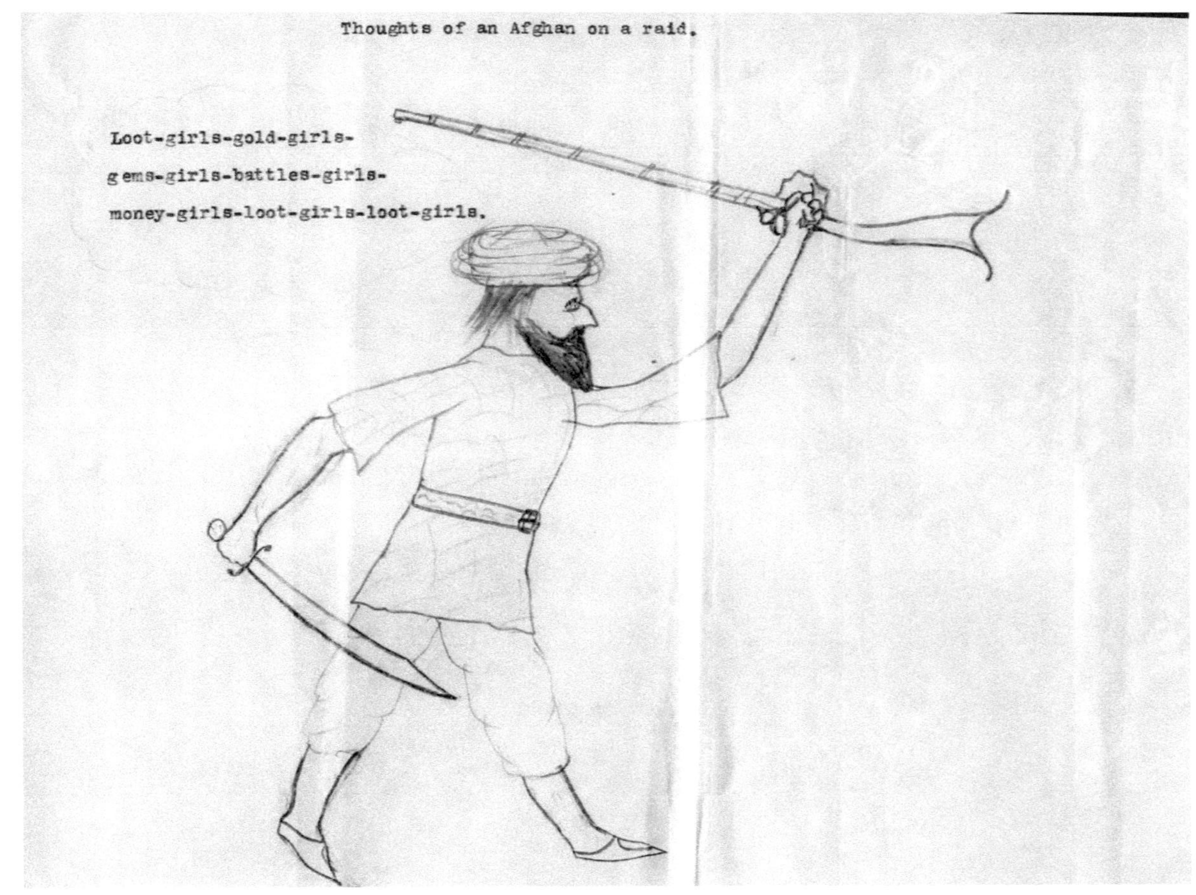

Thoughts of an Afghan on a raid.
Loot-girls-gold-girls-
gems-girls-battles-girls-
money-girls-loot-girls-loot-girls.

WHERE THE EAST AND THE WEST SHALL MEET.

Afghanistan --- Amir

Arabia ---- Sultan

Algeria --- Dey

Abyssinia ---- Sultan

Bokhara --- Amir

Baluchistan ---- Sultan

Cashmere --- Sultan

Arabia -- Sultan

Turkey -- Sultan

Afghanistan -- Amir

Persia -- Shah

Turkestan -- Sultan

Bokhara -- Amir

Oman -- Sultan

Kurdistan -- Sultan

Sarawak -- Rajah

Algeria -- Dey

Morocco -- Basha

Egypt -- Khedive

El Borak
North of Khyber
Winds of the Sea

~~Frat~~

El Borak
Bagheela
Borak

Frank Gordon
Steve Allison
Drag Buckner
Lal Singh
Yar Ali Khan
Ahmed el Kadour
Abdul El Kadour
Hal Slade
Akbar Khan
Mustapha el Hamid

Gordon,
Allison,
Buckner,
Yar Ali Khan,
Ali Khan,
Ali Beg,
Khoda Khan,
Yar Hyder,
Rahman Akbar,
Abdul El Kadour,
Abdullah Dost,
Ahmed Hyder,
Yar Mahommed,
Yussef Yar,
Lutuf Mahommed,
Akbar Khan,
Habibullah Yar,
Mahommed Ali,
Sulieman Ali.

Lal Singh,
Narendra Mukerji,
Ghopal Mukerji,
Jugnara Nath,
Ahmed El Kadour,
Amir Singh,
Ibrahim Ali,
Ramm Baksh,
Ananda Lal,

ROBERT ERVIN HOWARD (1906-1936) grew up in the boomtowns of early twentieth-century Texas, eventually settling in Cross Plains where he lived for the remainder of his short life. Deciding early on a literary career, he spent the bulk of his time crafting stories and poems for the burgeoning pulp fiction markets: *Weird Tales, Action Stories, Fight Stories, Argosy*, etc. Howard's literary reputation was assured with the publication of "The Shadow Kingdom" in 1929, which featured a unique blend of Fantasy and Adventure which has since been termed Heroic Fantasy. The creation of Conan the Cimmerian in the pages of *Weird Tales* has earned him lasting recognition.

ROB ROEHM has edited more than a dozen Howard-related books for the REH Foundation Press as well as a couple with his own Roehm's Room Press. He has won multiple awards for his research and writings in a variety of Howard-themed publications. He has traveled to every location in the United States that Howard mentions visiting—from New Orleans to Santa Fe, and dozens of Texas towns in between—verifying and expanding our knowledge of Howard's biography. His research has also uncovered lost Howard stories, letters, and poems. He writes about these discoveries, infrequently, at howardhistory.com.

PAUL HERMAN, long-time engineer and intellectual property attorney, began publishing REH in 1999 via his own Hermanthis Press and later, Wildside Press; he has edited well over one million words. His etexts have been the starting material for a significant number of REH books published in the last 17 years. His REH bibliography, *The Neverending Hunt* became the new standard when it was first published in 2006, and is the basis for the HowardWorks website. His wife of 38 years, Denna, continues to tolerate his hobbies. Paul currently resides in Weatherford, Texas, a few miles from Robert E. Howard's birthplace.

MARK WHEATLEY holds the Eisner, Inkpot, Golden Lion, Mucker, Gem and Speakeasy Awards and nominations for the Harvey Award and the Ignatz Award. He is also an inductee to the Overstreet Hall of Fame. His work has often been included in the annual Spectrum selection of fantastic art and has appeared in private gallery shows, the Norman Rockwell Museum, Toledo Museum of Art, Huntington Art Museum, Fitchburg Art Museum, James A. Michener Art Museum and the Library of Congress, where several of his originals are in the LoC permanent collection.

DAVID A. HARDY has written essays on El Borak and other Robert E. Howard characters in The Cimmerian, the Del Rey anthology El Borak and other Desert Adventures, REH: Two-Gun Raconteur, and other publications. He is a former member of the Robert E. Howard United Press Association. David Hardy lives in Austin, Texas.

STÅLE GISMERVIK has been passionate about REH since discovering Conan in 1990. He established one of the earliest and largest Conan-focused websites, and currently manages the comprehensive REH resource at reh.world. Ståle also administers the Robert E. Howard Foundation website and its Press counterpart, and oversees the curation and editing of Foundation eBooks. Recently, he has taken on the role of preparing the new Ultimate Books for publication. His work contributes to the preservation and promotion of Howard's legacy.